And I Loved Them Madly

And I Loved Them Madly

Matthew Parkhill

a&b

First published in Great Britain in 1995 by
Allison & Busby
an imprint of Wilson & Day Ltd
179 King's Cross Road
London WC1X 9BZ

A catalogue record for this book is available from the British Library.

ISBN 0 74900 261 1

Designed and typeset by N-J Design Associates
Romsey, Hampshire
Printed and bound in Great Britain by
Redwood Books, Trowbridge, Wiltshire

For Sara (26 August–29 October 1966)
and our parents

Gnothi Seauton

1

God knows how many thousands my parents paid in fees, but you'd have thought the school could at least supply some half decent lights. We were at our desks, straining our eyes under the dim lamps, earning headaches. Exams were two weeks away. Make or break time. No second chance. I was twisting the broken spine of yet another Hitler biography, scrawling some notes on his sexual predilections. Blatch, the history master, loved him; said he was a madman and a genius, said he was a genius precisely because he was a madman. All geniuses are mad, have to be, by definition; that's what gives them their insight, their understanding of the way things really are. We spent most of the year on Hitler, in one form or another. Blatch said he wanted us to see the world through his eyes. He was mad: Blatch, that is. But he was no genius. At least, if he was, I never got to hear about it.

Hitler liked to be dominated by Eva Braun. Blatch liked to be dominated by Hitler. Braun and Blatch should have got it together. A question on Hitler's private life was a sure thing in the exams. Blatch set one every year. He once asked the senior year to explain Hitler's foreign policy via analysis of his sexual tastes. Glibb's parents complained to the Head, said the question demeaned those brilliant young men who sacrificed their lives in the war. No greater love is there. They said so themselves. Blatch was taken to task, rapped on the knuckles. But he didn't care. He was retiring next year anyway, going off to Bavaria to drink beer, wear lederhosen, and write a book.

Peter sat in the far corner of the room, staring over the top of his books at the religious postcards his mother sent him. Some miracle or annunciation came through his box every day. He was no great scholar. The masters said he was too introspective to achieve the required objectivity of academic study. His work was self-indulgent. They told him to get his head out of the clouds and shape up.

Peter was the token oddball of the school. We shared a room. I was devoted to him. He was quiet; we didn't have much in common. He never bunked over the wall to chase the village girls, didn't play sports, just watched life from the sidelines. But he had an extraordinary sensitivity which went right through me, like he was constantly disappointed by the world, like something was always letting him down. He was looking for something. You could see the pain of the search in his eyes. He saddened me and I suppose that was why I loved him.

I would have done anything for him.

Then came exams.

Success was everything, I couldn't afford to foul up. Cambridge was riding on them. Nothing could get in the way.

Peter always lacked discipline, never could get down to serious work. But he was more distracted than usual in the weeks before it happened. I did notice that. It wasn't like it came out of the blue. But I had exams, I didn't have the time to give. I should have, I know that now. But I thought I could postpone it, thought he could hang on.

He couldn't.

I turned the page and watched Hitler's libido blitzkrieg into Poland. Peter had been sitting at his desk since dinner. It was unlike him to be still for so long. Once or twice I looked over. He was staring at his mother's cards on the wall

Then, whilst Hitler was rampaging into France, Peter started to take them down: martyrs, saints, miracles, nativity scenes, passions, annunciations, Christs on crosses, they all began to pile up on his desk. When he had finished he took out his pencils and started to sharpen.

I can still hear it now. Scratching. Scraping. Woodshavings tumbling to the cold floor. Once one was sharp, he would begin another.

I didn't stop to see what he was up to. I had work to do. Had to succeed. Time. No time.

How long he sat there after he'd finished the last pencil, I can't say. Hitler was marching down the Champs Elysées, no doubt wishing he was back home with Eva, by the time I turned round and saw Peter trembling slightly, his hand splayed out across images of the crucifixion.

Looking back, the hardest thing of all is that he didn't look at me. Not even a glance. He grabbed a pencil and before I could move rammed it into his eye.

His devil's scream brought the whole dorm crashing through our doors. Blood sprinkled across the Christ.

I turned back to my books.

The ambulance came and took him away and I sat at my desk taking notes. Hitler was unstoppable.

Peter was committed for treatment. I got straight As, received the school's coveted Taylor scholarship, and won a place at Cambridge.

I wasn't happy even then, not like Peter.

2

The whole world's looking for a story to tell. Not me. Had I known how this was going to end, I never would have started. Nothing would make me happier than to have nothing to say. No comment. End of story. What's so great about getting fucked up? If there was any way on God's earth I could have avoided this, I'd stop right now. Pack up and go home. I don't look for stories. Stories look for me. Damn it, they hunt me down.

And nowadays it's all about self. Everyone has something to say about self. Jesus, wherever you look people are discovering themselves, taking on inner journeys, seeking out true meaning, understanding, enlightenment, 'is-ness', kidding themselves that it all adds up, that they're going to find an answer, that it's all going to slot into place. All they have to do is read a few books, burn a little incense, hum a little, meditate here, take a drug there, don a funny outfit, fly to Tibet and, voilà - AWARENESS. Mysticism. More like madness. You play with your mind, you take the consequence. It's not a game you win or lose. It's not something you can take or leave. You buy the ticket: you never, never get off the ride. I've had enough selves to last me a lifetime.

I'd intended to go to Italy from the start, stay with Charles in his family home in the hills to the north of Florence: lying on the red tiles in the sun, toasting our little white English arses; women, curly-haired Italian women, playfully shy, painfully beautiful; the odd intellectual or artistic pursuit thrown in, a gallery here, a concert there; nothing too strenuous, the way it should be.

But my plans changed. I got a first in my end of year exams at Cambridge. I was eighteen years old. On top of the world. And I wanted to enjoy the view. So I went to New York, on a humid Monday evening in June.

'Fuck you too, brotherman!'

Horns, engines ripped the early morning air. Humidity encasing sweat. Stench from exhausts, steam from manholes torched my throat. I couldn't even spit. I blinked. Once. Twice. Light whipped my eyes. Bruises stamped on my face. I stink. There's vomit on my jacket. I'm in a gutter. What the hell am I doing here?

'Fuck me. Fuck me! No. Fuck you. Fuck YOU!' A second, angry, faceless voice echoed the first. There was the slam of a car door and someone started to sing in high vibrato. 'Jesus Loves You', I think it was. A little waveringly perhaps, but yes, Jesus loves you.

'Are you all right?'

Bones groaned.

'You don't sound too hot.'

Arms snapped.

'Come to that, you don't look too hot either.' I wiped the gunge from my eyes, white and crusted, and saw a tall, thin woman in a smart grey skirt standing over me. 'Here, let me help you up.' She reached for my hand.

'I think I'll sit.'

'Are these your things?'

Scattered across the pavement were my belongings. The thick white aran sweater my grandmother had knitted for those chilly summer evenings, trampled into the gutter. A dog had shat on it.

Cowards.

'Yes. Yes they're mine.'

She set about picking them up, scurrying to and fro in her pretty white blouse, folding the clothes as best she could and putting them back into my bag, lines of concern furrowing a petite face, surrounded by a mass of auburn hair which touched the ground when she crouched down.

'How do you feel?'

'Sick.' Lips caked in salt.

'Let's get you inside. There's a diner across the street. Come on.' She helped me up.

I stumbled. 'I'll be fine. I'm a little dizzy, that's all.' My head felt as though it had been squashed into a tiny box and locked in for the night.

'You look terrible.'

'Thanks,' I smiled and felt something crack in my nose.

She hauled my rucksack on to her thin body, almost vanishing under it's bulk, and we set off at a fragile pace to the café at the end of the block.

New York was going to love me. Have no doubt about that, not even for a moment. New York was going to fall at my feet. So call me arrogant, who cares. It was true. People did love me in those days. It's just the way it was. I felt great, looked better: composed, in control. I was handsome, interesting; what should I do, apologise? Could I help it if things were going my way?

You look at me now, you'd think I'm spinning a yarn, giving you a line, bullshitting. Maybe I am. That's something you'll have to judge for yourself. But then it doesn't really matter I suppose, because you're never going to know the truth. There isn't one. Let me tell you something right now: don't try and figure this all out, you'll go crazy.

I was good at bullshitting then, had a knack for it; people fell into my words willingly, followed me, believed in whatever role I dangled before their eyes – shy, confused; humorous, idiotic; confident, dominant – I wasn't deceiving, they were aching to be led. Now it's different. I've no one to bullshit anymore. That's why I'm telling you. You think I'd be lying here couched in my own shit, shivering at the screams, waiting in line to die, telling you all this if I didn't have something better to do? But I don't. That's the sadness. There's nothing. No visitors (who'd want to visit me). No distractions. I've forgotten how to read. No radio. No television. We're not here to have fun, you understand; we're here because we're the dregs, the dreams that never quite made it. We had potential, everyone does. That's the death knell, the fast track to failure. So here I am, mixed up in some sort of oblivion. Even the nurses don't bother talking to me. They just wipe my pitted arse about once a week (and not very well at that – my piles could be charted). They think I'm deaf. They know I can't talk. Sometimes they smile at me when they rocket the pills down my throat (ricocheting against my windpipe, making me retch), but that's just sadism, that's why they're nurses.

So I'm here telling you, in a voice you're imagining in your head. Can you hear it? You can't see me. You don't even know if I'm real. Maybe you're making *me* up.

You see, it's not like then. Then, I was real.

I'd just finished my first year at Cambridge, came out straight from the May Ball. What a year. I trumped them all: academics, sports, society; I left them standing, couldn't see me for dust. I was the toast of the whole damn place. No one could touch me, even come near me. It wasn't easy, I worked hard. I just made it look effortless, that's all. It was bluff, most things are.

And so, here we are, New York. The ultimate city. I can hear it now, beyond these walls. I won't be going there any more, can't get out. But then: adventure and experience loitering on every corner, kicking their heels, longing to whizz you away from whatever you chose to leave behind. No trace. Drunken forgetfulness oozing up through the sewers. Oceans of possibility breaking on the island's shores. No past. Only present. Maybe future. You see, I had a future then. I would have dazzled the shit out of you. You've never seen someone with a brighter future. Only now I'm trying to figure out were it all went. Somewhere along the line it took a wrong turning, lagged behind, and we got split up. So I turned back, retraced my steps, went in search of it, spent most of my miserable life looking for that future. Never found it, never crossed my path again.

Take. That's all I had to do. Take what was mine, and take what wasn't. And what did I do? I got taken. Jesus, if only I could leave all this behind.

You ever had a dream? I mean a real dream, someone you thought you could be.

Listen. Dreams are demons: run from them, get the hell out while you can. If you don't, they're going to come after you and then you'll be sorry. I had a dream – look what happened to me.

I bounded off the bus at Port Authority, Midtown Manhattan, and dived headlong into the boiling cauldron of the New World: rush-hour traffic blocking the avenues, gnarling gridlock, horns blaring, taxi drivers cursing, passers by passing by, street-hawkers hawking, drunks arguing and a fat man with no shirt on the corner singing an unknown song out of tune. I stood on the curb, didn't even notice the vicious city heat, just stood there, watching, unable to take it all in, my lungs sodden with metropolitan madness.

A sweaty bum in a ripped suit and fingerless mittens approached with an outstretched hand, lurching from side to side, scratching his groin with the hand that wasn't begging. He smelled of shit. He'd get nothing from me. I pushed him away and hurried into the nearest café. The bum wandered aimlessly, until his legs decided it was no longer worth the effort and he slid to the ground, just gave up, no point going on. His trousers were too big for him and the crack in his grubby arse flashed me a slanted smile.

On the pavement outside the café window an elderly man (a

cracked face) sat on a suitcase, turning his head with the passing cars. Each time the lights changed to red he grinned and noted something down in a tattered green book. He saw me watching him, mouthed something vicious, shook his fist, stood up and wandered off, dragging his suitcase behind.

There was a mirror on the far wall, an ornate frame with chipped cheap bronze paint. My mother had one just like it, in the back sitting-room (though I suppose her paint must have been more expensive). I looked at that mirror every day, watched myself grow up in it. She never cleaned it and my reflection grew musty; on dark winter days I could barely see myself. When grandfather died she threw the mirror out. I heard it go shattering into the rubbish shed at the side of the house: my youth. I asked her why. She cried and never told me.

I stared long and hard at myself in the far wall. The mirror made me look smaller, younger, lost somehow in the mayhem around me; unable to reflect. My face seemed to move, ripple as though I were looking into a pond, for ever caught looking at myself.

A lady with a bundle of paper bags tied with a string sat down at my table, taking off her cream stilettos and rubbing her callouses with a silk handkerchief. She started talking. Not to me in particular. Just talked, babbling away as if she were the only person in the whole city. She was mad. Starkers. And no one even gave her a second glance. She had a patchy moustache, blotchy raw skin. She sat between the mirror and me, looming large, obliterating the view. I caught her breath: putrid.

I guzzled the half-filled cup of lukewarm, Fairy-Liquid-tasting coffee, slung my jacket over my shoulder and, leaving the baglady with my reflection, stepped out on to the warm street, heading for Times Square and a cheap hotel.

Night barked, chasing away leftover light, and street lamps began their transformation of an eternally restless city: immense towers of concrete reaching out to the dark, connecting with nothingness; runways of lights speeding into nowhere. New York climbed inside my head, dancing, zig-zagging through the furrows and burrows of my mind. Brilliant beams blasted blackness – the Empire State.

A thousand times, at least, I must have wandered that island; over and over, until each corner began to look like the last. The bag dug deep into my shoulders. The glittering maze lost its shine and I thought of a bed that I knew, somewhere, waiting.

Weary. I shuffled through tattered newspapers, plastic bags and discarded underpants (Calvin Kleins). A lonely neon beer sign buzzed in a bar window. A group of teenagers loitered on a corner, an exhausted radio playing at their feet, watching the street in silence. Nearby, a tall skinny boy (a wiry mop of black hair, dirty skin) danced out of time with the music, waving his arms in the air like a drugged gospel preacher, howling at the sky.

'Hey, mutherfucker!'

I stopped. A grubby leather hat slunk from the depths of the half-darkness, bringing with it a bulky confusion of shadows. Silent skyscrapers cowered behind.

'Sorry?'

The figure didn't answer. A fist up and down, arms folded. He nodded and waited for me to respond. I tried a smile.

Laughter, like a hyena on heroin, tapped on my shoulder. I looked round. There were two more, smaller than the first, standing in the exact same position. They jerked their fists and folded their arms. The hyena had a missing front tooth and a fresh scar on his upper lip.

'Sorry!' he sniggered.

Time passed. No one spoke. The snigger died. The sun set. Traffic passed. Lights. Shrieks. Laughter.

I ran for it.

Didn't even make it to the curb before I was felled by a kick. I shrieked. A gloved fist smashed into my teeth, grimy leather mingling with blood, drowning my tongue. The hyena leered into my face and spat into my eyes; salt, nicotine blurring vision. He kicked me in the stomach. I curled into a ball. He kicked me in the small of the back. I opened. He kicked again. I tried to grab his foot. Nothing there. And again. He stamped on my hand. Runways of lights sped into the sky and towers of blackness lay down to die. The bag was wrenched from me. I scrambled to my feet. I was up. Running. For a second. Until a final blow brought me crashing to the curb and I watched New York sink into the ocean.

She seemed excited, charged, the smart lady in the grey skirt; she seemed terribly excited, as though finding me in the gutter had made her day. I was dirty, dazed, full of aches, and she stood there with this proud smile on her face. I must have been the most exciting thing that ever happened to her, poor woman. She took my arm and ushered me into the café. It was stuffed with men in suits, horn-rimmed spectacles and meaningless initials stitched into shirt cuffs, poring over boring papers, gallons of caffeine pouring down their throats, stimulating them just enough to lead some sort of life until retirement.

'I'm Aimie,' the woman said as we took a corner booth by the window. There was a half-finished breakfast on the table, morsels of overcooked bacon (oink oink) swimming round (piggy paddle) in grease, alongside an open *New York Post*. "Our City Is Dying", whined the headline. (Jesus, if that place ever keels over, where the hell are they going to put the corpse?)

'I'm Benjamin.'

'So, Benny...'

'Benjamin.'

'Benjamin, tell me what happened.'

A young waitress bounced up with an empty smile, pen poised. Ready to serve. 'What'll it be?'

'I'll take a bran muffin and a decaf.'

'And for you?' She stared at the dried blood on my shirt, then shoved her smile back into her pocket, shuffling her feet so she could look down on me. Her nose turned up so far I could the beginnings of a brain.

'Coffee, please.'

'Regular or decaf?' She sniffed at my filthy clothes.

'Ordinary coffee, please.'

'Like I said, regular or decaf?' She didn't like me.

'He'll take a regular,' Aimie laughed, embarrassed for my sake.

'Anything to eat?'

'Do you have an English breakfast?'

'Is this England?'

'No.'

'We have ham, eggs, fries, browns...'

'Fine. I'll have one of those.'

'Fine.' She snapped her pad shut, writing nothing, looked again at the blood, then at Aimie, and left. Perhaps she thought I was a bum. Perhaps she thought Aimie was being kind to me. Perhaps she disapproved of charity.

'Come on then, tell me what happened.'

'I was attacked.' I gazed out the window at a taxi driver leaning on the bonnet of his cab, reading the paper, waiting for... who cares.

'When?'

'Last night.'

'Who by?'

'I didn't catch their names.'

'Okay, wiseguy.' She smiled and leaned forward, staring into my eyes. She had a soft face, the kind that longed to be taken home and cared for, though the years hadn't been gentle with her. She looked dragged out, ever widening circles hanging obstinately under her eyes, weary. Or was it boredom?

The waitress with the monopoly on bad attitudes placed Aimie's breakfast gracefully (or as gracefully as a personality disorder utterly devoid of grace can manage) on the table, then slammed mine down in front of me, grease slopping into my lap.

'Enjoy your meal,' she said to Aimie.

'What are these? I asked.

'Browns.'

'Browns?'

'Hash browns, mister. Just like you ordered,' she replied curtly and left, trotting down the aisle, her tail-arse high in the air like a stuck-up Parisian poodle (stopping occasionally to cock a leg).

'So, what are you doing here?'

'Being mugged.'

'Besides being mugged.'

'I've come for the summer. Come to take a bite out of the Big Apple.'

'Seems the Big Apple's taken a bite out of you. Now what?'

'Now? I've no idea.'

At the next booth two middle-aged women stared silently at each other over their milkshakes.

'You know anybody here?'

'No.

'You travelling alone?'

'Yes.'

'Have any contacts?'

'No.'

'Nobody?'

'No.'

'Nothing?'

'No.'

'Benjamin?'

'Yes.'

'Are you nuts?'

'Perhaps.'

One of the ladies opposite got up, flicked a pile of notes on to the table and walked out, tapping the reading cabbie on the shoulder and getting into his taxi. He folded his paper, slung it through the front window, spat, picked his nose, chewed on the bogey, savoured the flavour, then got in the other side and drove off like a maniac. Her companion sat alone, staring at the money. After a while, she rolled it up, put it in her handbag and ordered another milkshake. Chocolate.

Aimie hurriedly drank her coffee, then went to piss it all out so she could make room for another.

While she was gone I checked my things. My passport was still there (giving the wrong colour of my eyes; they were, and still are, just, blue, not grey. Blond hair, if you're interested. Not that it matters, it didn't hang around, there's none of it left now. I had beautiful hair in those days; full, slightly curly, it was my trademark, people used to say... Oh, sorry. I guess I'm reminiscing again. I slip into that kind of easily. Selfish of me, isn't it. I suppose I should get on with the story. After all that's why you're here.

Where was I?

Ah, yes – New York diner, bruises, dried blood, passport, my passport – I still had my passport, though the bastards had taken my money, all of it bar the few hundred dollars I had rolled up inside a sock. I thought of going home, or at least picking up the phone and getting some money wired out. But I had this pride with a thing about independence and it kicked up a fuss, insisting I stand on my own two feet for a change.

I shoved the things back in my bag and stared on to the Avenue.

New York City.

Shit Creek. And not a paddle in sight.

Aimie hurried back from the toilets, flustered. She was late for work, hadn't realised the time. She gabbled (swallowing her words), did her hair (brush tangled), bolted down another coffee (another piss), burnt her tongue (cursing), and offered me a place to stay until I sorted myself out. When I refused she asked why the British had the perversity of being so damn polite, picked up my bag and almost dragged me out of the café.

'I've come about the job.'

There was a high food counter, its plastic covering cracked and split, dirt ingrained in the wood beneath. I stood in front and coughed, hesitant, polite. Behind me, balding men with identical paunches huddled around a dozen cheap Formica tables, cigarettes and grubby glasses glued to their hands. Others leant against a broken jukebox, chewing and flicking ash to the floor in time with the music which barely made it out of the speakers. On the yellowing wallpaper hung faded pictures of horses and greyhounds, fat greedy men in tasteless silk shirts standing proudly next to the beasts, cigars in their hands and chunky rings on their fingers.

'What job? What ya talkin 'bout?' The fat slob in the grubby vest eyed me suspiciously from behind the counter. He scratched the thick hairs on his chest and coughed violently, his belly quivering.

'The job advertised in the window.'

'Aw that.' He took a long drag on his cigarette, then stubbed it out, scattering ash on the till. 'Well, what 'bout it?'

'I'd like it.'

'You ain't from round here are ya?'

'No. I'm from London. England.'

'And you ain't American neither are ya?'

'No. I'm not. I'm English.'

He opened a small tin, took out another pre-rolled cigarette, lit it and stared at me, long and hard.

I'd been at Aimie's three days, recovering. She had a small place, bland paintings of New York in pastel shades and white horses by the moonlit sea covering the walls, bookshelves filled with accountancy magazines and journals on how to manage stress, and a record collection dominated by Dire Straits. It kind of made me want to cry.

She took me out to dinner on the Upper West Side and we talked about what I could do in New York. She promised to find me a job. We drank. She asked me what I did. I told her about Cambridge and we drank some more. She was fascinated, wanted to know everything: the dates, the places, the people, the society, the sports, the parties and May Week, she especially wanted to know about May Week. She'd always dreamed of going to a May Ball. She had an affair, once. He was an anglophile and promised to take her to an Oxford Ball, told her they were the height of civilisation. He even managed to get tickets. But the the week they were due to go, he ran off with his shrink and took him instead (took him on the flight over, took him in the men's at Oriel and took him all the way back to America). Aimie still wanted that Ball.

So I played a role.

'They're wonderful,' I told her. 'Simply wonderful. Champagne fountains, food mountains, dancing till dawn on the lawn, ferris wheels riding high, dodgems, fireworks. Heavenly surroundings; college courts, riverside gardens, deer parks. Everything you could ever wish for. A fulfilment for every dream.'

'Which is the best? Which would you take me to?' she put down her drink, letting her fingers fall lightly on to my hand.

'That depends what you're looking for,' I said, watching her eyes flirt with mine. 'Trinity is vast and wild, Clare is petite and romantic, Peterhouse is refined and suave.'

'I want to go to them all. I want to go now.' She pulled a face like a spoilt child and tugged at my arm.

'They're all over. This time last week I was at Trinity. Now there's a night I won't forget: huge ballroom, full orchestra, hot-air balloon taking you high into the night sky, chauffeured punts under coloured fountains.' I looked at the bottom of my empty whiskey glass and saw Charles pulling down Annabel's dress, her white rounded breasts bouncing before the whole marquee. Annabel was head of the Christian Union, her mother had warned her about wearing a low-cut, strapless dress. She'd danced so carefully all night, petrified, one hand constantly pulling up the bodice. Then Charles came along and it was all over in a flash. God, how we laughed. She gave him one hell of a slap, his cheek was still red the next morning. But it was worth it. Annabel threw away the dress, vowed to listen to her mother in future, and resigned her position: the Christians were headless.

'What are you smiling at?' Aimie giggled.

'Oh, nothing special. Just the Ball.'

I talked and talked, letting her fall into a society of delightful ludicrousness, of self-indulgence taken to delicious extremes: of a party where naked male models of classical proportions stood on a podium for guests to inspect over cocktails, whilst the host pranced around the room dishing out lollipops of all imaginable flavours, swan's wings strapped to his back; of punt-driven picnics, sozzling in fields with no horizons; of my celebrated victory over the Oxford sabre captain, winning us the Varsity match. I had my Blues jacket on then; it was a little grubby from my night on the pavement, but it shone all the same. I loved that jacket. Tale followed whiskey. Whiskey chased tale.

'You're so lucky,' she said, her eyes alight. 'I wish I was there.' She moved closer, gently touching my bruised cheek.

'Let's have another drink,' I said, swinging my stool round and calling the barman. 'After all, this is New York.'

By the time we got back to her apartment she was stone drunk. I carried her to her room, where she tried throwing her arms around me, but her co-ordination was none too sharp. 'Stay with me. Sleep with me. We could have a Ball,' she laughed, and promptly collapsed on the bed.

I undressed her down to her cotton bra and panties (yellow roses) and stood over her, listening to the traffic on the avenues humming endlessly into the night. She was older than I thought, little mounds of unwanted flab between her thighs to prove it.

I did think about it, for some time. I even had a hard-on. But it didn't seem fair.

The next morning she wouldn't stop apologising. 'I feel so terrible. It's just that, well I don't normally drink and, last night... Well, I just, I'm sorry if I behaved badly.'

'Not at all. I had a wonderful time.'

'But I mean later, I...'

'Forget it. It happens.'

'Thank you for putting me to bed. You were the perfect gentleman.'

Later that morning I paid a visit to Aimie's doctor for a check-up. It didn't take long. He stripped me to my waist, tapped me in a few places and asked me to follow his finger with my eyes. Total: seventy dollars.

'You're in good shape,' he told me as I buttoned my shirt. 'That helped. But you've been lucky, you've nothing that won't heal in a week or so. Come and see me in three weeks.'

Clearly he was short of cash.

I left the surgery and was strolling around the neighbourhood when I came across the sign in the window of Henry's Luncheonette.

'Give the kid a job, Henry,' one of the men by the jukebox shouted.

'Where d'ya get them bruisings?'

'Somebody punched me.'

'Ya punch him back?'

'Of course.'

'Hard?'

'Want me to show you?'

'All right. Ya got the job. Be here seven tomorra. A.M. And don't be late.' He poured himself a gin, squeezed out a slice of mouldy lime, and disappeared into a back room, coughing up phlegm.

The next morning I was outside Henry's Luncheonette at a quarter to seven. Henry didn't come 'til a quarter past, by which time I was deep in some dream or other: the University Library full of delicious, edible women, all of whom were at their desks, studying hard, deep in concentration, with no clothes on. I came into the Reading Room (high, mighty, learned) and they looked up from their books, turned towards me, each and every one of them, gasped, opened their legs, moist, and said ... 'Don't lean on the glass! What ya leanin' on the glass for, ya make it dirty.'

I opened my eyes to see Henry's yellow teeth sunken into his flabby, unshaven face. He was wearing the same clothes as yesterday, only now there were several dark stains down the front of his vest and blood smeared around his crotch.

'What you gawpin' at? Ain't ya never seen a woman's calling card before? Ha! Kids!'

'Sorry, I was just...' but he was already inside. 'I've been a waiter before,' I hurried after him, 'I've had lots of experience, so I shouldn't have any problem.'

'You cuckoo? What ya talkin' 'bout, waiters? What ya talkin' 'bout waiters for? I ain't got no waiters here. People don't come here for waiters, they come ta eat.' The room smelt of sweat, stale cigarettes and chips. Henry went behind the counter and switched on the air conditioner, which rattled and clunked laboriously to life, then picked up a bucket and went from table to table emptying the ash trays, replacing them without so much as a wipe.

'So...' I hesitated, waiting for him to speak. He lit a cigarette, flicking ash into the newly 'cleaned' ash trays, and carried on with his work. 'So, what will I being doing then?'

'Jeesuss! What d'ya mean what ya doin'? What ya think ya doin'? Dishes. Ya doin' the dishes. Here.' He led me into a dark, narrow room behind the counter, on either side of which damp boxes were stacked floor to ceiling. At the end was a wooden draining board and a small enamel sink, above which, sticking out of the wall, was one solitary tap. 'Here,' he repeated, handing me a fouled grey cloth with holes in, 'there's still some stuff from yesterday. We open in ten minutes.' And he went back into the other room.

I followed behind. 'Excuse me,' I coughed politely.

'Ain't you started yet? What ya want now? Can't ya see I got work ta do?'

'I was wondering if it might be possible to have some gloves.'

'Gloves! What for? What ya want gloves for?'

'For washing up.'

'Fa washing up?'

'For doing the dishes.'

'What ya want gloves fa dishes for? I ain't never used no gloves fa doin' no dishes.'

'Perhaps I could buy some. Is there anywhere near here I could get some? I'll be quick.'

'So longs as you pay for them, I can't see no harm. Across the street, there's a hardware place, they got some. Sure they have.'

'Thanks very much. I won't be a moment.'

'Better not. Gloves!' he snorted. 'And close the door! Ya lettin' all the cold air out.'

I did as he asked, turned and ran down the street to the nearest café, went in, sat down by the window and ordered a coffee.

An hour and two doughnuts later I gave Aimie a call and told her my career with Henry was going nowhere.

'Forget it. I've found something for you. There's a guy here who knows about these summer work programmes for foreign students.

There's some organisation which fixes them up, arranges everything. You got a pen?' I beckoned to the waitress, grabbed a pencil from her breast pocket and took down the details.

The YMCA was a miserable place to find God. It stood alone on West 46th Street in the midst of a derelict block, two abandoned Mercedes smashed up against a wall, half a Volkswagen burnt out behind. It was an enormous, filthy, red-brick building with dozens of tiny windows strung along each floor like dirty washing hanging in a cramped backyard by a railway line. On the corner hung a huge neon crucifix in pink. I looked for the neon Christ, but he seemed to have disappeared, climbed down off the Cross and just walked off.

A handful of people was gathered by the doorway, rucksacks in their hands, arguing with a stunted bus driver who stood by the open door of his vehicle, his stubby arms folded, refusing to let anybody on. It was baking on the street and the air-conditioned bus sat empty.

'You board when I say you board and not a moment before. Understand!' he bawled, his face bursting red with constipated bureaucracy.

I followed Aimie's instructions, negotiating the Christian crumbling corridors, and found my way to a small, cramped and sweaty office. There, I stood in line for two hours only to be told by an overweight, wheezing young girl with raging acne and an evil cold (in summertime) that there was nothing she could do for me (sneeze). She took a great deal of time, a lot of mucus, and not a little pleasure telling me this. The work programme was organised back in England, see. If I wanted a job (cough, phlegm) I'd have to go back there, see, sort out the details, then come back here and she'd see what she could do, though she couldn't promise anything - gurgle. See?

I shot her my best dejected look and regaled my story, the whole thing: from Cambridge Blue to New York gutter. She was stubborn, she took some charming. But fortunately the bruises on my face still shone and she took pity on me.

There was a place by the name of Veda that needed staff. She handed me a huge glossy brochure, the kind that advertise cheap holidays next to building sites miles from the sea in Southern Spain. Veda looked like some sort of summer camp for children with learning difficulties. Reading, writing, that kind of thing. It was paradise:

upstate New York in the Catskill Mountains, an Olympic-size swimming pool, tennis courts, baseball field, river running through the grounds, stacks upon stacks of photos of colourful faces. I'd never seen so many happy children. I guess that should have made me suspicious from the start. But I was just thankful that something had turned up. The season lasted ten weeks. I'd get 200 dollars plus full board and lodging. It was just what I needed.

I filled out the necessary documents and by four o'clock I was official. The overweight girl told me (snort) to take a bus from Port Authority. She even managed half a smile, or was it a grimace? I would have bowed low and kissed her hand, but she had the clam.

There was an Adirondack bus leaving at nine thirty the next morning for a town by the name of Madingdale, from where I would be picked up and taken to Veda. Aimie and I had breakfast in the café where we'd first eaten, she with her bran muffin and I with my hash browns. The strop of a waitress wasn't there, thank God, and there were fewer horn-rimmed spectacles, just some jogging suits reading the weekend news. New York was still dying, the papers said so. Not that I cared, I was out of there.

'It's been good having you around. Different, you know. This kind of thing doesn't normally happen to me. I think I'm even going to miss you.' Her voice was sad and tired. 'Still, I'm happy for you. Sounds like you're going to have a great summer.'

She started to tell me something of her love-life, speaking low, taking me into her confidence. She was the kind of woman who carried her hurts around in her pocket, taking them out every now and then for inspection, just to see if anything had changed. I'm sure it was interesting. I would tell you, but I didn't hear what she was saying. I wasn't paying attention, I was watching the clock on the wall, worrying about the time. When she came to a suitable break (I think her first boyfriend had just left her because she would only go missionary), I told her to write the rest down and send it to me.

We jumped in a taxi and honked our way through short-tempered traffic to Port Authority.

'Well, you won't forget this place in a hurry. New York gave you one hell of a welcome. Let's hope you'll have better luck here on out.' She kissed me quickly on the lips. 'I'm glad things have worked out for you, really I am.' She looked at me awkwardly, unsure whether to kiss me again.

'They wouldn't have had it not been for you. Thanks for everything.'

'Come on, you'd better get on the bus, I think the driver's about to leave. Maybe I'll see you at the Ball.'

'Maybe.' I climbed aboard the air-conditioned bus and sat at the back. Aimie flicked back her long auburn hair and waved, a sad smile on her face.

There was a hiss from the brakes and the bus shuddered forward. She blew me a kiss as it turned the corner into the New York traffic, the bustle, heat and noise safely on the other side of a large tinted window.

3

Brakes hissed and the bus pulled away, leaving me standing on a deserted garage forecourt in the bright sunshine. Across the road by a cast-iron bridge was a beat-up tin sign in dull red: *Be Sure To Drive Like A Snail In Madingdale*. Apart from the river, snaking down the valley, the road alongside, it looked like snails were the only things that moved in Madingdale: the place was empty. Dead. One huge corpse. No, come to think of it, that's a lie. There was a pair of legs, in dirty overalls, sticking out from under an old blue Chevrolet on the far side of the forecourt. I wandered over and banged on the hood.

'Excuse me. Can you tell me where I can find a phone?'

There was no answer. So I banged again.

'Don't hit the damn hood so hard,' a deep growl of a voice sparked up. 'What you hit the damn hood for? You'll dent the car.' (The car was nothing but dents.)

'Could you tell me...'

'So, you're a stranger,' the voice boomed, the body remaining immobile, wedged under the car. 'Ain't such a good idea to go round hitting hoods so damn hard when you're a stranger, now is it?'

'No. I don't suppose it is.'

'Where ya heading?'

'Veda.'

Something in the engine snapped, a jet of steam gushing out the side. The guy must have burnt himself, but he didn't make a sound, didn't move, save for a slight twitch in the left leg. There was a long silence. I wondered if he'd heard my question. So I asked him again, about the phone.

'Veda eh? So they're still sending people up there. Thought they'd shut that place down years ago. Damn well oughta.' The voice was loud, hostile, like it was blaming me.

I waited. I could hear something being unscrewed, metal on metal, grinding. Whatever it was didn't want to budge. The mechanic grunted. But no voice now. Just a motionless body under a car that was falling apart

I asked a third time for a phone. No answer. I waited in the shadowless sunlight, squinting, a cool trickle of sweat behind my right ear. In the distance you could hear the river, and the odd truck rumbling along some highway. A pair of hands appeared on the bumper, dirty nails chewed to the bone. I thought the mechanic was going to haul himself out, stand up, stretch out his hand with a smile, buy me a beer, at least talk to me. But I was wrong. He pulled himself further under the car, disappearing completely. There weren't even any legs. Nor grunts. I stopped breathing to listen. Nothing. I was going to bend down to look for him, but was suddenly frightened of finding nothing there. So I went off to look for a phone myself.

Ritch was proud of his red Cherokee Jeep. Not that it was a great piece of machinery, in fact it was pretty much a piece of junk; but then I guess Ritch didn't have a lot else to be proud of. Ritch was the director's son and it was he who came to pick me up.

'I'm proud of my red Cherokee Jeep. Isn't it just *it*?' That was the very first thing he said to me.

I agreed, it was.

'I'm Ritch. Hi.'

Then he didn't utter another sound until we were out of Madingdale.

We trundled down Main Street (overtaken by snails): a grocery store which sold nothing but washing powder (the only one in the Continental United States), a Mexican bar run by Chinese teetotallers, and a boarded up cinema which closed right after it premiered its first film – not so much a ghost town as a town in the grips of rigor mortis – and passed on out into the country (no better). The road straightened, thick woodland on one side and a large lake on the other, rowboats scattered on the surface, fisherman gazing hopefully at the water.

'You fish, Benjamin?'

'No.'

'I do,' Ritch replied to a question I hadn't asked. 'Or rather, I did. My dad used to take me when I was a boy. Took me by the ear and yanked me down to the lake every Sunday morning, meant he had an excuse to skip church. He figured the Lord, being a fisher of men, would understand. I never been since. Fishing, that is. I still go to church, once in a while. You go to church, Benjamin?'

'No.'

'I loved fishing, sitting by the lake in the sunshine. It was catching the fish I hated. Interrupted the day. So I took off the hook and threw the line in. The fish didn't bother me so much after that. Never told my dad though, he'd have gotten mad.'

Over a hill and we came to a town even smaller than the last. Sageville: a few houses, the obligatory bar, a fleabitten mongrel of a dog (about to die), and an antiques shop where an old woman sat on the porch at a sewing-machine (manually operated - the woman, not the machine) with no material to sew, a cat perching on her left shoulder wishing it was a parrot.

We turned down a backroad, dipping sharply past a shack with a hawk shackled to a post in the garden, a man in a tattered green dressing-gown lying in the flower bed, and round a large bend which hugged a broad, slow moving river. The smell of stagnant water climbed so far down your throat it made you retch. We skidded into a gravel driveway, at the end of which a faded green sign hung loosely over a gate: *Welcome to Veda.*

'Could do with a coat of paint that,' said Ritch.

'What does it mean?'

'Veda? No idea. I guess my mom just liked the sound of it. Here.' Ritch handed me my bag and told me where I'd find the director welcoming the staff. 'Any time you want a ride in a jeep now, you just ask Ritch.'

An old man in frosted glasses, baggy trousers big enough for two and a hunting hat (fluffy sides pulled down over his ears) came out of a wooden hut marked HIGH COMMAND and shuffled past me with an absent stare. I said hello, chirpily, in an I'm-new-here-let's-be-friends sort of way. He ignored me, just shuffled on.

Ritch disappeared into the hut and I was left alone, standing in the midst of a vast sweep of forest and field. To the left a high razorwire fence separated Veda from the road, signs posted at regular intervals: STRICTLY PRIVATE. ALL TRESPASSERS WILL BE PURSUED. It was a vicious-looking contraption, huge spotlights and sirens along the top, something you'd expect to see around a military barracks not a children's camp.

I followed the path as instructed, passing a large hall, a payphone on the porch with no receiver, a basketball court with no nets, and a trampoline with no springs. I came to a narrow bridge (planks missing) over a tiny brook dwarfed by huge maple trees (diseased), what little water there was trickling into a tunnel under the road (cracked). In the distance long, thin, barren cabins, meticulously ordered and numbered, stretched up the hill to a second basketball court without nets. Everything looked disused, abandoned, left to rot, even the grass.

At the end of the path was another hall, much larger than the first with thick wire mesh across the windows. Inside a large group of people was gathered around long tables, listening to a petite elderly woman who was standing in the centre of the room, her frail voice buffeting the silence.

I opened the door. It squeaked. Everyone turned to stare. I stared back. The woman stopped talking and squinted. She took a while to focus and then croaked. 'You're *special*. Come in, come in. Sit down.' She opened her arms to receive me like priest. Behind her sat two fat women, one of whom smiled and nodded, the other glanced up at me and shook her head. It was dark in there and chilly. Nobody said a word. I felt uneasy, as though I were interrupting the funeral of someone whom nobody much loved. Avoiding the elderly lady's blessing, I went in and sat down. She waited a moment, her audience captivated, the heavy lines on her face framing a placid expression, her hands clasped in front of her, her grey hair resting neatly on her head, then continued. 'Remember. Veda is a *special* place. And you are *special* people. Know this: whatever happens to you here, the experience awaiting you will affect the rest of your lives.

'I think that's about everything. Thank you for being so attentive. I just know we are all going to have a good season.' She gave one long final smile, almost bowed, and sat down, putting her head in her hands, scratching, mumbling to herself, her voice wavering. I thought she was going to cry.

'Okay, that's all for now,' the fat woman with fair curly hair, the one who shook her head at me, jumped up and bellowed impatiently above the growing chatter. 'Meet outside for work assignments in ten minutes.' The staff filed out the door, two by two, regiment like, gathering into small groups on the grass in the sunshine.

'Who are you?' the fat woman demanded abruptly, thundering over to me at a hefty pace.

'Benjamin.'

'Benjamin?'

'Benjamin Ryan.'

'Ryan. Right. I'm Norma, your head counsellor. Now let me see, Ryan, Ryan...' she flicked through the files she held under her arm. 'Strange, can't find it. Ah, you must be the one who called yesterday. Leaving it late,' she snapped, a little angry.

'Yes, I suppose so. Well, you see, I...'

'You'll need this,' she handed me a blue folder with a heavy don't-waste-my-time-I-don't-give-a-damn sigh. 'Information on orientation. Introduction to Veda. Rules. Learn them. I'll get you a contract to sign,' and she bustled back to her table.

'See you got your orders.' A young man broke away from the group outside and came over to me, an impish grin lighting up his tanned face (gap between two front teeth), holding out a hand covered in garish bright green paint. 'I'm Joe.'

I shook it. Some of the paint came off on me. It was sticky and smelled, like vomit. 'Pleased to meet you.'

'Likewise,' he answered in a thick Northern accent. 'Just got in?' The sides of his head were shaved, unevenly, the rest of his hair short, standing on end, bar a long untidy pony tail sprouting from the back. Yet he didn't look aggressive, not at all; the half-hearted mohican rather sweetened his face. 'Ready for Initiation?'

'Ah, Joe.' Norma returned with a bark. 'Go up to the arts and crafts room and mend the picnic tables. Then move them out on to the cookout field. Arrange them in a circle, and make sure they're in strict numbered order. Here's the key.'

'No problem, HC,' he saluted, clicking his heels just loud enough for me to hear.

'Take Benjamin with you. Fill him in on what he's missed.'

'Will do.'

'Right then, see you later. Oh, I nearly forgot. The contract. Sign this. Give it back to me this evening. Don't forget.'

No abuse of Veda property or staff. No leaving Veda grounds without prior permission. No drinking. No smoking. No food of any kind in the Bunks. No girls in boys' bunks. No boys in girls' bunks. Veda ethos to be upheld at all times (Remember, you're special). Irregularities to be reported immediately... the list went on.

'There's a lot of rules here,' I said to Joe, closing the folder.

'Ah don't worry about those. Nobody else does. Except Kommandant Kolchak and Nazi Norma, and no one listens to them anyway. They run this place like a prison camp. But we ignore them most of the time.' He threw the file on the floor, sending up a cloud of dust. 'I bet no one's been in here all year,' he coughed. 'Well I suppose we'd better shift some of these things or it'll be the firing squad.'

We stood before a number of haphazardly stacked picnic tables in a dark, musty hut, pervaded by the stench of decaying leaves and dead animals. The walls were lined with battered tins resting precariously on worm-ridden, badly made shelves. In the far corner was an old enamel sink stained with all the colours of an ageing rainbow, under which lay a pile of twisted nails, dried pasta and a grotesque carnival mask.

'I don't know what Norma was talking about, filling you in. There's been nothing going on. We had the Kommandant's talk this afternoon, but that's about it and you didn't miss much there. Just welcoming stuff, you know, how good it is to see us, what wonderful people we all are, the normal crap. And you've met Norma, got the worst over with. She's a bitch. And a big one at that. Ellen's the other head counsellor, the other fattie. Nice girl though. Shit that's heavy!' We lifted the first table, dragged it to the door and carried it to the clearing next to the hut. 'This is the cookout field. That up there's the counsellors' lounge, completely unusable. And that over there, I don't know what that building is.'

'Is this your first time here?'

'Yep. Came in last week. Most of the others arrived yesterday. Kolchak brought a few of us over early to get the place ready. Jesus have we been working our butts off! She's a real slave driver.'

'Who's Kolchak?'

'Dr Kolchak to be precise. A doctor in psychology I think. Or is it psychiatry? Not that I can tell the difference. A bit screwy herself if you ask me. She's the director, the Kommandant, the one who gave the speech. Now she *is* weird. I can't figure her out. Don't know anyone who can.' We ambled back to the hut to fetch another table. 'She's really worked us. There's some old codger called Herbert who's supposed to be in charge of maintenance. He's the one who's supposed to look after this place, but he never does a bloody thing. Spends his time fishing down Redhill Creek. Stands all day up to his neck in water, grinning like a moron. God knows why she keeps him on. He's nutty too. Senile. In fact, come to think of it, so are most of the people who work around here. Wait till you meet Elmer, Kolchak's husband. He's in a different galaxy.

'Anyway, so we've had to sort this place out on our own. Eight 'til dusk every day this week, and there was only five of us. Kolchak said she'd hire some locals to help us out, said they could paint the pool, but she never did. She's stingy like that, never pays for anything if she can help it. Always cutting corners. Dishes out promises, never keeps them. We ended up painting it ourselves this morning. Look at me, I'm covered in the stuff.'

'You painted a swimming-pool that colour!' I stared at his garish green hands.

'It wasn't our choice, believe me,' he laughed. 'She's told us to do the basketball courts tomorrow, same colour. She's got some paint left over, wants to use it up. Waste not, buy not, that's her motto.' We lifted another table and carried it to the field. 'You should see the pool,' Joe continued after we had put it into place. 'It's hilarious.'

Veda's swimming-pool was indeed a joke: stunted, puke green and empty. Herbert was supposed to have fixed it up two weeks ago. That's another joke – Herbert couldn't fix his own dinner. I was expecting a sparkling blue, Olympic-sized affair, wide, fifty-metre lanes, basking in rolling countryside, that's what the brochure said. But then I soon realised that the brochure which had suckered me so completely in New York was little more than an exercise in creative writing: the river running through the grounds turned out to be the tiny brook I'd crossed earlier, a mouldy yellow trickle that smelt of urine; the baseball field was buried knee-deep in grass, the pitcher's mound an anthill; the tennis courts had weeds growing through their myriad cracks and (surprise) no nets; and the only smiling face I'd seen since my arrival was Joe's, and I suspected he was drunk.

Joe and I yanked the broken picnic tables from the hut and hammered and sawed and banged until most of them at least stood upright if not straight, then took a break. Over our heads an old light aircraft buzzed back and forth, sweeping low over the clearing. The pilot waved at us and did a loop the loop.

'Bloody show off! That's Patrick,' Joe said. 'He runs The Cuckoo's Nest in Sageville. He's a queer, but he's okay. Has his own landing strip up past the falls.'

We sat on a mouldy log and looked down into the wood; sunlight trickling through the leaves, birdsong scattering the calm. It was beautiful, in a rundown kind of way, like the colours which made up the scenery had faded. Nature needed touching up. But then maybe that's just my memory. I get a little lost sometimes. I'll forget you're there and stop altogether, it's nothing personal. It's gets hard, finding my way. Don't mind me, let me ramble; you just carry on...

'It's quiet around here, so tranquil.'

'You won't be saying that much longer,' Joe laughed. 'Smoke?'

'No thanks. I gave up. Bad habit.'

'So's life.' Joe took a packet of Winston from his back pocket, tapped out a cigarette, lit it, took a deep drag and let out a long, slow sigh.

'Yeah. You'll have a good time here. It's a laugh once you get off grounds. There's two bars up in town: The Cuckoo's Nest and Dotty's. Now there's a hell of a place. I've spent every night up there since I got here, the greatest pisshole I've ever seen. We'll go tonight. You'll love it. Then there's the river, the Redhill, great for swimming, and the falls for diving. And now the girls have arrived, looks like we're set. Boy are there some pretty girls! Did you see them?'

'I didn't really get the chance.'

'You must have noticed Natasha. Now she is what I call hot. Hot with a capital H. Long blond hair, blue eyes, they don't come much better than that. She's the prize, they're all after her. Me? I'm going for Claudia, tall German girl. Kind of big. But nice. Very nice. Yeah,' he nodded to himself in agreement, 'you'll have a good time all right.' There was a shout from the bottom of the hill, followed by another, the sound of wood splitting and howls of laughter. 'That's the infirmary down there. They're fixing that up too, or trying to; the place has dry rot. It's been condemned. Kolchak thinks she can hammer a few planks over the holes and that'll make everything okay.'

We sat and listened to the laughter fade. Joe smoked his way through four cigarettes, lighting one from the other, sighing contentedly after each stub had been extinguished as if a cigarette were the most exquisite pleasure the world had to offer.

'Is Joe short for Joseph?'

'No, it's short for Joe. Just Joe. Me mum chose it 'cos she thought it sounded American. She loves America. Never been here in her life, but she loves it all the same.' Joe talked about home. His mum and dad had divorced when he was a boy and he had a brother who was a postman and never spoke to him. Joe sent him a Christmas card every year. And every year, on the first post of the twenty-eighth it would be returned unopened. Joe came from some small town up in Cumbria and ever since he could remember he couldn't wait to get out of there. He had inherited the American Dream from his mom. Once Veda was over, he was going to hitch coast-to-coast, said it was something he just had to do.

Anthropology. I think that's what he said. Or was it archaeology? I can't really remember. He did tell me. But he seemed a little unsure himself. Not that he cared. Joe was studying at Coventry Polytechnic ('Cov Pol. You never heard of Cov Pol. Great place!'). He had a laugh there, said that's all that mattered: getting smashed, snogging the odd girl at the college sweaty (and they were usually odd), stealing police cones (he had a collection – one hundred and fifty-four), dressing up in drag for the *Rocky Horror Picture Show* ('seen it fifty-five times – Cov Pol record'). He knew the words, vaguely. He said he would have learnt them by heart by now, only he was pissed every time he saw the film. He growled to me: 'Everybody shoved him. I very nearly loved him. I said, hey listen to me. Stay sane inside insanity...'

Then he asked me what I was studying. So I told him.

'Philosophy!' he repeated, somewhat stunned. 'Jesus, that's a bit heavy, isn't it?'

'We all have to think.'

'Why?'

'Why! Well where would we be without thought?'

'Probably end up in a place like this.'

I wasn't sure what he meant. I was going to ask but Norma crept up behind and yelled at us for taking an 'unscheduled break'. She scared the shit out of us. We fell off the log backwards. Joe hit his head and Norma smiled. She inspected the tables and proclaimed our work 'unsatisfactory', treated us to a list of woodwork dos and don'ts, then lectured us on the perils of working too slow. Rome may not have been built in a day, she said, but at least they made a start. She told us we were useless, not to be trusted, then cracked us back to work. I clean forgot about what Joe had said. At any rate, I found out soon enough what he was talking about. Only now I wish I never knew.

At the cookout that evening, a feast of half-frozen, half-burnt hotdogs and hamburgers squashed into stale buns, our skilled handiwork and tireless effort let us down. Three of the tables collapsed, sending a large container of juice and several packets of hotdog rolls sprawling across the dirt in a sticky red mess.

'Joe! Benjamin!' Norma roared to cheers and wolf whistles from the rest of the staff.

Pissing Norma Off was against Veda rules.

We ran for cover amidst thunderous applause and ate our food round the side of the arts and crafts room, out of sight. We could hear Nazi Norma storm trooping up and down, frothing, muttering about incompetence and sloth.

'The problem with Norma is, she's never gotten over the trauma about the sex.'

At least that's what I thought Joe said. It took me a while to adjust to his accent. I only cottoned on when he started talking about the end of the world, which didn't come into any experience of sex I'd ever had.

Norma's father had founded a sect, not a very successful one by all accounts. He was a failed postman. Don't ask me how you can be a failed postman, but he was. He got the sack and, with his redundancy money, travelled round Georgia predicting armageddon for July 3rd.

God wanted to punish the American people, he preached, they'd disappointed Him. So He was going to wrap everything up on July 3 just to stymie America's celebrations for Independence Day, thus pissing off all those patriotic citizens who'd laid plans. Serves them right, they should have read their Bible more. Anyway, Norma's father waxed lyrical on doom, gloom, and hit upon the idea of the End Of The World Foundation™, for which he collected donations totalling $1,334. Not bad for two weeks' work; more than he earned as a postman. Sounds far-fetched? Remember, this was the Deep South. You can read about it in the *Georgia Herald* if you don't believe me, issue Nº 666/3, 4 July 1962.

When the great day finally came it proved to be a bit of a let down. Norma's father was hoping for the mass suicide of his followers. In the event, only three turned up. In truth, only two. One, George Jackson, Snr. (eighty-three years old) died of a heart attack climbing the hill on top of which the mass suicide was supposed to take place.

So there was only Norma's father and Martha, his housemaid (plus the journalist from the *Georgia Herald* who was covering the story). They considered calling it off out of respect for George Jackson, Snr., but decided, under pressure from the journalist, to go ahead with the suicide. The journalist (who later became a senior editor on the *New York Times*) had paid a fortune in taxi fares to get to the remote hilltop and he wasn't about to be short changed.

Arsenic, that's what they took. Small capsules. The journalist was disappointed. He'd been promised self-immolation (sells more copies), but Martha had forgotten the matches, left them on the kitchen table. So they popped a few pills instead.

Martha must have had a stomach of iron. She swallowed the arsenic, lay down to die, got up two hours later and went home to make the supper. She's as fit as a fiddle to this very day, Georgia's oldest living resident.

Norma's father wasn't so lucky. He keeled over instantly. Dead. End of the road.

So much for sects. (Stick to sex.)

Poor Norma. Not that Joe and I had time for a lot of sympathy whilst she was chasing round barking after our balls.

Eventually, Joe went back to the cookout field to face the fire. Not because he was brave, he just wanted second helpings of hotdogs. I slunk away to the bunk to freshen up for Dotty. I tried the shower, but all I got was brown water and thick clumps of rust. So I sat on the toilet to make a start on some of the books I'd brought (a blissful habit I picked up from my father who has curved floor-to-ceiling bookshelves surrounding the toilet bowl), but the seat was broken, plastic splinters lodging in my arse. In the end I forgot about cleaning up, lay down on my lumpy bed, pummelled the mattress into some sort of horizontal shape, and closed my eyes.

'Eeh! Meester Joa, you creezy bastard!'

'Stojan you old horse! Come over here, meet Benjamin. Benjamin this is Stojan, our resident nutter from Yugoslavia.'

'Montenegro. Montenegro. Titograd, Montenegro!' he roared heartily, slapping Joe on the back, spilling beer from his mug. 'Good to meet you, Bejamine. From London right? Right?' he prodded me and shouted.

'Yes, that's right.'

'I knew it, I knew it Meester Bejamine. What a city! What a city!' he bellowed in his heavy accent. 'My town. London. My town. What a city!' he threw his head back and laughed, revealing a mismatched set of dark, decaying teeth. 'Well come on then, let's sit and have a lettle drink my frieend. Just a lettle drink. Come, come, Stojan Radulovic at your servis.' He took a jug from the large oak table, filled our glasses, smashed his against mine, spilling still more beer, and emptied its contents in one long, thirsty gulp. 'That's goud. That's goud.'

'I love this place,' Joe said after Stojan had left to go and buy another pitcher. 'See that jukebox over there? The most modern thing on that is Sinatra.'

Dotty's, or rather The Old Rockcliffe, was a long, thin, dimly lit bar with a square back room, an upright piano with absent keys, an antiquated jukebox, and a dilapidated pool table. It was the kind of place where Real Men in short-sleeved checked shirts and grubby baseball hats (advertising the local mechanic) spat on the floor and shot pool until they died. Baseball played on a television high up in a corner with the colours so faded that you couldn't tell which team was which. Not that it mattered, no one was watching. Above the bar was a string of Stars and Stripes, behind it an enormous array of bottles: whiskey, gin, rum, martini, brandy, more whiskey, and – a bottle of moonshine in her hands – Dotty: the old lady of seventy-three with a full head of white hair who owned, ran the place, and drank, tirelessly.

'Turn it up, Dotty!' came a loud New York shout. Dolly Parton burst forth from the antique brown speakers hanging (barely) on the wall. I filled Joe's glass, then my own.

'Ellen, Ellen, come here.' Joe, already a touch drunk, beckoned wildly to the second large lady from the dining-hall, the other head counsellor. 'Why weren't you at the cookout? I missed you.'

'How sweet,' she kissed his cheek. 'The boss wanted to see me. But don't worry, I heard all about your little screw up. Norma was livid. She was still ranting about your incompetence down at High Command. I'm only sorry I didn't get to see it. So come on then Joe, introduce me.'

'This,' Joe took a gulp of beer. 'This is my brother, Benjamin. Ben for short.'

'Joe, you are naughty, you didn't tell me you had such a handsome brother.'

'I'm not his brother.'

'No,' said Joe, lurching slightly. 'He's my friend and a damn good one at that. Damn good!' He finished off his glass.

'Hi, I'm Ellen.'

'Pleasure to meet you. Joe was telling me about you this afternoon.'

'Oh yes, and what was he saying?'

'Lies, all lies,' Joe yelled, filling his glass again. 'Ben's from Cambridge. I suspect he might be a toff, but a damn good one. Damn good!'

'Joe,' Ellen interrupted. 'You're drunk.'

'Not yet. But I'm working on it. Have another drink,' he slopped beer into her mug. 'I always said, Ellen, never judge a toff before you've mended a table with him. Never. And I was right, wasn't I Ben?'

'DAMN!' A shout came from the pool table, followed by a long cheer. Dolly Parton gave way to Frank Sinatra, Frank Sinatra to Johnny Cash, Johnny Cash to Neil Diamond, who in turn gave way to Dolly Parton and the cycle began again. Glasses were emptied, filled and emptied, emptied and filled. Jugs were bought. Pool was shot. Even the out-of-tune piano was played (badly) by a thin civil-servant type in a striped shirt. 'That's Mark,' Joe told me. 'He's from Cornwall. Goes on about Cornish independence and the history of the pasty. Bit of a stiff if you ask me.'

A local took down a flag from above the bar, waved it aloft and yelled 'God Bless America'. He then bought all the counsellors a shot of whiskey, almost exhausting Dotty's supply. 'Cheers!' He got up on a table and shouted above the music. 'Welcome to the USA. Land of the free.' There was prolonged applause and whistling, then utter silence whilst everyone drained the contents of their glasses.

'You must be Benjamin.'

The young man who came up to the table looked tense, uncomfortable, his hand tentatively outstretched as though half expecting me not to shake it. He was smiling, but that was just formality, you could tell that right away. His jet black hair was offset by youthful red cheeks, capillaries running riot, and he was dressed not stylishly but with clear attention to quality, though a little stiffly, like his mother bought all his clothes. He was familiar somehow, though for the life of me I couldn't say why. Perhaps it was the whiskey.

'Must I?'

'Yes.'

'Why?'

'Joe told me. He said I should introduce myself. So, I'm Lucien. Lucien Diabolo, from Paris.'

'Ah, that great snarling city. Paris!'

'You don't like it?' Lucien looked offended.

'Like it? I love it. Paris is woman. How can I not like it? Woman. No more. No less. I always wondered why they called it Paris and not Helen. *Vous parlez très bien anglais Lucien, et avec un bon accent, très bon*.'

'Thank you. I lived in London as a child. My father worked at the Embassy for a while. And please, use tu.' He put his empty whiskey glass on the mantelpiece and sat down, looking at each of the counsellors at the table in turn before fixing his eyes intently on me, waiting for me to speak. His gaze was a little disturbing, like he was expecting something from me. The whiskey had started to go to my head, so I poured myself a beer to help it on its way.

I was just about to resuscitate our flagging conversation when Lucien spoke, cutting me short, as if on cue, stuttering nervously like a schoolboy up before the head.

'Joe, he tells me you study philosophy, at Cambridge.'

'Does he?'

'Don't you?'

'Yes.'

'So do I, study philosophy I mean. Just like you. Well, at least I try. Not in Cambridge, in Paris. I'm sure I'd know you if I studied in Cambridge. Or perhaps not. Maybe we wouldn't be friends. Though of course, I'd like that. I expect we're quite similar. Fascinating subject don't you think?'

'What is?' I said, trying to follow his twisted trail of thought.

'Philosophy. Philosophy is a fascinating subject to study. It's the only thing that comes up with any answers.'

'It has its merits, I suppose. Though it's all improvised wisdom, you do realise that, don't you? Like everything else, improvised.' I couldn't believe Lucien was serious. I was sure he was poking fun at me. So I took a swift gulp of whiskey, frowned heavily and leant towards him with a gruff snort, like my political thought tutor (who was about to snuff it and leave a fortune to his unfaithful wife) when he's on the verge of casting a pearl (though I only ever caught the swine). 'Who was it Lucien, eh?' I began in a slow, drawn out, pompous drawl. 'Montaigne I think, one of yours, who said "Philosophy, the search for knowledge, is to learn how to die".'

'Yes, yes, I remember that.' Lucien came alive, sparked, bolt upright in his seat, almost clapping his hands with excitement, wetting himself. 'A valid point, interesting. We are seeking answers to questions that only death can provide,' he pronounced with suffocating solemnity.

'Lucien!' I slapped him hard on the back, laughing, and gave him a beer. 'Please. Lighten up a little! This is summertime. I don't want to learn how to die. I've barely started learning how to live.'

It was then I saw what was familiar, something I recognised: it was the hurt in his eyes; it reminded me of Peter. My teasing was out of place. He smiled uneasily. I wanted to say something. But it was too late. The moment passed.

'Lucien!' Joe gasped urgently, grabbing his arm. 'Did you know your eyes are black? Never seen that before. He's got black eyes,' he leant over to Ellen, using her arm to steady himself. 'He's got black eyes. Amazing. Just like the devil himself.'

'Lucien, you old frog!' a stout man with a thin moustache and a large beer gut, stumbled into the bar, booming.

'Dave,' Joe raised his glass. 'Where've you been?'

'Over at The Cuckoo's Nest.'

'What's it like?'

'Well it ain't swinging like this place, I tell ya that. Fuck it's 'eaving!'

'This is Benjamin, got in today.'

'How do?' he said, licking some froth from his chin. 'Where you from then?'

'London.'

'London?'

'Hampstead.'

'Well that ain't London, is it, not London proper. That's snob's place. Full of pansies. Ya might as well be a bleedin' foreigner. I mean...' He stopped, mid-sentence, looking around, searching for something. 'Well come on then! What we waitin' for? Get the beers in.'

More jugs were bought. More glasses filled. More emptied. And the introductions rolled on: Chris, a handsome, wholesome American with the ageless white-teeth smile to prove it; Fergus, an ageing hippy with a tie-dye shirt, a hook nose and dye-tied thinning long hair; and Bjorn, a tall Swede with terrible English and drooping eyelids that made him look like he was permanently doped to the hilt. We drank and sang like old friends on New Year's Eve, starting with 'New York, New York', progressing after several repeats to 'My *Way'* and ending with 'Stand By Your Man', by which time most of us couldn't even stand up, let alone stand by anyone.

'That's Claudia,' Joe said during the intermission. 'Gorgeous, isn't she?' He pointed to a tall girl at the bar with short white hair and baggy dungarees, like Andy Pandy after an over enthusiastic trip to the barbers. 'And this,' he continued, not giving me a chance to speak, 'is Natasha.'

A slim girl with bright blue eyes, a mass of long blond hair and pouting lips emerged from the smoky crowd at the bar and sat at our table.

'Hi Joe,' she said in a soft voice, her pale skin flushed from the sun.

'Hi Natasha. How's things?'

'Great. I'm tipsy.' She crossed her slender legs, glancing at Dave who couldn't take his eyes off them.

' 'Ello darlin'. Don't waste ya time wiv them poofs. Why don't you come over 'ere and sit on my knee?'

'Not now Dave. But you could fill up my glass for me.' She passed it to him and he obediently carried out the request. 'Thanks, sweetie.'

'Anyfing for you darlin'. Anyfing. Anytime. Cheers!' He raised his glass.

'Cheers.' She raised hers. He gulped down a mouthful, she a small sip. 'So who's this then? Aren't you going to introduce me?'

'I was wondering when you'd ask,' Joe said with a wry smile. 'Say hello to Benjamin.'

'Hello, Benjamin. Having fun?'

'Yes, thanks. Joe's looking after me.'

'Where did you get those bruises?' Her eyes scanned my face, then looked into mine.

'I got into a fight in New York.'

'Oh you poor thing, are you all right?'

'Yes I'm fine now. It's looks worse than it is.'

'What happened?' She moved a little closer, turning her back on Joe.

'I saw someone getting mugged and tried to help...' and off I went, giving the longer version of my mishap. She sat and stared at me, her mouth slightly open, a drop of moisture on her lips. Music played and alcohol flowed. She asked me what I did. I let fly, racing over my routine. I told her about Cambridge: about my first in philosophy; how I was taking flying lessons with the RAF University Air Squadron; about the brilliant parties; the glittering intellects; regaling her with tales of fencing bouts and wild friends. I gave her everything. She took it all and still wanted more. She moved closer. I poured out another two beers. She asked me to go on.

'Well, Ben,' Joe lurched between us with smirk, 'here's to one hell of a summer eh.' He winked at me and we drained our glasses.

4

Joe was right. Kolchak was weird.

That night, after Dotty's, I couldn't sleep – too much alcohol. So I got up early to take a look around. I was the only one awake. At least, I thought I was. Then I heard this hullabaloo down on the edge of the woods, this tremendous screeching, like two animals locked in combat. I hate it when animals fight. I know they're supposed to, Nature's way and all, but I hate it all the same. When I was a kid I would lie in bed and hear tomcats tear each other's eyes out over some bitch. I'd open my window, grab a stone from my father's fossil collection and throw it at them, just to stop them scrapping. I couldn't bear the thought of their hurting each other. I didn't mind people fighting, I still don't. In fact I rather enjoy it, they deserve it. But animals, that's another story. So I raced along the edge of the wood, desperate to stop the fight. But the only thing that stopped was me – dead in my tracks. In a corner of Veda, where the ends of the razorwire fence meet, I saw the two Kolchaks: the Kommandant, and her husband, Elmer. He was a mirror image of her, petite and frail-looking, like he'd been awoken from death, yet a little chubby at the same time. It wasn't chubbiness from eating or drinking, you could tell that. It was baby fat that he'd never quite got round to losing.

Elmer Kolchak had a knife in his hand; not a poxy Swiss Army knife that you buy on holiday and give to your kids for Christmas, but a huge hunting knife with a fuck-off blade, shining long and sweet in the early morning light. You could do some serious damage with that thing. And he was running around, waving it above his head, lunging at a chicken which screeched in fear of its life. The poor thing was terrified, chased by a tired man in his seventies at six o'clock on a Sunday morning.

And the most bizarre thing of all was that Dr Kolchak, the Kommandant, was just standing, watching. Not applauding or anything, not even egging her husband on, just watching. I couldn't believe it. This was that sweet grandmother of a woman who gave us such a charming welcome yesterday; the kind of old thing you could only hug.

Elmer cornered the chicken, its feathers squashed up against the wire fence, squawking. For an old man, he was really quite agile. He raised the knife above his head, chuckling to himself, and was just about to bring it down across the chicken's neck, smacking his lips in anticipation of the bloodbath, when his wife piped up.

'Okay Elmer, you can stop there.'

And that's just what he did. He stopped. He lowered the knife, put it back in its sheath and blew his nose, calm and composed, even a little jolly, like he was discussing a good baseball result with the vicar after the Sunday service. Even the chicken seemed to relax.

Dr Kolchak stepped forward, picked up the chicken with expert hands, stroked it under the chin as though it were a cat and the three of them – the Kommandant, Elmer, and the chicken – wandered off together, no doubt in search of breakfast.

I said nothing. Not a word. I wasn't even sure of what I'd seen. After all, it was early, I hadn't slept well and I'd been drunk the night before. I couldn't swear that that's what really happened. Besides, soon enough there were other things to think about.

Veda moved up a gear. Norma span into action, in her element, dictating orders here, there, and just about everywhere. Sweep the bunk! Scrub the basin! (I can still see grime rings. Scrub some more.) Repair the toilets! (Nice smooth flush now.) Mend the mosquito mesh! (Not another little bugger in sight.) Cut the grass! (I want it looking like a carpet.)

My detail, along with Joe and Chris, was to paint the basketball courts using the left-over paint from the swimming-pool – bright green. The pool itself stayed empty. Herbert had forgotten to order the chlorine.

Norma was everywhere, all at the same time. You'd watch her disappear down the path in front of you, sit back and take a breather from your work. Then you'd hear the bark. Distinct. Rasping. It could only be Norma. She'd be behind you (God knows how she got there). 'Look lively! Look lively!'

Along with the omnipresence of Nazi Norma, each job came equipped with tools of a specific designer brand: Fucking Useless Inc. The paint brushes were more suited to boxtop watercolours than to a basketball court. Blunt garden sheers were expected to cut an entire baseball field, in and out. To put up the mesh, nails were carefully doled out from the store-room; each one had to be meticulously accounted for and was bent in at least two ways. And there was only one hammer (a rubber camping mallet) for the whole of Veda.

Two days of this and we were dead, each and every one. Barely enough collective strength to lift a glass of beer.

And on the third day, after a more than usually tasteless breakfast of puréed pancakes and sickly syrup, Norma said: 'Let them be allotted their bunks'. And it was done.

Joe and I were given Boys' Bunk 8, the largest cabin on the lower level of Veda. It stood on the edge of the forest in the far corner of the baseball field (now looking like a hacked up carpet), one of the few to have shade from overhanging trees, with only seven beds and one bunkbed where there was room for at least twelve. 'Looks like we've hit the jackpot Ben. Ellen's got a soft spot for you,' Joe said, throwing his bag on the bunkbed. 'And I, for one, am happy about that. I'll take the bottom if that's okay.'

We spent the day cleaning and arranging the bunk. We disinfected the bathroom, moved the beds along one wall to create maximum floor space, installed a small couch and table which we stole from the counsellors' lounge, and removed a dead grass snake from the shower. It snapped in two when Joe picked it up. He wanted to keep it as a souvenir, but I made him throw it away. By the end of the day B8 was habitable. All it needed was a toilet that flushed and a shower that sprayed water, not rust.

Natasha was our first visitor.

'Wow! You guys have struck it lucky. This place is enormous.' She bounced on my bed. 'Hmm, comfy,' she said with a wicked grin. I lifted her off and the three of us went to Dotty's where Joe sat in silence at the far end of the bar, ogling Claudia from a safe distance, inspecting his feet every time she turned round to try and catch his eye.

'Joe. Stop being pathetic,' I told him. 'Just go and buy her a drink. It's that simple.'

'I will. I will. Just have to wait for the right moment, that's all. The right moment. Timing. That's the name of the game. Timing.' He bought a whiskey, drank it with one gulp, stood up with pronounced purpose, marched over with a masterful manly strut to where Claudia was sitting and waltzed right past her, slouching down at Chris' table, deflated, gazing at her from the far end of the bar.

He looked over at me and shrugged apologetically.

'Can't you talk to Claudia?' I pleaded to Natasha. 'You know her. Tell her to give Joe some attention. He hasn't stopped talking about her. It's driving me nuts.'

'He's in love. I think it's sweet.'

'He's not in love, he's in lust. And the more whiskey he drinks, the worse it gets.'

'Okay I'll talk to her. I'll fix something up.'

Natasha and I sat and talked. Or rather, I did most of the talking. She cooed. I had her right where I wanted her. She sat opposite me, her eyes flitting from my lips to my eyes then back again. Occasionally she brushed her hand against mine, and spoke in a low voice as though pulling me into some forbidden secret. She told me a little about her home. She came from Wolverhampton, somewhere like that. Her father raced pigeons, or tried to. He was a lousy trainer and each time he let them go, they'd just fly away and never come back. Cost him a fortune. She talked mostly about her mother; she'd had a hard life, raised a family and went out to work to compensate for the useless husband she'd been given. She was the bread-winner; he was the bread-eater (along with his pigeons). The story had a sad end: fights, divorce, that kind of thing, I wasn't really listening, though I did hear the part about the mother pouring petrol all around the pigeon shed. One cigarette, carelessly flicked to the ground, and BOOM! No more pigeons, no more marriage.

I watched Natasha with vague interest. But what gave me the greatest pleasure was the barrage of envy oozing from the other guys in the bar. Dave watched her intently, eyes fixed, or rather he watched me watching her. I wasn't sure who he had the hots for: Natasha or me.

I didn't see Lucien again until the next evening. I'd been looking for him, couldn't figure out where he'd been hiding. I don't know why I so wanted to see him, but I did. He'd triggered something; a memory, a blur. I was on my way up to Dotty's and there he was, standing in front of Sageville church, staring up at the wooden tower. I stopped and waited. Every few minutes he would move his head gently from side to side, walk up to the door and shake his hands, before stepping backwards and staring up at the tower again. He was muttering to himself. I couldn't make out what he was saying, but he was clearly agitated.

A battered blue Chevrolet rattled along the highway, a young man in grubby overalls at the wheel. Lucien turned and saw me, then bent down and pretended to be tying his shoe-lace.

'Why don't you go in?' I called out.

'Go in where?' he replied, acting surprised to see me.

'The church.'

'Why should I?'

I walked over to him. 'I just thought you might.'

'Why?'

'No reason.' I wanted to say something about the other night, apologise for teasing him. 'Coming to Dotty's?'

'Later.'

'Lucien, listen, the other night, I didn't mean...'

'I have to make some phone calls,' he interrupted, looking past me, shifting from one foot to the other.

'Okay. It's just that, if I upset you...'

'Upset me. Why should you have upset me?' The fingers of his right hand shook, almost fluttering with the evening breeze. He started to walk away, turned, and came back. 'Why should you have upset me?' he asked again, fidgeting with the buttons on his jacket.

'I don't know. But if I did, I didn't mean it, that's all.'

'Upset? I don't see why I should be upset.' He turned away again and started walking down to the general store.

I watched him go.

'I have to make a phone call,' he shouted over his shoulder and broke into a run.

I stayed there for while, hoping he would come back, staring up at the wooden church tower. But the dark brought the cold, and I went to Dotty's alone.

'Let the orientating begin.'

That's what Norma said, at breakfast on Thursday. She stood up with great pomp, blobbling her way to the centre of the hall (stamp, stomp), clapped her hands, coughed, and shouted: 'Let the orientating begin'. God knows who she thought she was, Caesar or someone. And perhaps God knows what she meant. I certainly didn't.

I thought maybe we'd get maps, compasses, toggles, cub scout shorts, something like that (Akela we will do our best). I thought we'd get the chance to dress up as little boys and run around the woods playing silly games, pretending to be men.

But I was wrong.

All we were given were files and told to go away and learn them. I was excited, eager finally to find out what Veda was all about, find out exactly what we'd be doing. That was a mistake. I realise that now, looking back. But I'm not the kind of person who learns from mistakes. I should have taken my cue, got the hell out of there whilst the going was good, and maybe I'd have come out of this okay.

Dakota is severely autistic. Low functioning, self-abusive, can be violent towards others. Hyperactive. Sugar intake must be strictly regulated.

Mitchel has cerebral palsy. Relatively high functioning. Frequent seizures, sometimes severe. Prone to acute temper tantrums. Can be violent, occasionally vicious.

William is low functioning. On heavy medication to prevent damaging seizures. Problems with bowels, soils regularly. Overheats easily. Must have enforced periods of rest.

'Joe?' I dropped the file on my lap.

'What?' he lay on his bed, smoking a cigarette, reading my Nietzsche

The minds of others I know well;
But who I *am, I cannot tell:*
My eye is much too close to me,
I am not what I saw and see.
It would be quite a benefit
If only I could sometimes sit
Farther away . . .

'Have you seen this?'

'Seen what?'

'This!'

'What?'

I jumped down from my bed and threw the file at him.

'Jesus, Ben! What's the matter?'

'Take a look at that. First page. Introductions.'

He took a drag and opened the file. 'What?' he said, looking up at me.

'What? What do you mean, what? They're fucking lunatics.' I paced the bunk. Back and forth, floorboards moaning with each step. Back and forth.

'Ben, take it easy. Sit down will you, you're making me nervous. Jesus! What's your problem?'

'What do you mean what's *my* problem? I don't have a problem, Joe. This place has a problem. This place is a fucking loony bin. A madhouse. A crank farm. And you ask what's *my* problem. How can you be so damn calm. Why didn't anyone tell me? These are fully fledged fucking lunatics, Joe. Card-carrying crazies. Cuckoo. *Capisch?*'

'I know. What were you expecting?'

'What was I expecting?' I yelled. I didn't like yelling (lack of control, exposed weakness). But I did. Yell. Loud.

I stopped pacing and sat on a bed in the corner, listening to the shrill echo of my voice fade into the woods. Then I got up. Pacing again. Back and forth, rhythm channelling anger. Back. Forth. 'You mean to say you knew. All this time. You knew and said nothing?'

'Of course, that's why I came here. Benjamin, I work with "loonies" back home. What the hell did you think Veda was?'

'God, I don't know. Learning difficulties. Kids with learning problems. Reading, writing. Not violent, bowel-shifting, fucking crackpots.'

'Who told you that?'

'The brochure.'

'I told you about believing that thing. Jesus. You've been led right up the garden path,' Joe laughed.

I did not.

I kicked the wall, leaving a small hole in the thin hardboard that just about held up the roof.

Joe stopped laughing. He got up from the bed and flung his cigarette out the window. 'Sorry, Ben, I didn't realise. I thought you knew. I would've have said something, but I thought you knew.'

I stood by the door, looking out into the forest. It hadn't changed, not so you'd notice. Tranquil. The setting was the same. Everything was the same. But I didn't see the green fields, nor the wood. I didn't hear the birds, or smell the pines. I gazed straight through to the high razorwire fence. Joe was talking: muffled words. I heard the terrified squawking of the chicken, Elmer's knife raised high above his head, Kolchak's calm face, and behind, standing on the outside, looking in, looking for me, I saw Peter. He had a pencil in one hand and the sharpener in the other. He was smiling, faintly, beckoning. He said he wanted to explain something to me, talk. But I was afraid and moved away from the window.

'...believe me,' Joe went on, and on, 'you'll handle it. Why not try and calm down a little, eh?'

I sat down. He went back to his bed and picked up Nietzsche.

'Oh by the way, how's it going with Natasha? You're a lucky son of a bitch you know that. Everyone's after her.'

nobody wins all the time

At first I used to go home for weekends. Some of the boys on my dorm stayed; they lived too far away, or they didn't get on so well with their parents, but I would always go home. I would read to Mother while she cooked, the pages of my book damp from the steam in the kitchen. Or Father would give me extra fencing lessons in the summerhouse at the end of the garden. We fenced foil. Father never took to sabre; said it wasn't precise enough, too much chopping and slashing. Said if the school wanted me to succeed in life, it should be teaching me foil, not sabre. I still can't beat him at foil, but I'll trounce the old man at sabre.

I loved weekends. My parents belonged to me in those days and whatever we did, we'd do it together. I was never bored. When I had nothing to do, I would do it with them.

Then *they* came.

Mother had the feeling she wasn't doing enough for the community: guilt or some such other worthless emotion. So she thought long. She thought hard. Something local, that was what she wanted. And she took upon the idea of the kids from the psychiatric hospital nearby. Except it wasn't really a psychiatric hospital, more a psychotic hotch-potch.

The first time she invited them round was to make angel cakes one Saturday morning in May. I remember going upstairs to my room and one of them was there, lying on my bed, drooling on my sheets, chewing the ear of Bear. I asked him to leave. He didn't answer and he wouldn't budge. Just carried on drooling as if I wasn't there. I ordered him out and he wouldn't move. Ignored me. So I picked up my pillow and started beating him. Beat him so hard my hands turned blue. Still he wouldn't move. Mother heard the yelling and thundered upstairs. When she saw me hitting the crazy with a pillow, she slapped me clean across the face. That was the only time she ever hit me. She said he was *special* and I mustn't behave with him like that. *Special*.

They came every week after that. Crawling all over the bloody house. Playing with my toys, pretending to read my books, sitting in my chair in the kitchen. I took to sitting on my own in the summer-house. I don't think Mother even noticed. She was too enwrapped in her little angels.

I stopped going home for weekends. Spent all my time at school. At least my sabre improved.

5

Seven: Dakota, Mitchel, William, Robert, Charlie, Walter and Joshua. Seven files crammed with information: medical conditions; functioning levels; sexual habits (extra pages stapled on); tablets, medicines; forbidden foods and liquids; co-ordination abilities; speech difficulties; behavioural patterns; skin conditions; ear infections; and extensive details on toilet-training, right down to the last flush of the loo. Seven files to work on. Seven patients to learn. Seven lists of incomprehensible facts. Seven lunatics.

We read in silence.

After lunch, cold chicken and hot ice cream, came the first orientation session: we sat and listened; Norma stood (on a table) and snapped, rattling off disorganised lists of facts, any and every how, at a bewildering rate.

1. Veda is a special place.
2. You are special people.
3. Veda is split into two sections: higher level, lower level.
4. The higher level takes adult clients from institutions and care homes in New York (new group every two weeks).
5. The lower level takes adult and child clients from private families across America (one group for the whole season).
6. Those on the higher level are lower functioning.
7. Those on the lower level, higher functioning.
8. Reveille at seven-thirty, for breakfast at eight-thirty (sharp – lateness punished).
9. All clients expected to be up, washed, teeth clean, dressed, happy by that time.
10. Veda has seven daily activities: academics, cooking, drama, music, basketball, arts and crafts, sewing.
11. Swimming every day is compulsory.
12. Except when it rains, when films are compulsory.
13. Come to think of it, all activities are compulsory.
14. At nine-thirty counsellors are free until midnight.
15. Between these hours one counsellor is assigned to watch over bunks to ensure clients are safe, known as On Duty (OD).

15. a) N.B. Counsellors are never completely Off Duty (OfD), even when they are not fully On Duty (OD).

16. ODs will be given out as punishments if and when the head counsellors (HCs) so please.
17. Programmes are run by programme counsellors (PCs).
18. Bunks are looked after by bunk counsellors (BCs).
19. Bunk counsellors are required to go with their bunk to programmes to assist programme counsellors in the running of their programmes. They are, under no circumstances, permitted to BO (Bugger Off).
20. Clear?
21. Good.

The day dragged on in much the same way, a whistle-stop tour of lunacy, delivered with a pace and lack of coherence that only a lunatic could understand.

We were introduced to the medical staff: Dr Rosenthal, a woman even more fossilised than Kolchak, who could barely walk owing to a crooked back obtained from her lifelong habit of sleeping hunched in a wooden chair; and two nurses, Ruth and Rebecca, one with a limp, the other with an inhaler. Rosenthal had been struck off, so Kolchak got her on the cheap. As for the 'nurses', they were about to go to college to study medicine and hitherto had no more experience of medical practice than dishing out the odd aspirin.

The high point of bewilderment came when the Kommandant took the floor. She shuffled to the centre of the room, smiling benevolently at her staff. I tried to conjure it up, the chicken: her bestowing mercy, ordering a halt to her husband's slaughter, rescuing the dumb animal from imminent sacrifice. But I couldn't do it. The picture just didn't fit. Had you seen her, standing there in the dining-hall, a picture of aged gentility, you'd have thought I'd made up the whole chicken episode.

She held her hands high as if to bless us, waiting for silence, then began.

'Veda is *special*,' she smiled. (A titter from the back, an embarrassed cough.) We were supposed to return the greeting, 'You're *special*'. But no one did. Except Norma, a sole stupid voice ringing out across the dining-hall. Kolchak smiled at her second-in-command, thanked her for her example of understanding and kindness, then began.

'Veda deals with the mentally ill and retarded. However, it is our strict policy only to take clients above a certain functioning level. All applicants are thoroughly screened and we accept only those we feel can benefit from our programme. So none of you will have to deal with serious mental illnesses.' She spoke slowly and quietly, fearful we might not understand. She fixed her eyes on each counsellor in turn, granting an individual smile, just for them, because they were SPECIAL.

'Serious Mental Illnesses,' she said and stared at me.

'On the charts which I'm going to hand round are a list of the conditions which affect Veda's clients.' (She actually called them clients.)

There was no point going into these conditions in great detail, it would only confuse us. That's what she said, her words. Then, consulting her notes, moving a little closer, so we could see the varicose veins bursting beneath her tights, she went on to give a prolonged, highly technical and confusing introduction to the various worlds (known and unknown) of abnormality.

By the end my head was spinning. I couldn't tell what was Down's or ups, Autistic or artistic, Palsy or plausible. I had gained no knowledge of how to deal with the consignment of crazy cargo arriving at the weekend, could not distinguish between retarded and insane, deranged and demented, psychopathic and psychotic, schizophrenic and schizoid, manic and manical, catatonic, depressive, hyperactive, shell-shocked, defective, stark, certified, bewildered, bemused, unhinged, unbalanced, obsessed, possessed, crackers, cracked, scatty, screwy, nutty, nuts, bananas, batty, cuckoo, barmy, bonkers, loco, daft, dippy, loopy, potty, dotty, cranky, wacky, dizzy, giddy... Giddy. I was giddy. I couldn't tell the difference. Nor did I give a damn. I was thinking about my departure from Veda, planning my return journey to New York City on the next bus.

'I hope that has been of some help. Thank you for your attention.' Kolchak lingered for one last prolonged smile, a squint, then, instead of shuffling back to her seat, went and stood by the window and stared out on to the grounds. It was like someone had turned her off, put her on the shelf, and there she stood there until tea. Immobile. If you looked carefully, you could just detect her breathing.

'What was about all that?' Bjorn said under his breath.

'Don't ask me. I didn't understand a word,' Chris replied.

'Was English she speaking?'

'A lunatic's a lunatic,' Dave replied. 'Don't make no difference what you call 'em. Fancy language don't mean Jack Shit.'

'Thank you Dr Kolchak,' Norma rose, ignoring her director standing at the window, 'for a most interesting and informative talk. Now we've heard something of the theoretical side I'd like to focus on the practical.'

We were then subjected to seizures: *grand mal, petit mal*, causes, drugs, and what to do when your client starts spinning out of control. 'Do not put your hand near their mouth, despite what you may have heard in the past. If their head is on its side there's little chance of them swallowing their tongue. During a seizure muscles contract. Put your fingers in their mouth and you'll get them taken off.'

Rosetta, a smaller but fiercer model of Norma who was in charge of the kitchens, wheeled out two metal urns. Tea time. We stopped for a drink, biscuits and a cosy natter about epilepsy.

At Cambridge, I would buy Chelsea buns from Fitzbillies (rushing past St Cat's, pushing against biting winds) for afternoon tea and sit with friends in Charles's rooms over looking Old Court, lounging in rough leather armchairs which squeaked each time you moved, chatting about nothing until our conscience dragged us kicking and screaming back to the library. Charles never did like to work much. He was library-phobic. He never handed in essays and would have gotten into serious trouble long ago had it not been for old Squiggley. Professor Squiggley was the senior Classics don at our college, devoted his life to Hellenistic domestic earthenware, and he thought Charlie was the best thing that ever happened to the Classics faculty: not so much his mind or insight into antiquity, more a question of his butt. Squiggley wanted to get into Charlie's pants, everyone knew it, and that was the only reason Charlie kept passing his exams. All he had to do was drop his trousers. Once a term, not more, in the faculty museum, behind the Laocoön. That kept old Squiggley going (a pant, a grunt, and it was over), made sure the marks Charlie's supervisors gave him and the marks officially listed were somehow never quite the same.

The buns from Fitzbillies are sweet and sticky and when you eat them, nothing else matters. The tea at Veda was disgusting.

Lucien was sitting on his own, so I called him over to join us. Joe wasn't best pleased. He felt uncomfortable around Lucien, said he was a Grade A weirdo. But I didn't like the thought of his being alone.

He showed me his exercise book. It was full of notes, page after page after page. He must have written out every single one of Kolchak's syllables out in pro-long hand. On the front page he had drawn the cross section of the human head, with a crucifix and video camera in place of the brain.

Tea finished, break ended, we moved on to violent clients.

Rather than (as I'd foolishly presumed) running like hell from violent psychotics, Norma actually instructed us to go *towards* them and implement the restraining position. This she demonstrated on Ellen who was neither a) strong, b) violent, nor c) psychotic. It was the not the most reassuring of demonstrations.

I thought I'd met everyone. How I'd missed her, I don't know. The girl opposite, sitting stiffly in her chair; she wasn't exactly the kind of character you could overlook. It wasn't that she was beautiful, far from it. She had a gaunt, pale, almost white face and was dressed in shabby, mismatched clothes, a tatty skirt hanging awkwardly over thin legs, her head slightly bowed, gaze lowered, a sad air, a sombre spectre who didn't quite fit. I suppose it's possible you may not have remarked on any of this; just another weirdo, a little underfed perhaps, but something you'd come to expect from Veda. It was the hood you couldn't ignore. Not a rain cap or a hat: a large, pointed hood made of thick, coarse cloth in a dark, rich purple, set back on her forehead, casting her face in shadow.

She was there. No doubt about that. And yet absent, removed, as though standing back from us, watching from afar. I was fascinated by her. I wanted her to look up, to acknowledge me. I whispered, waved, called out loud, whistled, attracting everyone's attention but hers. She wouldn't raise her eyes, not to me, didn't even seem to hear. Seemed preoccuppied. Eventually Norma told me to shut up and I slunk back in my seat.

The afternoon lumbered to a tortuous close, dragging its heels, reluctant to let evening take over. The girl in the hood left before dinner and didn't come back again. We sat down to a lasagne with a cheese crust so heavy it sank to the bottom of the dish, followed by peach halves from a tin, the solidified juice of which refused point blank to leave the can.

After the staff had been allowed their one cigarette on the hill, Norma marched us back into the hall for the evening session, which was devoted to reinforcement: positive, negative, neutral – 'an effective way to ensure a working link between client and counsellor'. We had to encourage them, praise them, give them treats when they've been good, and take away things they like when they've been bad. I wouldn't bet on it, but I was sure Norma was reading to us from a dog-training manual.

Then Ellen stood up and announced that the onus of change rests principally with us (whatever that means). 'Most clients will have adapted to their disabilities. Begin activities slowly and build up gradually. Adapt your ideas to their abilities.'

We had to alter our expectations of what is and what is not possible. What constitutes success and what failure. What is important and what is irrelevant. What is central and what is peripheral.

To shoot a basket is good, but it is not the object of basketball.

Counsellors had long since started to grow restless. Norma had a way of stretching even the longest attention span to breaking point. She held on to her sentences, unwilling to let them go, making sure the point she was making was lost in a confusion of twists and turns into irrelevancy. It was growing dark outside. Herbert had yet to wire up the arc lamps in the grounds and a thick blackness surrounded the dim lights of the dining-hall. Norma promised not to keep us much longer. A weary cheer went up from the staff.

The session ended with a list of dos and don'ts as long as the line on a deep-sea fishing reel: physical checks had to be run on arrival; inventory forms had to be filled in for their belongings, from toothpaste to Tampax; incident reports had to be completed whenever there was a seizure, an accident, an injury, or an 'irregularity'. There was a form for everything and everything had a form.

And that was it. Over. One day of talks, lists, indeterminable facts, indistinguishable voices, jargon concocted to mystify, and we were expected to be ready. In two days I would have seven lunatics in my care and that was all the advice I got.

'You've listened a long time today,' Ellen stood again to inform us of the obvious, and keep us just that little bit longer. 'You've taken in a lot of information. Perhaps some of it is a little jumbled. But if you forget everything that's been said, remember one thing: your clients need you. They will be relying on you.

'That's all. Have a good evening.'

There was a scramble for the door and the counsellors rushed out to the darkness.

6

'PAUL! STOP!'

The boy stamped his feet on the wooden tiles of the dining-room floor, clapping his hands and shrieking.

'Ellen!' Norma yelled. Ellen jumped up and rushed over to help. 'Paul, calm down. It's all right, it's all right. Just calm down.'

Counsellors sat in their chairs. Watching. Dumbfounded.

Paul waved his arms in the air, like the frantic wings of a caged bird, ripping feathers against metal bars. 'AAIIIEEEE!'

Norma moved behind him, trying to reach forward for his hands, but they flapped so fast she couldn't get a hold. 'Paul! Calm down. It's okay. Calm down.' She eventually managed to grab his hands and pull them backward in the restraining position, while Ellen tried to lift his feet off the ground. The boy leaped high into the air with a fearful scream, shaking himself free, and flew to the door, banging his hands against the wood, splitting the panel. Norma ran over and opened the door. 'Go on then Paul. GO!' she shouted angrily.

He fled outside and sat on the grass, where he rocked gently back and forth, twitching his fingers in the air.

'Jesus Christ.'

We sat in silence, notebooks open on our laps.

Norma was clearly shaken, though smiled as though nothing untoward had happened. 'Well, as you might have noticed,' she laughed awkwardly, 'that didn't go quite according to plan.' She paused. Paul rocked quietly on the grass. 'Paul was a client here last year. I thought it might be a good idea to bring him along this afternoon for you all to get a chance to meet him. But, er, it seems he's a little upset.'

Nobody said a word.

'I think that's all for now.'

Counsellors remained in their seats. Only gradually did they get up and quietly leave the hall.

Have you ever dealt with lunatics? Have you? Maybe you have. Or maybe you think you have. Ever lived with them, night and day, slept with them? Perhaps. But have you ever been me and dealt with lunatics? No, I didn't think so. So don't sit there and presume to tell me what kind of reactions I should or shouldn't be having, what's reasonable, normal, believable, whatever. Don't you go hi-jacking my emotions. This is my story, not yours. Got it? Good.

At Dotty's that night the mood changed. People still chatted and played pool, you wouldn't have noticed anything different had you come from outside Veda. But something was missing. There was none of the singing or the raucous laughter which had characterised previous evenings, none of the lightness, only an inkling of what awaited us heavy in the smoky air.

Joe was over at The Cuckoo's Nest having a drink with Claudia. He'd finally plucked up the courage to ask her out in front of May's Ice-Cream Parlour up by the falls, but only after she initiated the conversation, with Natasha at her side. He was so surprised when she said yes that he dropped his ice-cream cone on her foot. She was wearing sandals, those Germanic comfort things. Joe mumbled apologies whilst luxury chocolate chip and cream melted between her toes. From that moment, she was his.

Joe wanted to have a double date with Natasha and me. Safety in numbers. But I convinced him otherwise.

'It'll be much better if you go out with her on your own. Be alone with her, talk with her, charm her, pay attention to her, spin stories of your childhood. Women love that. Come over to join us later. But only once you're already winning her over; *then* you can mix with your friends, play the popular guy, ignore her a little. She'll soon want to be alone with you again.'

So Natasha and I sat in Dotty's waiting for Joe, talking about nothing in particular. I had already charmed her. The chase was over. There was nothing more to say.

On the other side of the room Dave slouched in his chair, watching us, downing one beer after another. Every now and then he hauled himself up as if he were about to come over and say something. But he just swung round, sometimes throwing in a belch for effect, stood up and stumbled off to the bar to fetch another drink.

Three things about Dave, that's all I ever found out. And that was only because he told me them himself on my first night, waltzed right up and listed them as though I had a right to know. He came from somewhere in London (Elephant and Castle, I think he said), had just lost his job, and had a wife who left him for a young man with an hereditary peerage (or a 'cunt', as Dave put it). I asked around, trying to find out more, but I always heard those same three things: Elephant, no job, cunt. No one knew anything else.

One of the locals with forearms like cricket bats invited Natasha for a game of pool. He asked me if he could ask her. (They're sure polite in Hicksville.) No problem, take her. I almost told him not to worry about bringing her back. Dave looked annoyed. He glared at me as if it were my fault she'd been asked, then, when she had gone, stumbled over to where I was sitting, knocking down a chair on the way.

'What you say to 'er?' he splurted.

'Pardon?'

'You heard. What you say to her?'

'Nothing, we were just talking.'

'Talkin',' he sneered, taking a long swig from his beer. 'I know your type.'

'I don't know what you're talking about.'

'Yes you do. You posh gits are all the same. Think you can smarm yer way in 'ere 'n take what you bloody well like. Well I telling ya, you better watch your step.' He finished his glass. 'This place ain't like outside, you remember that, allwight?' and he swung his bulk around and lurched off to the bar, shoving Lucien aside as he went.

'What was that all about?' Lucien asked, hurrying to the table, looking concerned.

'Don't ask me. He's drunk.'

I poured him a beer from my pitcher.

'*Santé*.'

'Cheers.'

In the back room Bjorn could be heard trying to scrape together enough English to flirt with Alison, the arts and crafts counsellor from Adelaide. She had nifty hands, worked beautifully, that's what Bjorn said. And now he wanted her to work on him. Chris had given him a scrap of paper with popular chat-up lines in English. Some of them weren't bad. But Bjorn had mislaid them and was having to wing it. 'Nice is here. So do you do what?'

'It's quiet tonight,' said Lucien.

'That business with Paul has shaken people up. Norma's little plan backfired.'

'Quite a show, wasn't it? Never seen anything like it.'

'I never want to see anything like it again.'

'You look troubled.'

'I am. More than troubled. Lucien, I'm not cut out for this kind of thing. If I'd had to face Paul I would have been through those doors faster than he was. Did you see him? His strength. That look on his face. If the others are anything like him, God help us.'

'They say he can.'

'Who?'

'God.'

'Can what?'

'Help.'

'Lucien, are you trying to convert me?'

'No, it's not for me to do something like that. I don't believe you can.' He halted, unsure, waiting for me to interrupt. When he saw I had no intention of doing so he rushed to continue, like he'd been given the all clear, excited. 'You can't convert someone else, I mean. Either you convert yourself, or you don't believe. Yes, I think that's what I mean. You can't be persuaded about faith. What's the point? If faith doesn't come from within, then it's meaningless. If you have to persuade faith, or reason with it, then it's not faith. Is it?' Lucien stopped to draw breath. He wasn't talking to me, I just happened to be there. 'Benjamin, are you religious?'

'Well, let's just say right now I'm praying for a miracle to get me out of here.'

Lucien didn't respond. I don't think he liked my answer. He opened his mouth, words eager for the charge. I was expecting him to launch into another sermonette, but he got up and bought a drink.

The local was helping Natasha to hold the pool cue. He leant over and held her instead. She laughed and pushed him away, playfully, then waited for him to come back for more.

'Lucien, what are you doing here?'

'Having a drink.'

'No, I mean at Veda. You're an educated guy, from Paris and all that. There must be a million better things you could be doing with your summer.'

'No, this is of great interest to me. I thought you felt the same. The malfunctioning mind. You've got the chance to get so close here. These people, they're an education. I want to see them, be amongst them, learn from them.'

'Do you do this kind of thing back in France?'

'Not like this. It's always fascinated me, in books and things. But this time I want to see it for real, for myself. My brother, he's had some problems. Not that he's mad or anything, but, well, you know. And my mother, she's...' Lucien stopped, like he'd heard the ringing of a bell, warning him against overstepping the mark. He mumbled something about disloyalty and I saw anger in his eyes.

There was no sign of Joe. Things must have been going better than expected with Claudia. He wouldn't be needing the beer I was saving for him, so I drank it myself.

'I could ask you the same thing,' Lucien said finally. 'What are you doing here?'

'Wishing I was somewhere else.'

'So why don't you leave?'

'Because I'm too damn proud, that's why. Besides, I signed that bloody contract.'

'Then why come here in the first place?'

'I didn't know, not that it was going to be like this. I was brought here under false pretences. I've been hoodwinked.'

'Hoodwinked?'

'*Dupé*. Taken for a ride. Led up the garden path. And now I'm stuck there. I know how Peter Rabbit felt now. Only Mr McGregor isn't going to put me in a pie, he's got a straitjacket.'

'Peter Rabbit? Who's he? What are you talking about?'

'He's also a philosopher, Lucien. Like you. A wise old English philosopher.'

A coin rattled into the jukebox and a shaky male voice rang out, accompanied by an even shakier acoustic guitar. Strings twanged out of tune (out of time) and Lucien told me a little of his life in Paris and asked about mine in London. Nothing special. Conversational toe-dipping, testing the water of each other's personalities. Then he told me I seemed sullen and said if there was anything he could do, if I had any problems settling in, all I had to do was ask. He said he knew how it could get sometimes and someone who understood was the world's most precious gift. I told him he was sweet, and he blushed.

Natasha finished her game, refused the persistent offers of a drink from the local, removed his large hairy hand from her hip, and came back to sit down.

'I lost,' she said with a sigh and finished Joe's beer.

'Don't worry,' said Lucien. 'There's always next time.'
'Quite the little philosopher, aren't we,' she replied.
'Yes,' he winked knowingly at me. 'Just like Peter Rabbit.'

7

'Thirty-five pairs of spanking new Calvin Klein underpants! Thirty-five!' Joe repeated. 'This kid has a lot of money and a seriously bad set of bowels.'

On the floor of the cabin lay the open trunk of William Alexander Hunt, Fresno, California. Inside, the thirty-five briefs were still fresh in their packages.

'Look at this. Just take a look at this! New shirts, new socks, new trousers, the whole bloody lot. He's even got a silk dressing-gown. Two trunks full of the stuff. We'll have to give him the large cubby. Okay, I suppose we better note it down. Thirty-five pairs of underpants.'

Three chartered buses from New York would be arriving late that afternoon, full of loonies. The schedule stated the morning was to be used for 'final preparations'. Final preparations! There was nothing final about my state of preparation, there was nothing even remotely prepared about it.

I had spent a restless night tossing and turning. I dreamt Lucien was an American priest and he was baptising me in Redhill Creek. He got stuck in preach mode and couldn't stop saving my soul, went on pardoning me for eternity. I kept kicking the blankets to the floor. God only knows how many times I got down to pick them up. I didn't get much sleep.

At five I gave up trying. I pulled on a pair of jeans and a warm sweater and sat on the porch to watch the sun rise over Veda. It was cold and still. I sat and waited. I was lonely, a little afraid. When it eventually bothered to show, the sun was a disappointment. I paced the porch blowing into my hands, then after a while went inside to look for Joe's cigarettes.

Herbert delivered the bags and trunks to our bunk after breakfast in his battered rusting yellow pick-up, moving round the grounds at a lethargic walking pace. The pick-up was the official Veda vehicle; it had *You're Special* written along the side in chipped paint and wasn't legal on the road.

'There ya're boys,' he said, sitting on our steps for a smoke of his pipe (Kolchak paid part of his minimalist salary in tobacco) whilst we did all the work unloading the truck. 'Great day for fishin'. A day like this in sixty-five I hooked the big salmon up over t'ward Woodstock. Wife moved out the next day, left me like the wind. Had ta eat the whole fish my damn self. The doc says ta tell ya the rest of the stuff 'll be coming with the crazies.' He pulled the fluffy sides of his hunting hat down over his ears, hitched up his baggy trousers and drove off slower than he had come.

Unpacking was tedious. Lists had to be made of everything they brought. Then it all had to be arranged neatly in their cubbyholes. I didn't see the point. What difference would it make to them whether their things were tidy? Nor could I understand why they had so many possessions, and such expensive ones at that. Such a waste.

The excessive luxury of William Hunt's trunk was almost matched by Charlie Wise from Colorado. He possessed the most beautiful woollen sweaters and thick cotton shirts I had ever seen.

'The kid's got style,' said Joe, trying on one of his pullovers.

I thought about diverting some of his possessions to my cubby, just a shirt or two, but my conscience (what little I had) stood stubbornly in the way, arms folded.

The next bag we unzipped was a green army duffle with a heavy dank odour. It belonged to Joshua Art Hoses of Oxford Avenue in the Bronx and was full of the shabby, grubby clothes you find in a charity shop; darned socks and patched-up jeans. He only had two pairs of trousers for the whole summer and when we'd finished unpacking his stuff his cubby still looked empty. I folded his bag and put it under his clothes to make it seem like he had as much as everyone else, then went to the bathroom to wash the filth from my hands.

After an untouched lunch of overcooked spaghetti and undercooked meatballs we unpacked the two remaining bags. The collection of New York Mets paraphernalia (shirts, pyjamas, towels, toilet paper) belonging to Dakota Slide and the neatly pressed clothes of Robert Booker Adams, New Hampshire, including a set of matching shirts and ties, and even a blazer. At the bottom of his trunk was a bag full of hangers and a beautifully written, annotated list of instructions from his mother about how to fold his shirts and trousers to avoid creasing. We threw the hangers in the back room, scrunched the clothes into the cubby and shoved Mrs Adams' letter in the wastepaper basket.

'That's it. That's the final pair of socks. Note them down and we're done.' Joe and I put the trunks and bags away then sat together on the porch, watching the comings and goings from the bunks to the HCs and back again, waiting for the buses that would change our lives.

'Well, I'm glad that's over,' Joe said, lighting up a cigarette.

'Me too.'

'Mark and Nick over in B6 have got eleven. And their bunk is smaller than ours. Rather them than me.'

'Yes.'

Neither of us felt much like talking, so we sat in silence.

There was a large gap on the porch where banisters were missing. Herbert had promised to replace them last week, though nothing had been done. ('A job like that takes a lot of preparation, boys.' Herbert's life was one long preparation.) Through the trees I could see inside B3, where Frank and Johann were busy filling their patients' cubby holes whilst sharing a spliff, exhaling through the wire mesh and wafting away the smoke with their hands as best they could. On the porch of B2, opposite the HCs, Berg and Thomas sat deep in conversation, occasionally stopping to write in the files on their laps.

'Too serious by half those two. Smoke?'

'No thanks.'

Joe lit up again. He looked at me and smiled feebly. 'It'll be fine, you wait and see.' He wasn't convincing, and he knew it.

I leant my head against the bunk wall and thought of home: rooms in college, with their view over the Backs; slumbering in the stalls at Wednesday Evensong at King's; bustling down Silver Street on my rusty bicycle, late for one of philosophy's rare lectures; friends at Trinity and long evenings spent conquering the world; Charles's summer in Florence and the invitation I never took up. I thought of Father sitting reading in the corner of the kitchen underneath the hanging plants, while Mother baked bread or prepared dinner, the large oak table filled with pots and herbs and covered in flour, steam rising from the stove, misting up the windows. She liked baking bread, said it was the only time she was ever truly relaxed.

Frank and Johann finished their unpacking (and their spliff) and Berg and Thomas their writing. The stream of counsellors to and from the HCs dried up until soon there was not a soul at the foot of the hill.

'Attention all staff.' Norma's voice whistled over the tannoy, cracking the shallow solace I had found. 'The buses will be arriving at the gate by the HCs' office in ten minutes. The buses will be arriving in ten minutes. All staff to make their way to the HCs now. All staff to the HCs.' The tannoy crackled then faded away. And then there was silence.

Slowly, in hesitant dribs and drabs, counsellors started to emerge from their bunks and gather by the track. A few chatted, though most just stood and stared down the road, waiting for the buses to come into view.

'Well, Ben, old buddy. Looks like this is it.' Joe got to his feet. 'We may as well go down. No point waiting around.' He stood watching me, dragging on his third cigarette.

'Never such innocence again.'

'What?'

'Nothing.'

'Come on, tell me. What did you say?'

'Larkin. I was quoting Larkin: "Never such innocence again". I was thinking of one of his poems, that's all.'

8

Lucien wished me luck.

I said nothing.

Natasha squeezed my hand.

I did nothing.

My mind was fixed on the three silver Greyhound buses rumbling down Sageville Road. Three sharp horn blasts and there they were. Stationary. Behind the HCs. Waiting. Tinted windows concealing their cargo. I didn't need to see to know what was inside.

'Listen up everyone!' Norma yelled, her voice hoarse from a week bellowing instructions. 'As they get out the buses we'll call their bunks. The counsellors responsible will come to collect them one at a time. When you have all your clients, take them to the bunk. Dinner will be at seven.'

Most counsellors stood in silence, awaiting the opening of the doors. Orientation was over. No more medical files to learn, no more clinical classifications, no more theoretical lunatics. Disorientation was about to begin.

Dr Kolchak and Norma approached the first bus, clipboards at the ready, and tapped on the window. High overhead, glinting in the sunlight, a silver plane flew without sound, its white trail cutting deep blue in two. The door swung open with a relieved gasp and the riptide flooded out, drowning the tranquillity of summer, inside came outside and lives turned upside down: shrieks, shouts, cries, wails, laughter, sobs, songs, all mingling in a single suffocating salutation. The handful of counsellors that were still talking stopped and stared at the door.

Ellen came down the steps, looking worn and dishevelled, and handed a folder to Kolchak. She signed some papers, then took a step back and looked up at the heavens as though ready to pronounce judgment. 'First bus is for the upper level. E3, can we have a counsellor from E3, please.'

Then came the first: a tall, skinny man, moving forward with great difficulty and apparent pain, slow, burdened step by slow, burdened step. On his head was a white plastic helmet, its strap tied tightly under his chin, contorting his face. Patches of white stubble marked his cheeks, with fresh scabs in between. He held his quivering hands

His head leant to one side, his eyes gazing through the back of Joe's neck. 'Robert, this is Benjamin. He's going to be your other counsellor for the summer.'

I reached out my hand with a smile. 'Hello Robert, pleased to meet you.' He didn't respond. 'Did you have a pleasant journey?' He stared right past my shoulder, his mouth open slightly, revealing thick braces, food caught in the metal. 'Well, we're going to have a good summer. I expect you're looking forward to it.' The skin on his arms flaked away in thin sheets.

'Why don't you say hello to Benjamin, Robert?' Joe said. His stare did not alter, nor did his lips so much as quiver.

'He'll be all right,' Joe told me.

'B8.'

'I'll go. You look after Robert.'

I took his hand. It was limp and moist. I gave it a squeeze. 'You must be hungry?' He said nothing. 'You've chosen a beautiful day for it.' He did nothing.

'Eye contact', that's what Ellen had said. 'Establish positive eye contact.' I bent down and tried to catch his eye. He just turned and looked away. I thought about physically turning his head, but was reluctant to touch him.

'Walter, this is Benjamin,' Joe repeated his introduction in the same slow voice.

'Eeaaoo,' said the boy holding Joe's hand, smiling and nodding vigorously.

'Hello, Walter. Welcome to Veda. Did you have a nice trip?'

'Eauuh,' he replied, dribbling on his shirt and scratching his stomach. As the saliva fell from his mouth he tried to suck it back in, making a long, low gurgling noise.

'Sshloouugoop.'

'Good.'

He nodded to me and looked down at his bandy knees. 'Ireed,' he pointed to his feet.

'Yes,' I replied, pointing at mine.

'Yerz, ya man. Hey ya man what's fur dinner yas what is?' I looked up to see Joe with yet another by his side.

'Dakota, say hello to Benjamin.'

'What is fur dinner what is fur dinner yas what is?'

'Dakota, say hello to Benjamin,' Joe repeated.

He screwed up his face and shook his fists at me. I stepped back, raising my guard. He forced a 'Hullo' from his tightened lips and lowered his hands. 'What is yers what is ya man?' His face was all out of proportion. There was not enough room for the enormous ears, nose and mouth, his cropped hair accentuating the peculiarity. His long arms drooped almost to his knees, the fingers on his huge hands closed tightly together. 'Ya man,' he began, then shook himself free from Joe and went to sit on the grass under the tree, where he picked up a twig, peeled the bark off, threw it down and picked up another.

Joe shrugged, and went back to the bus. I looked at Robert. He looked past me. I looked at Walter. He nodded and smiled.

'Eunoh.'

'Yes,' I nodded back.

Dakota sat on the ground, peeling twigs and mumbling to himself.

The next to arrive was a lanky boy with a wild mop of black wiry hair.

'Joshua, this is Benjamin,' said Joe.

He walked up to me on his toes. 'Well, hello there Counsellor Benjuman. I am Client Joshua Art Hoses, and how are you today?' He spoke slowly, a soft chuckle underlining his words. 'I'm very well thank you, well you know I had a nice journey, well yes I did. Very pleasant. It's nice to get away from the city, well yes it is, don't you find? I live in the Bronx, well yes I do, and, you know, that's not always the most quietest of places now is it?'

'Good.'

He laughed a laugh both carefree and menacing, showing his missing front tooth, and shook my hand. 'Well you know I think that's Client Dukota Slid over there Counsellor Benjuman, well I do think he was here last year, yes I do. I'll just go over and say hello to him if that's okay with you. Just a little hello. I'm sure he'll be more than bestest pleased to say a little hello to me.'

'Sure, Joshua. Go right ahead,' said Joe.

Joshua wandered up to Dakota, sat down next to him and started talking, chuckling with almost every word. Dakota scrunched his face, shook his fists and continued to peel.

'Benjamin. Joe. B8.' Ellen called out.

'That's the last one,' Joe said. 'Do you want you go?'

I didn't.

'Er, okay.' I let Robert's hand fall and made my way through the chattering, crying and singing to the door of the bus.

'Right ya'll motherfuckers, which one you sonsabitches belongs to ME!' A short, stocky boy leapt from the steps and hummed meanly at the Kommandant, blinking his eyes rapidly.

'Benjamin,' Ellen laughed, 'he's yours. William Hunt, California.'

'Yeah that's me, yes sirree. That's me. William Alexander Hunt. Here I am. William Alexander California Hunt,' he shouted in a rough voice, bounding up to me.

I retreated a few steps, holding out my hand from a safe distance. 'Nice to meet you William.'

'Ya momma's a pig!' he jumped forward with a grin. 'Hhhhnnnnn!' He had two chipped teeth, a squashed nose and large cabbage ears which reminded me of Blinker, my old maths master, who came to look that way from years of boxing (and losing) in the British Army.

'Well then, William,' I said softly, 'why don't we go and meet Joe and the others? I expect you'd like that wouldn't you?'

'Pig!' he yelled. I took his hand but he shook free and slapped my arm. 'Oh no no no no no ya don't.'

I walked on ahead of him, just out of range. 'Why don't you follow me then?'

'Yes sirree. Here I come.' William stomped behind, opening and shutting his mouth like a psychotic carp.

'William, this is Joe. He and I will be looking after you this summer.'

'Uba uba uba. Pig!' William let out a loud burp.

'Looks like we've got a live one here,' Joe laughed.

'Ya sister's a prostitchewee.'

'Okay, that's the lot. Let's get them up to the bunk. Come on,' Joe called to Dakota and Joshua who were still sitting on the grass. 'Let's go!'

'Yas I do like tweegs yeas I do yers I do like tweegs...'

'Well now Client Slid, I think Counsellor Benjuman and Counsellor Joa want us to go now, well, you know, yes I do.'

'Ee o zo da unk.'

'Yes, Walter,' I answered. 'Robert, are you ready to go?' He stared past me and said nothing. I set off up the hill, Walter at my side, smiling, nodding and dragging his feet along the grass, scuffing his shoes.

Dakota and Joshua sat on the ground. Robert gawped into space. William charged around, grinning at everyone.

'Well come on then, what are you waiting for?' I shouted.

'Go ta Alabama, ya fat monkey!' William shouted back.

'Okay. Let's go, let's go. Come on come on, move it. Move it!' Joe ran behind them, weaving in and out like a bewildered sheepdog.

'Well, doesn't he look funny, doesn't he just?' Joshua said, without laughing.

'All right Benjamin, let's leave them here. Let's go and have our dinner,' Joe said loudly so they could all hear. 'You watch this,' he whispered confidently as we walked up the hill. 'Negative reinforcement. Works every time. They'll soon follow.'

We got to the top and looked back.

'Oh, shit.'

They hadn't moved an inch. Not one of them. Not an inch.

We marched back down the hill.

'You take Dakota and Joshua, I'll take the other three.' Joe strode over to William. 'Okay William, let's go.' He grabbed his hand.

'Get offa me, ya pig punk!' William pulled away. 'Hhhnnnn!'

I went to fetch Joshua. 'Come on then, up you get. Let's go to the bunk.'

'Well you know Counsellor Benjuman, I think I might just do that,' he replied, getting up, wandering over to another counsellor and introducing himself. 'Well hello, I'm Client Joshua Art Hoses, well yes I am and I come from the Bronx, that's in New York City, well I do. You know, Counsellor, your face seems familiar...'

'Joshua!' I bawled. 'Get up the hill.' He turned and walked away, continuing his conversation with no one. I pulled Dakota to his feet, took his arm and dragged him behind me. He followed for about five yards, then sat himself down again, picked up a twig and started peeling.

'WILLIAM!' The boy rushed past me, Joe in hot pursuit.

'ROBERT!' He stood by the tree, the exact same spot where he had been left. I went down, took his lifeless hand and pulled him after me. Walter dragged his feet up and down the hill: to Joe, to me, over to Joe then back to me again.

'To the bunk, Walter.' I pointed towards B8. He nodded, and wandered over to Joe.

I snatched the twig from Dakota's hand, threw it away and tried pulling and shoving him up the hill bit by bit, blade of grass by blade of grass. Finally we arrived at the top.

Robert! I'd left him down below.

By the time I returned with Robert, Dakota had wandered off in search of his discarded twig.

'Hi, Benjamin,' Natasha trotted up in her tight shorts and kissed my cheek. 'How's it going?'

'Don't ask.'

'You don't sound too happy. Why don't you come over to my bunk later? I'll cheer you up.'

'I don't think that's a good idea, Natasha.' I yanked Dakota to his feet and pulled him up the hill. 'Give him a push would you?' I shouted to her, pointing at Robert. She glared angrily, turned her back and stormed off.

'Well I go to school right there in the Bronx, well you know now that's the truth, and I'm not lying neither...' Joshua was talking to a patient who was lying with his ear to the ground, patting the grass.

'WILLIAM!' Joe's voice rang out across the grounds.

Veda had come alive and tranquillity ran for cover. Counsellors rushed to and fro, chasing patients, chasing each other. A specialised population stood muttering, mumbling and twiddling its ears, rocking on the grass, humming and whistling, jumping up and down, running round in circles, triangles, hexagons. I watched one boy patting his large stomach ceaselessly. 'Ah yeah! Bagels and cream cheese!' A girl scratched her shins and squealed. A man wandered aimlessly, a guitar slung over his shoulder, stopping occasionally to point at it and grind his teeth. A woman picked up a branch and started firing at the trees. Then she reloaded and took a pot shot at me.

I sat down next to Dakota and picked up a twig.

9

Bastards.

Crazy.

The bastards were driving me crazy.

I was tired, hungry and acutely pissed off. I had slept hardly a wink, kept awake by a cruel combination of snores, moans, grunts and groans. Most of the night I sat on the edge of my bed watching William as he sat watching me, a malevolent grin peeking from the shadows. To reassure myself I grabbed the wooden Louisville Slugger baseball bat from Charlie Wise's trunk and stuck it under my pillow. Eventually, however, William got bored with his game and fell asleep, leaving me and Captain Insomnia to spend the night together.

I lay in bed and cursed.

Aimie. Damn! No-good do-gooder, why the hell did she have to find me this job? What business was it of hers, poking her nose into my affairs? Veda. What a stupid idea! Henry's would have been better than this, at least there I'd get a decent wage. Why wasn't I in Florence with Charles? Bet he was having a great fucking time! Why did the shit always foul up my fan? I sank irretrievably into the mud of self-pity, where poisonous thoughts lulled me to sleep.

Dawn came rattling impatiently at my door before I had the chance to draw barely one undisturbed breath, bringing with it B8's matins: inane muttering and sonorous farting. On the otherside of my eyelids I saw my own room, back home: a snug duvet; Mother's paintings; my dog, Samuel, curled tight in his basket; and a cup of warm, real coffee on the bedside table.

I opened my eyes.

There they were. Exactly where I had left them. All five. Present and incorrect. Unwashed and unwelcome. Sweet is the shattered dream.

It was only seven, breakfast was not for another hour and a half. I tried to go back to sleep, but every time I closed my eyes Norma's words poked me in the ribs: 'You'll need all the time you can get on the first morning. Be sure of that. They have to have their routine established from the start. No routine, and they can't function.'

Five pairs of vacant eyes stared, waiting for me to do something, longing for routine. I pulled the covers over my head and tried ignoring their existence. Please God, make them quietly disappear, let me start the morning over again. I'll do anything. I'll believe.

'Well yes, you know I think he's awake now, well yes I do. Well, you know, I think he's talking to himself. Counsellor Benjuman is talking to himself. How strange. Don't you think that's strange, well yes I do.' A slow voice answered my prayers.

I sat up and stared back, without the faintest notion what to do, until I was forced to concede they weren't going to wash and dress themselves.

'Okay everyone.' I jumped down to the cold floorboards, trying to drag up a little spirit. 'It's a beautiful day. Rise and shine. Time for breakfast.'

No one moved. Not even Joe.

I waited for them to get up.

Nothing.

Pronounced inactivity.

I pulled covers off beds in the hope that the cold would shrink their balls and shift them. Joshua was the only one to move. He swung his legs out of bed and sat on his hands. There he stopped, awaiting further instructions.

'Go to the bathroom, Joshua.'

'Well, yes I will, thank you for asking Counsellor Benjuman, most considerate, you know I think I might just do that, yes I think I will, such a nice idea.'

'Hey ya man what's fur bweakfwast?' Dakota sat up with a sudden jerk as though someone had flicked his ON switch, his mouth moving even before his eyes opened.

'I have no idea Dakota. Why don't we go and find out?'

'What's fur bweakfwast what is?' he persisted, screwing up his face.

'I don't know Dakota,' I repeated louder.

'Yerz ya man yerz what's fur bweakfwast yerz?'

Was it him?

Or was it me?

'Yes what is fur bweakfwast what is...?'

'Come on Dakota.' I interrupted his one-sided dialectic, pulling him out of bed, pointing him in the direction of the bathroom and giving him a shove. He followed obediently, shuffling across the bunk, muttering to himself and scratching his bottom.

'Morning, Walter.'

Walter opened his mouth to answer and produced a mouthful of saliva which dribbled on to the blanket despite noisy efforts to suck it back in.

'Ehnouuh,' he said, smiling at me, a faint hissing escaping from his throat.

I left him to his own devices. 'Let's go, William. We don't want to miss breakfast now do we?'

'Go ta Alabama,' he growled.

I didn't need telling twice. I beat a retreat to my bed, glancing over my shoulder to make sure he wasn't following.

I guess it was an awakening of some sort, devoid of consciousness; eyelash by eyelash, a melodious collection of mutterings, mumblings, gurglings and dribblings: Walter in earnest conversation (a form of heavily salivated squeals) with Robert, who lay in his bed incapable of paying the slightest attention; William humming erratically to himself; Dakota ranting in the bathroom, accompanied by the incessant undertones of Joshua's life history. '...did I tell you, Client Slid, I come from the Bronx, yes I think I did...' Although he spoke slowly, painfully slowly, Joshua was difficult to understand. He had this habit of stressing the wrong syllables and words which meant you had to translate each sentence. '...well *you* know, I did*n't* tell you my *par*ents have a hou*se* on *B*lock I*sl*and, well *as* it *hap*pens yes they do, they *go th*ere from time *to* time, tha*t's ok*ay if...'

Joe opened one eye, cast a dubious glance across the bunk, then wisely shut it again.

'Oh no,' I prodded him, 'you're not getting out of it that easily. Get up and face Bedlam.'

'That bad huh?'

'Worse.'

'Sleep well?'

'Sleep? Well? What does that mean?'

'What you need is a good solid breakfast. Nothing a good breaky can't cure.' Joe jumped out of bed, pulled on his jeans and strode forth. 'Right then,' he bellowed with severely misplaced confidence. 'Let's get to work on this lot.'

More than happy leaving him to tackle William, I went to the bathroom to find Dakota standing before a wash basin playing with his erect penis. '...lunch we go hey ya man what's fur bweakfwast yas...' Neither soap nor flannel in sight.

'Dakota! I asked you to wash your face,' I said, trying to keep my eyes off his abnormally large dick. 'What do you think you're doing?'

'What's fur bweakfwast yeas?'

Think = misnomer.

'I don't give a damn what's for bweakfwast. Just wash your face. *Comprenez-vous*?' I turned to leave but was blocked by a smirking, naked William standing in the doorway.

'Get out of here motherfucker punk!' I know when not to argue and stepped aside whilst he went into the toilet and relieved himself on the floor. It was disgusting. But the thought of going into that cramped cubicle to help him improve his aim was even less appealing.

'Walter! What are you doing?'

Dumb question. It was perfectly obvious what he was doing. He had pulled all his clothes out of the cubby hole and was sitting on his bed trying to put his left leg into the right sleeve of a small white T-shirt.

'Walter. That's a T-shirt and those are your legs – no connection.' Walter shrugged his shoulders, one leg in a T-shirt, smiling and nodding, his head lolling loosely like one of those pathetic plastic dogs that some people insist on putting on the back shelf of their car.

'I'll dress him,' Joe said, trying to untangle the mess. I returned to the bathroom to check the progress of the arse-scratching and floor-pissing fraternity.

William had finished target practice and was standing next to Dakota at the wash basin busily searching for something in Dakota's navel with his toothbrush.

'Why aren't you washing like I asked you to?'

'Suuuuck an egg!' William squealed.

There was nothing else for it. I didn't want to, but they were going to be there all day. I rolled up the sleeves of my nightshirt, soaked a flannel and started to scrub.

'No no no no ya don't! Get off me ya fuck sonfabitch mama!' William shook himself free and spat at me. I jumped back, slipped on the urine and fell, hitting my head on the toilet bowl.

'Hhhhhnnnnnnn!' he grinned, baring his chipped teeth. Dakota stopped mumbling and allowed himself a brief chuckle. They were having the time of their lives.

'GET THE FUCK OUT OF HERE!' I shrieked, jumping up, desperately trying to subdue my ardent desire to throttle the little freak. (Oh, to see William in pain, if only for a moment.) 'Go on. GO!'

I took the mop and started to dry the floor.

Brilliant rays of sun shone through the thin bathroom window, scattering patterns on the urine, gently easing into a new day. Outside leaves fluttered calmly in the morning breeze. A sparrow hopped his unhindered way from branch to branch, stopping for a moment to glance at me on the inside, then flew away.

I pulled down the blind and squeezed out the mop.

Joe was still struggling with Walter, trying to make parts of his body fit into places he did not want to, or could not, put them.

'...look yas I playing with my toes yas I am ya man I playing with my toes yers...'

'Well done Dakota. I am happy for you.'

Robert was still under his covers. Intelligent choice. I left him, at least there he couldn't cause any trouble, and went to attend to Joshua. His long, emaciated body lay naked on top of his bed, his skin so filthy it seemed dirt were permanently ingrained in its pores. The mattress was too small for him and his malformed feet (corns, bunions) jutted over the end. He laughed as I approached, his eyes following my every movement.

'Right then, Joshua,' I said, a little apprehensive, 'let's get you dressed.' I took a grubby T-shirt from his cubby and widened the opening for his head. He stared blankly at me, then spoke as if to a child.

'Well, Counsellor Benjuman, you know, I can dress myself thank you very much, I don't need no help, I ain't no baby, I can dress myself thank you very much.'

He sounded so sad. I gave him the shirt and went away.

Joe had finished dressing Walter, who sat on his bed happily bouncing his head, and was now focusing his attention on William, approaching him with caution. 'You won't catch me taking chances with this maniac.'

'...yeas I am I playin wiv my toes yeas little toes I playin...'

'Dakota! Put your toes down. You can play with them after breakfast, you have to get dressed now. What do you want to wear?'

For the briefest of brief moments he was silent.

'I do believe I've stumped him,' I said, proud of my first achievement.

'What's fur bweakfwast?' The elation was short.

'Books.'

Another momentary pause, a tiny hesitation, a disruption to routine. 'No no yeas what's fur bweakfwast yerz what's...' and he was off.

Ignoring him, I pulled a New York Mets shirt over his head, his voice echoing from inside Shea Stadium. 'Dakota, pull down your shirt.'

'Tomorra bweakfwast yeas tomorra bweak...' I pulled down the shirt for him and struggled with his socks.

'Dakota, stop moving your toes.'

'My toes ... yas they are my I like play wiv my toes my toes yas I do like...'

'I know they are your toes Dakota, just stop moving them so I get your socks on.'

'...my toes...'

'STOP!'

'...ya man yerz what's...'

'TROUSERS!'

'fur bweak'

'Come on, Dakota. Help me will you! Put your leg straight.'

'...fwast...'

'No straight. Look. Like this.'

'...yerz it is ... yerz ... ya man...'

'Straight I said. What are you, stupid? Is it so bloody difficult to understand?' I pushed his knee down and quickly zipped up the fly over his seemingly permanent erection. 'Now. Put your foot in here. No. No. Your other foot. No not that one, the other one. This one. *Voilà!*'

'...then we go yas we do ... yerz ya man...'

'Push your foot in. Stand up and push your foot in.'

' ...No's not ... ya man!'

'Dakota! For fuck's sake, stand up and push your foot in!'

'...ya man yas we do...'

'Wait, stay still. I haven't finished yet. STAY STILL!'

'...ya man when...'

'Dakota. My name's Benjamin, not "ya man".'

'...bweakfwast yeas what is...'

'Ben-ja-min, Dakota. The name is Benjamin.'

'...yas we go we go fur bweakfwast yeas ya man...' He flapped his arms.

'Okay I'm done,' Joe said, standing triumphantly next to (at a safe distance) a fully dressed William. 'Let's go and get some food. I'm starving.'

I didn't bother about Dakota's sweater. It wasn't worth the effort.

We had won. The struggle had been long and hard. But they were dressed. Finally.

They sat on their beds, exactly as they had been over an hour before, except no longer wearing pyjamas. Muttering, mumbling, gurgling and dribbling. The same vacant expressions on their faces. Waiting for someone to do something. Had they noticed the change? Was it worth it? Had they really noticed the difference?

My stomach rumbled.

'Me too. You go down, I'll be with you in a moment. I'm just going to wash my hands.' I went to the basin to wash away the sense of dirt (scrubbing, scraping) but it didn't make any difference. It was under my skin. I threw the towel on the bed and left the bunk.

Lights!

I went back to switch them off and there he was, lying motionless, under the covers.

One hour. That's what I spent getting Robert Booker Adams out of bed. And I failed. Sixty prolonged minutes of frustration. Three thousand six hundred exhausting seconds in a game I didn't even want to play. And final capitulation. I couldn't get him to so much as lift his little finger. The little bastard beat me, lying there, motionless, his wide infuriatingly passive eyes gawping at the rafters. He didn't have to move, didn't even have to open his mouth and I was reduced to pathetic incompetence.

Beaten hands down by a retarded pubescent.

'What happened to you?' Joe bounded into the bunk with a disgustingly happy face. 'You missed Cheerios. And the pancakes were edible, almost. You should have...' He looked at me, then at Robert. Maybe he read my mind. Maybe he didn't need to. Maybe he saw ANGER and FRUSTRATION carved two inches deep across my brow. At any rate, he saved me from doing something to Robert I would surely have lived to regret. (Then again, maybe not.) 'Why don't you come outside for a moment?' He put his arm around me and led me away.

We wandered up to the top field into the morning air. The day was clear, cold. The sun had yet to decide whether the world was worth warming.

Away from the bunk, from them. All it took was a few planks of old wormed whitewashed wood between us and I calmed.

'Smoke?'

'No.'

Joe lit up. 'Come on, Ben, don't let them get to you like this. It's the first morning. So you're having a few problems, so's everyone. You should've seen the shit going down in the dining-hall. You're not the only one, nobody knows what they're doing at the moment. Take it easy, don't let yourself get drawn in. It'll get better.'

I felt so useless. I couldn't even get them to piss straight. 'Joe, you saw me in there. I don't belong here. This isn't my scene at all.'

'You're not quitting are you?'

I didn't reply.

'For Chrissakes Ben, don't take it all so damn personally. It's not you against them. You're not fighting a battle here. There's nothing to win.'

We walked round the field twice whilst Joe had his quota of post-breakfast nicotine (puff, drag, puff, drag), dew soaking our feet. He tried his best to convince me not to leave, really put his heart into it. I had to give it another try if only for his sake.

'We should be getting back. Benjamin, give it a chance. You'll see.'

I promised him I would and asked for some time alone to clear my head.

Further up the hill were the small falls where the brook which divided Veda tumbled its way down to the Redhill. Beside it was a steep bank covered in layers of dead pine needles and open cones – at least the weather was going to be fine. Patients' cries and counsellors' shouts didn't penetrate that far into the forest. There was only the sound of running water, accentuating the silence. There were no vacant eyes, no erect penises, no grimy clothes, no pools of urine – just me. I sat and watched the water as I always sat on the Erasmus lawn in Cambridge at night. Alone. Watching the dark reflections of college buildings sinking into the Cam. I would sit on that lawn with a mug of coffee after finishing at my books, gazing at the cold winter stars, thinking of far away places and of the myriad adventures awaiting me. I would dream of being elsewhere, always elsewhere, of something different.

I looked into the brook and thought of home and of what I knew.

In fencing, there is a move which helps you face the unknown. You are on the piste, your opponent runs at you full pelt, flailing his sabre. You have no idea what he's going to do, what attack he's going to make; a head feint, flank or a belly feint, head. You need the point to win the match. He has nothing to lose. You have about three seconds. Pressure is on.

The way out is the most simple move imaginable. It is also the most difficult. All you have to do is remain calm. Steadfast. You wait for the final moment until he is just about to cut into his attack. Then you merely take the smallest of steps backwards at the precise moment his sabre whizzes through the air. All he will cut is an empty space, you will force him to fall short. Then he is wide open for your counterattack which, if you are fast enough, cannot fail.

There, when you are in danger of losing it, when you are in a position of weakness, you keep your head, take a tiny step out of the action and you are transformed into a position of unbeatable strength. And you've hardly done a thing.

I imagined my five retards running down the piste toward me, sabres flashing. And I imagined the joy with which I methodically took them apart.

Joe was wrong. Everything is a battle. Everything can be won, and everything can be lost.

I wasn't going to lose.

At the foot of the falls lay a small pool in which turbulent water calmed itself. Leaves and twigs were gathered at one end, coated with a thin layer of scum. In the middle was a small animal about the size of a kitchen mouse. I got up for a closer look. It was a vole, trapped in the detritus, belly up – dead.

It seemed a good idea. Get them outside, running around, exhaust them. Have some fun, play a little, work with teams, establish leadership. Raise spirits, regain self-respect. A game of basketball seemed a perfectly good idea.

'Great!' said Joe when I returned with the suggestion. 'I'll go fetch a ball.'

He was sitting quietly on his bed, fully clothed, as though nothing had happened, vaguely smiling, triumphant.

I rushed outside. 'How did you do it, Joe? Robert. I mean, how?'

'I didn't do a thing,' he laughed. 'I was cleaning the bunk. He just got out of bed and dressed himself. Didn't say a word.'

The little bastard.

Right. No more question who was in control. I marched them out to the basketball court with a determined command.

'Okay, Joe's the captain of Team A and I'm the captain of Team B. Dakota, Walter and Robert, you're on Team A. Joshua and William, come with me. First one to twenty. Right teams, who's going to win?' I raced around the patients, circling them, yelling like a cheap and cheerful cheerleader, waving my poms-poms.

No one answered.

Undaunted, I dragged my team down the far end of the court for a pep talk – tactics, that's the name of the game. Everything comes down to tactics in the end. 'Right boys, we can take them. Stick together and pass the ball. Remember, teamwork. Now, the first move, what we're going to do is this...HEY WILLIAM! What the hell are you doing?' He charged at me like a bull on heat and tried wrestling the ball from my arms. 'William, we're on the same team!'

'Go ta Mississippi!'

He won the ball, ran to the end of the court, then kicked it high into the air. He looked liked one of those subuteo football players, the one which takes the corner kicks; you press the head and the leg raises into the air without bending, a cross between a Can-Can dancer and a Nazi on parade. He gave the ball one hell of a wallop, sending it flying over B3 and into the trees.

'William!' Joe yelled angrily. 'What did you do that for? Go and get it!'

'Ya go and get it!'

'No William. You kicked it, you go and get it.'

'Suck a egg!' he screeched and ran off the pitch, flapping his arms.

Joe fetched the ball and we restarted the game – minus one player.

Joe dribbled down the far side. I ran to intercept him. He passed me with a skilful turn. 'Dakota!' He called to his team mate, ready for a one-two to set up a basket.

'What's fur lunch yerz what is...' The split second the ball left Joe's hands, Dakota saw an unpeeled twig in the middle of the court and bent down to pick it up. 'I like tweegs...' The ball flew clean over his head, rolling all the way down the hill to the dining-hall.

'Shit! Not again. Dakota, pay attention, will you. Now go and get it. Hurry hurry! We've got a game to play here.'

Dakota took his twig and dawdled down the hill, mumbling to himself about the day's menu. He reached the bottom, looked at the ball and, like a badly trained retriever, decided not to come back, preferring instead to squash his nose against the dining-hall windows and inquire about the *à la carte*.

'What *is* fur dinner yerz what *is*...'

'Dakota! The ball. Fetch the ball Dakota! The ball.' Joe stood at the top of the hill, yelling instructions to his errant team mate.

After fetching the ball once again, Joe got the game under way. Same move, though this time down the other line, spinning past me like an old-time Globetrotter. 'Walter!' It was only a short pass, a couple of feet at most, all he had to do was catch the ball, the basket would have been a sure thing. My defence was running round in circles at the other end of the court. Walter dribbled and held out his arms, neither one in the same direction.

Whilst Joe was retrieving the ball for a third time, I tried to inject some enthusiasm into the teams. 'Come on. Let's go! Remember, it's all about winning. No prize for second place.'

Robert hadn't moved since the beginning of the game. He stood on the centre spot, his mind trying to catch up with the fact that his body had got out of bed. Joshua stood underneath the basket, informing the posts where he went to school. William ran around in tiny squares like a dog chasing his tail, shouting 'I'm gonna get you, I'm gonna get you, ya pig, I'm gonna...'

'Let's give it one more try, eh?' Joe said, anticipating my request for a permanent time out. 'You never know, it might work. They just need to get into the swing of things.'

'Okay. First basket wins.'

This time I anticipated Joe's little set move and ran down to block him. He had no choice but to pass. 'Robert. Catch!'

Catch what? 22?

It was beautiful. Slap bang square on the face. Joe threw the ball at a fair old whack and Robert stood motionless, watched it coming right to him. I wish I had it on video. I'd play it over and over, frame by frame. All he had to do was put out his hands, that's all. WHAM! Right in the face. Blood poured from his nose, streaming down his pressed shirt, which he'd put on back-to-front. Back to reality. It must have hurt. It was a damn hard pass. No reaction, not even a hint of one. Robert just stood there and stared straight ahead. Though I thought I saw him blink. Once.

My humiliation had been avenged. The basketball gods had ordained to punish him for my suffering. I smiled.

Game over.

Lucien wanted to see the church up in Sageville. But he didn't want to go alone. Christ knows what he thought would happen to him in there. Still, I had no objection, so I went with him during our lunch hour. I was thoroughly exhausted, in need of a dose of religious silence. Churches are great places for flaking out, as long as there's no concerned priest lurking in the corner yearning for a soul to save.

We left the noon heat behind and stepped into the cool church. It was Protestant, even I could tell that. There were none of the fancy trimmings the Catholics enjoyed, just a few hard wooden pews and a bare stage with a table for an altar underneath a modern cross with no Christ. What with their candles and costumes, smoke and songs, strikes me the Catholics always have a better time of it, a real party.

Lucien crossed himself at the door, bowed in the aisle and curtsied low before sitting down, like some sort of holy aerobics instructor.

Lucien knew about churches. I think he'd been inside every single one in Paris, and that's more than most priests go to in a lifetime. He used to go with his mother (hand-in-hand in the pew, praying for the good of the family), but he'd stopped sometime ago and now preferred to go alone. He wouldn't tell me why, just said he no longer went with her. In fact, come to think of it, most of Lucien's conversations seemed to culminate in mention of his mother, and there he would stop. No matter how I tried to lure him, he'd go no further.

He'd had somewhat of a constipated upbringing. His father held some high post in the French diplomatic corps, and that restricted the things Lucien was allowed to do. He spoke about his childhood with a nudging resentment. His father was a firm believer in the Church of French Cultural Supremacy. He even forbade his son to watch American movies, said they would lead to cultural contamination. Lucien loved American movies; he fell asleep in French ones. They may have been culturally correct and wonderfully artistic but they were, well, boring: a constant introspective analysis of one relationship after another. He tried to find them interesting, really he did. But he couldn't. Then he took to sneaking out on Saturday mornings to catch the latest American film (a sacrilegious offering from the cultural agnostics). His father thought he was going to dance class. He never could figure out why his son stood out as the most appalling dancer at the grand Parisian Rallyes, thereby committing social suicide. He even objected to his son's trip to America, but I got the impression that he no longer cared enough to stand in Lucien's way.

For his part, Lucien seemed to be having a ball. He loved Veda. Wouldn't stop talking about his patients. He kept a notebook, a catalogue of abnormal behaviour. Everything his patients did was noted meticulously. There was no personal comment or reflection; just the facts, a logbook of insanity. He worked up at B12, over the far side of the baseball field. That was a hard bunk, the lowest functioning male group on the lower level. It had a lot of flappers and screamers, you could hear them as far down as B8. God knows how he managed to stay sane in there.

Lucien beckoned me to join him on the front pew, so I took a silent seat. He was repeating the Lord's Prayer in French. But he didn't have his eyes closed. He was watching me instead. *'Notre Père qui êtes aux cieux...'* I joined in. 'Hallowed be Thy name...' I wasn't even aware I was doing so at first, just an old school habit from assembly. You'd get detentions if you were caught not following the head's lead.

Meaningless prayers out the way, we sat back in the pew. Lucien gave a huge sigh as though he'd just completed a daunting task, happy he'd pulled it off without a hitch. The sunlight sprinkled through the windows, illuminating the cross. On the rare occasions I found myself in church, marriages and things, I passed the time by studying the stained glass, testing my parables or saints' lives (Sebastian was my favourite, all those arrows – I never could figure out why none of the archers shot him in the groin, that'd be the first place I'd aim for) but in Sageville the glass was plain and there was nothing to distract me.

I thought he'd finished. I was just about to stand up and leave when Lucien once more went down on his knees. This time he did close his eyes, his lips taut. He took my hand in his, squeezing it tightly as though he were afraid. His palm was smooth and I could feel a sharp pulse racing inside him. The tighter he shut his eyes, the tighter he held my hand, almost pulling me to my knees. I resisted, staying in my seat.

His eyes flinched. In haste, he crossed himself several times, then sat up, expelling one long low burst of breath, like a free-diver coming up for air, like he couldn't breathe and pray at the same time.

He wiped some sweat from his eye and looked down seeing our hands still joined. Suddenly, he pulled his hand away, shocked at what he'd done.

'Sorry, I didn't realise. It's my mother. You see, she likes the odd prayer.'

'It's okay, Lucien, I didn't ask.'

From the next town down the valley came the shattering wail of the fire siren.

'Lucien, what...?'

He jumped up from his seat, startled by the noise, and hurried down the aisle, heels echoing in the rafters. 'Come on, Benjamin, we're going to be late!'

The queue for dinner started early. Though why is beyond me: the food wasn't worth eating, everyone knew that.

In front of the dining-hall was a small paved clearing where a short man stood with his hands clasped behind his back, his face nothing but a mean snarl couched in heavy stubble. He wore a white capped T-shirt, his arms and neck covered with thick hair and faded, self-inflicted tattoos, and nodded his head gently, in a 'Fuck me! I'm cool' sort of way. He reminded me of the Italian guys I'd seen hanging around the street corners of New York, drooling after each female leg that passes their way, rubbing their crotch with subtle charm, yelling 'Hey, baby! You and me! You and me baby! How about it, uh?'

A boy leapt around on one foot, earnestly studying his right index finger which wouldn't stop moving. He leapt into Al Pacino's space.

'Get the fuck outta here,' he bawled, shoving him to the ground.

The terrified boy scampered to his feet and ran off.

'That's enough, Tony!' Norma shouted.

'Rambo. Name's Rambo. This is my space, and no one comes into it. No one.'

'Okay, Rambo. But if you can't guard the doors without hurting people, Rosetta won't let you do it. Understand?'

'Rambo.'

'Understand, Rambo?'

'Yeah that's me. Rambo' He strutted a little, re-establishing his territory, and then resumed his post.

'Somewhere over the rainbow...'

A deafening screech ripped through the air.

'Way up high...'

A short woman with an untidy mass of white hair rampaging down to her waist was trying to rip out her vocal chords, one by one.

'There's a land that I dream of...'

She had the most enormous mouth I had ever seen; when it opened her face simply disappeared. And her teeth! Her mother must have been a horse.

'Once in a lullaby...'

Her fingers were covered in large plastic rings, her lips smudged with rouge. She held her wrinkled hands to her wrinkled face and whinnied at the top of her voice.

'Somewhere over the rainbow...Oh, you beautiful man, come here. Come to Dorothy. A kiss. A kiss!' There was no time to escape. Puckering up with a ferocity that put Mick Jagger to shame, she launched herself at me with a cackle.

I turned just in time. She missed my mouth, her lips slobbering against my cheek, rows of teeth taking a layer off my skin. I disentangled my arms and pushed her away. 'Come on you lovely man. Just a kiss.' I managed to duck the second one, dragging a patient in front of me to take the full impact of the embrace.

I could taste her in my mouth, the flavour of decay.

It was while in line for another of Veda's culinary catastrophes that I found the invitation in my pocket. It was left over from Michaelmas term.

You are cordially invited to partake in
The Heavenly Experience of Dining with Ye Cherubs
Sunday Noon **Old Hall**
Dress: Vulnerable

It was crumpled and slightly faded, had been through the wash a few times, but it was still legible. I read it and sank back into the self-deluding warmth of memory, trying to shield myself from my present, unfortunate circumstances. Society dinners at Cambridge were the one place where you could find all the infamy which nowadays (in our oh-so-correct times) gives the University a bad name. They were presumptuous, pretentious, spurious, pompous, affected, conceited, totally unnecessary - in short, marvellous. They were the one place where you could ensconce yourself in the ludicrous nature of existence, where you could keep at arm's length, if only for a short time, the unfortunate seriousness of life. So many people frowned on these dining-society events that, inevitably, there had to be something wonderful about them.

A young girl shat on the grass and it was time for lunch.

Rambo swung the doors open. 'Okay move it out. Let's go. Come on.' The mess of a mass pushed and shoved its way into the dining-hall, scrambling to tables whilst counsellors chased patients in a futile effort to exert a minute modicum of control.

'Don't sit there!'

'Don't slap him!

'Don't start yet!'

'Don't eat that!'

'Put your trousers on. Now!'

'Benjamin, how lovely to see you. So glad you could make it. Beaujolais Nouveau! How did you get your sweet little hands on that? I didn't even know it was out yet. And what an outfit! Are those *real* feathers?'

'What's fur lunch ya man?' Dakota clicked his tongue and shook his fist. 'Yeas what is fa lunch?'

Baked ziti.

Our rickety table (made, badly, by Herbert) was at the far end near the kitchen door. Plastic coating, plastic cutlery, paper plates and paper cups. The hall had the odour of bodily fluids, diced and stewed. And the noise! You couldn't hear yourself yelling. Patients were everywhere: climbing on tables, chairs, tongues in the food, hands down trousers, fingers up neighbours' noses.

The long mahogany table stretched the entire length of the hall, behind which, in the huge medieval hearth, a lively fire crackled a warm welcome on a wintery afternoon. Spread along the thick white cotton cloth were baguettes, fresh meats (blood running), crisp, steamed vegetables (butter melting), bottles of wine from the college cellars, port, Belgian chocolates and fruits so exotic that no one had the slightest idea of their names, nor cared. High overhead spotlights illuminated the brightly painted eighteenth-century ceiling, with its carved angels dancing merrily amid the rafters and...Joe plonked two paper plates on the table, each piled high with queasy-looking pasta and a watery red sauce which slopped over the edges.

'Right then, who wants some of this muck?'

'Me me me me me,' William stuck both his hands in the air. 'YEAH!'

'Well, you know, Counsellor Joa, perhaps I might have just a little, after all, you know, we have to eat don't we, yes.'

'Eauh ee oo.'

Joe slopped out ziti for the brave.

William plundered with a vengeance, shovelling the food into his mouth with the serving spoon, squeezing it in with his fingers. Robert sat with his hands in his lap staring at his fork, still under his mental covers. I tried eating, but Walter was too close; his face covered in red sauce, a thin layer spread on his right ear lobe. He was having difficulty establishing a connection between the fork and the mouth. There was more pasta on the table than on his plate.

'Walter, what are doing? Can't you be more careful.' He looked up and nodded, overturning his fork, spilling ziti sauce down his shirt.

'Uah weo,' he smiled proudly.

Gone. My appetite vanished. I pushed my plate away, into the waiting arms of William, who seized it eagerly, devouring my lunch in a matter of seconds.

'...wed yeas wed wed joese I want wed...'

On the next table was the pale-faced girl I had seen during orientation, the one with the pointed hood. She was wearing it again. It was a sunny day, hot and stuffy in the dining-hall, and here she was wearing a hood. And no one but me seemed to notice anything amiss. Everyone else seemed oblivious to her. She sat impeccably still, barely blinking, a paragon of patience, whilst a dumpy patient with frosted glasses flicked baked ziti at her, using her spoon as a catapult. The girl sat calm, graceful, whilst red pasta sauce splattered against her white blouse.

William burped. Joshua farted. Laughed. Then farted again.

'But Francesca. Come, come. You don't need to *dress* vulnerable. You're in a permanent state of vulnerability.'

'Orlando, you know you're so terribly wrong. She presents herself as vulnerable, that's the veneer she wishes us to see. That's precisely her hidden strength. She would like to convince us that she revolves around us, meek and mild. But in reality it is *she* who is the sun, we are merely the planets; subject to her silent powers. It is the perfect disguise, and she wears it perfectly. Am I not right Francesca?'

She blushed and took a small sip of red wine.

'You see, even her embarrassment is staged.' Old Hall echoed to our laughter.

'I think we're ready for dessert now, Hodgkins.'

'WED JOESE!' Dakota brought his fist crashing down on the table, ziti scattering in all directions.

'WHAT DAKOTA!' I shouted, wiping sauce from my eye. 'What the hell are you going on about?'

'Wed joese yeas it is wed yeas it is I want wed yas yas I do...' He was hyperventilating, shaking in his chair, waving his fists in the air.

'Red juice.' Ellen brought a portion of enlightenment to our table. 'He's saying he wants red juice. There's some in the kitchen. Ask Rosetta.'

I took the jug, filled it and placed it in front of Dakota: he poured. The cup filled and still he poured, juice overflowing on to the table, stopping only when Joe told him to. He finished his drink in one mouthful, then poured out another, spilling yet more, then another and another until 'Finished wed joese more wed joese we need more yas we do need more finished...'. I returned to the kitchen, refilled the jug, gave it to Dakota and waited. He poured. Spilt. Drank. Not a pause even for breath, guzzling on autopilot.

Five times I repeated that journey.

Wine bottles lay empty, the port decanter upturned. The cloth was a mess, the floor worse. The food fight had gone better than expected. I had chocolate sauce on my tie. Orlando had mustard (grained) in his hair. We were drunk. Tired. It was growing dark outside the hall, the lights in Old Court shining through the crested windows. The clock above the library struck a heavy seven and we fell into a silence as the echo resounded in the hall. Cigars were lit and conversation left to find its own way. We huddled closer to the fire, drifting helplessly into our own thoughts. Hodgkins came in and offered the cheese one last time and then went home to his flat above the boathouse, where he had lived alone for forty years, waking at six every term-time morning to unlock the gates for over-enthusiastic boaties.

'Sunday afternoons in winter are such a solitary time.' Orlando mused as he refilled his glass.

'And yet the perfect occasion for good company.'

'I wish it could always be like this,' Francesca sighed. 'Why can't it go on for ever? I never want to leave.'

'Let's get out of here,' I said, as Walter knocked a runny Angel Delight into my lap. 'I've had about as much of this as I can take.'

'Can't yet,' Joe replied. 'We've got to wait for medication.'

'...wed joese I want...'

'No Dakota.'

'Yas what's fur dinner yas what is ...'

'Oh, shut up.'

After the nurses had distributed pills to B8, a whole chemist shop going down William's throat, we shovelled everything from the table into a rubbish sack, disinfected the floor underneath Walter's seat and got the hell out of there.

Back at the bunk we found Walter standing on the steps pointing at his ziti-covered clothes. 'Irty, irty, irty, irty.'

'No shit, Sherlock.'

Joe was in need of nicotine, so he crashed out for a while whilst I took a flannel and tackled Walter's face. I might as well have taken a broom, gone to the beach and swept up the sea. Ziti everywhere: on walls, in hair, in soap. I threw Walter's clothes into a sack and shoved him under the shower. That only made things worse. The shower head went into spasm, water spurting every which way but down until I was plastered with cheap pasta sauce and rust. I yanked Walter out, dressed him, then jumped in the shower myself.

I only caught a glimpse at first. Then I looked again. There was an eye peeking through the crack in the door, spying on me: Joshua. He stood there, rubbing his inner thigh, grinning at my naked body, muttering softly to himself. 'Well, you know, Counsellor Benjuman,

I don't think you have anything to hide, well, you know, I was just wondering...' I yelled at him and slammed the door, catching his fingers. He howled and scampered back to his bed, chuckling. I'd had enough of that shit in the dorm back at school.

'I just don't know.'

'What?'

'Well, I just don't know.'

'What don't you just know?'

'I just don't know if this what you need right now.'

'What are you talking about? Who the hell are you anyway? Go back to your bunk. Can't I get a moment's peace around here.'

That evening, after having clocked up another day crammed to the hilt with yelling, impatience and anger, I collapsed on the porch. Just a moment to myself, away from the patients, that was all I wanted, a tiny stolen moment. But they got everywhere, that was the worst thing about Veda. Don't ask me where they came from: the bushes, the trees, from under the floors, out of the showers, they came at you from every direction, sneaking up on you when you weren't looking. They'd somehow sense when you were off guard and that's when they'd go for you; crowding round you, prying, demanding, touching. You'd be sitting on the toilet, in the midst of a nice private crap, look up and one of them would be there, standing right in front of you, grinning, mumbling or playing with his penis. Even now, on the porch when I was trying to escape, there was one, biting his fingers. He wasn't even one of mine. Some guy I'd never seen before.

'What bunk are you from?'

'Now don't you go get angry with me. It's ain't my fault you having so damn a miserable time. I just don't know.' He was long, thin and black, with wide eyes and hair that looked like it'd been cut with a pair of blunt garden shears. 'I just sitting here, figured you could use the company.'

'I don't need anyone's company but my own. And I especially don't need yours. You're a patient, for Christ's sake. Now go on. Scram! Get out of here! Go find your counsellor.'

He stared off into the distance, ignoring me, fixing his gaze on something in the forest.

'What are you staring at?'

'I just don't know. I just figured you could use the company. Seem you need all the help you can get.'

'What the hell are you going on about, you miserable crazy? What the fuck do you know about me anyway.'

'I just figured...'

'Well, don't just figure, get out of here.'

'I just figured.'

'Jesus Christ! Why can't you leave me alone? You people are driving me MAD!' I stormed back into the bunk, slamming the door with a mighty thwack, grabbed the heaviest blanket I could find and buried myself under it.

The following day, Joe and I were ordered down to High Command. We couldn't figure out what we'd done wrong. Sure we'd broken some Veda rules. In fact, we'd broken most of them, but then who hadn't? In the end our worrying was wasted effort; we hadn't done anything. The Kommandant had a present for us.

Outside, in the reception area, we found a crooked figure hunched over a picnic table. He fixed us an angry stare as we walked to the door.

'Hello,' Kolchak greeted us with her choicest of bland smiles. 'And how are my two boys?'

'Fine, thank you.'

Her office was not what you'd you expect to find at the heartbeat of a mental asylum. It was small and cluttered. It seemed to be against her religion to throw anything away. Bric-a-brac of all unusable kinds lined the shelves, hemming you in: rusty fencing foils hung on the wall alongside a stuffed eagle with a missing eye; glass cupboards full of antiquated electrical equipment, frayed wires and bits of transformers; broken wooden skis cluttering the doorway; a pile of faded, holed lampshades stacked on a springless armchair. God knows how she got any work done in there. The only sign that it was an office was the antiquated typewriter and three phones on a large metal desk in the centre of the room.

Harriot, Kolchak's personal assistant, stood in the far corner and stared at us as though we were intruding on her privacy. She had a masculine face, the beginnings of an unwelcome moustache and a nervous tick in her left eye. At first I thought she was winking at me and almost winked back.

'No problems with your clients?' Kolchak asked.

'Er, well, now you mention it,' I began.

'No,' Joe interrupted, standing on my foot. 'None at all. Everything's fine.'

'Yes. Just fine.' I echoed feebly.

'Good. I am glad.' She smiled at us. We smiled back. Harriot didn't smile. 'I have something special for you.'

'Special?'

'Yes. Your new arrival.'

'New arrival?'

'Mitchel Luck. He's waiting for you outside. I'll have his trunk sent up. I'm sure you're going to have a wonderful time with him,' she rubbed her hands together, just like my father used to do before he walloped my backside with his slipper. 'Remember, he's *special*.'

'Great,' I heard myself say. 'Thanks very much.'

'Goodbye,' said Harriot and winked.

'Goodbye.'

Outside we were greeted with an impatient sigh and a grunt.

'Hi Mitchel, I'm Joe. This is Benjamin. We'll be your counsellors this summer.'

'I know. I've been waiting for you for twenty minutes.' When he spoke (or rather whined), only the left side of his mouth opened, dragging the other half reluctantly with it. 'Is Joshua here this year?' he demanded.

'Sure is.'

'Oh Jesus, not that asshole!'

'Yep, that arsehole,' Joe laughed. 'Well then, let's get you up to the bunk.'

'What about my duffle?'

'Don't worry about that,' I said. 'Herbert will bring it up in the truck along with your trunk.'

'No,' he squeaked angrily, 'I want it now. It's got my music in it.'

'Okay, okay, no problem. We'll take it now.' I slung the bag over my shoulder. Mitchel stood up and took Joe's hand and we set off on a slow, arduous journey, dragging our new patient (our special present) to B8. By the time we arrived, our patience had been left way behind, sitting crooked outside High Command.

One side of Mitchel's body was withered like a dying plant, his leg and arm contorted inwards at painful angles. He walked more with a side-to-side movement than a forward one, dragging his left foot behind, scuffing his shoes. Every few steps, he would snatch his hand angrily away from Joe, stop and curse, his voice wavering from high to low with each sentence. 'The bitch didn't let me bring my chair. They always let me have a damn chair at school. Always always always! But the bitch wouldn't let me bring it. Steve. That's what it is, that fucking Steve.' He would huff and puff his way a little further, then stop again, little beads of sweat running off his pimply skin. 'Fucking bitch! Where's my chair?' Halfway we swapped; I took Mitchel's hand, Joe took the bag and on we went, suffering in silence.

Mitchel turned to me and smiled. There was spittle in his bum fluff and food between his teeth. 'You know guys, we really could save all this trouble.' There was sudden friendship in his voice. 'All you need to do is get me a wheelchair. That's all.'

'It would be simpler,' Joe agreed. 'I'll go down to the infirmary later and see what I can do.'

After negotiating the assault course of abuse, we finally dragged Mitchel Luck up the steps of the bunk.

'I want the things from my bag,' he snapped.

I opened the duffle and took out two Walkmans, dozens of mangled cassettes, eight pairs of training shoes, three tubes of toothpaste and a large pile of heavy metal and martial arts fanzines.

'Well, hello there, Client Luckee.' Joshua had been watching Mitchel from the moment he came through the door, but it was several minutes before he spoke to him. 'I see your broken arm hasn't mended yet. Now that is a shame, don't you think? Well, yes I do.'

'Shut up, Joshua, you fucking asshole!' Mitchel screamed.

'Take it easy, Mitch,' Joe said.

'Well, you know I was just saying that it's a terrible shame. And, well, you know, I think you're the asshole,' Joshua replied, unruffled.

'I said shut up. Get out of my face!'

'Well what do you know? all I'm trying to do is be polite.' Joshua stood at the end of Mitchel's bed, a nasty grin on his face. 'And there he goes again, just like last year, being horrible, well, I don't know, I just...' A shoe whizzed into Joshua's stomach, sending him into a fit of melodramatic coughing. He bent double, glancing at Joe and me out of the corner of his eye, waiting for us to pull Mitchel into line.

'That's enough, Mitchel,' I said.

Joshua stopped coughing and smiled.

'He started it, that asshole. Why don't you tell him?'

'Well, I was just saying hello, I don't suppose Counsellor Benjuman and Counsellor Joa think there's a problem with that. Well, I was just being friendly, Client Luckee, and saying that you should get your broken arm mended, that's all. Well, yes I was.'

'Get out of here!' Mitchel yelled, veins in his neck popping with fury.

'Oh shut up, both of you!' Joe shouted. 'You're giving me a bloody headache.'

Dakota started laughing, bouncing on his bed. The louder the others shouted, the more he laughed. He was a mischievous son of a bitch.

'And you shut up an' all, asshole,' Mitchel bawled at Dakota.

'I laffin' at Joshwa yas I am I am laffin' at Joshwa...'

'Shut up, Dakota.'

'Yeah!' William joined the fray. He wandered over to Dakota's bed, slowly raised his enormous fist and brought it crashing down on top of Dakota's head. 'Yeah. Shut up. PIG!'

Dakota fell into stunned silence, his eyes open wide, trying to connect William with pain. 'Willy heet me yeas he did Willy did heet me yeas there,' he pointed to his head, 'there he heet me...' It wasn't a protestation, nor even a complaint, merely an observation of fact. 'Willy did heet me cos I laffin yeas...'

'Cut it, Dakota!'

'Well, do you see what you've done now, Client Luckee, you've gone and upset the whole cabin, and just because I was trying to be friendly. Yes indeed, and we was going fine before you came along with your broken arm.'

'Get the fuck out of my face. NOW!' Another shoe went flying through the air.

'Well, I really don't know...'

'PIG!'

'ASSHOLE!'

Joe and I quietly got up from our beds and tiptoed out to the porch, closing the door behind us, leaving the special population to be special alone.

B8's happy family was completed later that afternoon when our last charge arrived. A fat kid from Colorado, stubborn as hell, Charlie had Down's Syndrome, I checked it in my notes. His face was chubby and flat, as though it had been squashed against a wall. Slit eyes and pudgy nose hid under a mass of blond hair. He didn't say anything when I went to fetch him, didn't even look at me. I tried taking his hand but he wouldn't let me, nor would he come to the bunk. For half an hour I tried luring him out of his seat until, exasperated at having another Robert on our hands, I left him to his own devices and set off alone.

Fuck 'em.

After a few steps he began to follow, keeping the same distance behind. Each time I stopped, he stopped and sat on the ground. Every time I started, he started, playing some infernal game he and his twisted mind had invented to send me skitty.

Stop. Start. I dragged Charlie to the bunk. Start. Stop. He sat alone on the porch for hours, staring at the same picture in one of Mitchel's *Kerrang* magazines whilst the rest of the bunk boiled and bubbled with shout and scream. I tried to think of elsewhere. I tried to take myself back to Cambridge: to old rooms with sloping floors where the doors of cupboards never closed; to feast-filled candlelit halls; to idle academic chatter over port with fumbling professors; to cold courtyards, the air pervaded with chapel voices; to falling down narrow, uneven stairwells in drunken heavens. But they had contaminated my thoughts. Their faces. My mind. Their voices.

When the nurses came at dinner that night Joe and I put in an order for large quantities of aspirin.

Two paper plates of cold chicken weighed down our table, daring us to eat. We wheeled Mitchel as far away from Joshua as possible. 'I wanna sit next to Joshua,' he whined.

'But you don't like Joshua,' Joe protested. 'You hate him. You think he's an arsehole.'

'I wanna sit next to Joshua.'

'Well Counsellor Joa and Counsellor Benjuman, don't you think that Client Luckee should be allowed to sit where he wants? I do, don't you and...' Joshua droned on.

'Okay, okay!'

So we put them together. Joshua told Mitch about his parents,

Block Island and his new teacher at school, whilst Mitchel ripped his cold chicken to shreds, attacking it as though it were still alive.

'Well you know Miss Kerschbaumer...grunt...will be...snort...very happy to see...slurp...me, well, I think...burp...she will...asshole...'

Within minutes, William's plate was an abattoir, a wasteland of carcasses; Walter had a wishbone in his hair; Dakota had downed three jugs of juice and was demanding more; and Charlie had joined Robert in eating nothing, saying nothing and being nothing.

There was a short sing-a-long-come-get-to-know-each-other planned for that evening. One of Kolchak's things where we could get together and all be jolly friendly and celebrate how special the special population were and how wonderful, dedicated and saint-like the counsellors were (Remember, you're *special*).

Fortunately, it never got off the ground. A woman from G6 who sucked her tongue overturned a table at the far end of the hall, sending food, juice and hot coffee everywhere. Like a pack of dominoes toppling one after the other, a chain reaction of excited patients ran amok with cold chicken. A boy from B6 spat at Robert. A patient from Lucien's bunk urinated in the middle of the hall. Rambo ran wild with a wet mop, shoving it in people's faces yelling, 'Don't move! Or I blow you away.' Joshua jumped up and did a quick circuit of the hall, skilfully dodging the pandemonium. 'Ohlolololololololololo!' he screamed. Counsellors relinquished control. The law of the dining-hall reigned supreme. Someone threw a chair and Norma decided to abort dinner. Medication was rapidly distributed and we were sent packing to the bunks to calm down. Evening activity was cancelled.

We rounded up the bunk, dragging William from the kitchen where, the chicken having run out, he was in the process of constructing a gargantuan peanut butter and jelly sandwich (all jelly, no sandwich). Dakota refused to leave, stamping his feet, hollering for 'owaange joese yas I do owaange...' William punched him again, sending him scurrying to the bunk like a frightened deer. 'Willy gonna heet me again yas he is heet me Willy gonna...' Joe lifted Mitchel into his wheelchair and we pushed him through the debris on the floor.

'Man! Did you see that, you guys?' he hollered. 'Did you see that girl? That thing went flying. Oh boy, that was great! And Joshua! He was cool. Man he's so cool!'

'Mitch,' Ellen blocked our path. 'What are you doing in that chair?' Mitchel stopped laughing. 'So, you did it again huh?'

'Aw come on Ellen, leave off,' he said meekly.

'Don't "Aw come on" me. Out you get!' She hauled him out of the wheelchair. No curse, no protest, no temper. It wasn't the same Mitchel. 'He does this every year,' she explained, 'tricks the counsellors into giving him a chair. He doesn't need one.'

'Don't, Ellen. Stop.' Mitchel looked guilty as sin.

'Not only does he not need one, his doctor specifically said he shouldn't have one. Didn't he Mitch? And you know why, don't you Mitch?'

'Ellen,' he pleaded.

'Don't you Mitch?'

'Yes,' he submitted.

'Well, tell Joe and Benjamin what he said.'

'Aw, Ellen.'

'Tell them!'

'He said if I use a chair my leg will never get stronger.'

'Exactly. Now get up to the bunk.' He obeyed without a murmur. Crushed. 'You got to be sharp. He's a tricky one.' She laughed. 'Same moves every year, though.'

'Well,' Joe shrugged, 'he certainly pulled large quantities of wool over our eyes.'

'How did you do that Ellen? I mean, how?'

'Do what, Benjamin?'

'Make him do as you say.'

'Giving you trouble is he? You just gotta know him, that's all. Give it a little time. You'll soon get to figure his ins and outs.'

Joe and I watched Mitchel practically run up the hill. A miraculous recovery. Jesus couldn't have done a better job. Cunning bastard.

10

'Get a load of this!'

'What?'

'William's language.'

'What about it?'

'Says here his parents used to leave him in front of the telly when he was younger, hardly ever spoke to him. Picked up his vocab from the TV. No wonder he's got a mouth and a half on him.'

Joe and I were on the porch flicking through the files we'd been given during orientation. I wanted to see how they compared to reality. It was hard to believe that any of what we'd witnessed could be depicted on paper.

Veda was abed, the volume finally turned down. All that was left was a quiet residue of demented dreams and abandoned awakenings. From inside B8 came the hushed solitary conversation of Joshua and the heavy snores of Charlie, his rhythmic mucus gently rocking the bunk. Up at B12 someone was having an almighty fit. Screams tore through the blackness and pierced the moon. The stars were more distant than I had ever seen, frightened of coming too close.

Putting B8 to bed proved more of a battle than getting them up had been. They were determined to stymie you at every instant, like that was their one concern in life. They sensed your weaknesses, the things that pissed the hell out of you, and they headed straight for them, snapping at frayed nerves, holding on, twisting, shredding them.

Robert climbed under the covers immediately. I thought he was at last trying to be helpful, told him what a good boy he was, then saw he still had his clothes on and had wiped Joe's boot polish across his pillow. William and Walter had a water fight, filling their cups from the toilet basin after Dakota had taken a piss and forgotten to flush the chain. Mitchel lay in bed pulling his cassettes to pieces, chewing on the tape, scowling at the world, occasionally stopping to cuss Joshua. Joe lost his cool for the first time and shrieked like crazy, bawling him out like there was no tomorrow. It was getting to both of us.

Nor did it finish after lights out. Charlie wheezed and spluttered so violently I thought he'd swallowed his windpipe. I panicked, grabbed the torch and rushed to his aid. He was bent double, a fat contortionist gone too far. I turned on the lights and pulled on a coat ready to head for the infirmary. Only then, when I took a closer look, did I see that Charlie was sleeping peacefully. The rest of the bunk, however, were now wide awake. It took me an hour to settle them down again. Finally, as I was tiptoeing out to the porch, ready for a snooze, came a resounding thud. Once more I sprang into action, charging inside, waking the bunk, only to find William lying on the bathroom floor: sound asleep. Then there was the sniffling. Mitchel was sitting up in bed crying. Unfortunately, he wasn't asleep. He was missing his mom. So was I. I was missing his mom. I was missing my mum. I wanted to cry. I sat comforting him, telling him everything was all right when I knew it wasn't. Eventually the sobs snuffed themselves out and B8 fell into a fragile calm.

'What was it this time?' Joe asked when I came back to the porch.

'Mitchel. He's missing his mother.'

'That's funny, I was just reading about him and his mum. He beats her. There's a dozen incidents here about his violence. He broke her arm once.'

'Wonder if she's missing him?'

'You know what happened to him? "Cerebral palsy induced by accident at birth." The doctor delivered him with forceps, squeezed a little too hard and, whoops, crushed part of his head. Led to oxygen deprivation, or something. Sixteen years like that 'cos of one tiny slip.'

I didn't want to think about it. At first I tried sympathy for him. But I kept seeing his whining face and thinking of his mother, of Mitchel hitting her, yelling at her, day after day after day. Perhaps he blamed her. After all, she brought him into this world.

'I looked up Joshua too.'

'And?'

'Born normal, so they say.'

'So what happened?'

'His mother abandoned him on the streets when he was a kid. They found him when he was about seven years old, couldn't tell how long he'd been on his own. Listen, "Mental irregularities recorded when found. Deteriorated over the following two years". Poor kid.'

'Hello, my friends.'

Lucien stepped out of the darkness and up on to the porch.

'*Salut. Ça va?*'

'Not so bad. Tired.'

'Aren't we all.'

'How's it going with B8?'

'Like a recurring nightmare, Lucien and the night's just beginning. I've had it and they've only been here two days. You can't get through to them. Can't communicate with them. It's like you're not here. I spend most of the time talking to myself. I'm going to end up like them if I'm not careful.'

'I can think of worse fates,' Lucien smiled.

'Can you? I can't. They're veggies. Out and out. I thought Kolchak was supposed to have screened them. She must have had her eyes closed. I was expecting something like Billy Bibbit or Mr Harding, *Cuckoo's Nest* and all that. But these! You can't even hold a conversation with these.'

'It's worse than I thought it would be,' Joe spoke for the first time. He didn't feel comfortable around Lucien, never said much. 'I've worked with retards before. You got to be patient. You've got to take a little time, tune to their frequency. Still, I got to admit, I wasn't prepared for anything like this.'

'Nobody was. Orientation didn't prepare us. Theory. That's all it was. Words and smiles.'

'But at least the work is intriguing,' Lucien protested.

'Intriguing!'

'No, I'm serious. These people have the potential to educate us, teach us. I'm learning a great many things.'

'That's funny, because I get the feeling my entire education is in reverse. Another week and I'll be learning to read.'

'No, but Benjamin, try to look at these people in an objective light. How they behave and interact. How they respond to us. That's what you need to do. They're a world apart and yet here they are, right next to us. A world within worlds; and we're on the outside, not understanding. It's not they who need to understand, it's us. Don't you ever wonder what's going on in their heads? Don't you wish you could enter their world, see it from the inside? Find out what they know?' Joe stamped on a spider which was making a dash for the door. He was tiring of Lucien and his ideas, you could see it. 'You must look at it like that, Benjamin. These people are fascinating. They are cases to be studied, and we have the perfect opportunity to...'

'Case studies!' Joe interrupted, irritation sharpening his voice. 'For Christsakes, Lucien, will you give it a rest. There's a fourteen-year-old kid in our bunk who's fucked up simply 'cos no one else wanted him. And that's that. I don't call that a fascinating case study. I call it a fucking tragedy!'

'I just meant...' Lucien began, then faltered.

Lucien was too sensitive for his own good. He was the only guy I ever knew who cried in a McDonald's. Imagine that, blubbering over your french fries in the home of the clown. Lucien hated McDonald's, he only went there to spite his father. He was sitting at a sterilised table, lost in the deadend alleyways of his thoughts, when he heard this voice. It came softly; apologetic, guilty. 'I'm sorry darling. I forgot. It's my fault. Really, I'm sorry.' Lucien looked up and saw this man sitting next to a little girl, stroking her hair, both of them staring at a hamburger unwrapped on the table, the inside of the soggy bun covered in glup. There was radish on it, ketchup, all kinds of plastic bits and bobs. The girl liked her hamburger plain. Her father knew that, only he forgot. She was about six. A girl that age shouldn't have to remind her father she doesn't like bits on her burger; he should know these things, that's what it means to be a father. So he apologised a little more and, feeling terrible, went to buy her another. Lucien looked at the girl: there she sat, huge hazel eyes, little reddish plaits running down her back, staring at the burger her father had, in his absent-mindedness, bought; two simple tears forcing their way down her cheeks like pebbles on a shore. That burger was all that mattered to her and her father had let her down. Lucien wanted to hold her, he felt so miserable. But he was frightened the father would think he was interfering with his little girl. He couldn't even comfort her because of the suspicions of a dirty world. So he just sat there, all alone in McDonald's, and cried his little heart out. Like I say, Lucien was too sensitive: what wouldn't so much as graze others drew blood from him.

And here he was, reeling from Joe's rebuff.

'It's okay Lucien,' I said, trying to console him, seeing the hurt in his eyes I'd seen at Dotty's on that first night. I could almost feel his stomach tighten. 'You have a point. I just think we're a little tired to discuss it this evening.'

Joe lit a cigarette and the rest was unspoken.

'Oh boy,' Joe broke the awkward silence, his boyish smile lighting up the porch. 'Look who's coming. Heya gorgeous!'

'Hi Joe. Hi Lucien. Hi Benjamin.' Natasha was coming up the path. Lucien stood to kiss her, remembered he was no longer in Paris, and sat down again like a fool. 'So what are three handsome men talking about on a starry night?'

'Insanity,' Lucien replied.

'Seems that's catching. Claire and Charlotte have gone on about nothing else all evening.'

'But now you're here,' Joe said, 'you've brought a little sanity into our lives.'

'Well I was bored, so I thought I'd take a walk. It's a beautiful night.'

'Even more beautiful now you're around.' Joe was overdosing on flattery. But he was doing it for my benefit. He thought I needed help with Natasha.

'Joe, you're too sweet.' Natasha paused and looked at me. 'You're quiet.'

'I'm tired.'

Joe and Lucien waited for me to go on. But I didn't feel like talking, at least not to Natasha. She belonged to drunken evenings in the bar and hot summer days at the river. There wasn't a place for her on the porch of B8, with the files and the patients who had exploded into our lives. She didn't belong there. I'd brought her into a world where I didn't want her to be. I'd been selfish. And? I couldn't want her anymore for that. I couldn't hold her in my arms for the sake of my conscience.

Natasha stayed and chatted a while, shooting the crap about who was doing what to whom and why. Bjorn had finally made it with Alison the arts and crafts counsellor from Adelaide, his dreadful English notwithstanding. Mark from B6 was trying it on with Ellen, but he was a creep, everyone knew that. The drama counsellor, Suki, had been scene practising with Chris in the social hall. And Lorraine, the evening activities counsellor with an ever-ready smile and a nice word to say about everyone, was gunning for Ritch the director's son (riding in the Cherokee Jeep) and making a fool of herself by all accounts.

I remained silent.

The screams from B12 stopped. Veda was calm; a peace all its own. At length Natasha left, shooting an accusing glance at me as she got up. She waited for the offer to walk her back, but it didn't come and she set off down the hill alone.

'Why did you do that?' Joe asked

'Do what?'

'Behave like that with Natasha.' He wasn't angry, he just didn't understand. 'You can see she wants to be with you. Why are you horrible to her?'

'I'm not horrible to her, at least I don't mean to be.'

'You don't talk to her.'

'I don't want to be with her, that's all.'

'You weren't saying that at the beginning.'

'That was different. I was chatting her up, having fun, playing games. I didn't mean anything serious by it.'

'You could have fooled her.'

'Well maybe then, but not now. Things are different now. I don't want to be burdened by a relationship. Not here. Did you see that look in her eyes? She'd suffocate me.'

'I don't understand you, Ben. Most guys would give their right arm to be with her, and their left.'

'Maybe, but that's not enough.'

'You want to watch yourself. Dave's been asking about you. He's got the hots for Natasha, thinks you're fucking her around.'

'Dave's welcome to her. He can fuck her around. Because from here on out I'm having nothing to do with her.'

High over the trees from the girls bunks on the other side of the brook came a screeching laugh. A solitary voice started to sing: 'Follow the Yellow Brick Road'.

'I'm tired,' said Joe. 'I'm gonna hit the sack.

'I better be off too,' Lucien said miserably. 'See you tomorrow. Goodnight.'

I waited for Joe to go inside and then took Lucien's hand. It was tense, a little sweaty. 'Don't take offence from Joe. That's just the way he his.'

He made an attempt at a smile, kissed my cheek, lips like a child, and ran down the steps into darkness

I listened to Joe climbing in to bed, weary springs creaking. It was cold on the porch and the river's echoes were lonely. I thought of nothing. I thought of everything. Restless. Spinning. It was a long time before I slept that night.

11

The next morning I was awoken by the pervasive smell of excrement. It was early. A light mist enveloped the bunk. Dew hung lazily on the grass. Tranquillity poked her head around Veda's door to see if it were safe to come in. Beauty stepped tentatively out of the forest. A dark brown slush oozed from between William's sheets – Nature's triumph to tragedy in one foul bowel movement. Gingerly, I lifted the covers to be welcomed by a lumpy mess festering in the bed, smeared into his pyjamas, entwined with his body hair, little streaks of green amid dominant brown, identifiable remnants of last night's dinner. William slept peacefully, couched in his own shit, oblivious to the stench. For a moment I toyed with the idea of creeping back to bed, having seen no evil and waking with a surprised look on my face when Joe told me that William had soiled himself.

'Oh really, Joe?'

'It was gross. Took ages to clean up.'

'How terrible. You should have woken me, I would've helped.'

I couldn't do it.

I showered William, took the lumps out of his Calvin Kleins, threw the sheets into a plastic sack and took them down to the rubbish area. They were beyond saving. Even the mattress was stained. By the time I'd finished it looked as though I were the one with serious sphincter malfunction: my hands were darker than Michael Jackson's, my body reeked.

When I came back *he* was there again, the skinny black guy from the other night, sitting on the porch, staring at something in the trees.

'I just don't know.'

'You again! It's too early for you to be wandering around alone. Where's your counsellor?'

'Well I figured I'm allowed a morning walk once in a while. What you think, I crazy or something? Ha!' He laughed loudly and bit off his thumbnail. 'You figure I so crazy I can't even take a walk. You one sonfabitch judge, ain't ya. I just don't know.' He stuck out his leg, preventing me from passing.

I eyed around for a stick in case of trouble.

'No, I just thought...'

'Well that the damn trouble with you people, you think just a little too damn much don't ya? You think I crazy, don't ya? Well of course I'm crazy. I lived in a crazy home all my damn life. Who wouldn't be crazy? And I just figured you could do with some company. You an ungrateful bastard, ain't you?'

He spat out the thumbnail and stood up. For a moment I thought he as going to hit me and I backed down the steps.

'Well, I just don't know,' he sighed, and wandered off across the hill, without so much as a glance in my direction.

I couldn't wait for breakfast. I no longer cared what I ate. It didn't even have to be edible. I was famished.

But I never made it. It wasn't Robert this time; the smell of shit succeeded where I had failed before and he got up of his own accord, washing and dressing himself into the bargain. It was Mitchel. Moaning and whining about every shirt I chose for him, he took an age to dress. By the time I'd finished, the others had already left in search of Cheerios.

'Come on, Mitchel. We're late.' I was helping him down the steps (shoving him a little) when he started to quiver. I thought he was cold, so I let go of him to fetch a sweater. The side of his mouth fell open, saliva running on to his chin. His eyes rolled back in his head. A surge of violent spasms welled up from nowhere, crowding round. He shook and tumbled down the steps in a series of heavy thuds, twitching in the dirt at the bottom.

'Mitchel! Mitchel!' I panicked. His head lolled to one side, his arm beating on the ground like a broken butterfly wing, his legs knocking together, knees bleeding. 'Help! Somebody. Up here!' I called out. Yelling.

Nobody came.

I watched as the convulsions threw him from side to side. 'Please Mitchel, stop.' His teeth started chattering and a shade of blue swept into lips, a twist of agony distorting his face.

Sudden. Unexpected. It stopped as it had started.

Life came back to his eyes and he gasped for breath, sucking his saliva, biting his lip. 'Mitchel, are you all right?' He tried to sit up, but tumbled backwards. He was covered in dirt and blood. Straining his neck, he looked up at me and smiled feebly.

That was my first seizure. My rite of spring. *Grand mal, petit mal*, what did it matter - I thought he was dying. And what had I done? Nothing. I hadn't known what to do. I saw life running before my very eyes. I saw them coming to collect the body from the bunk, zipping up the black bag, his mother piling up his magazines and taking them away. And I had watched him. Guilt. Thrashing. In pain. They had told us about seizures, but they didn't tell us it would be like that.

A day of learning. Veda was up, running, and fully dysfunctional. It was the first day of activities. Our schedule started at 10 a.m. sharp with academics. Like most things in Veda, this wasn't what it seemed.

Academics was held in the academics room, a chicken run next to the infirmary, and was taught by the academics teacher, a girl by the name of Claire who had just finished school and was waiting to go to Liverpool Polytechnic, with no more experience of teaching academics than Walter or Dakota. Claire was small, with breasts of direct inverse proportion to her size. Joe was taken with her right away. Though, strictly speaking, it wasn't her he was taken with; it was the breasts (the rest of her he could take or leave). If he could have detached her breasts and waltzed off with them he would have been quite happy. But as there was no sign of Claire and her wazoombas parting company, he had to make do with the whole package. He'd been looking forward to academics all week; one hour when all he got to do was stare at *them*. He tried creeping through the forest, round the back of her bunk, to see if he could see her taking a shower. But what kept out the mosquitoes also kept out Joe (the dirty peeping Tom): the wire mesh on the windows of G4 was too thick for him to see anything. So he had to make do with seeing the bouncers through Claire's thin Marks and Sparks pullover in the academics room, imagining them ballooning into his ecstatic face, suffocating in paradise.

We only just made it to her class on time. William was also up and running that day. He soiled himself again, producing even more shit than the average politician. 'I don't know why his parents buy him underpants,' said Joe as I threw away yet another pair of Calvin Kleins. 'He needs thermo-nuclear nappies.' What with the clean up operation and another seizure from Mitchel, we almost missed our first lesson.

The academics room was even smaller inside than it looked from the outside. A rickety table with a glued-on extra leg to hold it steady was Veda's centre for studious activity, the core of curricula confusion. Around the sides were a few homemade bookshelves with some homemade books and tupperware bowls with ill-fitting lids, which contained various instruments for the pursuit of academic excellence, such as odd jigsaw pieces and milk straws.

'Good morning, B8,' Claire stood up, babashkas bub-bub-bouncing, clicking her fingers, relishing her newly found authority.

'Good morning,' Joe replied, eyes wide.

'First I want you to introduce yourselves so I can get to know you.'

'I'm Joe. Get to know me.'

'No, not you. The patients.'

'Academicslady sschedle I wanna see da sschedle...' Dakota was off and Claire was thrown. First blood to B8. We were her first class and I don't think she was fully prepared for the Slide.

'Er, yes, good, okay, so,' she began. 'What's your name?'

'Lady lady sschedle I see da sschedle yas I do lemme see it yeas...'

'Now Client Dukota, why don't you be quiet for a moment, I think the counsellor is asking me, well yes I do. My name is Client Joshua Art Hoses, and I live in the Bronx, well you know, that also happens to be the place where I go to school and when...'

'Okay, thank you. Just a name will do for now.'

'Ssche...'

'And Dakota, what's your name?'

'Dakota Slide, five four fwee Lincoln Avenue, Silver Spwing, Maryland, YUSA. Five five seven fwee two eight nine sschedle.'

'Good God!' Joe sat up. 'Did you see that Ben? He answered a question. He actually answered a question. Dakota, what do you want for lunch?'

'Lunch yas I do...sschedle I wanna see...'

'Dakota, what's your name?' I asked.

'Dakota Slide, five four fwee Lincoln Avenue, Silver Spwing...' he reran the self-identification programme.

Joe shrugged. 'Oh well,' he said, disappointed. 'At least it's a start.'

Claire went round the table asking names (leaning dangerously low over Joe). But her academic exercise was drowned out by Dakota's persistent and increasingly frantic demands to see her schedule.

With each request came a little more agitation – a rock of the chair, a shake of his fist, a flap of his arm – the by now familiar signs that he was getting acutely pissed off. The more he was ignored, the more angry he grew. 'Yas I will yas I will see it yas I will I will...' he banged his hands on the table defiantly.

'Why does he want to see my schedule?' she asked, bemused.

'Don't ask us,' Joe laughed. 'We just wash him, dress him and help him piss straight. Dakota stop now. That's enough.'

'Nuh nuh nuh I will yas I will nuh nuh nuh...'

'Stop! Enough I said!'

Dakota flipped. He shook his head and started slapping his ears. Furious. Whacking himself. Slapping his face. Grunting uncontrollably. The noise was terrific. Charlie slipped off his chair and hid under the table. William covered his face and squeaked.

'Make him stop,' Claire cried. 'He can have the schedule. Benjamin, please make him stop. He's hurting himself.'

I grabbed Dakota's hands. There was a lot of power there, it took me a while to bring him under control. His ears were red and his lips swollen. 'Okay Dakota, calm down, just calm down. Here look, you can have the schedule.' His shaking slowed. He started panting. 'The academics lady will give it to you. Here. Look, take it.'

Joshua chuckled to himself. 'Well won't you just look at that Client Slid. Now he is what I call one crazy momma, well don't you know it, yes he is.'

Dakota spent the rest of the lesson reading the schedule and asking Claire which groups she had when. 'Academicslady who you have at fwee yes who who?' Walter tapped Joe on the shoulder, pointed at Dakota, laughed, and asked 'Wi?'. Joe shrugged, not unlike Walter. William sat snapping pencils until I summoned the courage to confiscate them.

So much for academics.

Next was music, which turned out to be as unmusical as academics had been unacademical. The music teacher was a wholesome, chubby girl named Violet with the voice of a small-town church choir. She was from Nebraska and proud of it. Little pure curls on her head and the original rosy cheeks. She had a guitar all her own (which she slept with) and was pleasant. Way too pleasant for B8. They reduced her to complete confusion in a matter of minutes, refusing to sing along to 'Jesus Wants Me For A Sunbeam', preferring instead to snap the drumsticks, take the dried peas out of the squeegee-bottle homemade-shaker and chuck them around the room. (If Jesus was smart, he wouldn't want anything to do with them.) Mitchel and Joshua had a fight, turned the air blue with a string of highly inventive curses and sat on one of the tin drums which Walter was trying to bang out of time.

So much for music.

Next on the list was cookery class, where the teacher, Alexandria, an economics student from Greenham, informed us that she was 'Going to instil a respect for safety in the kitchen and a basic knowledge of the culinary art'. It was going to be an uphill struggle. B8 hadn't yet learned how to consume food properly, let alone make it.

The cookery room was downstairs in the cottage where Rosetta lived. The stove was a museum piece, the fridge leaked, and the basin only had a cold tap. Alexandria suited the environment perfectly: dyed orange, cropped hair, several ear rings, a pierced nose, a mean pair of legs and one hell of an unfriendly face. She read the kitchen rules like she was reading roll call in Auschwitz. Those not washing their hands before touching food will be shot.

'And always remember,' she instructed, goose-stepping in front of the pasta stores, 'the kitchen is a dangerous place. Do as you are told and only leave your seat when you have my permission.'

Dakota's timing was impeccable. He stood up and wandered over to the notice board. 'Sschedle,' he whispered, as though exacting a pagan ritual, 'sschedle sschedle sschedle...', warming up for the next performance.

'Young man,' Alexandria snapped, 'what did I just say?'

'Sschedle cookinglady I wanna see da sschedle...' He had that determined glint in his eye.

An almighty clash was on its way, and I didn't rate Alexandria's chances of survival.

In the event, I never got to see the titanic struggle. An all too familiar smell drifted from William's end of the table. Calvin Klein pair N° 4. I had to leave to clean him up. Well, to be fair, 'NO SHITTING IN THE KITCHEN' wasn't on Alexandria's list.

The following evening, seven seizures, six fits, five pairs of Calvin Kleins, and two packets of aspirin later, when frustration was on the point of despair and desperation had nowhere left to go, the Veda

Council was convened on the hill outside the dining-hall. It was an informal group – Joe, Dave, Chris, Bjorn, Fergus, an Irish mature student who never stopped talking about the 'revolution' back home but who had no intention of ever going back there to help fight it, Thomas, our resident counsellor-in-earnest who kept the minutes (for what that was worth), and some guys whose names I never bothered to learn – which got together every now and then to catch up on gossip. They'd sit, have a coffee and a cigarette, bitch a little, then go their separate ways. But tonight there were more serious things on the agenda.

It had been a hot day. The sun was only just becoming bearable; that welcome time of the evening when it is warm yet cool, bright though soft. The buzz of Patrick's Bulldog could be heard from the other side of the river, its yellow wing-tips occasionally peeking over the tree tops. He flew every night at the same time, then landed and went straight to The Cuckoo's Nest for a Guinness, always putting J5 on the jukebox: 'We Are Sailing' by Rod Stewart. He had wanted to live in Cape Cod, run a fish restaurant and sail a wooden-hulled yacht with a red spinnaker. Instead he ended up in Sageville, running a bar and flying an old canvas plane with yellow wings. 'Somehow,' he told his customers every night before he went up to bed, 'somehow dreams never quite work out the way you intended.'

I lay on the grass, Lucien at my side, staring into the day's dying haze. Every second you could grab away from the patients was a precious gift at Veda, and most of my free seconds were spent with Lucien. He didn't come to the bunk much anymore: Joe wasn't too fond of him, so he stayed away. Whenever we had free time, he'd wait for me down by the main gates. I'd always find him tugging at the wire, as though he were trying to pull down the fence. We'd go up to the church together for a quick Lord's Prayer. Then he'd hold my hand while he sat and mumbled his own prayers, either in an agitated silence or an angry French so rapid I couldn't understand. Afterwards we'd visit May's Parlour where he'd buy me an ice-cream (vanilla, with added fresh cream and hot fudge sauce if he were in a good mood) and take his grubby, well-thumbed, original edition of Jacques Prévert's *Paroles* from his pocket (a present from his father, given on the condition that he never tell his mother) and read to me. Lucien loved reading aloud: he was good with other people's words, that was the only time he didn't stutter or falter, the only time he lost his awkwardness. But it was this, this artlessness, this jarring with his surroundings, that drew me to him; that and his kindness. He knew I was finding it tough at Veda and it troubled him. He did everything he could to make things easier for me. The previous day, after lunch, at the start of our free hour he came to see me. We had planned to go swimming in the Redhill. There was this huge aspen tree which hung right over the water; you could climb almost to the top branch and throw yourself off, flying through the air, crashing into the river. Lucien had been looking forward to going all morning, excited: that was the child in him. Only we never got to go. William had the squits, running down the back of his legs, unstoppable. It started in the dining-hall, carried on all the way up the hill and was now in full flood. I was exasperated; I couldn't deal with it any more. William's bowels were driving me skatty. When Lucien arrived I was sitting on the floor in the corner of the bathroom, head in hands, rolls of dirty thick-grained toilet paper at my feet, tears waiting to fall. He took one look at me, helped me up, sat me on a bed and took over: cleaning William, changing his clothes, mopping the bathroom floor. Not once did he mention our trip to the river. You could see he was disappointed, but he didn't mention it. All he cared about was me. I would have been lost without Lucien.

Every day he would show me his notebooks, his progress report. He was proud of them. He was trying to figure out if the autistics in his bunk had a way of communicating with each other and, if so, whether it could be used by the world outside to speak to them. Listening to Lucien was never boring. Don't ask me where he got his ideas from. Sometimes he came out with the craziest notions. He told me once he'd noticed that none of his patients had imaginary friends in the way ordinary kids do. He wondered whether they themselves *were* the imaginary friends of ordinary kids: imaginary friends as a kind of foray into mental abnormality. Lucien figured that we were all born with a little madness inside, but that most of us had it squeezed out of us while we were growing up and it never surfaced again. Someone should get a hold of those notebooks one day: a little organization and they'd make a great read.

'The point I'm making...' Thomas was lecturing the Veda Council, wagging his finger at his audience. Thirty, balding and from Hamburg, he was on his way to a stress-induced heart attack. 'The conditions here are not what we were led to believe. I find it unacceptable.'

'Unacceptable!' Dave interrupted. 'It's a fuckin' disgrace! The facilities are shit, the organisation's from the Fird bleedin' World and the patients are a bunch of veggies. The toilets don't work, the flids shit themselfs all the time. I mean they can't even feed themselfs an' we're supposed to be doing, what, "arts and crafts", "music", "drama". Give me a fuckin' break, willya. I don't blame Simon for leavin'. He did the right fing. I tell ya, tomorra I'm pickin' up what Kolchak owes me an' I'm out of 'ere.'

'Dave's got a point,' said Fergus. 'We were lied to. We weren't prepared for this. Orientation was joke.'

'High functionin', that's what we was told. My arse is 'igher functionin' than them lot.'

'And she said she checked them before they came.'

'Bullshit.'

'So we all agree,' Thomas continued, 'we've got reason to feel aggrieved. Let's try to do something about it. Take some action. Change things.'

'Come off it,' Mark sneered cynically, 'what are you going to do?'

'I don't know. Contact the agencies who sent us here. Call in the health department. Organise a petition. There must be some kind of regulatory body we could complain to. We could approach Kolchak, all together, collective power.'

'Collective power!' Mark laughed at the absurdity.

'That won't do nofin'. I'm going. An' if you're smart, you'll do the same.'

Temperatures had been rising from the moment the patients stepped of the bus. Counsellors felt cheated. Most of the anger came from those on the higher level. I hadn't been there yet, but we'd all heard the stories. They had it worse than us. The institutionals were vegetables, couldn't do a thing. And up there counsellors had to deal with violence on top of everything else. Chris had already received a nasty black eye for his efforts.

Simon had walked out that morning, stopping off at High Command to give the Kommandant a piece of his mind. Everyone knew what he said, you could hear the shouting down by the social hall. A crowd gathered to enjoy the show, despite Norma's flustered attempts to disperse it. Kolchak wasn't fit to run an institution, that's what

Simon told her. Veda should be closed down. There were blind and disabled patients having to negotiate steep gravel tracks to get to dinner. It took them half an hour and they were constantly falling over. Activities were a farce: counsellors weren't trained for the job and didn't have anything like the right equipment. Corners were always being cut and it put the safety of counsellors and patients at risk. The bunks were a disgrace, a breeding ground for disease. There were too many patients with too severe conditions for the place to cope with. Veda was a joke and he demanded to know how much money Kolchak was making out of it. She threw him out of her office. Simon worked in a care home in New York, he was used to dealing with the mentally disabled. He wasn't whingeing and she knew it.

'Okay, so we've all got it tough,' Joe spoke up. 'But we should stick with it, make the best of a bad job. What good's leaving going to do? How's that going to help the patients?'

'Fuck 'em! That's what I say. I ain't cleaning up no more shit. I've 'ad it.'

I wouldn't have put in quite the same way, but I could understand Dave's point of view. I couldn't see me lasting ten weeks. I'd have to go sooner or later. Might as well be sooner. My reasons were not as worthy as Simon's. I wasn't thinking of the patients. I was thinking of me.

If I am not for myself, who will be?

Hillel. I'd written a paper on him in my exams. But that was just philosophy. Only now did I understand the real meaning of his proverb.

I chose to ignore his second line.

If I am only for myself, what am I?

Protest faded and the revolutionaries went back to speculating about who was sleeping with whom. Dave, eye fixed on me, spoke loud and long about Natasha's physical assets. Thomas promised to organise a petition and form a delegation to see Kolchak with a list of concerns. But by now most of the Council had switched its attention to Bjorn, who was propagating more interesting material: the naughty nocturnal activities of Alison the art counsellor.

'And what a work of art she is!'

It wasn't that the subject didn't interest me but, with the restless nights and early mornings, I'd missed out on a lot of sleep over the past days. Tiredness followed me around like a relentless companion. So I headed to the bunk to put my head against a pillow.

A lonely moon drifts its worn way across Cambridge spires. Echoes run riot round courtyards, ancient buildings tormenting each other with stories of days long gone. In a Master's Lodge a chaplain frowns a moral frown and pours himself another glass of dry sherry. Ageing Fellows wrestle with Fenland winds, their swirling gowns threatening to carry them away. Professors sit in tower rooms before dying fires with earthenware mugs of lumumba, dreaming of those hazy days of summertime youth. The gentle Cam cuts through Clare Gardens, watching two aspiring lovers as they listen to the night. The punts are moored for Michelmas, waiting for those magical moments of May.

I sit in the barren rooms of Professor Bardhaw, overlooking the barren orchard, listening to his thoughts on Plato. Seven undergraduates, all with a glass of wine in their hands and the seminar paper on their laps: 'The Soul and its Thirst for the Good'. Professor Bardhaw's thick white hair flops over his eyes as he nods at 'a valuable objection indeed' from a young man with a runny nose just up from St Paul's. The Michelmas Term cold: obligatory for all Cantabridgians. On the walls are two Gaelic crosses from the monastery outside Cork to which Professor Bardhaw scurries for intermittent retreats.

'But for Plato,' he answers the sniffing undergraduate from St Paul's, 'the Soul has three parts – Reason, which is located in the head; Courage or Spirit, which is located in the breast; and Desire which is located in the belly.'

My belly desires more wine, so I help myself from the college decanter, and take a few notes. Reason. Courage. Desire.

'Of these,' he continues, 'Reason is incomparably the most important, for it partakes of the eternal.' I blink. I thought I saw Professor Bardhaw dribble. 'Whereas Courage and Desire belong entirely to the world of time and space.' He did. He did dribble. Look. He's doing it again. 'It is Reason, therefore, which sees the truth.' He turns to me and smiles, his head lolling slightly. 'It is Reason which is "the inward man", the rational element in us that is our real personality.' He flaps his arms. Professor Bardhaw flapped his arms!

'Courage is, on the whole, obedient to the dictates of Reason and will help it to establish its ascendancy.' Now he's dribbling again, rocking in his seat, nodding his head up and down. Twiddling his ear. I hold tight to the arms of the chair and look around to see if the others have noticed, but they just carry on taking notes as though nothing out of the ordinary is happening. 'But Desire is strong, wilful, contentious, turbulent, and chaotic.' I know that smell. Someone's farted. No, it's too strong. Excrement. Professor Bardhaw has soiled himself, I see it running down the legs of the great oak chair, slopping on to the threadbare rug. 'So Reason is like the charioteer who is driving two horses, one tractable and one wild. In this idea you see that Plato did dwink wed joese yeas he did yeas he did. Weason has a sschedle. Courage is going, well, at least, I think it is, to Block Island and Desire is a mutherfucking fat PIG!' I leap from my chair, sending my notes and wine sprawling across the table, knocking the crystal decanter with the boar's head crest to the floor, where it smashes into thousands of tiny pieces, each one laughing, mocking me. I make for the door, but before I can get there Professor Bardhaw collapses on the floor and starts thrashing in violent spasm. I stand and watch as his lips turn blue. He swallows his tongue and chokes whilst the seven undergraduates take notes.

12

'I got candy on my neck.'

'That's good.'

A large man stood before the fire in a sou'wester pointing to a thin red strip of sugar-covered candy he had licked and stuck to his neck.

'I got candy on my neck and potato chips in my boots.'

He wouldn't leave me alone. Everywhere I went he followed, stumbling after me, leaning over me, his flabby face almost touching mine, his stale breath burning my nose. 'I got candy on my neck.'

'I don't give a damn!' I got up again and tried losing him in the crowd. The cackle of the campfire fought to be heard above the night time crackle of the patients. Voices flew with the flames, sparks singeing the trees. Shadows writhed on the forest floor. Dorothy, the one who kissed me outside the dining-hall, stood in the clearing and started to screech. 'Somewhere over the rainbow...' Her mouth looked larger in the dark, her eyes wild, her hair rampaging out of control. 'Way up high...' The fire spat fiercely, trying to drown her song. 'There's a land that I dream of...' Beside her stood a boy, attentively playing an accompaniment on a guitar with no strings.

'I got candy on my neck.' The man found me again.

'Leave me alone.'

He wore an enormous raincoat, as thick as an elephant's hide, black wellington boots and the bright red sou'wester. In the light of the flame I could see sweat pouring from his face. He flashed me a crooked smile, licked his lips and pointed to the candy.

Eventually I managed to find Lucien, sitting on a tree stump on the edge of the crowd.

'Who's your friend?' he asked.

'No idea. He keeps following me around.'

'He's got candy on his neck.'

'I can see that.'

'I got candy on my neck.'

'I think he belongs to Thomas. B2.' Lucien tried to send the guy away, turning him and pushing him in the opposite direction, but he kept coming back. So in the end we just left him, standing in front of us in his raincoat in the hot summer night, an unwanted statue, pointing to his candy.

'Enjoying the sing-song?' asked Lucien.

'Wonderful.'

Dorothy's screeching came to a halt and Norma introduced the next act. Joey, a patient from B2 with lop-sided glasses, his head strained at such an angle that he was permanently looking at the sky, tuned his branch and began. 'I been a working on the railroad,' he sang, with no real notes. 'I been a working on the railroad.' His voice grew louder. ' I been a working on the railroad...' Now he was shouting.

On my left sat a girl amid a pile of leaves. The fire lit her eyes and I could make out a soft, sweet face that reminded me of my cousin Josephine. I would read to her when her parents went out in the evenings. They were out most of the time: dinners, concerts, always making connections, always. They had a firm. Consultants, a husband-and-wife team. They never had time for anything but business: 'You can leave work, but work never leaves you', that's the kind of crappy thing my uncle used to say. I never understood why they bothered having a kid. She was growing up right under their noses and they didn't even realise. Still, I liked reading to Josephine, watching her smile come and go with the turning of each page. *The Lion, the Witch, and the Wardrobe* was her favourite. I'd lost count how many times I'd read it to her. She never could understand how anyone could be so horrid to nice Mr Tumlus. But she had faith in Aslan, she knew he'd put the world to rights. She just wished he could do something about her dumb parents. When I put the book down, Josephine would take me by the hand and we would search each and every cupboard in the house on the off chance that there might be a snow-covered street lamp at the end of one of them. Narnia, that's all she ever dreamed of. I warmed at the thought of her and watched the girl amid the pile of leaves. She shook slightly and put her hands down her trousers, winking to herself. She pulled something out and held it up to the light. Then she put it to her mouth and, slowly, started to eat. I stared hard. And then I saw. What it was. It was excrement. She was eating her own excrement.

'I been a working on the railroad.' Joey went on. 'I been a working on the railroad...' He'd been singing the same refrain for the last five minutes and there was no sign of him moving on or stopping. Norma dragged him away by the collar so someone else could have a turn. 'I been a working on the railroad...' he yelled, wandering through the trees.

I told Lucien about my dream. He wasn't surprised. He interpreted it for me, proceeding to dissect it piece by piece as though conducting some biological examination. Veda, he said, had started to permeate every aspect of me; my thoughts, my memories, my subconscious. He told me it was significant that I had dreamt of Cambridge. For me, he said, Cambridge was sacrosanct, untouchable, and that Veda could enter this world showed how much I'd been affected by what was going on around me. Nothing in me was sacred anymore, Lucien concluded, internal frontiers had started to crumble.

Neat analysis. But I remained sceptical. After all, a dream's just a dream.

'You can't make sense of nonsense,' I told him.

'There's a reason for everything and everything has a reason,' he answered, warming to his subject. 'Imagine for a moment, just imagine that madness is infectious. You can pick it up, catch it just like a common cold. So, you come into contact with these people and you catch what they've got, become crazy like them. And so it goes on. Thriving. Spreading. What we need is inoculation, a jab to prevent insanity.'

'I got candy on my neck.' The man in the sou'wester leant over me.

'You can't tell me,' Lucien went on, 'there's no reason for your dream. Of course there's a reason. Look around! Just look at this place. It's in the very air we breathe: madness.'

'Specialness.'

'Retardation, insanity, whatever you want to call it. You're still infected.'

'And what about you, Lucien? How come I'm the only one around here catching a cold?'

'Because you're exposed. I'm standing well back, an observer in a medical mask. There's nothing to worry about, Benjamin. Veda is another world, another language. It takes a while to learn, and it can be frustrating at first. But imagine, once you've mastered it, think of all the possibilities it will open up. You're beginning to understand madness, and madness is beginning to understand you.'

A log rolled from the fire, sending flames racing along the earth.

There were screams of fear and cries of excitement. Patients ran and danced, whipping themselves into a frenzy, until Joe kicked it back into the inferno and they died down.

'Your reality has become a dream. So now your dream takes on reality.'

Having explained it away to his satisfaction, Lucien sat back, content. His black hair shone in the firelight. But there was no reflection in his dark eyes. They were dead to the world, obscuring the whirring and grinding inside his head that never seemed to cease.

I was OD that night. I had to go prepare. Lucien offered to come over and keep me company, sit together on the porch. I declined. Some time alone, for a change, wouldn't be a bad thing.

'I got candy on my neck.'

I stood up, went over to the guy in the sou'wester and ripped the thin red strip of sugar-covered candy from the side of his neck. A drop of blood oozed from the small tear in the skin.

'Not anymore you haven't.'

He was there. Again. The skinny black guy. Sitting in the same position, on my porch, staring out into nothing, chewing his fingers.

This was the last thing I needed.

'You don't look too well,' he said, not turning to look at me as I walked up the steps.

'I got a cold.'

'I just don't know. That's too bad. You should wrap up some more warm on a night like this.'

'Look, I appreciate your concern. But you're somebody else's patient. You're nothing to do with me. You shouldn't be spending all your time sitting on my damn porch. What is it with you? Why don't you just fuck off?'

'I just figured you need company. Someone watching over you, that's all.' The whites of his eyes stepped out of his dark skin and danced around the porch, goading me. He smiled, rubbing his chin with the back of his hand. 'You see, I know how it gets. All alone, can't figure it out. I'm crazy, remember. Spent me whole damn life at the butt end of one treatment or another. They always be trying out some experiment on me, nothing ever stay the same. So, I figure I in a position to help. What with you having a hard time settling in n' all. Need someone like me to show you around.'

'I don't need anyone,' I yelled at him, shoving my mouth right close up to his ear. 'And even if I did it certainly wouldn't be anyone like you, you can be sure of that. Now you better leave before you start to piss me off.'

He didn't move. Just sat there, looking out, muttering about his time in various New York homes. I didn't want to know. I told him so. I asked him again to leave. I asked him several times. I tried lifting him off the porch, but he was too heavy. His voice was driving me nuts: incessant, dreary, sodden. There was nothing else to do.

I went inside to fetch a pillow.

Then I beat the shit out of him, hard as I could. He didn't flinch. I don't think he even stopped talking. I hit him again and again. Each swipe harder than the last, the cover on the pillow splitting. I beat the frustration the hell out of me. When I'd finished, he asked if that was all I'd be needing then, nonchalantly, like he was leaving a small-town bar after a few noontime drinks, he stood up and wandered off.

There was no moon. Ominous shadow clouds swept across the nightscape. I watched the counsellors disappear down the path by the social hall and off up Sageville Road. And I was alone. I had wanted some time to myself, even Lucien had been claustrophobing me. I needed OD, time to unwind, regroup my forces. I sat on the steps of G7 and stared into the darkness.

I no longer wanted my solitude. I wanted people around me. I hoped Lucien would ignore what I'd said and come and sit with me anyway. It was comforting having him around. Veda without him was an eerie place. Night confiscated the security of sight. Alone with the patients, the hushed disquiet enveloped me, sealing itself around my fears. They were closer somehow, suffocating. I could feel their uneven breath. Deranged whispers swirled through my head. Lucien rocked. Joe dribbled. I stood up and looked across to the adjacent bunks, hoping to see someone with whom I could share out the solitude. Someone who would turn the light on my darkness, sending my dreaming distortions fleeing for cover. But there was no one. G7 was set slightly back in the trees, you couldn't see the other porches from there.

I sat down with *War and Peace*. I had decided it was to be my summer Campaign before leaving England, but had yet to open the first page.

Well, Prince, so Genoa and Lucca are now just family estates of the Buonapartes.

It all seemed so far removed, so irrelevant. Or was it my state of mind that was removed? My peace had been shattered. If only it were war, I could surrender.

I flicked through the pages.

Love hinders death. Love is life. All, everything that I understand, I understand only because I love.

Tolstoy should try coming to Veda.

I put the book down and looked again into the darkness. Only then did I notice there were no crickets. Veda had silenced their song. Even the fireflies flashed their momentary messages from outside the gates. It was deathly quiet. I shone my torch on the trees to comfort myself that I knew what was there. Their twisted, scraggy faces taunted me. I saw the head of Medusa which hung above my bed as a child and which, despite the terror it reduced me to, I could never bring myself to pull down (it was still there when we moved house ten years later). I turned off the torch. The darkness was even thicker, clinging to my body, pouring in through the cracks. I heard the Gorgon laugh.

I looked at Joe's watch. I had never owned one, didn't like the idea of time passing on my wrist. Only two hours to go.

There is solitude and there is solitude. One is light and productive and is welcomed with open arms. The other is heavy and unbearable and extinguishes spirit.

I needed Lucien.

I stood up and was about to go look for him when I heard a faint noise coming from inside the bunk, barely disturbing the breeze. I listened, but couldn't make it out. If I could just ignore it.

Slowly, I climbed the steps to the screen door and peeked into virgin blackness. I flicked on the torch. Assorted bodies lay in beds in a variety of contortions. The noise was slightly clearer. High pitched. Coming from the other side of the bunk. I stepped inside and waited.

Waited.

It was rhythmic, constant, a simple refrain over and over again. It was neither sung, whistled, nor hummed. More a combination of all three. Or perhaps a squeak. I shone the torch on the floor and followed its light to a doorway at the back of the bunk. It was almost religious, like satanic Gregorian chant, innocent and menacing. It droned on and on, a sweet hypnotism of bitterness. And on. I stepped through the doorway into the bathroom, the beam of my torch catching rusting faucets and stained enamel. I heard a creak and spun round to catch a glimpse of Professor Bardhaw in his monk's habit scurrying across the bunk and out the door. The torch fell to the floor. The chanting stopped for a moment. There was the laugh of a child. I rummaged in the blackness for my light, found it and switched it on, illuminating the bright blue eyes of a young girl. She was sitting on the toilet sweating, chewing her matted blond hair, chanting. I froze in the eternity of her gargoyle's stare. She rocked gently. Her hand was between her legs, moving fiercely up and down, tearing at her insides. On the cracked floorboards lay a small pool of blood. The faster her hand moved, the higher and more beautiful the chant, the sweeter her smile.

I dropped the torch and fled the bunk.

The following morning I decided to leave Veda.

13

I shifted the van into gear and it climbed unwillingly up Sageville Road, spluttering in protest, threatening to stall each time my foot so much as brushed the accelerator. After a while we reached a compromise and trundled along the winding road at twenty-nine miles per hour, doing our best to avoid the cavernous potholes. It was a beautiful morning, none of the closeness of the previous days. Clear. Fresh. We passed by the old gravel pits which had been turned into lakes, where Ritch said carp big enough to feed a family sat just below the surface, waiting to get caught (though no one had ever hooked one). The road climbed and dipped through beauty, swerved and swung through calm. I wound down the window and let the wind dry the sweat from my shirt. Joe was drumming on the dashboard, singing along to Otis Redding who crackled from inside the radio. He was in a good mood: Joe, not Otis. Otis was dead. Things were going well with Claudia and Joe was on a roll. Which was more than I could say for the van. It even slowed when freewheeling down hill.

'Can't you make this thing go any faster?' said Joe.

'Only if you get out and push.'

Ellen had asked us to pick up some new counsellors who were arriving at Madingdale after lunch. We were highly favoured. Kolchak trusted us with her van (mercy be), though she still asked me five times whether I had my driving licence and gave me an annotated rundown of the highway code, followed by a short practical quiz.

I hadn't told Joe about the previous night. I didn't know what to say. It didn't seem such a big deal outside of darkness. But the eyes, the voice. I could still hear it, echoing through my shaking hands, and it scared me half to hell. I had run down to find someone and met Norma on the path. She smiled at me pitifully when I told her the story and strode up to the bunk: bulky, bold and fearless. I stayed where I was. Nothing would have dragged me back in there.

Neither had I told Joe about my decision to leave. I knew he was going to be disappointed. I didn't like the thought of letting him down, but I couldn't stay anymore for that.

I wasn't sure what I was going to do. I'd give Aimie a call in the afternoon; I could stay with her for a while until I found something.

Perhaps I'd go West. California. Surely that had something to offer? Maybe Joe would come with me, it would be good to have him around. I looked at him. He drummed. 'I left my home in Georgia, headed for the Frisco bay...' No, he wouldn't leave; he'd stay no matter how bad things got. That was the way he was.

We crawled round a sharp S-bend, avoiding an upturned truck lying in the dirt and a squashed racoon, and came out on the main road. It seemed much longer than two weeks since I was last there. Or was it that time no longer meant anything? Main Street, Madingdale: the old cinema, the Mexican bar, I felt I was revisiting an old childhood haunt. An elderly man with a hole in his hat watched the van as it trundled down the street. He stood on the curb, aimlessly, clicking the fingers of his right hand. I waved. He looked at me with empty eyes. After we had passed by I saw him wave in the mirror. Was he from Veda? I couldn't tell anymore.

If I was to make the trip to New York City, I'd need the bus times. They had schedules at the garage. I was a little uneasy about getting hold of one without letting Joe realise what I was up to. I'd tell him in the evening; things are always easier over a beer.

There were not many cars on the road that day. I saw the iron bridge over the shallow river. But it no longer seemed as beautiful as I remembered, as though something had got in the way. I came to the crossroads and waited. Trucks rumbled across America. The last car that passed was a beat up blue Chevrolet.

She was standing.

The others were sitting on the grass at the side of the garage forecourt, their rucksacks strewn all around. But she was standing. I was aware of her existence a fraction of a second before she was of mine. She wore a simple white T-shirt against an endless blue sky and I watched her watch a white cloud pass by. She brushed her hair from her eye and looked at me. For the tiniest of time she shot through me, then looked away, fully aware of what she had done. I took my foot off the accelerator and my hands fell from the wheel.

'Ben, are we going to sit here all day or are we going to cross this road? I'm thirsty, I want to...' Joe looked at me, then at her. He said nothing. He knew.

14

'AWAY! AWAY!'

Bewildered patients tumbled through the door, herded by confused counsellors into the light rain which had been falling since sundown. Institutionals ran into the night, their eyes lighting up the darkness. Some fled in panic, others fumbled in fear. A man carrying a toothbrush fell to the gravel and started to cry, toothpaste smeared across his cheek. Lights came on in the other bunks. Cries went up and pandemonium cracked his whip. One large woman with breasts drooping to her waist and wild wet hair refused to move. It took three counsellors to lift her. She struggled so violently that they dropped her, her back hitting the edge of the steps with a thud. She didn't make a sound but sat where she had fallen, holding her head calmly as though contemplating some inexorable problem.

Fergus rushed past me.

'What's going on?' I shouted after him.

'It's Michelle. She's flipped.'

It was well past lights out. I had been climbing to the higher level to find Chris when an almighty shriek stopped the rain in its tracks. Several crashes followed in short succession and the door of E1 burst open, spewing out a procession of panic, flying into the night like exorcised spirits.

I made my way through the chaos and up the steps. Some savage colossus had run amok: beds had been flipped over, cubbies knocked down, mattresses sprawled across the floor, clothes in the rafters and a pretty pink blanket lay outside an open window in the mud.

A petite half-cast woman paced circles around the wet floor of the bunk, her dark eyes flashing in anger at the inanimate objects she had slain. In her hand was a clump of thick black hair which she guarded as though it were the prized scalp of a warrior. She hung her head low, a panther's rhythm, breath short, but deep like the bull before a charge.

Suddenly she ran to the door and spat through the wire mesh. I watched her saliva fragment into a thousand little pieces and sail into the night air. 'BASTARDS!' she screamed, then retreated to the other end of the bunk. Her voice was unnervingly normal, reaching high above the trees and falling as rain on the heads of those she had frightened away.

'She just needs someone to talk to her,' Slim said, 'to be kind to her. Look at her! She's scared.' Slim was OD for E1. He always said he knew how to handle 'these people' and felt a embarassed that he'd let this whole thing get out of hand. He opened the door and stepped inside. 'Michelle, it's okay. Nobody's going to hurt you.' She was panting heavily, holding the clump of hair up to the light, examining it. Slim walked towards her confidently, trying to hush her as though she were a distraught kindergarten child. Michelle squinted, backed up a little, then sprang, grabbing a cubby twice her size and tossing it like a matchstick. Slim jumped back as the cubby crashed down in front of him. He forgot her fear and, remembering his own, turned and ran, trying to shift his considerable bulk as fast as it would go, his gut quaking underneath his shirt, spilling out the edge of his trousers. She was soon upon him. She tore at his hair, pulling out ginger tufts, throwing them to the floor. She stopped, picked them up and added them to her collection. Slim reached the porch. She took another swipe. He slammed the door, catching her hand in the hinge. She howled and collapsed in a heap, sliding down in a pool of water, hissing.

Fergus charged up the steps, soaked through to the skin.

'I just spoke to Kolchak,' he panted. 'She's on her way, says we've got to restrain her until she gets here.'

'Restrain her!' Slim cried, nursing his head, and pride. 'She needs to be put down.'

Michelle crawled away and lay in the middle of the bunk, staring at the ceiling, listening to the floor. Fergus, Slim, Bjorn and I stood watching her with a single collective wish that Kolchak would arrive before we were called upon to act.

The rain grew heavier, rattling hard on the roof, disturbing the caged beast. She rose and started prowling once more, pulling the contents of cubby holes to the floor. She picked up a radio and smashed it against the wall.

'The bitch! That's my Walkman,' Alison said, looking up at Bjorn. Unfortunately for us, Bjorn was A Man and his machismo (against his better judgment) stepped into the breach.

'I think something should we do. Of us there are four. She is little and one.' The three of us smiled uneasily. Love is such a dangerous thing in the wrong hands. 'Why not Slim and Fergus take her attention? Me and Benjamin can power her over when she is away looking.' Bjorn's years in the Swedish army were beginning to show.

'Okay, Bjorn,' we heard ourselves reluctantly agree, each looking round for an excuse to leave.

'Get lost! You won't catch me going in there again,' Slim said. 'No way, not while there's still some hair on my head.'

'Chris, you?' Bjorn turned to his bunk partner who was standing at the foot of the steps.

'Sure. I'll go.'

Gingerly, Bjorn opened the door. Before stepping in he turned and smiled at Alison as though he were marching off to the trenches. I half-expected a short speech.

Chris and Fergus took one flank, trying to stick as close to the wall as possible. The enemy lay in the middle of the bunk, watching them curiously. Bjorn and I took the other, trying not to draw attention to ourselves. The plan seemed to be working. Michelle's eyes remained fixed on the decoy. We were outsmarting her. Bjorn winked, the signal to go over the top. We rushed at her. But she wasn't there. Military intelligence had failed us. Michelle span round and attacked from behind. A flying leap. A screech. And she was on top of me, tumbling on to a mattress, yanking at my hair, her broken nails ripping into my scalp, saliva of excitement dripping onto my lips.

'GET HER OFF ME!'

I only stayed because of her. The moment I saw her standing in the sunshine on that garage forecourt in that small American town, all thoughts of leaving Veda simply vanished from my mind. I had never seen anything like her. I had dreamt her, searching for her in my waking hours. And she had come, finally; that longed for relief of soft summer rain, a slight breeze in its wake, displacing everything.

Driving back from Madingdale with her in the back of the van I could hardly keep a steady hand on the wheel. I drove slowly, not wanting the arrival to end, trying to burn those first moments indelibly into my eyes.

I said nothing to Joe. He never knew of my plans to leave, nor the reasons for my desire to stay.

That was five days ago. Five long tortuous days in which her presence only served to make my existence in B8 even more miserable. The greater my infatuation with her, the deeper my repulsion for the patients. They were everywhere, trying to mar her perfection: in her smile, her eyes, climbing out of her skin, in the unending longing, in the hope without foundation, in the shattering desire. Five days, and I had yet to proffer her one solitary word.

'Hold her still! You must hold her still.'

We held Michelle down whilst Kolchak prepared the shot. She didn't like doing this, she told us so, repeatedly. It went against all her methodological principles. But she realised that with twenty institutionals standing in the midnight rain she had little choice. The beast kicked and screamed, spitting at us until her mouth ran dry. It took four of us to steady her. The needle went in. She struggled, tried biting, and then her jaw relaxed and her body went limp, its spirit passing on to the night.

Chris and I carried her to the Kommandant's jeep and took her down to the infirmary, where we left her on a bed in a large white room, a twisted smile of calmness terrifying her face, a clump of black, blond and ginger hair tight in her hand.

Benjamin, are you all right?'

Lucien and I were down by Redhill Creek, under a tree in the rain, watching Herbert in a T-shirt, getting soaked, standing in a rowboat, motionless, fishing. No bites. No fish. He didn't even bother to reel in, check the bait and cast again. Not once. Just stood there, believing his patience (or stupidity) would eventually be rewarded. One fish, even a tiddler, a minnow, that's all he ever wanted. He told us the Lord was watching over him, the Lord was the Provider (it said so in his Bible) and the Lord would provide the fish. By the look of it the Lord was even more of a lousy fisherman than Herbert.

The man in the radio said it was going to brighten up, so Lucien and I sat waiting for the sunshine.

'Why do you ask?

'You seem, well, miserable. What's the matter? Is it that business with Michelle?'

'Yes. And no.'

'How do you mean?'

'It's this whole place, Lucien. This place is the matter. And now it's worse than ever.'

'Why?'

'Because *she* has come.'

'Who?'

'That girl on the higher level. You must have noticed her.'

'No.'

'Up in E2.'

'Oh, her. What about her?'

I watched the raindrops fall on the river, the ever expanding circles carried downstream until they were destroyed in the rapids.

'Lucien, do you know the Plato myth about love being the longing for the half of ourselves we have lost?'

'No. We haven't done Plato yet.'

'Well when you do him, let me know. In the realm of spirits we are one. When we come to this world we are split into the two halves in which we now find ourselves: male and female. And Destiny dictates that we wander the earth until we find our missing half.'

'And this *girl* is your missing half?' he said with disdain.

'Until I saw her, I didn't know I had a missing half.'

Lucien was silent. He was holding some insect, a horsefly, by its wings, watching it struggle.

'Are you sure about this?' he said at long last. 'I mean, don't you think you're over-reacting. She's just a girl.'

'What would you know about it anyway, Lucien?'

'What do you mean by that?' he demanded, ripping the insect's wing.

'I just meant...' His eyes searched mine, accusingly, longing to know what I knew, daring me to speak.

'Yes?'

'I just meant that, well you're a man of reason.' He sighed, deflating, relieved. 'The heart has its reasons Reason itself does not know.'

'That's not fair,' he reached for my hand. 'You make me sound so cold.'

'Not cold, just detached.' I let him wipe the rain from my hands. He had soft fingers, tender, made for a young girl who had yet to know hardship. Even in the cold, they were warm. 'You're an observer, you said so yourself.'

He smiled, placed his open palm against mine, and squeezed. Rain dripped from my skin. 'Besides, I don't think she's right for someone like you.'

'You *know* her!' I withdrew my hand. 'Why didn't you say anything, why the hell didn't you tell me?'

'Benjamin, don't get angry; it didn't seem important. I've only spoken to her once or twice. She didn't make that much of an impression.'

'Well what's her name?'

'Gabrielle de la Rosiaz,' he said, grudgingly.

'A name like that in a place like this. It doesn't fit.'

'A name's a name's a name.'

'What's she like?'

Lucien didn't answer, not at first. I knew him when he was like this. You had to tread carefully. Hurt would crawl into the whites of his eyes, and if it made it to the centre you'd lose him. He'd go all defensive, clam up. I picked up some stones and started throwing them into the river, close to Herbert's boat. He didn't seem to notice. Then I asked Lucien again, 'What's she like?'

'She's all right. I don't think you'd like her, though. For one thing, she's religious.'

'Why should that bother me?'

'Well, you're not.'

'I come to church with you, don't I?'

'That's different. Besides, you only say the Lord's Prayer and that doesn't count.' A dull pain soaked Lucien's face.

'I pray.' I flung the stones against a rock and listened to them scattering down the valley. 'In my own way.'

'Not properly.'

'Oh well I *am* sorry. I didn't realise prayers were graded.'

'Besides, I thought you said you didn't want to be burdened by a relationship, not that kind anyway.'

'When? When did I say that?'

'About Natasha.'

'That was different. That was just a game.'

'And when *isn't* it a game for you Benjamin?'

It was the first time I'd heard Lucien shout. He tensed and shook a little, putting his hand to his forehead, squeezing the skin into a frown. There was a squeak. Almost inaudible, it seemed to come from elsewhere. He stood up angrily and stormed down to the water's edge, alone in the rain.

I sat for a while, throwing stones, feeling miserable. Then I followed Lucien to the water and put my arm around him.

'I'm sorry, Lucien. I didn't mean to upset you. I was just asking about her, that's all. I didn't mean anything by it.'

'I just don't think she'd be good for you.' He spoke in monotone, not looking at me.

The man in the radio was wrong. The sun wasn't going to shine. Rain reigned supreme. We didn't talk for a while.

'Come on Lucien, let's go back.'

'I just don't want to see you hurt.'

'I know. I know.'

I took his hand. It was limp, wet and cold, and we left the river behind, Herbert waiting for the Lord and his fish.

And the rain came down.

Rain came again the next day. It had barely stopped since she had arrived, pausing long enough only for the clouds to refill. The rain soaked Veda in a tired melancholy, even the trees grew sad. Swimming was cancelled, the one activity where we could relax and take it easy, and we were forced to spend our time climbing the walls of the bunk. William's bowels kept on the move and I was becoming accustomed to living in a toilet. Wise old Dr Rosenthal said it was caused by the heavy dosage of his medication, not that it really mattered: shit was shit. Dakota was developing an uncanny ability to annoy people. He was a born talent, I swear, standing at the end of Mitchel's bed, laughing at him and playing with his ears. 'I stand near ya bed Mitkal Fluck yas I do I do stand near ya bed, look, look, I near ya bed...' This would piss the hell out of Mitch, who would bawl and try to punch or kick him. But Dakota had calculated the distance perfectly. By the time Mitch's deformed body responded (wasted joints creaking to life), Dakota was out of range, laughing. Mitchel would then take it out on Joshua, who was lying in the next bed minding his own business. Curling up the magazine he was reading, Mitch would thwack him across the head. Every now and then William would join the party and thump Dakota just for good measure.

In the evenings Mitchel asked if he could call his mother. Begging, cursing, screaming until we gave in. It was against Veda rules (N° 39). Patients and parents spoke once a week, on Saturdays. But neither Joe nor I could put up with Mitchel's tantrums. We'd refuse for a while, let him stew, then take him down to the payphone just before he turned violent, where he'd complain and bitch to his mother until his voice gave out. They were long calls. Once, feeling a little sympathy for his mom, I took the receiver away from him and put it to my ear: dialling tone. She'd hung up. God knows how long Mitchel had been yelling at no one.

Robert and Charlie started to eat, though rarely at the same meal; one would have breakfast, the other lunch, upholding some secret pact. Neither of them had spoken to Joe or me as yet. Though once, while I was having a crap, I heard them mumbling to each other in the bathroom. 'Don't you go do do that now Charlie Wise,' Robert whispered. To which Charlie replied, 'Do it. Do it', and stroked Robert's behind. Then they realised I was there and they hushed up, washing their faces in silence.

The roof leaked and the walls wept. The rain shrunk the bunk. Being couped up with them was too much. Even Joe yelled more than before. Mitchel whacked Joshua one too many and a fight broke out, Mitch scratching and biting with a venom exceptional even for him. Joe shrieked and clouted them both round the head. After which we all lay on our beds in a sullen silence.

I couldn't stand it in there any longer. I took off. Went for a wander under the overcast sky, up to the higher level just to try and catch a glimpse of her.

I stood on the porch of E6 with Chris, counting the rain drops. The triangle between the bunks on the higher level was like an undecided graveyard, a dozen old men standing around full of purposelessness, unsure whether to live or die. Rain poured from their sunburnt faces. They could have been anyone's grandfather, left there accidently, forgotten.

One balding man stood by a picnic table, rocking backwards and forwards in an awkward rhythm. He held his fingers to his mouth and pretended to eat. Long white socks were pulled up to his knees, great bulges protruding at odd angles underneath, like varicose veins unleashed. He stopped rocking, bent down, reached into his left sock, yanked out a hairbrush, placed it on the table, picked up a small rock and put it into his sock where the hairbrush had been. Then resumed rocking.

'...an' an' an' an' and I was in the shower, an' an' an' an' and they came in an' an' and said if I was good they'd give me candy...' A great hulk of a man with an enormous stomach span slowly around and around, yapping excitedly to the heavens. His shorts were too big for him and his shirt was on back to front. On his face was fixed a smile which was everything but a reflection of happiness. '...an' an' an' and I was in the shower an' an' and they came in and took my pants down, an' an' an' and they shoved this stick up my ass, stick up my ass, an' an' and they made this yellow pus come out an' an' an' and they said I was good. Yeah, an' an' an' and they said I was good.'

'Frank!' Fergus bellowed from the porch of E4. 'Come over here. Get out of the rain.' The man stumbled towards E4 without the slightest physical co-ordination, scratching his stubble. A few paces from the porch he grabbed his balls, stopped, and trundled off in the opposite direction. 'An' an' an' and I was in the shower, an' an' an'...'

The balding man bent down, took out a matchbox, exchanged it with the hairbrush on the table, shoved it into his sock and rocked.

Coming from the lower to the higher level was like crossing a frontier, moving up a level of madness. Down below was just preparation; this was the real thing. You could smell the insanity, it oozed up through the earth with the worms. Abnormality had gone beyond its own limits and come back the other side, penetrating normality so the two were no longer distinguishable. There was something strange up there and for a long time I couldn't figure it out. Maybe the raindrops were larger or the sky further away. Then I realised: there were no children up there to soften the blow.

'Why don't you bring them in?' I asked Chris.

'Can't. We've tried. They won't stay in the bunk, they throw a fit. It's not worth the trouble. So we just let them stand outside. They're there every day, sunrise to sunset, rain or shine, decorating the place. They're happy enough.'

Behind us a short fat Down's man sat on the porch, banging his back against the wall with brisk movements. *Bom bom bom bom.* His legs squeaked in protest as he slammed himself against the wood. *Bom bom bom bom.* His face screwed with pain. *Bom bom bom bom.* Chris saw me staring at him.

'It takes a bit of getting used to up here.'

We stood and watched the rains drain the human wasteland.

'She's gone.' Chris said.

'Who?' I panicked for a moment, thinking of Gabrielle.

'Michelle.' Relief. 'They came from the institution this morning and took her back. Not before time, I say. Apparently she was here last year, did exactly the same thing.'

'She should never have been allowed back.'

'That's what everyone is saying. Scott left this morning too. Said he couldn't stomach it any longer.'

'How many counsellors have you lost up here?'

'With Scott, that makes ten.'

'Ten! Kolchak's not going to have any staff left soon.'

'She's thought of that already. Ellen was saying people leave every year. Kolchak knows that in advance, so she employs more counsellors than she needs. She's way ahead of us.'

'What happened to Thomas and his revolution?'

'Nothing as far as I know. He made some calls and drew a blank. Said people didn't want to know. He's still talking about petitioning Kolchak. Can't see it will do any good, myself.'

In the middle of the triangle stood a familiar figure: skinny, aimless, biting his fingers. I stared hard at the black face beneath the sodden cap, the white eyes looking out for nowhere.

'Who's that?' I asked Chris.

'Him? That's Louis.'

'Is he from up here?'

'Yeah, he's in E4 with Dave and Fergus.'

'Well I wish to God he'd stay up here. He keeps coming down to my bunk. Sitting on my porch morning, noon, and night, pestering the hell out of me. Won't stop talking.'

'Louis?' said Chris, surprised. 'I don't think so. Not Louis. He's a Grade A Veggie: non-verbal, can't hear a thing neither.' Chris called out to the guy to prove what he said was true. He got no response. 'You must have made a mistake, Benjamin.'

'Maybe. But I could have sworn that was him.'

Just then, the door of E2 opened and Gabrielle stepped on to the porch, her beauty instantly out of place. Behind her, she dragged two fat ladies, taking their hands and leading them down the steps. Her eyes were fixed on the ground, rich brown hair draping soft shoulders. I could feel her gaze reflecting off the dirty gravel. She knew I was there. Bright colours swam in the rain around her, a fresh breath in a stagnant world. I felt her body as though it were lying next to me, its scent drifting across hours of stillness. She walked through the higher level as if she were superimposed, an afterthought. The two fat ladies waddled behind, folds of flab bouncing up and down, the one picking at the other's crotch.

'She's quite something.' Chris said, watching me watching her. 'So that's what explains your presence up here. And all this time I thought you were coming to see me.'

I was going to go after her, find the courage, talk to her, bring the whole thing to a head, get it over with, only then the door of Gabrielle's bunk opened once more.

I thought my eyes were lying.

He came out, pulling a sweater over his head, pushing back his thick black hair, looking around, then ran down the steps. And there he met my incredulous gaze and stopped dead, staring at me, standing in the midst of the wasteland, the dozen empty bodies hemming him in. For a moment, he was one of them – Lucien.

He stared right at me. He stared right at me and said not a word.

Bom bom bom bom. The fat Down's slammed his body against the wall. *Bom bom bom bom.*

He didn't smile, didn't wave. I saw him sway slightly, as though the breeze were about to knock him down, then he ran off into the trees. Gone.

Bom bom bom bom. The door squeaked and a tall rake of a man came out on the porch behind us, excrement running down his pale legs. *Bom bom bom bom.*

'Shit.' Chris said. 'Geoffrey, not again! Look Benjamin, I'll speak to you later, okay. I've got to go clean this guy up.'

I followed the track through the trees to the lower level. The rain had washed the autumn leaves from the forest floor, mud replacing the bright carpet that once lay there. Streamlets ran across the path, the mountain's tears soaking my feet. I kept hoping I'd meet Lucien. That I could hold his soft wet hand, pull him close, and realise I was wrong, that I'd made a mistake. But the forest was empty.

Misery fell from the sky and soaked me to the skin.

At the foot of the hill a patient in a large green poncho was sitting in a puddle. And standing over her was the counsellor in the purple hood, the one with the pale face, wearing the same tatty skirt in which I'd seen her at orientation. I thought she'd left with the others: despaired, packed up and gone. I'd asked Joe about her, but he didn't seem to know anything. He wasn't even sure who I was talking about. I wondered if she had something to do with Kolchak and that was why we didn't see much of her, because she spent all her time down at High Command. Or perhaps she was simply a hermit, didn't like people, ate alone.

'Come on, Mary,' she said softly to the patient, caressing the girl's cheek. 'You don't want to sit here in the rain. Let's go inside into the warm.' She spoke with a heavy Slavic accent, with the patience of one who is used to suffering.

The girl grunted, sat on her hands and refused to budge.

'Hello there,' I said. 'Having trouble?' She looked up, heavy clouds passing across her green eyes. Rain dripped from her nose and she stared through me with expressionless expression.

'Come on, Mary, you will catch a cold and then you will be sick. Why don't we go back and I'll tell you the story about a boy who lost his way?'

'Do you need any help?'

'No. Do you?'

She looked past me, as though speaking to someone behind. I looked around. There was no one there.

'Do I! Why should I need help?'

'Mary, come now. There's nothing more to wait for. It's all over.'

I asked again. 'Why should I need help?' But she ignored me. Or maybe she didn't hear. So I tried to help her, started to lift up the patient.

'Don't touch her!' Sudden anger rose in the counsellor's voice, her eyes soaked with accusation. 'I don't want help from *you*.'

Now she did look at me. Straight at me. She said *you*, but she didn't mean *you*. There was no mistaking that. She meant *someone like you*.

The patient looked up and smiled. It was the girl I had seen masturbating on the toilet in G7. She laughed the same laugh and again there was blood on the floor. Her poncho shrank to a monk's habit, smeared with mud. She took the counsellor's hand and stood up. They stared at me, each in an identical way, as though there was something I had not done for which I should be sorry. I wanted to ask their forgiveness, but I didn't know what for.

They turned and left, disappearing through the trees, leaving me alone.

Stretching out an open palm, I watched the drops gather in my hand. But soon, even they began to slip through my fingers.

15

Fever granted me a rare audience over the next days. I lay in a lone sweat watching distorted faces come and go. Shivering by day from the heat, burning by night from the cold. Father came along in his fencing gear, foil at the ready. We fenced and I lost, soundly. He said he was disappointed in me, that my parries were weak and, when he took off his mask, he had the malproportioned face of Dakota. Then Mother came with buckets of honey and lemon and she poured them over my blankets, sweet and sticky. She read me stories in the slow, muddled voice of Joshua, chuckling at my confusion. I even saw Charles, riding down Silver Street in Cambridge behind an Italian sun. His arms and legs were withered and they kept getting caught in the spokes. Then the skinny black guy was there, standing by my bed stroking my hand, smiling, telling me pillows are for sleeping on, not for hitting people.

On the last night of the illness I woke to find Elmer Kolchak's face squashed against the mosquito mesh of the door, the flesh of his fat oily nose pushing through the wire. The bunk was quiet, save for Charlie's snoring, and I could hear Elmer breathing heavily, as though exerting himself. 'The director was worried about you,' he panted. 'She wanted me to check if you were all right.' When I got up to thank him and tell him the illness had passed and that I was fine, he ran off, and I found his trouser belt on the porch.

Lucien never came to visit, as I'd hoped. That hurt, more than I thought it would. I didn't expect him to be Florence Nightingale, just be there, for a while; talk to me, hold me. But all I felt was his absence. Even deep in delirium I would have known had he been by my side. He told me later that he couldn't stomach being close to illness. It made him sick. He said he asked after me, constantly. When I told him I'd heard nothing, he blamed Joe for not passing on the messages.

Once I was up and about Lucien made a special effort, he couldn't do enough for me. He sat ODs with me, took me for ice-creams, read French to me, indulged my vanity. Granted, we didn't spend as much time together as before, but he seemed a little tired and distracted. Besides, the time we were in each other's company was wonderful: paddling in the river (Herbert still waiting for his first catch – Lord, hear his prayer), making a driftwood raft for our escape from Veda, diving off the falls, sneaking out to Dotty's during lunch hour, explaining his crazy ideas, showing me his notebooks, sharing some poem, running off into the forest to be alone. The incident outside Gabrielle's bunk was never mentioned. He didn't bring it up and I never spoke of it. I convinced myself I'd been mistaken. I didn't want to know otherwise.

Independence Day came stumbling along to greet us. A time of cutting loose, of celebration, albeit temporary.

Fading sunlight sparkled the red, white and blue faces. Cheap crêpe streamers hung from porches. Coloured paper fluttered on the tennis courts where Herbert still hadn't put up the nets. Homemade banners wilted from arc lamps.

The battered yellow pick-up edged its way lethargically on to the top field, a balloon pinned to each corner; Herbert at the wheel, lonely in his Uncle Sam hat; Ritch in the back, distributing tiny flags to outstretched hands with that all-American smile; patients going crazy, rushing at the truck with independent excitement. They had been making costumes all week and were running wild with red noses, blue cheeks and white chins, tall hats, striped trousers and starry shirts, a riot of colour looking for co-ordination.

Ritch switched on the tape machine and 'Born In The USA' ignited a whirl of halloos and hails, screams, shrieks and wails. Every face joined in. Every nose. Every eye. Hands flapped. Bodies bounced. They all knew the words, even those who couldn't speak. The field became an indistinguishable mass of colour and noise, the retarded blending with the insane, the autistic with the palsy, the downs and the disturbed, spinning in an untrammelled fever of illogical joy.

Lucien was confused. He couldn't understand why they should get so excited about the Fourth of July when for most of them it could mean absolutely nothing, how it was that they couldn't even feed themselves yet knew the words to 'The Star Spangled Banner'. The irony escaped him, it was simply another item on his list that needed a reason.

Natasha held the liberty lamp aloft, walking tall behind the truck, patients following her like ducklings waddling after mother. She blew me a kiss as she passed. Lucien laughed and pinched my bum.

'Ben!' Joe called out. 'Come here. Check this out.' He rushed over and grabbed my hand, pulling me to where Dakota stood chewing the Stars and Stripes.

'Listen to this! Dakota, where were you born?'

'In da usa yas I was in da usa born in the usa yas I was...' Dakota mumbled in time with the song.

'Look! He's enjoying himself,' Joe said, astonished. 'He's actually enjoying himself!'

Dakota twiddled his ears in celebration.

The parade wound its way up the hill. The song played over and over, accompanying us past the pool, through the trees and on to the higher level where Violet, the music teacher from Nebraska, was organising a Fourth of July sing-song with her favourite guitar. Joe put his arm around William and sang at the top of his voice.

You had to laugh, he hated Springsteen.

Violet's sing-song torched the insides of the unfinished social hall on the higher level, you could see the wood buckling under the strain of a hundred screeching voices which had never known a tune. Lucien and I sat together, as far away as possible, our offended ears threatening to up and go.

He took out his notebook and wrote down some observations whilst I told him about my times in Paris with Charles. His parents had an apartment in St Germain. Lazy afternoons in the Luxembourg, watching jealous Polyphemus devour Acis and Galatea in the Medici Fountain. Coffee behind the clock in the d'Orsay café, taking a break from Renoir's fulsome breasts. Sunsets on the Pont des Arts, solving the problems of the world, laughing at lovers. Dinner in the Polidor on rue Monsieur le Prince, where the old white-haired woman with a nasty temper gave us free ice-cream. Dancing at Les Bains, by which time we no longer cared.

Then I mentioned the strange dreams I'd been having. Lucien logged in and off he went, never happier than when he was analysing.

'You see, it's like I told you before, remember? You've been infected. You've peeked over the border, looked into the land of the insane,' he rambled excitedly. 'The frontiers between dream and reality are melting away. Your fears, your doubts, your insecurities are wearing the mask of lunacy. Your demons are dressing up in new clothes. The subjects of dreams don't change, just the form they take.'

I told him that they were no longer dreams, that these things came to me during the day, like visions, that I was less and less sure of what I actually saw and what I didn't. He picked it up and ran.

'Your dreams are spilling out of their own confines, ignoring their own limits. Your mind is infected with new experience and your dreams follow. Emotions don't confine themselves to night. Experience doesn't operate solely during the day. So why should dreams?'

He wanted to know more. He wanted to know exactly what I had been dreaming. It was all raw material to him, waiting to be hammered into theories

I loved Lucien when his mind ran overtime. But sometimes it got too much; his rationality suffocating. In his effort to understand he was slaughtering his subject: the unknown. I didn't want my dreams analysed. I didn't want them rationalised. They belonged to me, they were mine, whatever they were. Understanding isn't a process. You can't arrive at it simply by questions and answers. Logic has its limitations, reasoning its restrictions. You have to feel.

Feel your way. Tentatively. Delicately.

Clarity needs kindness.

The iron grip of reason tightens and twists until there's nothing left to understand but understanding itself. A dry process which can prove nothing about everything and everything about nothing. An empty satisfaction.

The over-examined life is not worth living.

I didn't want that happening to me. If confusion was what it took to understand, then confusion was welcome. Nor did I care if the conclusions would be ragged, thin and humble, unsupported and unsubstantiated. Feelings don't need to be watertight.

There are more paths than reason.

Lucien's words twisted in my head. I didn't hear the sing-song deteriorate into a shambles. Nor did I see one of the patients grab Violet's beloved guitar and smash it over the barbecue. The first I knew of it was when Ritch asked me if I'd help set up the Veda sound system and play some tapes to keep them occupied until lights out. I was more than happy to oblige. It wasn't them I wanted to keep occupied, it was my mind.

The disco, as the ad hoc gathering around the tape machine turned out to be, was a surprising success. It came from nowhere, took hold of counsellor and patient alike, and shook them to unified exhaustion. Twisted bodies shouted as music pumped into veins like drugs. Patients came alive in a way no one could have imagined. They flung themselves into dance with abandon, leaping into the air, unwilling to come down. They spun outside themselves. Physical disabilities were cast aside, limitations forgotten, expectations shattered, boundaries vanished – everything gave way to dance.

Two shrivelled old men put their ears to the enormous speakers and closed their eyes, their fingers tapping lightly on the tables whilst volcanic noise blasted their ear drums. Doug, a teenage rockerbilly Down's from B6, led Charlotte, a buxom inmate of G5, to the middle of the hall, circling her proudly, his face filled with primitive lust, whilst she shuffled and swayed, the centre of attention, overwhelmed by tears. She lifted her arms high into the air and shrieked with delight. Mitchel danced with Joshua, playing his guitar, jumping up, crashing to the ground on his good leg, stumbling, falling down. He sprung up with grazes on his knees and joy in his eyes, yelling at me, 'It's all right. It's all right'. Jumping up. Falling down. Dakota sat on a bench at their side, trying to hide, flapping his hands out of time with the music, giggling. Even Charlie got up and got down, bobbing and flobbing with endless energy. He took Robert's hand and pulled him up, whereupon that great master of practised inactivity burst upon the dance-floor like a spirit possessed. And they danced. Together.

Darkness fell and the hall filled with light. Flies, mosquitoes, moths, gnats, more bugs than science has labels, hustled and bustled around the yellow bulbs. Music leapt into the forest and set the leaves alight. The hall burned like a beacon of confusion understood. Sweat. Noise. Smiles. Counsellors danced. And danced. With one another, with patients, with themselves. Fergus jitterbugged with Bradley, a mild autisitic with a phenomenal weight problem. Chris jived with Joseph. Lucien waltzed with Dorothy. And Dave, he took the hand of the man in the sou'wester, spinning him round and round with mesmerising speed, a'howling and a'hooting, candy flying from his neck.

And I. I was playing the music.

For a moment the two worlds merged and I glimpsed, for the first time, their smiles as smiles, their happiness as happiness, their tears as tears.

And that, was that.

Redhill Creek wasn't the same at night; its roar was fierce, its blackness threatening. The cold rush of the falls sent a chill down the valley which swept through every bone. The sky was clear and wide. Fireflies lit up the forest into a thousand pieces, like a fallen galaxy. It was a lonely place, even with friends.

Exhausted counsellors huddled round the fire on the rocks, drinking beer and watching flames, excited voices flying in the dark on the backs of fiery ashes. There wasn't an ounce of dance left in them. Their smiles were worn out, their laughter in need of rest. On the edge of the warmth Fergus played some broken tunes on his guitar, disparate notes carried away downstream.

'Eeh Meester Bejamine, you creezy sonfabitch. What a show! What a show! Sonfabitch, I knew it. Who else? Meester DJ from London. Am I right? Am I right?' Stojan handed me a frothy beer, slopping it down my sweater. 'A toasta, to Meester DJ.' He held his plastic cup high in his shaking hand, the fire burning in his dark smiling eyes. I raised mine aloft. 'Meester DJ,' he repeated and we downed our beer. 'Ooo that's goud, soo goud. Anothera. I geet you anothera,' he chuckled to himself and staggered away for a refill.

Something changed during the disco. Those yellow bulbs shed a strange light on what we were living through, set us apart from all that was outside Veda. I faded out the last song and counsellors and patients stood in the silence, echoes dying in the trees. It seemed a long time before anybody moved. They were reluctant to go, unwilling to relinquish the moment, frightened it might never be recaptured. Finally, they dispersed to their bunks. But the counsellors carried that inexplicable and elusive mood with them down to the rocks where they used it to light the fire for their own party. It sparked the fire, fizzed the beer, warmed the conversation, kept out the cold and lit the fireworks. Sam had brought over dozens of handheld rockets. Sam came over to Sageville every summer from his home in Poughkeepsie to hang out with the counsellors in the evenings at Dotty's. He had a thing about Europe. He'd buy you a beer if you sat and told him about where you came from. Straight exchange. He'd want the detail: you'd get the alcohol. Said it made him feel like he was travelling. We took turns lighting Sam's rockets, which whizzed and banged into the night above the river and over the trees, proclaiming an independence that none of us understood.

I looked at the counsellors, their half-lit faces, and tried to imagine their other lives, their homes and occupations. I tried to construct a world for them outside these grounds, where they would work, drink and sleep. But it wasn't possible. They weren't a part of anywhere else. They belonged here, with the broken toilets, the tasteless food, the seizures, the shit, and the dancing patients. Their identities formed in an irregular world of mental instability. Their personalities defined through abnormality. All terms of reference removed. No Cambridge. No Cov Pol. Just Veda.

'Hello. Stojan asked me to give you this.'

Gabrielle. I knew the voice even though I had never heard it. She stood on the edge of shadow, her smile a little unsure of itself. So close.

'Thank you for tonight. The disco, it's the first time I've smiled since I arrived.'

I took the cup she offered with an unsteady hand and held it to my lips, froth dripping on to the rocks. I stared, thankful for the cover of darkness. She was beyond perfection. I had been over this moment a thousand times, but when it came fortune found me disabled. Confidence, my casual friend, whirled in a tailspin of silent panic. I took a mouthful, but couldn't swallow. Cool, wet beer obstructing speech. We stood in stillness, eyes locked, whilst billions of stars burned over our heads, the distant rush of the falls echoing between us.

Just one word.

I swallowed.

She turned away, and I caught the corner of a stolen smile.

'Well, goodnight then.'

She left. She took my silence and disappeared into the wood.

I dropped my cup into the fire, watched it melt, and went to the water's edge. The river roared with greater ferocity. The leaves fluttered like nervous hearts. Fireflies flashed brighter. The air was colder, the night calmer. And water smashed into the pool at the foot of the falls with a deafening scream, drowning everything.

Out of a battered rock in the rapids, with the river swirling, tumbling, leaping all around, every possible direction, no conceivable reason, in the midst of confusion, in the thick watery blackness, grew a tiny plant, a solitary fragment of green in an unlikely world.

16

My chance had come.

And gone.

I had been over that situation a thousand times. A hundred thousand times. A thousand thousand times. A thousand million... I knew exactly what to say, precisely how to act, how to be, what to do, the smile, the bashful look away, the modest turn of head, the shy shuffling of feet. Tactics. Strategy. Every possible development had been considered. Plan A. Plan B. Plan C. All the way through to Z. Nothing had been left to chance. I knew it backwards. The whole routine. And when it finally came, the one thing I had been praying for since her arrival, what did I do?

Nothing.

Zip. Zero. Zilch. I stood there like a moron. Not a word! Not one single word. And all the things I had to say to her. Charm her. Woo her. Make her laugh, make her cry. Throw her a line. Possess her. Obsess her. I knew the rules. I'd written the damn things myself.

And?

Nothing.

I stood before her like a bumbling idiot. No wonder she smiled, she probably laughed all the way back to her bunk. I must be the joke of E2 by now. Arty Farty Benny. More fart than art.

But I'll win her, sooner or later. Just have to have the right opportunity come my way, launch into seduction mode and she's history. You wait. I'll win her.

The only problem was Lucien. Would he understand? It was different with women, different leagues. She couldn't touch the feelings I had for him. They were out of reach, on permanent reserve. I didn't want to lose him. But I wanted her. Jesus, I wanted her.

Then Chris told me.

Lucien had invited her to Poughkeepsie at the weekend. They were going waterskiing on the Hudson. Open betrayal. He didn't even speak to me about it. How could he.

I spent the next days avoiding him. I made sure our paths didn't cross, B8 took a different schedule and a new table at mealtimes. If I saw him coming to the bunk I hopped out the back window. I patronised The Cuckoo's Nest rather than bump into him at Dotty's.

How was I to know?

I felt such a fool.

How was I to know he was doing the whole thing for me?

One afternoon at the pool he cornered me, said I was acting like an idiot. Sam, the guy who'd supplied the fireworks for our party, had a boat at his home in Poughkeepsie. Lucien had arranged the whole thing: for me. On Friday night Sam would pick us up and on Saturday, our day off, Lucien and I would go waterskiing – with Gabrielle.

He was so good to me. All he wanted was to see me happy. I hugged him, pulling him close, right there in front of everyone at the pool. Mistake. Dave bombed us in the water, screaming: 'Arse bandits!'.

At nine-thirty on Friday night Sam's long black Cadillac stood purring outside Veda's gates. I was impressed. Lucien and I got in and waited for Gabrielle, bathing in luxury. I told Sam I couldn't wait to see his house. He told me I'd be disappointed. He was a car salesman, he'd borrowed the Caddy just for the evening.

'Oh well, can't have it all.'

Sam wanted to know what Veda was like. He knew it was some sort of funny farm, local gossip told him that, but he'd never yet dared set foot on the grounds. I told him it was impossible to describe. Unless you worked there, lived through it, you could never believe what went on within those grounds. It couldn't be imagined.

'Try me!' he said

So we shared a few stories, took him through some of the more memorable incidents: a seizure here, a fit there, and shit just about everywhere.

He didn't believe it.

The Cadillac hummed its opulent way through Madingdale, across the iron bridge and on up to New Paltz where we stopped to fill up with gas and nachos. Then, as we headed out into the American night, headlights lighting up the country, I made my move: clicked into seduction mode. I tried drawing Gabrielle deep into my world. I led her through Cambridge's well-worn grooves: fencing bouts, soirées, brilliant minds, Balls, punts, lawns, champagne, ferris wheels, fields of youthful extravagance, indulgence. I trotted off the lines, stretched out in the Cadillac's leather front seat and waited to reap the rewards.

And waited.

The harvest was a long time coming.

Gabrielle didn't respond. I tried leading her down different paths, seduction lying in wait for her. I threw in a few childhood stories. They never failed. But she wouldn't come. I tried harder. Pulling her here. Pushing her there. Talked about my dreams, my hopes, my ideals. Still she stood firm. She asked no questions, laughed not once. Eyes were not lowered, blushes not forthcoming. She just sat. In silence. Unmoved. Unimpressed. I was losing her. So I tried harder. The more I gave, the less she returned. Lucien knew what I was up to, he'd seen me playing the same roles with Natasha. He stayed silent, saying nothing beyond trying to change the subject every once in a while. I was making a fool of myself. Even Sam looked uncomfortable.

Finally, long after I should have, I dried up. I'd miscalculated. Crickets on the roadside hummed louder than ever, accentuating the embarrassed silence in the car. Sam shifted down a gear and started up a hill, the engine roaring with laughter. I couldn't understand it. It was a surefire method. It had never failed before.

Then, hammering the final nail into seduction's cushioned coffin, Lucien asked about her.

Gabrielle lived in a small village on the north shores of Lake Geneva, between Lausanne and Montreux. She'd spent most of her youth somewhere in the south of Spain where her father owned a ranch. Her family had moved around a lot, the ranch was their home, but her father didn't like running it. He'd been some sort of professor at an American school and she'd been born in South Carolina, but she didn't seem to want to say much more. She spoke affectionately about her village: the weather-beaten old men who worked the vineyards, standing in the steep fields, watching a world go by which was no longer theirs; the apron-clad women, who kept house with an open door and a closed mind; and the machine-guns of the boys on military service propped against porches on homecoming weekends. Her brother led expeditions in the mountains and sometimes she went with him, long lonely hours trekking in a silent line across hostile glaciers, ropes from waist to waist the only link. She said she could understand why some people found Switzerland boring. Not for her. Everything she wanted was there, though she missed Spain from time to time.

Sam and Lucien broke forth with streams of questions and a warm, lively three-way conversation sparked up. She was soft spoken, yet sure of herself. Not on the surface, not in an arrogant way, it was more solid than that. You could tell, it went right down to the bone. She had no need of effects.

I sat in silence, the fourth man, out in the cold, watching the cats eyes in the middle of the road light up for a brief moment, only to disappear underneath us, swallowed by darkness. One after the other after the other.

The weekend went downhill from there.

Sam's house was on Mill Street, leading down to the Hudson. It was an old wooden building, nineteenth-century, with a swingchair on the porch. He called it The Pleasure Dome. His front room was overrun with guitars, African drums and musical gadgets of every description (a hurdy-gurdy his prize possession), but it was the giant video screen which dominated. When he wasn't selling cars he made music: recording live concerts, watching them time and time again until he'd figured out every last guitar rift. I suspected he might be a hippy, but he was a nice guy nonetheless.

Gabrielle picked up his clarinet and played a Mozart concerto, straight through, faultless, without so much as a blink. You couldn't hear her breathing even though the reed was split. That clarinet hadn't been played in years and Gabrielle blew the dust right off it. Sam said he didn't even know it had such sounds in it (he'd bought it second hand for $50 off an old ex-Mormon woman and thought she'd cheated him, he could barely get a note out of the thing). It was beautiful. And the worst thing of all was, Gabrielle did it without showing off. She just picked up and played, like it was the most natural thing in the world. And when she was modest about accepting our applause, she really meant it. She didn't play to impress. She just played.

I sat and watched her. Wretched as hell.

We slept early so we'd have more time on the river the next day. I wanted Lucien to stay in my room, but he wouldn't hear of it and took the couch. Worst of all, he didn't mention the journey.

First thing in the morning Sam took us to his boat. He filled her up, lowered the engine into the water and we were off. I was the first to go, skimming along the river between tree-lined banks, the homes of yesterday's rich and famous perched on top. I have to admit it was beautiful, even if I was having a miserable time.

The Hudson was dirty, though it was cleaner than it used be. Sam told the story of a guy a few weeks ago who swam all the way down to New York City in protest against the pollution; stirred up a lot of publicity, then fell sick.

'That was Roosevelt's place,' Sam shouted as he pulled me on board.

I sat in the back of the boat and watched Gabrielle weaving through the wash. I tried to pull myself together, telling myself that I was blowing the whole thing out of proportion. Maybe she'd been impressed by me after all. Maybe she just wasn't showing it. Maybe she was better at the game than I gave her credit for. But I doubted it. Beyond necessities, neither she nor Lucien made any attempt at conversation with me.

We skied until our legs could no longer bend, then cruised down the river in silence. Exhausted.

'Take Mitchel for example, in Benjamin's bunk. He's high functioning, and he's miserable. That's what I mean. Do you see?' Lucien asked again.

Sam had to work that evening. The world turned and cars had to be sold. Gabrielle, Lucien and I sat by a darkened Hudson with a couple of bottles of summer wine, light and easily forgotten. The banks were shadows, the odd illuminated window whispering through the trees from the mansions lining the riverside. New York lapped at our feet.

Lucien and Gabrielle were talking about the patients, had been for a while. I was drinking, had been for even longer. She was so calm, gentle, and yet there was power. You couldn't mistake that. When she spoke, you listened, even when it hurt, even when you wanted to turn away. Words soothed from her as if they were carved in stone. Every move she made, every mannerism was an exercise in quiet confidence and natural grace. Her cheeks were flushed from the sun, burning gently behind the dark hair which framed her face. Her brown eyes were fixed on the water, following the ripples as they swam up the bank. Lucien was watching her, avoiding my eyes. I sat on the edge of them, as though watching a play in which I had no part.

'He has the most temper tantrums, sulks the most, cries the most.

And why? Because he's the most intelligent, self-conscious, aware of his limitations. That frustrates him and leads to his unhappiness.' Lucien was on form, I had to hand it to him. Gabrielle warmed to him. 'And who is the happiest in the bunk? Dakota. Why? For precisely the same reason. He's not conscious of his predicament. He doesn't know there's anything wrong with him. He's happy.'

'You have a warped idea of happiness, Lucien,' she said.

'He's subject to a purer form of happiness than us.'

Lucien was a Romantic, despite his adoration of reason. Wandering in his forests of observation, he couldn't see the roots of reality.

'It's all very well,' Gabrielle answered, 'you coming up with neat little arguments. But would you change places with Dakota?'

I was beginning to believe he probably would.

'Ignorance is bliss,' he smiled. 'Empty your head of what causes pain: knowledge. Then you'll find peace of mind.'

'That'ssh crap Lucien! And you know it.' I finished off another glass of wine and immediately wished I'd kept my mouth shut. Gabrielle and Lucien turned to me, as if surprised I was still there. I was slurring, I could feel it. But I no longer gave a damn. 'Yer just playing yer bloody intellectual gamesshh! Cansher of the intellect, that'sh what you got. For Chrissakes, how can yer pretend to play at ignorance? Yer can't empty yer damn mind. Dat'ssh the trouble with people like you, think think think think think and then think yer dealing with reality. Think yer ssolving problems. Well think again! Yer'll never find peace of mind 'cos yer can't empty yer damn head. Yer can't undo knowledge fur Chrisssakess.' I tried to fill my glass, but the wine kept slopping over the side and into the Hudson.

He waited until I'd finished, the echoes of my alcoholised anger fading downstream.

'I don't agree, Benjamin,' he said, devastatingly composed. 'The patients have things to teach us. In their lack of self-awareness, their simplicity, they have things to teach us. If we can step back from consciousness, we can find contentment.'

'So bloody well go live like them and see fer yershelf!'

Lucien finished his wine, trailing his fingers in the water, staring into the river as though he were expecting to find something.

'Benjamin,' he said, after a long awkward silence. 'Do you have faith? In anything but yourself that is.'

'And what the hell doyer mean by that?'

'Did you have a religious upbringing?'

This wasn't a question. It was a challenge. He knew it. And I knew it. He was starting to piss me off. 'Lucien, what the bloody hell are yer on about now? Give yer preaching a rest fer once.'

'I did,' he said, ignoring me. 'My mother thought religion was the solution to everything. It gave her the questions and provided the answers. It was her comfort, her security. She tried to make it mine, force it down me like medication to ease a cold. I remember her telling me it would meet all my needs, it would be my beginning and my end – I was seven years old. The Bible got everywhere in our house: from breakfast to bed, upstairs, downstairs, attic, basement, her Bible covered every inch, more pervasive than the cockroaches. She fed us on scripture, dressed us in parables and took us into the world of miracles. Morning Mass, evening prayers, we were there more often than the priest. It's no way for a child to grow up.

'It was the same for my brother. We suffered together, and then her Bible told us that was good. Though she left my father out of it. He never came to church with us, never prayed, never lit candles. I don't ever remember him picking up a Bible. She left him alone, I never knew why. And they never argued. Not once.' Lucien's melancholy voice rambled into nowhere, as though he were alone, wandering across the waves and into the night. He turned the bottle in his hands. Over and over. And over.

I watched Gabrielle watching him, her eyes lighting up in a way I never could have hoped for.

'When I got older I ran into a Mass of contradictions. What felt good was proclaimed bad, and bad good. You went into our house and everything stood on its head. She hadn't prepared me for that.

'I wanted to go my own way, think for myself, ask my own questions, find some answers that weren't prophesied. I couldn't make my mother understand I wasn't rejecting what she had given me, I wasn't turning my back on her. I just wanted to find out a few things for myself. She never could understand. How can you explain to someone when they answer you with quotations from the Book of Revelation?

'And then came the guilt. The righteous look in her eyes, the silent accusation. She would stand over me while I ate, just watching. I showered myself in guilt. Guilt got me up in the mornings and guilt put me to bed. All the while my resentment grew and grew, until one day I woke up and I could no longer tell which I hated more – my own mother, or her religion.

'Don't get me wrong. My mother was a good woman. She was just religious that's all.'

Lucien shoved the cork back into the bottle and threw into the river. It disappeared downstream. Empty.

'Three years ago my brother had a sort of breakdown. Manic depression they called it, though I can't see how depression can be anything else. I always knew that my mother thought the wrong child had been punished. It should've been me. She never said anything. She didn't need to.

'She's been seeing someone ever since. Once a week. Same psychiatrist every Thursday. For two hours he fills her head with shit and takes her money. He's become her crutch. He analyses every last drop of emotion until she's dry, and she swallows it whole. She needs him now, he's made sure of that. She'd go mad without him. Psychiatrist on one side and God on the other - I'm not sure she can tell the difference anymore.

'My brother's training to become a priest. He writes to her twice a day and never comes home. I saw a letter once. Full of scripture.

'My father's the only one who came out okay. He doesn't spend much time in the house. I think he's got a woman.

'Faith!

' *"Notre Père qui êtes aux cieux, restez-y."*

'I wish my mother had read more of Prévert and less of St John.'

A long uncomfortable silence greeted Lucien's final word. I knew full well what he had done. We sat. Silent. Still. Nothing to say. It grew cold. If only I'd had more wine.

Finally I asked him. 'Why tell me this now?'

'I'm not really sure. I suppose I wanted you to try and understand what I was saying before. I wanted you to understand why I want to forget, empty my head and start again. And you told me I was talking crap.'

Both he and Gabrielle turned to me, each looking in an identical way. Guilt seeped in through my pores. I wanted to apologise. I wanted to say something, anything. I wanted to tell Lucien that I knew what he was feeling, that I understood what he was going through. But I didn't. I had no idea.

17

I hadn't been mistaken. Lucien, that time when I saw him coming out of Gabrielle's bunk, I hadn't been mistaken. The night I got back to Veda from Poughkeepsie, cold, drunk and miserable, Joe told me. Though why he never said anything before I still can't figure out.

Ellen had decided not to take any action. To let it slide, to overlook it. She was easy going like that, Ellen. She said it didn't really matter, only they mustn't get caught again. At first I didn't know what Joe was on about. Then he cleared it up for me and I was no longer confused: Lucien and Gabrielle, they'd been caught together, in bed, last week. Tuesday to be exact, several days before Lucien had arranged the Poughkeepsie trip: for me.

Forget the bastard. Ignore the little Judas. That was Joe's advice. And though I knew he had my interests at heart, I knew also he couldn't understand. You lose someone, they betray you; you'll hurt, but in the long run it rarely matters. What you found in them – what they brought you, the things you shared – was temporary, you'll find it in someone else. Whatever we may like to think, the sad truth is: people are replaceable. Look around, we're replacing them all the time. Put your hand in a bucket of water, the water parts and makes way for you. Take your hand out and the water closes over, there's no trace of the space, the hole has been filled. That's how permanent people are to one another. But that wasn't the point with Lucien.

'You don't need him.'

That's what Joe said, told me I'd be better off without him. He told me to think about it: on balance, it was good thing. Think about it? On balance? It makes it sound so trivial. Here I am reeling from a punch to the gut, retching at the thought of them together, Lucien inside Gabrielle, leaving me behind, pissing on us, trying to understand how he could do such a thing and Joe tells me to 'think about it'. Emotion is not an objective instrument: it's doesn't weigh up and balance, it doesn't stand back and reflect: here we go, into the fire, and if you burn then fuck you! – that's emotion. You think it gives a toss about you? It's in cahoots with the mind; they make their own rules, don't even stop to ask your consent. And if you don't agree, they shit on you. It's not about need, it's about holding on, about not going under. Have you ever gone under? Let me tell you, it's paper thin; there's no crucial factor, no deciding moment, no explanation. Cause and effect just melt and merge into one. It builds up, quietly, creeping, a landslide of the past into one present moment. Then you slip. You're down. And you don't know what you're doing down there, you look around and you haven't the faintest idea how you got there or how you're ever going to get up. There are no outside voices, you don't let them in. There's only you, fucking up into a spiral you can't figure out. I guess you do kind of realise what's happening, in a distant way, a fading awareness, and you know the way out – but you don't take it, you just don't take it. That's all.

I'm not sure how things went then. In fact from here on out it all becomes a little unclear. I remember not leaving the bunk much, trying to avoid Lucien. I even recall Joe telling me how worried he was that I was becoming too withdrawn. I lost weight. I still ate, just didn't finish the meals very often that's all. That was the fault of the Veda food: once you'd tasted the first mouthful, you didn't see the point in going on. My cheeks hollowed. Not a lot, but enough for me to notice and that's all I cared about. And I grew tired, probably because I slept more. Joe was good to me; took the patients to breakfast so I could lie in. Norma noticed my absence in the dining-hall and flew into a minor rage (she didn't have time for anything else). But Joe convinced her I had the flu and just needed a little rest – she gave me four days to get better: Joe negotiated a week.

Joe'll tell you this is when I started acting strange (too much time with Lucien, that's what he'll say) but he was drunk or hungover so much of the time I don't think he really knows. Besides, even if he could remember, he wasn't seeing what I was seeing. He wasn't the one slipping. Or at least if he was, he won't say anything. I suppose that's only natural, after what happened to me.

The one thing I am sure of is that the day I saw Peter was the day Mitchel had the big attack. *Grand mal*. Lasted several minutes. He collapsed in the bathroom, thrashing about on the wet floor, smashing his arm and shoulder against the toilet door, helpless. I stood and watched. I could have cushioned him, could have prevented the cuts and bruises. But I didn't. I just carried on brushing my teeth. Well they were dirty. Joe was furious when he found out. Not about my teeth being dirty, but that I'd stood by whilst Mitchel seized.

Said I was fucking crazy. (What does he know about crazy?) He wouldn't speak to me the whole day. Though I kept hearing his words ringing around my head, piercing the hollow. And I kept watching myself watching Mitchel bouncing around on the floor, sliding back and forth in saliva and piss. I kept seeing myself. I kept trying to figure out that expression on my face. But I'd never seen it before, it was foreign to me. I counted the number of strokes I used to brush my upper front teeth. There were three strokes for every one time Mitchel's arm smashed against the door. I think he split the wood. But I couldn't say for sure. I was too busy watching me.

And then there was this voice, soft at first, like the distant hum of an insect. Then it came closer and I recognised it. It was Blatch, our old history master. He was sitting in our room talking to Peter and me about Hitler, said he caught his testicle in a goat's mouth. Said he was playing dare with a young Jewish boy and the young Jewish boy dared Hitler to put his testicle in the goat's mouth. Hitler, being Hitler, went ahead and did just that. The goat chomped off the ball. That, said Blatch, was why Hitler hated the Jews. At least, I think that's what he said. You see, I wasn't really listening. Or rather I was. But not directly. I was listening to me listening. I sat in my chair taking everything in, whilst I sat over at Peter's desk making sure all his pencils were sharp.

Pencils.

A humming came. Then went away.

I heard Peter beseeching me, asking for help to prevent what was coming. I was the only one he'd listen to. I could've stopped it and he would've been all right. I turned away. I couldn't change what would soon be the past

The skinny black guy came that night and sat at Peter's desk, which for some reason was now on the porch of our cabin. I saw myself go out and sit with him, talk with him. Why would I do that? I hate him. He showed me some pencils, said he could sharpen them for me. Said he figured I needed someone to sharpen pencils, otherwise they wouldn't go clean in the eye. It wasn't the eye Peter wanted, he told me, it was the mind. He wanted to go clean through the mind, but the eye got in the way. He said he knew how Peter felt: sometimes it could get so you'd have so much inside that it hurt. Everything you had stored in your mind doubled because you had the original knowledge and then its reflection, so in fact you had it all twice.

Well the mind wasn't built to take that. No room. Each time you watched yourself do something from afar, a closed-circuit consciousness, you were doubling what the poor mind could take. There was you, and a reflected you. If you could just put a tiny hole, a pinprick through the mind this would relieve the pressure, give you more room. Then the hurt would go away. The problem was a pin wouldn't reach the mind. So you had to use a pencil and had to go through the eye. Only way. You see, the skinny guy knew about pencils. Said he could sharpen some for me if I liked. A man shouldn't have to sharpen his own pencils. He said the least I should've done for Peter was sharpen his pencils.

And then there was this camera, kept following me around, like it was strapped to my shoulder. I didn't see the machine itself, just the image it filmed. And the image was me. Every laugh, frown, twitch of the eye, everything I did was simultaneously played back. In the end I couldn't tell which I was watching, the real thing or the playback on the screen of self-consciousness. It's a funny thing the mind. You figure it's on your side, work with it, co-operate. Only then do you see it for what it is: the enemy within. It's the foe you've been trying to beat all this time. Only you've been fencing with the wrong partner.

I watched myself on the camera give Dakota the wrong medication. He went into overdrive. Hyperactive. Had to go under observation in the infirmary to prevent self-inflicted damage. A simple error. Could happen to anyone.

Then I followed Gabrielle through the trees at night. There was a humming and I wanted to see myself watch her. She walked alone. The sun had failed to show that day, it was becoming lazy, and now the moon was drowning in the clouds. A slice of light danced through the trees and I could hear footsteps sinking in the earth. A plate shifted and there was an earthquake, somewhere. Though I didn't see myself see it. Her eyes were in the sky, seven of them. I tried to grab one to keep as a souvenir. I called her name and answered myself from high in the treetops. She turned. She had the bright blue eyes of the little girl from the toilet in G7. The Slavic counsellor in the hood stood beside her, a halo of sorrow, and there was no one beside me except myself. I gave the girl a sharpened pencil just like the skinny guy said. She used it to rip open her womb and out stepped Lucien in Professor Bardhaw's habit. He told me I was my brother's keeper. I said I had no keeper.

Humming.

There was no more room in my head. Full up. The skinny black guy was right. That's when the hurt came. He gave me a pencil. 'For Hitler!' cheered Blatch. I watched myself wrench open my eye.

Humming.

The needle went into my arm. I tensed. My jaw relaxed and I entered the sun.

The humming didn't stop, not for billions upon billions of seconds.

I sat on the hill and the sun shone on Bradley, a fat patient with a squashed nose from B5. 'What's in here?' He kept punching himself hard in the stomach, coughing up yellow phlegm, spitting it out. 'Bagels and cream cheese,' he squealed. 'That's disgusting. Ah yeah!' He punched himself again 'What's in here? Bagels and cream cheese. That's disgusting. Ah yeah!'

He came over to sit with me and I pushed him away, sending him back to his bunk.

Dinner comprised pizza with a crust as thick as *War and Peace* and a smidgin of half-cooked tomato paste on top. The rain got bored with pouring and paused for a breather. I sat on the hill, sipping my cold, decaffeinated, detasted coffee.

'You ain't a nothin' but a houndog...' A bald black patient stood on the table outside the HCs, swinging a dirty dish cloth and singing into a raw hot dog Rosetta had given him from the kitchen. 'Cryin' all the time...' They called him Elvis. They called him Elvis because that was his name. He knew the entire Presley repertoire upside down, never stopped singing it, one song laboriously after another, even when he was shitting, which was most of the time. Elvis had the runs. 'Well you ain't nothin'...' Mitchel stood behind him strumming his invisible guitar, screwing up his face, just like in his *Kerrang* magazine.

Rock

and

roll.

Chris and Joe were chatting about Kolchak. 'She seems so gentle, so sweet I just can't square it.'

Some sensational piece of news had been revealed about her. Something about her past. I tried to listen, but it got obscured by the humming.

'You know what I think her problem is? She's not nasty or malicious or anything, she's just naïve. She doesn't know what Veda's really like. She's never spent a night with the patients. It's all just a report or schedule for her.'

'Perhaps she doesn't want to know.'

Then I saw the humming. It was the Mad Mozzy, the bastard from B3 who kept us all awake at night with his screaming. He was down the bottom of the hill, by the dining-hall, slamming an old leather medicine ball on to the grass, picking it up and slamming it down, humming softly so that it shot around my head, high-pitched like fingernails scraping across an eternal blackboard. He had thighs like tree trunks. The only other pair I'd seen like that belonged to a sabre fencer on my team whose thighs were so big he couldn't cross his legs when he sat down. I hated him, the Mad Mozzy – the fencer was okay.

The low overcast sky trapped me here on the earth. Alone with the humming. I closed my eyes and tried to turn off the camera.

Pain. Glass shattering pain. Reflections flooding out across the grass. Myself in a million different roles, each one a lying mirror of truth. I sat down with my myriad selves, trying to call order. But they wouldn't listen. They were viciously angry. One of their own number had tried to elevate himself above the others. They wanted him out. The mind throbbed as I tried forcing it back into its box. The medicine ball slammed into my face. Red, white and blue. Independence. Purple. Rainwater poured into my eyes. My head span off its axis, rolling down the hill, vowing never to return. Humming. The Mad Mozzy stood over me, hands outstretched, waiting for his ball. Far away, wherever it was my head was going, the humming drilled into my skull.

I leapt up and raced after it.

He scrambled up the hill, clawing at the grass, shrieking. I saw the whites of his eyes. Chris and Joe roared with laughter. I'd stop the bastard's humming. Damn son of a bitch, I'd swat him like a fly. I'd stop the bastard's humming. I threw myself at his legs. He reached up in confusion, trying to grab something. We tumbled across the wet grass. 'Shut the fuck up now! Just shut the fuck up!' I grabbed his arm and wrenched it behind his back. Still he hummed. I twisted harder. Still he hummed. Harder. Hummed. I saw my mind in the corner of his eye. He struggled. Kicked and bucked. Incensed blood came bursting through my skin, drowning the humming. 'Come on you son of a bitch. Hum a little more. Just a little more.' I twisted. And twisted. And twisted. He fell silent. For a moment. He retched with pain. That's it. Finally. There it is. Hurt. His lips exploded.

Joe wasn't laughing anymore. 'BENJAMIN! That's enough. You're hurting him.' Only just. He could take more. I twisted again. Just a little more, almost a crack. 'Jesus Ben! Enough!' Joe threw his arm around my neck, throttling me, yanking me away. I didn't want to let go of the arm. I wanted to take it with me. 'Ben! IN THE NAME OF GOD!'

I let go...

Joe and I tumbled backwards, my head over his heel. And we lay there, in the wet grass, side-by-side, exhausted.

'What the fuck are you trying to do?' Joe panted. 'What the fuck's got into you? Have you gone mad?'

I didn't answer. I tried to wipe the grass stains from my legs. My head was heavy.

'Jesus Ben! You're fucked up.'

The Mad Mozzy sat on the grass shaking his hands. Gently rocking. Humming.

Joe pulled me up and we walked to the bunk together, where we sat on the porch until the rain started. He didn't speak for a long time, not until he started to calm down.

'Look Ben, you can't let them get to you like this.'

I never thought I would see Joe cry. Well he didn't cry, not really, not as such. But it was there in his voice, a moisture that betrayed a sadness or hurt. It was hard to understand what he was saying, his words were top heavy, falling over one another.

'We've been over this. You've got to get a hold of yourself, while you still can. Stop fighting them. You're not listening. Let them in. You must let them in.'

So many words.

I looked up at him, too tired to speak.

'Why don't you take a rest or something? Lie down. I'll keep an eye on the patients.' He tussled my wet hair. 'I tell you what you need, a good night out, that's what. Have a rest. Get yourself together. We'll go up Dotty's tonight and get absolutely wasted. What do you think of that eh?'

I was something of a celebrity that night up at Dotty's. Seems I had been cast in the role of vigilante: The Counsellor That Struck Back. Scott, the Mozzy's counsellor, was actually jealous. 'He's been a pain in the arse ever since he arrived,' he said as he bought me a beer. 'I just wish it could've been me that landed him one.'

'Well, surprise, surprise!' Dave taunted. 'You sure showed that crazy son of a bitch. So ya got some spunk in ya after all. I didn't fink you poofs had it in you.'

Mind, fame had its price. I had been eating humble pie with Kolchak all evening. 'It is a very serious matter,' she told me. 'Very serious.' I said I was sorry, many times, told her that I wasn't quite myself at the moment, what with Michelle flipping out in E2, I was shaken up, unbalanced, wasn't sailing on an even keel, but there were calmer waters up ahead. She smiled at my analogy. She said she was prepared to overlook it, against her better judgment. I think the grovelling helped. I told her that I had learnt a valuable lesson, that it would never happen again. Truth was, she couldn't afford to lose another counsellor. Afterwards I had to go through a counselling session with Norma at the HCs. She told me that I should never bottle things up again, that if it ever got too much I should talk it over with someone. I agreed and hurried up the road to talk it over with Dotty. All I needed was a few beers.

By the time Natasha came in I'd had more than a few and was well on my way to that wasteland to which Joe had enticed me. I bolted down another whiskey and went to join her.

She sat staring at me, playing with her blond hair, twisting it around her finger, letting it fall on her tanned shoulder. Her face was red. She'd been out in the sun too much.

'So how are you?' she asked, picking up her beer.

'I'm okay.'

'Haven't seen you around much.'

'I've been busy.'

'In fact I haven't seen you at all, since that girl arrived.'

'Who?'

'You know who I mean. That Spanish snob on the higher level.'

'I've been having a few difficulties, with the patients.'

'It's all right, I understand. It doesn't matter,' she told me, in a voice that said it did. 'I heard about your little performance.'

'Seems everyone has.'

'I'm not judging you, you know.'

I leant forward through the hazy cigarette smoke and gently kissed her exposed neck. I kept my lips there, hovering just above her skin so that she could feel my breath. Then I sat back and drank. She didn't know where to look. My eyes. Her hands. My lips.

'What,' she hesitated, 'what was that for?'

'Because.'

She searched for something to say.

I laid my hand on the table, just in front of hers, almost touching her fingers.

We sat for a long time in our corner of thick silence, amidst the drunken shouts and unprovoked laughter. On the far side, next the piano, sat the Slavic counsellor, the purple hood glowing like a shroud, her eyes fixed in a book. And yet I knew she was staring at me, egging me on, daring me.

I finished another beer. And another. Natasha reached out to hold my hand, but I moved it away. And another.

'Let's go,' I whispered.

I got up and Natasha followed me out of the bar.

We didn't speak on the way to the bunk, not a word. There was no need. The trees hung low over B8, as though they were trying to drag it into the forest.

We stepped inside and stood by the door, listening to the buzz of the fluorescent light in the bathroom. We left it on for Dakota. He couldn't sleep without it. I turned it off and slipped into silence. The arc lamps outside illuminated Natasha's dull shadow. Seven shapes slept soundly under seven covers. She felt uneasy about their being there, I could that see that, but she said nothing. I caressed her face, lightly tracing the outline of her lips with my fingertips. Charlie started moaning. I gently bit her top lip, coating it with a drop of moisture. She tried to kiss me, but I leant back and watched her lips strain in emptiness to find mine, wrinkles of frustration crowding her brow. William coughed. Natasha opened her eyes and looked round, alarmed. I put my fingers to her lips to stop the words. She kissed them. I let my hand fall, brushing her nipple. Her body tensed. I lifted the vest over her head. Hair, darkened by sweat, fell around her naked shoulder. I put my hand around her neck and squeezed her throat. A hint of terror ran from her eyes. I squeezed a little harder and felt the rough windpipe wall. Her lips quivered, unsure whether I would caress them or strike them. Pinching her neck, I led her to the couch where I ripped the laces from her shoes. Slowly, very slowly, I pulled down her trousers, exposing the vulnerability of her flesh inch by inch. I pulled her up and kissed her, my tongue forcing its way into her mouth, leaving me behind. Then I stopped and pulled away. I took down her panties and stepped back to inspect her nakedness. Her frightened fingers ran to hide her crotch. I stared at her, up and down, her eyes following mine. Then I crouched, watching her stand tall above me. She stood high on the tiptoe of unfulfilled expectation, the eyes of a child misplaced within a woman's body. Charlie sat up and spluttered. You could hear the phlegm thick in his throat. Natasha started. He grunted and snored. I knelt, just like I'd seen Lucien do in church, closing my eyes and running my fingers up the inside of her legs. She was wet. I tried to pray. But the altar of my mind had been emptied long ago and there was nothing there I could use. Natasha reached out to hold me. I jumped up, pulling her hands toward my shirt.

'Undress me. Now.'

Taken aback by the sound of my voice, she glanced nervously around the bunk, frightened the patients had woken, then unbuttoned my shirt, her fingers working with a speed that betrayed her impatience. She caressed my chest, laying light kisses upon my nipples. I took her hands away and put them on my belt.

When I too was naked I led her to the couch. She smiled. I lay my hands upon her stomach, gripping it tight, and turned her round. Her eyes caught the light. They were empty now. I held the back of her neck, placed my other hand on her moist pubic hair, and entered her, pushing until I could go no further. There I rested, looking around the bunk. Dakota muttered something. Joshua flipped over, the iron legs of bed scraping the floorboards. I turned Natasha's head. 'Eye contact', that's what Ellen had said. I started to move within her, running my nails across the small of her back. I grabbed her buttocks and thrust beyond her wall. She gasped. I pushed to the end. And withdrew. She turned around and held on to me, confusion shadowing her face.

Mitchel's head poked out from beneath the blankets. I led her to the centre of the bunk and lay her down on the cold wooden floor. There I opened her legs and entered her once more. Deeper. Clean.

All the way. She grimaced and whispered something I couldn't hear. I rose up and pushed in again. I pushed and pushed but she still she lay there, beneath me. Sweat ran in the cracked paint of the floorboards. I dug my nails into her. Her eyes opened. I pushed harder. She moaned and opened wider. Faster. Deeper. Harder. Still she would not go. I reached out for the pencil and saw myself guide it towards her closed eye. She lay back and smiled, unaware. I tried to remember what the skinny black guy had said. Clean through the eye. Relieve the pain. In the distorted light of lust I saw the brown hair of Gabrielle upon soft shoulders. Vicious grace. I could feel her insides harden, so I thrust harder. I closed my eyes in her pain. Just had to get the pencil in the eye. She beckoned to me. But when I tried to follow the Slavic counsellor blocked my way. She sat with the little blue-eyed girl on her knee and told her stories: stories of glittering minds, wild parties, fencing bouts. The little girl laughed and blushed and lowered her eyes and opened her legs, inviting me. But when I tried to enter the womb Lucien stepped out, accusation in his eyes. Then came the guilt. I'd let him down. Could have done something. Guilt, spiralling into the darkest corners of the bunk where not even the rats will go. Faster. Faster. Harder. Gabrielle looked up at me, sad, disappointed. AND THAT DAMN CAMERA! Never leaves me alone. Observes me. Reflects. Watches me. See my fucking self. On the porch of G7, amid the shadows, stands the Slavic girl, staring through me with righteousness. Mitchel was awake now. Natasha threw her arms round my back and thrashed on the floor. I stood over her and called for help as her arm beat like a broken butterfly wing in the dirt. Her eyes rolled back in her head and her tongue slipped from her mouth. Saliva poured on to my lips. Nails dug into my scalp. She buried herself in my skin and groaned. Tumbling forward in spasm after spasm after spasm. Gabrielle called and I ran away. Running so fast that I never stopped disappearing. World without end. I thrust harder and harder, faster and faster, ripping myself against the splintered glass of the womb. Natasha's back arched. I rose up. She let out a cry. I came. Over. She shuddered, kissing me violently, dragging out my tongue and carrying it deep into the forest.

We collapsed in dried paint and sweat. Panting.

Mitchel watched and Joshua muttered.

Natasha sighed and smiled sweetly.

I withdrew.

On the floor of the bunk, beneath her leg, lay a small pool of blood.

I yanked her up and gave her her clothes.

'Let's go.'

18

One of the institutionals made it. Got away. Escaped. Must have been when we were playing baseball. The game was a foregone cock-up from the first pitch. On the rare and long-celebrated occasions when a patient actually connected bat and ball, the ball vanished in the long grass which covered the field (Kolchak had asked Herbert to cut it the previous week). Then the hunt would start; patients and counsellors rummaging around like a pack of tracker dogs with no sense of smell. Often as not, when a patient found the ball he'd get so excited, running up and down whooping and wailing, he'd drop it. Then the search would start all over again. In the meantime the hitter would be running around the bases with a hero's smirk, clocking up dozens of home runs. When the umpire tried to enforce a maximum of one home run per hit, a fight broke out between Joseph and Doug, and they weren't even playing. By the time the final score was added up (somewhere between 83 vs 144 or 482 vs 617, depending on whom you trusted), the institutional was long gone. His absence wasn't even noticed until evening showers. He was one of Chris' up at E6. Non-verbal and deaf. He stood six feet seven and was as low functioning as they come. A huge hulk of a man who's frenzied looks put the fear of God in you.

Kolchak went spare. It was the first time I'd seen her lose her cool. Boy, she was steaming. Her face swelled up, capillaries bursting all the way down her thin nose. Her upper lip (burning rose red) quivered, you could see it some distance away, her hands quietly shaking. And the angrier she grew, the more dishevelled her hair became, slipping from its clip. She didn't shout, not once. That wasn't her style. Besides, she didn't need to. She frightened the hell out of the counsellors as she was. Her voice was still frail, but had a jagged edge to it; you knew she could cut you any moment she chose. Never have I felt so much power in such a little body. That was some fire raging inside her, some dragon roaring.

She called a big meeting in the dining-hall where she stood in front of a hushed staff, silent at first, letting us feel her anger.

'You have disappointed me,' she said quietly. 'I expected better from you.'

No one dared step out of line, not even Dave. We knew our place.

Even those who hated her bowed before her that night. The Kommandant: you could see where she got her name. She said she could only hope that, somehow, in some remote light, we could redeem ourselves. Then she stood, all eyes fixed on her, quiet and calm, as I'd seen her that first morning by the razorwire fence standing passively whilst her husband chased a chicken with a hunting knife. The power she'd held over that chicken, power to be merciful, she held over us now. She stayed a while, just long enough to be sure we recognised it, felt it, then left.

I was surprised how timid Norma could be, she's not a woman who took fright easily. Kolchak had even shaken her up (there was a lot of her to shake up), and she must have been used to her boss' strange ways. She waited some time after Kolchak had gone, making sure she wasn't coming back, before speaking to us. And even then she was nervous.

Norma droned on about counsellors' responsibility for twenty minutes before finally getting round to organising search parties. And then we spent another fifteen minutes running checks: no group must cover the same area; watches must be synchronised for reporting back; strict adherence to team leaders' commands must be observed; local residents must not be alarmed. By the time we set off, torches, maps and flasks of coffee at the ready, the police had phoned to check if we were missing a deaf, dumb, dishevelled black giant.

They'd found him in some old woman's kitchen a mile or so up through the woods. She was in hospital, recovering from shock. He'd broken into her house. She was a Catholic. Thought her time had come, began last confession, arranging her icons, kneeling by her candlelit bed, praying fervently before she was brutally raped and beaten to death. Meanwhile the institutional was in the kitchen, raiding the larder. And after Veda's dodgy diet, who could blame him? Any counsellor would've done the same. It was four hours before the old lady dared venture out of her room. She fled screaming from the house, charging down the street in her nightgown. Must have seen too many horror movies. The police surrounded the house with sharpshooters, yelling down the megaphone for the intruder to give himself up peacefully and no one would get hurt. It's the most excitement Sageville has had for years, you should have seen the crowd that gathered. It was only when the deputy in charge of the siege checked his watch and realised he was late for his poker game (which he always lost) that he decided to storm the house, guns at the ready. They found the institutional in a deep, satisfied sleep on the kitchen floor. Completely stuffed.

It wasn't easy avoiding Natasha. She was everywhere, an omnipresent memory with a hurtful pout. Whichever nook and cranny I chose she'd be there before me, foraging for some sort of explanation, never uttering a sound; just waiting, staring. It was there when I slept. The faces. The blood. I watched myself over and over again, a playback I couldn't switch off running haywire on the screens of my mind. Thrashing about on the floor whilst Mitchel looked on. And wherever she went the Slavic girl followed. I didn't even know they were friends. But every time I saw Natasha, those righteous eyes set deep in that sad, pale face weren't far behind, prodding me, breathing life into a guilt I had suffocated.

Lights out. Joe and I were on the porch preparing the medication. Natasha was skulking around just down the hill from the bunk, keeping her distance. It was only by chance that we'd discovered Mitchel was receiving the wrong medication. He'd been seizing a lot recently, throwing himself all over the place until he was just a bundle of bruises. We couldn't figure it out. He used to swallow his pills direct from the bottle, all our patients did. Then one evening at dinner he and Joshua were having a tussle and the pill bottle went sliding across the floor, a colourful kaleidoscope of colliding capsules. That's when the mistake was discovered. Mitch said his pills were orange; the ones on the floor were red. We checked his medical card. Joe was furious. The nurses had screwed it up. Dr Rosenthal said it was an easy mistake, and not a serious one. 'Trying telling that to Mitch when he's bouncing off the walls in a seizure,' Joe yelled at the decrepit doctor. From then on he wouldn't trust the nurses and we doled out the medication ourselves.

'What's got into her?' Joe asked, staring at Natasha sitting on the edge of the soggy sandbox behind B3.

'How do you mean?'

'Well, look at her. Always hanging around. She never comes up here no more, just sits down there, waiting for God knows what. And that look she gives you.'

'What look? I don't see anything.'

'Well it's sort of...'

'Yes?'

'Oh I don't know. Maybe I'm imagining it.' Joe counted out some pills and popped them into a plastic bottle. 'What the hell happened between you two anyway?'

'Nothing.'

'Well why's she acting so strange?'

'I don't bloody know. Go ask her!'

'Okay, Ben, don't get stroppy. Jesus, I was just asking.'

'Joe, you know women, there's no telling what they'll do if they can't get their own way.'

'Yeah, I guess you're right. A woman spurned and all that. She must have it pretty bad for you.' Joe waited for a response, but none came. We finished counting the pills and then flipped them down seven throats, drugging them into bed.

'Coming out tonight, Ben?'

'No, I don't think so.'

'It'd do you some good to get out of Veda for a change. You spend too much time on your own in this place as it is.'

I mumbled some excuse about bars getting boring, drinking being an eternal repetition of the same. Truth was, I didn't want to run into Lucien. He'd be up there with Gabrielle and seeing them together wasn't my idea of fun.

Joe went out every night, I don't think he'd ever stayed in. Even when he was tired and miserable, he preferred to be tired and miserable in the bar. Seems Claudia was as enthusiastic about getting paralytic as he was; together they'd share the burden of getting absolutely legless (isn't love sweet). He was lucky to find someone with whom he had so much in common. They were happy getting hammered together and I didn't want to intrude upon their contentment. Claudia said she felt sorry for me, being on my own so much.

'What do you do all the time?

'Oh, I have myself.'

And my self had me. My self had a vicious hold on me, its hooks deep into the bone, no intention of letting me be. From time to time, I'd try to sneak away, become self-less. But it would always be there, the camera rolling, images on a screen in place of emotion. So I'd let it have it's way. My self and me would spend our evenings together, sitting on the porch, or wandering through the woods, charting mazes of understanding, the layouts of which altered at each intersection we came to.

Joe asked me why I was behaving so oddly. I couldn't tell him; I wasn't aware I was. Nothing out of the ordinary as far as Veda was concerned. He took my silence as a snub, thought I didn't want to take him into my confidence. That only made things more difficult. Already Joe and I weren't speaking much, not beyond what was necessary to keep the patients' routine going, more my fault than his.

But we would at least always share a cigarette and a few sighs before bedtime, sitting on the porch listening to the sleepless voices which shadowed the Veda night. Then one evening, way after midnight, when he staggered back from Dotty's, Joe stumbled past me without a word and went straight to bed.

I followed him into the bunk and asked what was wrong. He told me he was sorry. So sorry. I thought Claudia and he had had a fight. Then he said he knew it all. Natasha. What I'd done. Exactly. Dave had been up Dotty's, telling everyone. Natasha and he were an item now. He took each sordid detail and passed it around with a pitcher of beer for open inspection. Said I was a snobby, arrogant, self-righteous cunt who'd get what's coming. Joe peeked from his drunken stupor, his eyes sunk in the pillow, longing for me to deny it. I started to, told him he shouldn't believe what jealous people say, then stopped. Joe reached out.

'Why Ben? Why'd you have to go and do a thing like that, why? First you take it out on the patients, now this. She's one of *us*, Ben, one of us. What's happening to you? Where's all this going to end?' His voice was low, unwilling, despondent; he was giving up on me.

I sat with him most of the night. He was throwing up and I was frightened he'd choke on the vomit.

It got worse the next day. Much worse.

Kolchak got a call from the BCCI, the Brooklyn Care and Concern Institute. One of their patients had been up at Veda during the last week, a middle-aged man, good-natured, quiet, low functioning. They'd found cigarette burns on his testicles and signs of serious sexual abuse. He'd only been back one day and the marks were several days old. They wanted to come up and ask a few questions. Kolchak promised them full co-operation.

All this was rumour of course. We were never told anything directly. But word got out all the same. The Veda Council met on the hill, buzzing with speculation.

I wasn't there. Hadn't been for ages. But I heard about it afterwards, word for word. Dave led the conversation, crafting it skilfully into accusation, moulding it into condemnation. You had to admire the way he manipulated the facts, would've made any politician proud.

He started out by saying he was sickened to the core (gaining the moral highground), that he, as a God-fearing and just man, would like to castrate the bastard and string him up. He whipped up a bit of fervour, got them baying for blood. Then he started throwing some thoughts around. Just one or two, nothing connected, as yet.

Benjamin. Now let's take Benjamin; now we all know he has a temper, look what he done to the Mad Mozzy. And his tastes, sexually speaking, not exactly, well, straight, are they? (Resigned agreement.) We've 'eard the stories about him and Lucien. And look at that little episode up at the pool, throwing their arms round each other in front of everyone. (Shame.) Proof. Ya just can't tell wiv them sort can ya? (Thoughtful nods all round.) It ain't natural. And his latest escapade. Him and Natasha. (Poor girl.) Well it ain't what you call normal, not like you and me, is it?

Dave didn't say anything direct, not at first. He just sowed a few strategic seeds of doubt in enough minds. Veda's grapevine did the rest. By the end of the day I was Suspect N° 1. After all, I had been OD on the higher level. In fact, I seemed to spend most of my time hanging around up there. And, well, Dave had a point, it wasn't exactly inconsistent with my track record, was it?

Joe was horrified. Even though we hadn't been getting along so well recently, he still tried standing up for me. He said outright he thought I'd been a bastard over Natasha, but physical abuse? Benjamin? But he was howled down. No one blamed him, they said so, they admired his loyalty. But it was no use protecting me. I was only getting what I deserved. Joe refused to believe it. He was one of the few. Veda came alive with accusation. Suspicion fell from the clouds. Even the trees whispered my name.

I knew it would go all the way to the top, I realised that from the start. Kolchak had ears among the counsellors, we'd become aware of that when she'd broken up Thomas' attempts at mass protest. But

I didn't expect her to act on it, not on gossip, didn't think she'd take it seriously.

These things take on a life of their own. What is absurd allegation one moment is sober fact the next. I remember Blatch, my history master, trying to explain how something like the Holocaust could so easily happen in so many countries. He told us not to be surprised that it *did* happen, but that it *doesn't* happen more often: people sway with the wind, they're fickle, they'll applaud the loudest voice with the grandest echo. It wasn't that a whole nation actively supported Hitler, it was just that the majority silently followed the minority who did.

Two days later I was called to High Command to answer some questions for the BCCI team. And not one person came forward in my defence.

I was never told the name of the institutional, nor did I discover who it was. All I knew was that he was from E4. I was shown colour close ups of the the evidence. Small round purple blotches on the testicles and around the groin. Blistered skin. Charred pubic hair. Broken blood vessels by the entrance to the anus.

'Those marks, Mr Ryan,' said the senior doctor from the institution, a short-sighted old man with dandruff and a glass eye, 'those marks are the result of cigarette burns. And this,' he passed me another picture, 'this shows the marks caused by forced anal entry.' He emphasised the words *forced anal entry*, relishing them, then sat back and waited for my reaction.

I said nothing.

'Note particularly the breaking of the skin. We've circled the marks for you to make it clear,' said his assistant after a while, a carbon copy of his colleague, except he had boss eyes. One glass and one boss, I could look them both in the eye without turning my head. They showed me the pictures again and again and again, like they expected me to comment on their artistic quality.

Kolchak sat at her metal desk pretending to be deep in paperwork, but watching me. I couldn't believe she let me go through this alone. No representation, no advice, no information, nothing. She just shuffled papers whilst I was getting nailed. The two doctors were smarmy as hell, smiling and joking as if we were having some genial chat when I knew damn well what they were up to. The questioning was hostile from the start. They had a file on me (Kolchak kept files on us all), flicking through it as if they were reading the Sunday supplements with coffee and bagels, firing off the odd condemnatory salvo. Yes, I'd had problems settling in at Veda. Yes, I did find it difficult working with these people. Yes, frustrating. Yes, it made me angry. Yes, I lost my temper and attacked a patient. Yes, I'd been seen embracing another male counsellor in public. Yes, I'd been withdrawn over the last weeks... I was getting burned. They asked me to come back later in the day, after they'd spoken to some other counsellors. They didn't even ask me outright if I did it. Nor did I tell them.

Two days I roasted over that spit. Two fucking days. Everyone, even Dotty, knew I was being questioned. I was a pariah. I went into the dining-hall and tables emptied, dived into the pool and it cleared within minutes. I even tried going up to Dotty's and had the door slammed in my face, laughter ringing around the bar as I turned and trudged across the gravel back to Veda. And no Lucien. I couldn't believe it. He didn't even come to see how I was. I thought crises were times when you bury the hatchet, pull together, realise what you really value. Maybe that was it. Maybe Lucien had come to just such a realisation: he simply had no value for me. Never have there been such long nights. Never have nightmares spilled into waking hours with such virulence. Joe kept the patients away from me, for my own good. And (and this was the last thing I'd expected) never have I missed my patients more than during those lonely days. B8 was empty, hollow, an echo of what I'd had and not realised.

Veda was sodden. The brook was in flood, somehow making the whole place seem menacing. At night I wandered, too numb to think, watching counsellors grouped on porches, pale lamplight shadows, watching me pass, silence jabbing at me.

Even my self stayed away.

Dave played out his role to the end, doing his best to ensure my conviction, feeding out more details of my night with Natasha. I even heard one rumour said I'd been smoking during sex, playing around with the cigarette.

Only on the third day did Kolchak think to look up the past OD schedules. THE THIRD GODDAM DAY. I had never been OD for E4. In fact I hadn't been OD throughout the week when the abused institutional had been present; Norma had given out so many extra ODs as punishment, she didn't need me. Then Fergus came forward and told the BCCI team that as far as he could remember, I'd never even been in E4. And Joe said that I hadn't been away from B8 for any extended periods, lying to save my hide.

I was cleared.

Not that it made much difference. Nothing sticks like circumstantial conviction. Unofficial, prejudged, it can never be undone. It's not justice we seek, but consensual opinion. If it sounds good and, more importantly, feels good, then truth can go fuck itself. Kolchak's posted letter stating that I was cleared of suspicion meant Jack Shit. My ostracism was complete.

Serves him fucking right. Had it coming. That's what was scrawled on Kolchak's letter. And that's all that mattered.

And maybe, just maybe, they were right.

The skinny black guy came that night, on cue, as if he had direct access to my thoughts. He sat on my porch, gazing off into his customary nothingness. He hadn't been around since I'd beaten him with the pillow, thought he'd finally got the message and left me alone, left off pestering me.

Boy was I glad to see him. I sank down next to him and breathed his company deep.

'Well I just don't know, you look like hell. Those guys give you a shit tough time? Don't surprise me none. They're nuts. I should know, I lived with them all my damn life. Used to ask me questions all the time. Never stopped for one damn moment. Damn stupid questions too. Some sort o' psychotherapalysis, whatever. Told me they could make me better. Wanted to know what my deep-rooted problems were. I told them. I'm crazy. That's my problem. Don't need no deep-rooted problems nor no deep-rooted cure. I just plain crazy. Simple as that. Why they got and go complicate things all the damn time. Then they got to asking me all questions about when I was a boy, you know, little n' all. Said it was important, remembering my childhood. Shit! Now how I supposed to go remembering that? I was just a kid! Think they know it all, see. Think if you understand your childhood, you understand your present and everything's A-Okay. Bullshit. Problem is, they ain't never been no crazy, so they don't know what it's like. Got no idea. I told them. I'm crazy. If they want to find out why, then they got to go be crazy too. Don't need no psychotheraputicalysis, whatever, to figure that one. Well I just don't know. Shit!

And now they on to you. You better watch your hide. An' I figure you getting to know some about being crazy. Well, it won't harm you none. Might even do you some good. Damn, sure it'll do you good. Understand a little. Being crazy's underrated. Few more crazzies an' we'd being doing okay.'

I wrapped his voice around me and pulled it tight. Charlie was snoring his lungs out inside the bunk, same as every night. But only now did I really listen. No muffling, moaning or groaning. Nothing abnormal. Just snoring, like my father. The skinny guy nattered on, his voice running around the night sky, going nowhere and I wondered if I had done it.

'...cause you see, up in E4 it's the same damn thing.'

The words clicked.

'What did you say?'

'Just telling you some about the boys they got up there in the bunk.'

'Which bunk?'

'E4.'

'So that *was* you I saw, standing on the higher level in the rain: Louis?'

'So you finally figured it out, took you damn long time.'

'But, I thought, Chris told me you were Grade A.'

'Grade A! Now what the shit is that?'

'Veg. Say nothing, hear nothing.'

'Well I's speaking now ain't I?'

'But you're not supposed to. They say you can't.'

'Well there you go. They says I can't 'cos they thinks I'm crazy. Can't go disappointing them now, can we? Make a hell of a mess, drive them nuts.'

'And that patient, the one who was abused...'

'George.'

'George. He was in your bunk?'

'Sure was. Nice fella. Too trusting, if you know what I mean.'

'Louis?'

'What.'

'Did I do it?'

'HELL NO!' He roared with laughter, his teeth shaking. 'Think I'd be sitting here chewing the fat with you if you did? Think I'm crazy? Shit! You didn't do it. No sir. That fat fuck of a counsellor of mine was the one.'

'You saw it?'

'Why of course. I was on the shitter.'

'Well, who was it?'

He didn't answer at first. He tweaked his lips up and down with his dirty fingers, rubbing his gums, as if he were trying to conjure up the words. A scream fluttered with the birds through the trees. 'Well, I just don't know...'

'Louis, please. You've got to know this time. You've got to tell me.'

'Dave.'

'Dave?'

'Ain't that what I just said. Slammed the poor bastard all over the damn place. Gagged him up while you boys were all down at the pool, swimming and splashing. Knew the little fella couldn't say a word. Said he had it coming. Fat fuck.'

'Louis, you've got to say something. You got to tell Kolchak.'

He grabbed the porch railing and hauled himself up. 'Oh no, you ain't getting me with that. Well I thought you'd try. Oh no.' He started to wander off down the steps.

'Wait! What do you mean "no"? You've got to say something.'

'I ain't got to say no thing. Oh no. Not me.'

'Why the hell not? You saw it! You saw the whole thing.'

'No and no. I ain't speaking nothing.'

'Louis, if you don't speak, Dave will get off. Nothing will happen. God knows what he'll do. He might even go for you.'

'If he comes near me I'll break his fucking head. Now you listen to me. I'm real sorry an' all for what they done to you. I wish it didn't have happened. But I ain't speaking nothing. I ain't responsible for what you boys do. It ain't my affairs. You want to go around hurting people all the damn time, that's your problem. I ain't playing no saviour. No sir, not me! Besides why don't you stop and think a minute before you go a'pleading and a'hollering. They think I can't speak, can't hear shit neither. Said so yourself. I like it like that. Just fine. No one bothers me and I don't go bothering no one. Sure comfortable. Taken me a long time to get this far. Now if you think I gonna go right on in there and ruin it all 'cos of some fat fuck of a counsellor, well you gotta think again. 'Cos I ain't speaking.'

'Louis.'

'Don't you go no Louis me. Why I start speaking, next think I know they'll be trying all their damn cures again, trying to re-in-tegrate me back into society, sending me out, messing me about. Sooner or later I be putting up with all that shit you got going. Drive me crazy. Now I'm sorry for you, like I say, but I ain't speaking out. Not now. Not never.' He smiled at me, 'No hard feelings now', and wandered off, chuckling to himself.

19

Autistics turn in on themselves, focus upon a microscopic pinpoint of an inner universe. They never quite make it to the outside world, never cross the bridge to the uplands the rest of us inhabit. At least, that's what it says in my notes, the ones I took during orientation. I had the file of a boy who was a human clock; he'd tell you the time whenever you asked him, right down to the last second. Never looked at a watch. Never wrong. Tick. Kind of impressive until you realise anyone could do it: all you have to do is exclude every last item, thought or action from your life but the counting of seconds. Tock.

No one's quite sure where autism comes from, Kolchak told us so herself. Some used to believe it was a condition brought on in young childhood, laying the blame squarely at the feet of the parents. A more user-friendly theory suggests the traits of autism are there when you're born. What's difficult to fathom is what exacerbates those traits in some and not in others. Why Dakota and not you?

A lot of work has been done on trying to reach autistics, to bring them out of their world, trying to make them connect, tempting them, motivating, shoving. None of it has been very successful. But that's not the point. The point is, we've never tried their world. It always did seem to me the height of arrogance (perhaps pardonable ignorance) to assume that they should want to leave their world and enter ours.

I keep asking myself why, lying here in this bed, watching the paint peel. I keep wishing I could see you in person, touch you, watch your reactions (if you have any); the thought of that keeps me awake at night, I don't want to sleep when I have so little time. But of course I can't. We'll never meet. And you'll soon forget everything I'm telling you. You'll close the last page and go on as before. We rarely change our lives. But the hope that, for a moment, it could make a difference, even the slightest one, I suppose that might make some of this worthwhile.

And so I keep asking myself. And now I'm asking you. Because I guess this is where it really began: slip-sliding down to a change in perception. And to tell you the truth, I can't figure it out, not exactly. Somehow my little chat with Louis revived a small section (long passed over) of my heart. Not that I looked at it like this. I mean, I didn't suddenly feel my heart was bigger or stronger, it didn't beat faster or harder or anything, not like in a poem. But I figured this kind of language, heart and soul, might make it easier for you to understand. Or maybe it was like the opening up of a part of an eye that I'd never used. Maybe that's how a poet would put it, a change of focus, a seeing of something to which I'd hitherto been blind. Or perhaps it was a whole new discovery.

Not that it happened suddenly, not like turning over the page and starting out on a new chapter. Nor painlessly, like in the poet's world of words. Words don't convey pain, people do. But looking back, I think it was somewhere around here that things started to change. Only, and I ask myself to this very day (I have nothing else left to do): was it for better or for worse?

I started to go to activities again. Only a couple at first, drama and academics, but at least I was outside the bunk, doing things with the group. For the most part the programme counsellors would ignore me and I'd sit in the corner, reading to one of the patients. I was no longer speaking to any of the counsellors apart from Joe. Or rather, they weren't speaking to me. I did try. Once. It was after dinner. Instead of disappearing straight up to the bunk as usual, I went and sat on the hill to drink my coffee, where counsellors gathered to chew the cud before evening activity. I didn't expect them to talk to me, not right away. But I thought they might at least condescend to ignore me.

It was pleasant there, the sun shifting into yellows and reds, stroking the tops of the trees on the far side of the Redhill, people littering the hillside, chattering, laughing. I convinced myself that I belonged, part of the group.

Dave was the first. Well that was no great surprise. He up and left almost as soon as I'd sat down, muttering about arse bandits, perverts and the like. Natasha, taking her cue, followed soon after. Then, slowly at first, but gathering pace, one by one counsellors stood up and left. Some looked at me disdainfully, turning their noses up and sticking their arses in the air. Others seemed a little embarrassed by the whole thing, but obviously felt it expected of them. They left *en masse* and went to sit elsewhere. Within a few minutes, the time it took the sun to set, the hill cleared. There were a few half-empty plastic coffee cups, the debris of rejection, cigarette butts, and me.

Alone. I tried to appear nonchalant, like I didn't give a damn. I wasn't going to give them the pleasure of seeing me cry.

I prayed. Not to God. At least, nothing you'd recognise as a prayer; more a plea with inner tears, longing for just one person to return. One person to sit with me and talk.

In the end, one did.

It wasn't exactly what I prayed for.

Bradley, the fat patient from B5, plopped himself down at my side and slapped his stomach. 'What's in here?' He punched himself. 'Bagels and cream cheese. That's disgusting,' he howled. 'Ah yeah!' He repeated it a few times, his whole life dedicated to those few lines, slapping himself and laughing.

I was going to send him away; loonies like that can get on your nerves. But then, seeing as I had no one else to talk to, I asked him a question: 'What's in there?'

'Bagels and cream cheese.'

'That's disgusting.'

'Ah yeah!'

And I patted his stomach.

It's not what you'd call a conversation, but it wasn't half bad. I felt a little better and asked him again: 'What's in there?'

'Bagels and cream cheese.'

'That's disgusting.'

'Ah yeah!'

Eight times. Exactly the same: tone, pitch, rate, inflection, each aspect of the sentence identical, not even a slight variation. Eight times we did that routine. Not a word out of place. After which Bradley got up and waddled away, chuckling, a little happier. And I, much to my surprise, found that I was too.

And that's the way things were for a while. The patients were the only ones who'd speak to me. Normal conversation became a rarity. I became immersed in what Lucien had called 'the language of madness', my vocabulary increasing everyday. Somewhere along the line I cracked a code and caught a glimpse of their world. Just a foot in the door at first. But that's all it takes, isn't it. Sooner or later you're in. And WHAM! the door closes behind you. Insanity, imbalance, madness, lunacy, call it what you will: it can only be understood from the inside.

20

Bodies lay strewn across the grass, some withered and white, patterned by monstrous mosquito bites scratched raw, others with chunks of rampant red flesh, singed and burnt through lack of protection. A hairless old man sat naked under a bush by the lifeguard's chair, staring into the fierce sun until his eyes watered, his lids flickering shut in protest. He would rub them until they opened again and he would continue gazing into the ball of fire. A woman sat huddled by the pool's edge, tentatively dipping her toes. On making contact with the water she would howl, pull her foot away and sit stroking it tenderly, muttering condolences, before dipping it again.

The dozen statues I'd seen littering the inner triangle of the higher level stood in the shallow end in exactly the same positions, as though they'd been hoisted into the water by a crane and had yet to realise the change of scenery. Louis was there, biting his fingers, his lips twitching. I called to him, but he didn't acknowledge. On the far side by the lifejackets a fully clothed man stood in the water swinging his arms back and forth in an exaggerated front crawl, going absolutely nowhere. Every now and then he would stop and bellow at the top of his voice, 'I'M THERE!', clapping appreciatively. Then he would start swimming again, standing still all the while.

I opened the gate to the pool area and bustled B8 down the far corner, to Coventry, away from the counsellors.

Veda was over halfway through the season and that morning, for the first time, Joe and I had observed a change. A shift in patient behaviour. Nothing momentous, wouldn't even register on the Richter scale. Still, for us, it led to a landslide. And I guess, looking back, it was the kind of thing that really mattered.

Dakota answered a question.

Not his name, not self-identification, we knew he could do that. A real, honest-to-God question. A question, followed by an answer. A comprehensible answer which meets the needs of the question.

It happened in the bunk after breakfast. We were late getting up, had to scamper around trying to get them all washed before first activity. The bunk was a sty: water, toothpaste, magazines, mud, soap and clothes solidifying into a thick carpet which covered the floor. William had taken to throwing his soiled Calvin Kleins up in the rafters, hiding them. We didn't notice at first, didn't think to check where his underpants were disappearing to, figured the people at the laundromat must be giving up on them, too heavily stained, and throwing them away. Then one of them fell to the floor. Joe slipped on it, skidding across the bunk, smearing excrement over the floor-boards. We looked up and found six pairs coated in protective dust, all containing faeces in different stages of fossilisation. We ran around like loons trying to clean the place up; Joe bawling William out, William grinning, Joshua laughing, Robert and Charlie playing with each other in the loos, Dakota getting all het up over the day's menu – the usual morning procedure. '...Yas what is fur dinner what is what is yeas what is fur...' he droned on and on and on and.

Joe lost his rag, and squeezed the mop out over Dakota's feet. Dakota didn't even notice, just kept on about dinner. 'I don't bloody know Dakota,' he screamed. 'What *is* for fucking dinner?'

'Fisshticks.'

The voice was quiet at first, lost in the general mayhem. Then it came again, louder, with more confidence. 'Fisshticks.'

'What?' Joe stopped dressing Walter, leaving him with one arm lost somewhere inside a T-shirt. 'Dakota, what did you say?'

'Fisshticks. Fisshticks fur dinner yas...' he glanced around nervously, uneasy at being the centre of attention. Joe bolted over to the noticeboard and tore down the meal schedule. Rosetta (having nothing better to do) had handwritten each and every mouthful for the whole ten weeks of her tortuous diet and posted it in all the bunks.

'He's bloody well right! Ben, get over here. Take a look at this. Fish fingers. See? He's bloody well right.'

I looked at the schedule. Joe was right, Dakota was.

Joe tried another. 'Dakota, what's for lunch?'

'Bagels and colcuts yers.'

'Tomorrow. What's for lunch tomorrow?'

'Pitza.'

'Wednesday. What's for dinner on Wednesday?'

'Chicken.'

'Thursday?'

'Baked zeettee.'

Joe went through every meal. Every meal of every day. Dakota trotted off the answers instantly. Then Joe went through all the meals for next week. Dakota got it right. Every time. And the next week.

Not even so much as a momentary hesitation, right through to the end of the season.

Joe howled with laughter. 'The kid's a goddam bloody genius. A genius! I swear, I never seen the like.' Joe picked him up and swung him through the air. This freaked the hell out of Dakota who screamed. Joe thought he was enjoying it and swung him some more. Dakota screamed some more, sending William fleeing for cover. Then he started slapping himself and we had to go into the restraining position. Still, it was a hell of an achievement. Joe wouldn't stop asking. Mixed the days round, changed the mealtimes, even tested him backwards. He was like a kid with a new toy. But he couldn't slip Dakota up. Not once.

Then, during academics, we cracked it. We finally figured it out. For each question Dakota asked, he already knew the answer. You just had to ask him back. He'd ask – you'd ask – he'd answer. Simple.

'Academicslady who ya have next fur academics who?'

'Who, Dakota?'

'B fwee yeas B fwee.'

'Academicslady who ya have tomorrow at ten who who?'

'Who, Dakota?'

'G six yers G six.'

He was right everytime. Knew the whole schedule off by heart. We took him to drama; same thing. He knew it all. Music: ditto. What a smart arse! Not a foot wrong. You couldn't ask him any question, mind. He wouldn't be able to answer them. He had to ask the question first, then you could ask him back. Those were the rules. As long as you stuck by them, Dakota never gave a wrong answer.

'How many lifejwackets we need fur B8 how many how?'

'How many, Dakota?'

'Fwee. Fur who fur who fur?'

'Who for, Dakota?'

'Willy Walta and Dakota yes Dakota.'

'Who's Dakota who?'

'Who is Dakota?

'Me. Yeas me.'

Right again.

I kitted them out with lifejackets and pushed them one by one into the water, all except Mitchel, who wasn't allowed to swim. I didn't go in the pool myself, not when the patients were around anyway. It wasn't clean. You'd be splashing about, come up for air and find yourself face to face with a floating turd; long, thick and coming straight at you, a torpedo from Submarine Sewage. If you were lucky they sank to the bottom, reducing your chances of getting them in the mouth. But for some reason most retard turds seemed to float.

William stomped over to the diving-board, climbed the steps with great ceremony, beating his chest, opening and shutting his mouth, in total awe of himself. Then he stood, perched at the end, waiting for everyone's undivided attention. A few bows, a backward step and the maestro was ready to perform. 'UBA UBA UBA,' he screeched, running down the board, gathering speed. 'YA SISTER'S A PROSTITCHEWEEE!' He flung himself into the air, arms and legs flailing, a Catherine Wheel gone haywire, trying his utmost to empty the pool with one splash. Next up was Charlie, determined to outdo William; bowing to his left, bowing to his right, bestowing kisses upon us all. He posed, admiring his fat body, patting the plentiful flab with pride. Then he took off, howling down the board, curling himself into a ball, slamming into the water with graceful precision, soaking the maximum number of onlookers. William waited for Charlie to surface, spitting out great gulps of water, swallowing even more, then tried ducking him. But Charlie was too quick and slipped his grasp. Then Charlie tried pushing William under, but William had a lifejacket and just kept bobbing around, spitting out water. Robert jumped in after them with a pathetic plop.

'Don't you go do do dat Charlie Wise.'

'Yeah, do it do it.'

'Go ta Alabama.'

Charlie cut away from the others, slicing his hefty bulk through the water with the speed and ease of a sea-lion. I hadn't seen them so alive since the disco. They splashed, spluttered, swam and sank. It could've been any public swimming-pool in summertime, almost.

Mitchel watched from the sidelines, Joshua sitting next to him, goading him.

'Well, you know, Client Luckee, now why don't you go in the pool? Oh, I'm sorry, well, you know, I have such a bad memory, well yes I do. I clean forgot about your broken arm there, well yes I did. And, well, your leg isn't looking so good now, is it? Still, it must be nice to watch. I do like to watch.'

'Fuck off, asshole!'

The harsh sunlight accentuated the painful twists and turns of Mitchel's body, so thin the sun couldn't cast a shadow. A splash of water on that fragile frame and he would dissolve.

Dakota wandered around in the shallow end, weaving amongst the statues, chasing some patient by the name of Jack Gessler, annoying the hell out of him. Gessler was ugly, even by Veda standards: he had the buck teeth of a rabbit who needed dental work; a nose that pointed so far up you could see his tonsils; glasses so heavy they kept slipping off his tiny, lobeless ears; a stomach so concave you could see his spine through his navel; and even with those lenses he could hardly see a thing. He was the perfect target for Dakota. He'd follow Gessler around, always just out of striking range, until Gessler wasn't looking, off guard, at which point Dakota would slip forward and plant a great smacker on Gessler's shoulder. 'I kiss you on da shoulder Jwack Gessler yeas I do kiss you yas I do.'

By the time Gessler lined up for a swing Dakota would be safe out of range and Gessler would spin in circles, yelling and cussing, often as not clocking some other poor guy on the side of the head. 'You just get away from me, Dakota Slide,' he would squeal. 'Get away, you hear? Or I'll tell your counsellor, you hear. You hear me, Dakota Slide? I ain't afraid. I'll go right up there and tell your counsellor. I ain't afraid.' Problem was, Dakota's counsellor thought it was the funniest thing he'd seen in ages. Dakota's counsellor was having a whale of a time.

By the time I turned my attention back to the diving area Mitchel was already running down the board. Joe saw him the same time I did.

'Mitchel! Don't you dare!'

It was too late. Mitchel couldn't have stopped even had he wanted to. His contorted body flew against the air, taught and twisted, turning slowly like a underfed chicken on a spit

It was his hunch that slammed into the water first, echoed right around the pool. Kirk, the lifeguard, didn't so much as look up, too busy looking up Claire.

Mitchel surfaced, spluttering and coughing. Even with a lifejacket he could barely manage to keep his head above water. Joe rushed to the side of the pool, ready to jump in. But Mitchel started to swim to the ladder, thrashing from side to side, clawing his way stubbornly through the water, his face screwed in angry determination. I pulled Joe back. 'Let him have a go.' His head half out of the water, slowly sinking all the while, Mitchel reached up for the ladder. 'Come on Mitch. Reach out a little further.' He reached, the veins in his neck twisting with exertion. He missed and fell back into the water. Slipping under. Joe made to dive in. I held him. 'Let him try on his own.'

'He'll drown, Ben.'

'No he won't. Let him try.'

Mitchel took a while to come to the surface, kicking and flapping like a fish starved of oxygen. He tried hard to steady himself, reaching out again. But it just slipped from his grasp. 'Again Mitchel. Try again.' This time he grabbed hold, hauling himself up on to the first step, where he rested, gasping for breath.

'You want some help?' Joe held out his hand.

Mitchel ignored it, just started heaving that damn crippled body of his after him, pulling it up, swearing under his breath, yanking on his good arm until you could hear the muscles ripping. 'Come on. That's it. Come on.' The withered side fought him hard, stubbornly refusing to move, holding him down. But Mitch wouldn't give in. He pulled harder, biting his lip until it bled. Eyes shut, spittle running down his chin, his braces grinding. One more step.

And he was up.

He made it. Right to the top. All alone. Triumphant. Never has there been a greater smile. Panting for breath, he tried to wink at Joe and me, then collapsed at the side of the pool, cutting himself up on the concrete.

I carried him to the first aid post, his heart ricocheting against his ribs, echoing mine. He sat proud whilst he was cleaned up, cream and plasters pasted all over. I took him over to the shade, were Joshua awaited him with uncharacteristic sensitivity and admiration. 'Well, you know, Client Matchel, I think what you went and did out there was a fine thing. Well, you know, I always said you was a mighty fine young man, well now didn't I? Mighty fine!' Mitch lapped it up.

Thomas scored a victory in his campaign against Kolchak. He'd managed to convince some health inspector to come out and pay Veda a visit, hassled the department so much I think they agreed just to get the earnest German off their backs. The guy was due to come on Parents' Day. Thomas drew up a long list of points, itemising incidents of sub-standard practices on Veda. Then he ran round like a blue-arsed fly, trying to organise a delegation to see the inspector. He even asked me. I was shocked. It was hard to hold a normal conversation again after all this time, but I managed politely to decline without dribbling, flapping, or slapping myself too much. I didn't want to get involved. The last thing I needed now was to provoke the wrath of the Kommandant. Besides, Parents' Day was racing round the corner, I had too much to do.

I was excited at the prospect of finding out that my patients had parents. It wasn't obvious at first: families, homes, uncles and all that; like we come from, you and me. I didn't think about it that way before.

After our breakthrough with Dakota, Joe and I discovered a veritable wealth of lunatic assets. A landslide of talents was unleashed, fast and furious. I swear, it was just like cracking a code.

William could shoot a basket from the halfway line of the basketball court. He stood there, the ball between his hands, hands behind his head and flung the thing forward, powered it straight to the net. Clean in everytime. Then there was Charlie and his literary output. He'd pissed his bed so heavily one night we had to take the mattress out to air. That's when we found them, under the mattress: piles and piles of papers, all with Charlie's name on. He'd been copying out excerpts from the adverts at the back of Mitchel's wrestling fanzines.

Mud WReztLinG VIXEnz

God knows when he did it. I didn't even know he could hold a pencil.

Dakota and laundry was another one that took us by surprise. We knew Dakota had a thing about laundry, he used to prattle on about how many bags each bunk sent out to the laundromat in New Paltz and how many came back (rarely the same number). What we didn't know was that he'd developed a fully fledged obsession, become a sort of laundryholic. Everytime the yellow truck trundled back from New Paltz with a fresh consignment, Dakota would become agitated, aching to charge down and greet it. We always managed to keep him in the bunk, usually by sitting on him. But one time, when Herbert swerved the laden truck dangerously through the gates, almost knocking down blind Billy from B2, Dakota slipped our hold, burst through the door, smashing the window, and ran screaming down the hill to meet the laundry at the HCs.

He soon returned carrying the four bags of skidmarked clothes we'd sent out the previous week. Then, like a famished shark at feeding frenzy, he ripped them open and started identifying each item of clothing.

'Willy Hunt yeas it is Willy's yeas...' he screamed with terrifying excitement, his ears twitching, holding up a T-shirt. 'Joshwa this is Joshwa yas...' he shook a pair of supposedly clean underpants under my desensitised nose. He went through all the bags in the same way, brandishing clothes in a fever pitch of laundry paradise, identifying everything: trousers with no name, shirts with no distinguishing feature, even odd socks. If I could have mass produced Dakota Slide and sold him to all those households like my mother's where odd socks breed like rabbits, I'd have made a bloody fortune.

Veda underwent a transformation for Parents' Day. The place was unrecognisable. Norma brandished the whip and we scurried to our tasks. Wood was painted, toilets were repaired, windows fixed, nets put up on the tennis courts, cracks filled in, boxes and boxes of expensive sports equipment appeared from nowhere, even a line of young trees was planted, adorning the edge of the path. Thomas raged about the hypocrisy of it all. Kolchak was conning the parents, making sure the fees kept flowing. Still, ethical or not, it was wonderful to flush a shit down the loo for once without it backing up.

Kolchak was a sly one, no question about that. The health inspector came, as promised. But it was a fix from the start. Thomas wasn't allowed near him. He spent most of his brief visit having coffee with the Kommandant in High Command. Even then, he was only shown around the bits of Veda that had been spruced up for the parents. Nor was it any coincidence that he'd come on Parents' Day itself, the only time during the whole season when Veda was even vaguely presentable. He was well and truly in Kolchak's pocket. Fergus ran a sweepstake on how much it took Kolchak to pay him off.

Thomas was furious. Said he intended to expose Kolchak in front of all the parents. Of course, he never got the chance. The institutionals were being sent on a day trip to Lake Takarnac to keep them out of sight. Wouldn't do to have the severely disturbed dribbling all over the place. After all, Veda didn't accept them, did it, they didn't get past the pre-season screening. Thomas unexpectedly found himself on the list for the trip even though he didn't work on the higher level. Just so happened that Kolchak had mistakenly given one of the nurses the day off (oops) and Norma said they needed Thomas's medical experience at the lake.

With him out the way, Kolchak had nothing to worry about. We wouldn't stir up trouble. Season was halfway over and we were all too concerned about receiving our paycheques at the end. Still, just to be sure, she gave us a little pep talk before opening the gates to the waiting parents. She said the place looked marvellous and thanked us all for our hard, hard work. This was a *special* day. Veda was a *special* place. We were all *special* people. *Very* special people. Then she told us that the day could sometimes be hectic. The parents could be tiring, 'Naturally concerned about their little ones whom they have not seen for a very long time. It is up to you to allay their fears and ensure they don't worry excessively.' We were not about to go spoiling their day by giving them any 'unnecessary' details of Veda or their children's behaviour, were we? She fixed us a sweet stare, making sure we got her drift, then added, 'If any parents are too difficult for you, simply ask them to come and see me'. She lingered a while, silently daring us to step out of line. Then, when she was quite sure that we were all too yellow and spineless, the gates were opened and the flood issued forth.

It was like Harrods at 9 a.m. on the first day of the sales. There were obese, heavily made up aunties; thin, life-beaten uncles; mothers embarrassing husbands with their enthusiasm; husbands embarrassing mothers with their manners; bored brothers with pocket computer games, zapping the universe to smithereens; gum-chewing, pom-pom toting sisters. Shouts of greeting, cries of joy, tears of anger, squeals of pain, steaming, overheating patients.

Not all B8's parents were coming. William's wrote to say they wouldn't be making the trip from California, too far. Not that William seemed to give a damn. I braced him for the news, promising extra canteen as compensation. But when I told him he looked at me, confused, as if to say 'Parents? What parents?'

Joshua, on the other had, seemed a little more upset. His foster dad phoned, said he wouldn't be making the trip from the Bronx, then hung up. 'Well that's okay Counsellor Benjuman,' Joshua said when I told him. 'I expect they'll be going off to Block Island. Well, you know, they usually go off to Block Island this time of year, they say it's nice this time of year, well yes, and I think it is and, you know, they can go if they want, they probably need the rest,' then he broke off, a solitary tear creeping up from behind. I put out a hand to comfort him and told him not to cry. 'Cry? Cry?' he chuckled. 'Now Counsellor Benjuman, why do you think I would go and do a thing like that?'

Robert's parents were the first to arrive. His father stepped up and stuck out his hand stiffly, two prissily dressed girls giggling behind.

'And how do *you* do? My name is Booker George Adams. I am Robert Booker Adams' father.' (Shake hands. Stiff back. Hoity sniff.) 'This is his mother and his grandmothers. And these are his sisters.'

The two girls curtsied politely. 'How do you do?' they chirped in unison.

'And how is my son?' Robert's father was an enormous man, hands like baseball gloves. He had a high starched collar, a wide purple tie and a heavy woollen waistcoat. It was close on thirty degrees but not a drop of sweat soiled Mr Adams' brow. Robert, head down, shuffled over behind Joe and held on tight to his trousers, hiding.

A long, hot, sticky embarrassed silence followed.

'Robert Booker Adams!' his father boomed. 'You come over here this instant and say hello to your mother.'

The boy complied with a meekness which, even for him, was surprising, placing a punctilious kiss on his mother's cheek.

'Now I hope you've been behaving yourself.'

'Yes, Daddy,' said Robert, still not looking up. 'I have.'

'And not causing these two fine young counsellors here any problems.'

'No, Daddy. I have not.'

The man turned to us. He picked something out of his hairy ears and frowned. 'Well?' he said.

'Well, what?' Joe answered.

'Has he or has he not been behaving himself?'

Joe laughed. He couldn't take this guy for real. 'Yes. Yes, of course he has.'

One of the grandmothers stepped forward and started pulling Robert about; tugging at his clothes, rummaging through his hair, running her hands up and down his arms and legs. God knows what she expected to find.

Then the other grandmother pulled Booker George Adams' arm, seeking some sort of permission. The father nodded (once) and she came over to us with short, crooked steps.

'I see the rash on Robert Booker's arm has got worse.'

'Rash?' Joe said, surprised. We didn't even know Robert had a rash.

'Yes. Rash,' she repeated, mouthing the word clearly.

'Oh, that'll be the heat I expect,' I said, with excess politeness.

'And the gaps between Robert Booker's teeth.'

'Yes?'

'They've got food in them.'

'Ah, well I think you'll find that's because his toothbrush is missing some hairs. You know, just along the side. We tried putting them back in, but...'

'You have to brush his teeth four times a day.'

'Oh we do, we do. Sometimes five. Isn't that right, Joe?'

'Yes, absolutely Benjamin. Sometimes six.'

'And Robert Booker's ears.'

'His ears?'

'Too much wax.'

'Too much wax!'

'Has she checked his penis too?' I'm not sure if she heard Joe's aside. But if she did she didn't show it, the taut smile on her face remaining firmly in place.

It was over an hour before Joe and I managed to escape the Adams family. They demanded a thorough report on everything. His writing, his swimming, his toileting, his sleeping... They asked so many questions they clean forgot to talk to Robert. He just followed them around, in silence, eyes lowered. Though his father did shout at him. Once. When he got some mud on his carefully polished Sunday shoes they'd brought especially for him to wear for the day.

Charlie's family arrived, rescuing us with a boisterous welcome, homemade chocolate brownies and hugs all round. Mother, brother and granny. They came all the way from Denver, Colorado, just to see their little boy. Charlie didn't stop beaming all day, I thought the wind was going to change and his face get stuck. They stuffed us with brownies and fed us with laughter. Charlie won the boys' swimming race and then gave the medal to his mother. She burst into tears, excusing herself for being so sentimental. Joe laughed manfully, saying he understood, then turned away. I think he was hiding a tear.

When Cathy arrived, her son underwent an immediate transition. There was no loose nodding of the head, no bandy knees, no dragging feet. Walter walked tall and, well, almost normally. Every time he threatened to fall back into his sloppy habits she'd bawl him out in a good-natured way. 'Ya gotta be hard on them,' she explained in her heavy New Jersey drawl. 'It's for their own good. Pick ya feet up, Walt!' she yelled, correcting a physical defect with the power of her voice.

Later, when she was on the loo, I tried it too. Walter sat on his bed nodding uncontrollably. 'Walt!' I yelled. 'Stop nodding.' It worked. He kept his head perfectly still, grinning at his forgetfulness.

Mitchel's mother was two hours late. By the time she finally hurried across the basketball court, flushed, muttering excuses, Mitch was already seeing red, cussing and swearing.

'I don't want to hear it!' he screamed, even before she'd opened her mouth. 'It's that fucking Steve. I know why you're late. It's that fucking bastard Steve.'

'Honey,' she said nervously. 'No. The traffic was awful and...' she reached out a hand, trying to calm him.

'Don't you touch me!'

She looked around, saw Joe and me watching, and started mumbling. 'Hi, I'm Geena. Mitchel's mother.' It was almost an apology.

Mitchel didn't let up on the poor woman all afternoon. I was surprised she'd come at all. I wouldn't have. Steve was her boyfriend, Geena explained, trying to justify something. Mitch and he didn't get along. Mitch's father had left shortly after he was born, said he couldn't stand having a cripple for a son. Said he was going to find a woman who'd give him a real man. She told us every last detail, dragging on one cigarette after another, whilst Mitch dragged alongside. Geena looked haggard, like life and she were in permanent opposition, wearing each other down. Mitchel had received compensation for the doctor's mistake with the forceps, the culmination of a ten-year legal fight. Won millions. He wasn't so bad before that. It was only afterwards that he became so difficult. Kept saying it was his money and that if she wanted any of it, she'd have to do just what he said. She'd tried to keep him from knowing, storing the money in trust. But one day a kid at school read a news report about the award and told Mitch. It'd been living hell ever since.

Dakota Slide was a gold mine of information. Only on Parents' Day was the full extent of this talent revealed. His father was clearly a Slide, the malproportioned nose and mouth left no doubt about that. He towered over his son, re-asking him the questions Dakota had already asked. Dakota knew the entire line up of the New York Mets and their playing schedule, both home and away. His father managed to silence him for a while by giving him a television guide whilst he asked us about Dakota's progress at Veda. But Dakota soon consumed the guide and the string of questions began to stream out. Every channel, every time slot, every date of the week; he'd memorised the lot. His father didn't bat an eyelid, just carried on his conversation with Joe and me whilst asking his son the questions he'd previously asked. This was the only form of family communication we saw. Dakota didn't seem particularly excited about his father's arrival, simply launched into his first question.

'Who starts for da Mets next season who who?'

'Who, Dakota?'

'Daral Mayleberry.'

'Hi, I'm Dakota's father. Richard.'

'Who play first base yeas who play first?'

'Who, Dakota?'

'Short Spa Siddleberg.'

'Do I get a hug, Dak, or have I drove all the way up here to discuss the Mets line up?

'When da Mets play first game when when?'

'Give me a hug and I'll ask you.' Dakota shook his fist angrily, then extended his arm briefly around his father, barely touching him.

'When when?' he repeated, his side of the bargain complete.

'When, Dakota?'

'Weddsday sifth april yerz da sifth.'

The day went off without any major disasters. Except for one mother who found a dead racoon down by the rubbish area and withdrew her daughter from Veda, demanding the fees back. Kolchak refused. They had a slagging match, Kolchak calm and quiet as ever, unnerving her opponent. The woman was no match for the Kommandant.

She lost her rag, screamed, resorted to personal abuse (parents standing around, 'tsk-tsking') then jumped into her beige Merc and screeched out of the car park, bawling 'I'll see you in court, Kolchak!' from the window.

'Just a spot of family trouble,' Kolchak told the bemused parents who were looking on. 'Poor Gillie, we've tried to do our best for her.' The parents nodded in sympathy. (Fancy that nasty woman picking on such a sweet old dear.)

The girls' swimming race turned into a free-for-all when Serina, an inmate of G6 whose only disability seemed to be a permanently foul temper, refused to accept defeat, pushing Grace, the victor, in the deep end along with her sister for good measure. Patients followed the lead. Joey pushed Michael. Steven pushed Joey. Bert pushed Steven. And Bert pushed Steven's dad in. By the time the lifeguard raced round the pool to sort out the carnage, several parents were climbing up the ladder wringing out their shirts.

The talent show went like a dream. They loved Dorothy. She sung four encores of 'Over The Rainbow' and was going on for a fifth when she slipped and ripped her dress, exposing her backside. Christine, a high-functioning little snot from G1, spoilt rotten, made a great Sleeping Beauty, except she kept waking up before Prince Charming arrived, moaning about him keeping her waiting. Then, when he finally did kiss her, she ran of the stage coughing and spitting, shouting 'Yeuck! Ugh! He put his tongue in. He put his tongue in!' Snow White went off without a hitch, if you ignored the sixteen dwarfs, and the fact that Snow White had to be poisoned by a Snickers Bar as she was allergic to fruit. All in all, the parents loved it.

Time for goodbyes.

Mitchel cussed his mom more or less the whole afternoon. Joe blew his top, yelling at him to shut the hell up. It was a risky thing to with a mother around; parents can get touchy when you start badmouthing their offspring. Still, Geena seemed grateful. Even went as far as saying she wished Mitch got a bit more male discipline. Mitchel burst into tears, blubbering that he didn't want his mom to leave. He missed her too much. She kissed him, allowed a brief hug and seemed relieved when she could get away.

The Adams family's farewell was as forced and unnatural as their arrival had been. Robert kissed every one in turn, screwing up his eyes and puckering his lips with the air of a martyr. Once they left he brightened up no end, came bounding back to us and started wrestling with Charlie and his brother.

'Take it easy there, Robert,' Joe said after first blood had flowed.

Robert came over, biting his lip, staring at the grass. He tugged at Joe's trousers. 'Please,' he spoke softly, almost afraid. 'Will you call me Book?'

'We'll call you whatever you like. But why?'

Book managed the corner of a smile. ' 'Cause my daddy calls me Robert, he calls me Booker, he calls me Robert Booker, but he never, never calls me Book.'

So Book it was.

Richard Slide was the last to leave. He hadn't stuck around Veda. He'd taken his son off in the morning. They'd gone to watch a little league baseball game over in Madingdale. Dakota had memorised the line up of both teams and the complete list of Baskin-Robbins 32 ice-cream flavours, plus added extras at ten cents a throw. Wouldn't stop asking questions about them. In between asking them right back, his father thanked us for taking care of his son and said if there was anything he could do... Then he walked over to his car, trying to hold Dakota's hand. But Dakota wasn't interested in anything beyond questions.

'Dak, are you gonna give your pop a hug?'

'Who played batstop who?'

'Give me a hug, willya.'

'Who did play batstop yeas who did?'

'Hug me and I'll ask you.'

Dakota hugged his father quickly, then pulled away, waiting for the question. Richard lingered a while longer, his arms outstretched, as though longing for just one real father-to-son embrace. But Dakota wasn't giving.

'Love you, kid,' said his dad.

'Who did play batstop who?'

'Who?'

'Wobbie Barnes.'

Richard walked to his car alone. He started it up and disappeared through Veda's gates without looking back.

Dakota turned and stumbled back up the path.

'What we have fur dinner tonight what what...'

21

'Walter! What the hell are you doing now?'

Cheap, broken Bic razors littered the bathroom floor, water gushing through the overflow, shaving foam smeared down the shower cabinet. And in the middle, Walter. Walter with tiny pieces of toilet-paper dotted around the side of his head, soaking up the blood trickling from the cuts.

Walter was shaving.

Walter couldn't shave.

Walter wasn't trying to shave his stubble, of which he had none, and which he couldn't shave even if he had. Walter was shaving the sides of his head.

Ever since his mother had openly admired Joe's mohican on Parents' Day Walter hadn't stopped touching it, asking 'I?'. He was absorbed, wouldn't leave the thing alone. Joe didn't like having his head poked and stroked, not by Walter anyway. So he told him to go get one of his own and leave him be.

And here was Walter, standing in the bathroom slicing his ears, taking Joe at his word.

Joe took him down the infirmary to get him bandaged up, called him an idiot. Poor Walt was confused. Joe said he shouldn't take everything so bloody literally.

'If I told you to stick your head in an oven, would you do it?'

Walter nodded.

That was the day Thomas quit. He huffed and he puffed his way out of Veda, swearing Kolchak hadn't heard the last of him. He vowed to take the matter up with the German Embassy first thing the very next day. *Mein Gott*, he'd be back!

We never saw him again.

Parents' Day receded into memory and Veda returned to its run-down self. The toilets stopped flushing, as if by command. The boxes of sports equipment vanished. No one even so much as mentioned it. You just went to the store-room one day and the boxes had gone, replaced by the old deflated basketballs and split plastic baseball bats. The tennis nets stayed up, however, although there weren't any rackets to play with. The unscheduled inactivity of the activity schedule got under way and the normal routine of chaotic abnormality was quickly re-established.

The Adams family visit, or more particularly their departure, brought Book to life. He came charging out of his mental slumber, bouncing into position as the bunk's most boisterous inmate. Any time there was trouble, Book was there. He wouldn't actually get involved. He was too smart for that. He just lingered on the sidelines, egging on whoever needed egging on in order to do whatever it was they shouldn't have been doing. He'd encourage Dakota to go annoy Mitchel. Then he'd sneak over and encourage William to hit Dakota. The more Dakota annoyed Mitch, the more Willy hit him and the more this spurred Dakota on to annoy Mitch.

Book had taken a distinct liking to Charlie. Increasingly, wrenching my eyelids open in the mornings, I'd find Book lying in Charlie's bed shuffling cards under the covers. Whenever we bawled him out he went all silent, like he was when he first arrived at Veda; saying nothing and eating less. He'd withdraw into his cocoon until Joe or I would tell him that we weren't angry anymore. Then he'd be back to his new self. Larking around, causing trouble, sleeping with Charlie and we'd have to bawl him out again. As for Charlie, he spent most of his time copying from Mitchel's magazines. He'd sit at the table, head tilted, tongue sticking out, humming to himself, transcribing

Slut WHoReS in AngrY Action

with utmost care and precision, letters rampaging off the page and onto the floor. He took to displaying his handiwork all over the bunk. You'd wake up in the morning to find yourself smothered in 'hot vixen bitches'.

Pillow-fights started around this time. It wasn't an intentional addition to the schedule. It was Mitchel who introduced it, as an anti-Joshua device. Joshua would sit on his bed, bugging Mitch as he'd always done. Mitch would swing for him every now and then, but he could never score a hit: Josh was always out of reach. The half of Mitchel's body which didn't work slowed him down, so by the time Mitch was up and in fighting position, Joshua had bolted for the porch. Mitch had to do some thinking. How to extend his range? I guess it came to him one night when he was pummelling his pillow in his customary anger and frustration. The pillow!

In bed that night Mitchel tried it out. I saw the thing go swinging through the air, smack in the middle of Joshua's unsuspecting face. Perfect reach. All hell broke lose. Josh grabbed his pillow and started pounding Mitch. Then William grabbed his. 'Here I come! Uba uba uba! Ya momma's a Cadillac!' he yelled as he charged into battle, his secret weapon wrapped tight in a Thunderbirds pillow-case. I think Walter was the next to pile in, though I lost count after that. Joe and I tried to restore order. But it was no use. The loonies were out of control. So we grabbed our pillows and joined in.

The fight lasted at least an hour and we only had one nose bleed. We had such a laugh that we decided to add it to the schedule on a regular basis. Joe wrote it on the noticeboard: "6.30 – 7.30 p.m. Pillow-fight". Mitchel wasn't half handy with a pillow, made up for his bad arm. He'd swing the thing so fast you didn't see it coming. You wouldn't even know he was near and BAM! he'd catch you upside the head. Willy and Charlie were pretty nifty too. Dakota was the only one who didn't join the fun. He got scared. He'd sit on the toilet picking his nose and asking us all to stop.

'...na I don't like I don't like da pillow na I don't like...'

We built up a pillow-fighting élite and started challenging the other bunks. Crippled bodies were mercilessly beaten. Then up they'd jump and give as good as they got. Retards ran amok with feather coshes. Some of the counsellors complained it wasn't good for the patients. Joe said they'd lost so many brain cells that a few more wouldn't make any difference. Besides, our boys were having the time of their lives. This beat academics any day of the week. Screw Special Ed, this was summer. Norma got wind of what was going on and tried stopping it. But it was too late. The mentally sick pillow-fighting fad, a kind of Special Olympics, spread like a forest fire.

TT: Thump therapy, that's what Joe called it. He swore it had a positive effect on our boys. Joshua didn't bug Mitchel half as much as before; he'd just wait until 6.30 p.m. came round and beat the shit out of him. Mitchel's whining eased off as well. He'd go into pillow frenzy for an hour, gnashing like a rabid dog. Then for the rest of the time he'd calm down, actually turned into quite a pleasant guy. No more squealing, ranting or cussing. He even made it through a whole phone call to his mom without swearing once. Not only did our boys turn into wizard pillow-fighters, they started to act like normal human beings into the bargain.

We expanded the idea behind thump therapy and increasingly started to do our own thing, following a customised schedule. We more or less gave up on activities like sewing and music. We kept going to cookery because we always got something to eat. And Joe voted to keep up with academics because he was still fascinated by Claire's gazzumbas. But we swam more, played baseball and went for treks in the woods. The boys seemed happy enough. Dakota was the only one who was put out. The first time we didn't follow the set schedule he flipped out, screaming and yelling. 'Stts's not on da sscedule nuh nuh ssnot...' he gulped between tears, refusing point-blank to move from the bunk. Joe had to write out an alternative schedule on official Veda paper and post it up for him to learn. Once he'd learnt it, he'd come with us. Our activities were restricted by this slaving to routine. We'd have to decide on everything in advance, couldn't do anything on the spur of the moment. Still, we got used to it and it seemed a small price to pay to stop Dakota slapping himself black and blue.

Films were the favourite activity on our homemade schedule. We'd sneak into the cottage when we were supposed to do sewing. Victoria, the sewing counsellor, had a key to the video-room and she was happy to let us in. She was more fed up with sewing than we were and jumped at the chance to veg out in front of the telly. Veda only had two videos: *The Karate Kid* and *Grease*. Not that it mattered. Our boys watched them over and over and over again. If they noticed, they never said anything. The only problem was bringing them back afterwards. All of them except Dakota and Book would take on characters from the films, step inside them. Walter stopped answering to his name. We had to call him Danny from the T-Birds for a whole week. He wasn't play acting either. He *was* Danny. Dressed like him. Walked like him, or tried to. Flapped like him. Most of the time we went along with it. Though things got a little too serious one day whilst we were playing basketball, William chopped Book across the throat with a mighty HI YA! Book wouldn't stop choking. Gave us one hell of a fright. Thought he was on his way out. We tried telling Willy off. But he couldn't see what he'd done wrong. He was the Karate Kid. Why shouldn't he give someone a throat chop? The Karate Kid never apologised. William only snapped out of it after Joe had pinned him to the ground, forcing him to surrender his title by admitting he wasn't the best karate fighter in the bunk. Film fucked up our boys more than anything else. They escaped from one reality to another to another. No wonder they were confused.

I didn't believe it when Joe told me. I had to go hear it from Ellen. B8 were going on a trip to the Catskill Game Farm with some other bunks from the lower level. It was our first trip. The first time we'd taken the patients off Veda's grounds. Out into the big bad world. I was looking forward to it. It would be good to get out, see some animals. That was until Joe told me. It was his day off. Ellen said she was sorry, but she had no one else to help out with B8. All the other floaters were tied up. She had no choice. It would have to be her.

'Who?' I asked, bewildered at Ellen's embarrassment.

'Gabrielle.'

I raced back to the bunk, tried convincing Joe to take a different day off.

'Please. Not her. I can't face that.'

'Ben, I can't. I'm sorry. Me and Claudia have got tickets to see The Pogues in New York. They cost a packet. We won't get our money back. I'd like to help you out, really I would. You'll be fine. Just ignore her.'

I tried to get B8 taken off the list of bunks going on the trip. If we stayed at Veda I'd be allowed to cope with the boys on my own, wouldn't be required to have a floater. Kolchak refused. Said the parents had already paid for the trip. They had to go.

Friendship and passion don't mix: two emotions separated by an impenetrable frontier. And that's as it should be. You lust after someone, loving them with passion, it's just possible you may be able to be their friend. If you can, so much the better. But there needs to be a driving force: either passion or friendship. One must outweigh the other in order to define the relationship. Passion where there is only friendship or, worse, merely friendship where there is desire, leads to misery.

From the moment I first saw her on that garage forecourt in Madingdale, standing in the bright sunshine, desire and Gabrielle had been but two words for the same thing. My longing hadn't gone away, there wasn't a moment when I wasn't painfully aware of it. But for my own good I'd managed to subdue it, box it away. And now she was to be paraded before me. So close; out of reach. No doubt she'd want to be friends. ('I hope we can still be friends.' How many relationships fizzle out in such pathetic words, no more than a selfish attempt to ease the speaker's conscience.)

I didn't want to be Gabrielle's friend; I wanted to be her lover. I wanted to be Lucien's friend, his spiritual lover. And now I had neither. Worse, I had to suffer Gabrielle's company: the memory of Lucien and the untouchable presence of her.

As it turned out there was one extra place on the bus. Ellen said I could have it, choose one other person to come along, said she thought another counsellor might make things easier on me, a sort of consolation. She was kind to me, Ellen. She thought I'd had a hard time, told Joe she didn't agree with the way they'd treated me. I thanked her, and chose Louis. At least that would ease my fear of being alone with Gabrielle.

Louis should've left Veda weeks ago. He came with Institutional Group B. And they went back to their institution before Parents' Day. The only reason Louis was still around was because they'd screwed up his paperwork and the institution had given his bed to someone else. They had no place for him and asked Kolchak if he could stay at Veda until they'd sorted it out. So I took Louis. And Gabrielle came along for the ride.

Bouncing from one pothole to the next in the stifling heat, we wound our way along the neverending Catskill back roads in one of those American school buses, the kind Charlie Brown rides in. The driver must have sat for hours, poring over a map, figuring out the most uncomfortable route we could take. (*'Yeah, this one should make 'em feel sick all right.'*) I don't know who designed those damn buses, but whoever it was had one hell of a sadistic streak. The suspension dates back to the days before the spring, and the cramped sticky black seats are shoved so close together you can smell the body odour of the guy three rows in front. Someone told me they were designed specifically to prevent kids from doing their neglected homework on the way to school. Two hours of being thrown around in that yellow tin can and I was a wreck. No wonder Charlie Brown's neurotic.

I thought I'd conquered my feelings pretty well, showed them who's boss, put them in their place. But they'd been there all along, biding their time, lurking, just waiting for the right moment. And on the day of the trip they lined up, standing tall, and presented themselves to me, one by one.

Simply seeing Gabrielle again was hard. Stubborn emotion forced its way out of the box in which I'd locked it. I felt the wood splitting in my stomach, hinges shattering, splintering my insides.

I wanted her. And the more I wanted her, the more I missed Lucien. I missed the way he saw things, his sensitivities exposed red raw, his sadness making everything somehow more beautiful. Time slowed around Lucien. It was addictive; a longing to be confused, to feel a burden, to be touched, to be one on whom not even the slightest moment of life, however insignificant, is wasted.

I looked at Gabrielle and thought of what I'd lost.

He would have been fascinated by the things Joe and I had found out about our patients; would have filled his entire notebook in one go. It's not that I didn't want him back, but I kept telling myself it was he who'd made the break. Over and over again I repeated that, trying to make myself feel a little better. He'd made the break. He'd have to come to me. He'd have to come to me... Principles obstructing happiness.

Gabrielle took a seat at the front. There was spare place next to her. I shuffled past as quickly as possible (eyes down) and took a seat at the back next to Louis. He didn't speak throughout the whole journey, just stared out the window at the low leafy branches as they rattled against the bus. He was looking a little worn. His eyes weren't as bright and he'd developed some sort of rash on his face from where he kept rubbing his cheek whilst he stood for hours upon hours of silent statutery in that triangle in the midst of the higher level.

We arrived at the Game Farm with a violent swing into the dusty car park, coming to a halt inches from a towering pine with a jerk that catapulted me into the seat in front. My nose brushed the stubbly side of Walter's head, the potent aftershave he'd slapped all around his ears making me sneeze.

Norma bustled her bulk to the front of the bus and, while sweat oozed from forty excited armpits, gave a tedious speech on decorum. 'Remember! You are representing Veda. I expect you to conduct yourselves accordingly.' Conduct ourselves accordingly. We were a bloody loonie bin for Christ's sake!

I grabbed the tickets, rounded up my little diplomatic corps and we were let loose.

Gabrielle asked me what she should do. She felt uncomfortable, I could see that. She probably didn't like this situation any more than I did. I told her just to make sure B8 stuck together and to keep an eye on Dakota as he had a habit of wandering off. Then I took Mitchel's hand and we hobbled up to the main gates. In the end I needn't have worried about Dak. We found him a visitor's guide with a schedule of the animals feeding times. So it was just like being back at Veda.

'When they feed da zebwas when when?'

'When, Dakota?'

'At four yeas at four why?'

Why? Why! This was a new one on me.

'Why, Dak?'

'Cause they do.'

Well, what kind of answer did you expect?

Louis wasn't happy about something. He was agitated, kept biting his lip. I thought twice about speaking to him, what with Gabrielle around. But if she knew he was classified as a non-verbal, she didn't show any surprise when he answered my question.

'What's up Louis? Something the matter?'

'Well I just don't know,' he sighed, scratching his rash. 'All these people out here, kinda gets to me. Everywhere. People. They just gonna go staring and staring. Always the damn same. Whenever we come outside. People. There they are. Standing around. Lots of them. Staring. Like they got nothing better to do. Like staring's the only thing that matters. Kinda gets me pissed. I just don't know.'

'Don't worry, Louis. They're not going to do that here. They'll be considerate, you'll see.'

We went through the gates: Mitchel kicking up the dust; Walter dribbling, nodding uncontrollably; Dakota hiding behind Gabrielle; William uba-ubaing; Joshua on tip-toe, flapping like I'd never seen; Charlie and Book clinging to each other, afraid to let go.

Never have I met so many eyes. Every single pupil was directed our way. Every face. Even the animals seemed to be gawping at us from their cages. Louis was right, they stared. And stared. Eyes following every awkward step we took. I was right too: they were considerate. That was the problem. Too considerate. Everywhere we went people stepped aside as if we were some kind of funeral cortège, suspending their enjoyment out of charitable sympathy. I began to feel a little abnormal myself, watching my movements for signs I'd picked up the patients' habits. Wasn't I dragging my feet just slightly? Could that be a globule of spittle running down my chin?

I looked around at each of my boys. Staring at them. Mitchel's leg was more acutely contorted. Charlie's face was flatter. Book's eyes more absent. Joshua's skin dirtier. William chewed his tongue, I'd never noticed that before. They didn't stare back at the eyes fixed on their every movement. Not one of them. A few gazed at the dirt track we were following, the others looked at me. All except Louis. He stumbled along behind, muttering humbly, shooting out the odd angry glance. No trees to hide behind, just open space and dust. Colourful tropical birds on the left. Some type of mountain goat on the right, almost extinct. And us in the middle. Animals everywhere. But we didn't stop to look at them. Just carried straight on, trying to slide through the park as inconspicuously as possible.

'Shit.' Louis whispered it at first. I only caught the tail end of it. 'Shit,' he mumbled. 'Well I just don't...'

Then it came, the explosion. I'd never have thought he had it in him. Not like that. Louis span round and roared. Howled. Squawked.

'SHIT! What you starring at? YA DAMN DIRTY FUCKS.' He took off, charging all over the damn place, waving his arms, clapping like he was trying to frighten away a flock of birds. 'Go on. Go on. Get the hell outa here!' The onlookers stepped back a little, averting their eyes, trying to pretend they weren't really watching. Embarrassed. But they didn't leave. They didn't want to miss out on the show. Louis ran crazy, brimming with pent-up rage. Waving. Hollering. Wailing. Kicking up dust. 'This ain't part of the goddam zoo. Shit! Go watch the animals, ya damn fucks.'

A little boy in the crowd started to cry, bawling his eyes out. His mother yelled at me. 'Hey! You're in charge. Control the crazy little...' she hesitated, unsure what to call Louis. 'Control him, willya!'

'Ain't no zoo. Ain't no zoo.' William echoed, beating his chest like a gorilla. He thought it was hilarious. 'Ain't no mutherfucking zoo! No no no no!'

I called to Louis. Told him to calm down and come back. He told me to go fuck myself. So I took my boys and hurried on.

'Should we be leaving him?' Gabrielle rushed along behind.

'He's old enough to look after himself.'

'I don't think we should be leaving him.'

'Fine! You stay and look after him. Who asked you anyway?'

'He shouldn't be left alone,' Gabrielle repeated. 'He can't cope.'

'Can't cope! And I suppose you know, do you. You know Louis? I know Louis. He's fine. He probably doesn't even want us around. He'll have his say and then he'll catch up. Now if you want to stay, stay! But I'm not letting these boys stand around and get gawped at like some bloody freak show!'

I felt Mitchel's hand fasten around mine. At first I thought it was a gesture of gratitude, that he was thankful to be out of there. But his nails dug too deep for that. The body seized rigid and he fell, rolling around on the ground before I could catch him.

The crowd ignored Louis and surged forward. Standing over Mitch. Looking on as he thrashed about in the dust.

'Oh my God.'

'Look at the poor thing.'

'He's in pain.'

'Hey mister! Do something, willya?'

I took off my shirt and put it under Mitchel's head, cushioning him from the hard ground. Then I took off Willy's jacket and stuck under Mitch's bare arm, trying to prevent the worst of the grazing. It wasn't a long seizure. Nothing out of the ordinary. But out here, outside Veda, it seemed so dramatic, horrifying. The crowd sure got its money's worth.

It was only when it started to subside, Mitch sucking on his tongue, that it came on, surging out of nowhere: anger. Faces pressed all around. Pitying. Hawk-eyes probing. Invading. I jumped up and yelled. I can't remember what I shouted. Or even if it made any sense. It just pissed me off. All of it. Them. People. Their liberal lines of concern. Standing around. Looking down. Fascinated. Disgusted. A little sympathy thrown in for good measure. Pissed me right off. Fuck them.

I ran. Shouted. Not at anyone in particular. I just shouted. And had there been someone in my way, I would have knocked them down: man, woman or child. But there was no one. A space cleared in front of me. Wherever I ran, people got out of the way.

Willy chased around after me. Copying me. 'Yeah! Fuck you an all, ya prostitchewees. Suck an egg ya motherfuckers! Ya pigs. Ya funky fat gorillas. Go ta Mississippi!' He scared the shit out of them.

I stopped. Stood back and watched him take over, a warm sense of pride welling up inside. Jumping around, grinning and yelling.

'Ladies and gentlemen,' I began. 'Please don't be alarmed. This is just how Patient 154 gets when he's on the verge. About to flip, you understand. Please. Please stand perfectly still, exactly where you are. He won't hurt anyone if you stand still. Any sudden movement and he may get violent.'

I wish you'd been there. You should have seen it. The crowd dispersed like a shot, ran every which way they could. Scampering and scrambling. A few seconds and there was just us on that dusty track. Lone loons. I watched them run, every last one. Willy kept bolting around, yelling, even when there was no one left to yell at. He ran over to the big cats' cage and had a good shout, roaring as the lions fled to their den.

I picked up Mitchel and brushed him down.

The dust settled. The silence came. Louis was chuckling to himself, crying. And there was Gabrielle. Standing there. Staring. At me. Smiling.

Zoos are okay. But let's face it, animals are animals. And ice-cream is ice-cream. I knew which one the boys would choose even before I made the suggestion.

Louis had lost a shoe in the hullabaloo and went off to look for it. When he came back, huffing, he was grinning from ear to ear. 'Shit, haven't had so much fun since the home burnt down. Boy were they confused. Thought I was real nuts. I had 'em going. Ya see that? Had 'em on the run. Scared yellow. Shit! That was fun.'

We found the café up by the horses compound on the hill. A charming ivy-covered restaurant with crisp white cloths shining in the sunshine and crystal wine glasses. Gabrielle said she wanted to buy everyone an ice-cream. I refused at first, didn't want anything from her. But she just told me to shut up and went ahead and ordered. Not only that, she bought super-duper-double-deluxe for all the boys. Walter took her hand and made her stroke the unsuccessfully shaved sides of his head.

B2 were sitting outside on the terrace. So we joined them. They were down the far end, the pretty side, with a view over the park. Their counsellor, Berg, said it was packed when they arrived. Not a free table in sight. So he sent Joey down there. Joey started to sing – 'I been a' working on the railroad' – scratching his balls. B2 had a table in no time. In fact they had five.

The super-duper-double-deluxe ice-creams arrived and B8's face lit up with a uniform smile, except for Dakota, who was already too busy scoffing to find time to smile, bolting down the ice-cream to be ready for the next question. Gabrielle took out her purse to pay the waitress and that's when it happened: the start of something wonderful. What I'd long hoped for, but never dared imagine. Her keys fell out on to the table.

'No no. Please put them away,' Berg jumped up in a panic. Then he looked at Joey. 'Oh no. Too late.'

Joey had a thing about keys.

He reached down and unzipped his trousers. Out it came. Large limp and dirty. Didn't stay limp for long mind. He twiddled around a bit, shuffling here and there, then up it popped and masturbation started in earnest. Not that you'd have noticed anything from Joey's face. It remained passive, his eyes fixed on the keys.

The waitress screamed and dropped her tray. Still, it took a while before she ran away. I guess she just wanted to make sure she was seeing things correctly. And then there *was* the size. I don't suppose she'd ever seen one so big. Don't suppose she ever will again. I hope not, for her sake.

An irate man hammered on the window. 'What in God's name...?' Willy grinned. Mitchel howled. Joshua reached for his groin. Charlie couldn't take his eyes off it. And Book, he just sat there egging Joey on. 'Do it do it do it.'

The red-faced manager came storming out of the restaurant, steam billowing from under his toupée. He stood stationary for a while, unable to speak. Joey increased his pace. The offending keys were taken off the table. But it was too late. Judging by the speed of Joey's hand, it would all be over soon.

'What in heaven's name is that?' the thin lipped manager finally managed to utter.

'Shit!' said Louis in genuine surprise. 'Why, it's a penis.'

That sealed it for us. Howls of laughter broke out all around, Berg sliding under the table, paralysed, Gabrielle with tears streaming down her face.

'I KNOW IT'S A PENIS, YOU MORON,' the manager screamed at

Louis. Louis seemed quite chuffed at the compliment. 'What's it doing on my terrace?' About to explode if Joey's grinding teeth were anything to go by. 'Get it out of here! Before I call security. Get it out. Out! Out!' he ranted like a lunatic. 'Now. Now. NOW!'

Berg having been rendered incapable by fits of giggles, it was left to me to redirect the errant member back home. I took the menu card and tried pushing it back into Joey's trousers. But the damn thing was too hard. So I bent back the menu and whacked the penis as hard as I could.

I think I saw a split fragment of pain register in Joey's eyes. Either way, he stopped. The thing went limp faster than a stumbling drunk fumbling to get it up. I used the menu to guide it back home and we scarpered before the manager had a chance to find out where we came from, taking our super-duper-double-deluxe ice-creams with us, of course.

22

Masturbation worked wonders. Gabrielle and I were talking again. It started slowly at first. A word as we passed in the forest. Then two. A conscious, awkward effort to establish contact. Then there'd be a smile. Tentative. Forbidden. We had Joey's penis in our heads, a point of reference, a beautiful beginning. And we built on that. Lucien was like the dead: he wasn't spoken of.

Then came D-Day. She invited me out for a drink. We stood under a tree in the dark, rain tapping on our shoulders. She wanted to take me to Dotty's. She must have known I wasn't welcome there. I told her so. 'You worry too much. They've got other things to talk about now besides you.'

I was terrified. Terrified of putting a foot wrong, of bursting this bubble of exhilaration that had unexpectedly floated my way. I remembered Poughkeepsie, my disastrous attempt to win her, her rejection, brushing me from her shoulder like a mildly irritating insect. But I agreed nonetheless.

And so we went. I scuttled through the smoky air, thick with Sinatra, to the back room whilst she went to the bar and bought the drinks. No one spoke to me. Dave was there, sitting by the jukebox, slobbering over Natasha.

Dave was exceptionally pleased with himself and made sure everyone knew it. For a week he'd been strutting round, chest out, head high, championing himself. He'd received a letter, from London, the result of a job application (up and over the interview hurdles). Successful. He'd been accepted by a firm of stockbrokers as a trader in the City. *Just what we're looking for*, that's what the letter said. Within a year, he'd be making tens of thousands, wearing fancy clothes, going to overpriced restaurants (ordering dishes with names he couldn't understand), and people would look up to him and wonder how they could be like him. He announced the good news publicly, at dinner, then stood back and accepted (with humility, of course) the flood of congratulations. Even Kolchak said how pleased she was for him, said how thoroughly he deserved it and how he should be an example to us all.

He saw me come into Dotty's and grinned. How could I have been so stupid? Some people never learn. Now was his chance. He stood up, knocking his chair over like some cowboy in a Western. He may even have spat, I'm not sure (he certainly stank). And he had a swagger, one hell of a swagger. He'd been practising. And putting on weight (a floorboard creaked in protest), there was a third chin nestling under his jawbone with the prospect of a fourth on its way.

'Well, well, well, look who's shown 'is face! Come back for more of the same 'ave we?'

No sooner had he spoken than Gabrielle grabbed him by the collar, yanked him across the bar and told him to mind his own business. He gazed at her hard, startled (a woman!). It took him a moment to figure out what had happened. He half-smiled, thinking it was a joke. So she stood hard on his toes, grinding them, and shoved him backwards. He couldn't show the pain, not in public of course, though his eyes began to water. The others in the bar hushed and turned, eagerly waiting to see what would happen. It was so quiet you could hear the muffled sounds of the baseball game playing on the faded TV set over our heads. (A cheer.) Gabrielle and Dave squared up, she was taller than him. For a moment they almost came to blows, you could see their hands itching, just longing to whip across the other's cheek. Dotty stopped wiping glasses, folded her cloth neatly, laid it across the draught tap, and watched.

Gabrielle wasn't going to back down.

Dave looked around, grinning, seeking support from his chums. (Strike One.) But no one smiled back. You could reach out and touch the embarrassment, stretch it, mould it. And in that moment Dave seemed to deflate. His shoulders slouched as (air escaping from his lungs) it dawned on him, slowly: he'd been made a fool of. Right there in public, in the bar, a man's realm, he'd been humiliated, by a girlie. (Home Run.) The fight went out of him, slinking away, ashamed. He looked to the floor, shuffled his feet and then, mumbling something about not letting the likes of me in and taking his custom elsewhere, he went back to his seat.

I didn't thank Gabrielle. It wasn't necessary. She knew.

She brought over a pitcher and we sat and talked. About Veda. I told her stories. Stories of the boys. Stories I've told you: Dakota and the laundry, the pillow fights, Walter and the mohican. I did impressions of them. I can't put them on paper. But you'd like them. Gabrielle did. She laughed. Her smile set me at ease. I relaxed. It was the first time in a long while I'd felt comfortable away from the security of my boys.

She told me the latest news on the Veda grapevine, from which I'd long been excluded. The bush was buzzing with stories of Kolchak. Gabrielle dismissed them as sick rumours at first. But someone asked Ellen and she confirmed them. Kolchak was a holocaust survivor. Her family were Russian Jews, living in Poland, and were sent to one of the camps. No one seemed sure which, though some said Auschwitz. Said that was why she never came up to the pool, didn't want anyone seeing the number tattooed on her arm. She was separated from her father. He was put to work. Her mother died. Kolchak and her sister were freed by the Allies at the end of the war. The sister was living in France somewhere, Bordeaux I think. Kolchak went with her at first, then left. She said the French were too anti-Semitic; not open about it like the Germans, but anti-Semitic all the same; on the side, underneath all that trumpeted *égalité*. So she came to America. And here she was, forty years later, running her own camp with wooden bunks and a razorwire fence. And we called her the Kommandant.

The next evening Gabrielle gave me a present. Not new, not something she'd bought, but something of hers: Rilke's *Letters To A Young Poet*. She told me I could use an injection of simplicity. She took me to The Cuckoo's Nest, sat me down, changed a few words around to suit herself, and read to me:

> *You must not be frightened if a madness rises up before you larger than any you have ever seen. You must think that something is happening with you, that life has not forgotten you, that it holds you in its hand; it will not let you fall. Why do you want to shut out of your life any agitation, any pain, any melancholy, since you really do not not know what these states are working upon you? Why do you want to persecute yourself with the question whence all this may be coming and whither it is bound? Since you know that you are in the midst of transitions and wished for nothing so much as to change.*

Gabrielle put the book down. And both our minds, with the flick of a page, turned to Lucien.

'He's never stopped speaking of you,' she told me. 'Always said that you understood him, that you cared. He really hurt at what happened.'

'What happened wasn't my fault.'

'It wasn't anyone's fault. That's the hurt. Tragedy isn't the clash of right and wrong, but of right and right.'

'Right? Was he right to do what he did? I wasn't the one who...'

'Who what?' she said, accusingly.

'Who ran off with you.'

'You make me sound like a doll.'

'You know what I mean.'

'Benjamin, this might not make any sense. Lucien didn't want me for himself. He wanted to stop you from having me. He couldn't bear that. He thought you were making a mistake. He was thinking of you. He...'

'Thinking of me! So, he's got you believing his twisted logic has he.'

'No,' Gabrielle protested. 'He hasn't got me doing anything.'

'What the hell's going on between you two? Is this some kind of ruse to twist the knife? He runs off with a girl he knows I want. Then you come along four weeks later and tell me he did it for *my* sake. Please, Gabrielle, spare me.' I got up and went to order a double whiskey. No ice.

Patrick, the bar's owner, strolled in dressed in his flying gear, looking like some sort of bewildered Biggles. He stood at the bottom of the stairs and addressed his customers with a sorrowful smile. 'Somehow,' he said to the locals (counsellors rarely showed their face in The Cuckoo's Nest), 'somehow, dreams never quite work out the way you intended.' And with that he took off his flying goggles and went up to bed.

I had another whiskey, then bought an overflowing glass of murky red wine for Gabrielle, speckles of cork floating on the surface. She sat playing with the toothpicks on the table. Building them up into a precarious pile, seeing how high she could go, then knocking them down before they collapsed. Building them up. Knocking them down.

'You don't believe me' she said, knocking over the pile, 'do you.'

'It's not that. I just don't understand why you're telling me all this.'

'Because you should know.'

'Should I?'

'Yes. Lucien needs you.'

'Well I was here for him. I didn't go anywhere. *He* choose to forsake me. And where the hell was he when I was going through all that shit over the abuse? Where was he then?'

'He felt for you. He was worried.'

'Worried! Worried! I went through hell. And he was worried. Well that's nice to know.' Some of the other customers turned around to see what all the yelling was about.

'Benjamin.' Gabrielle came closer, lowering her voice, her breath making the candle flicker. 'Lucien and I never made love.'

'I didn't ask.'

'No, I know that. But I'm telling you anyway. Lucien and I never made love.' She drank some wine, red darkening her lips. 'You know what he told me? Do you know?'

'No. How could I?'

'He told me that holding me was like holding his own mother and that he couldn't make love to his mother. He told me that when he got sexually excited, when he wanted me,' Gabrielle's breath blew out the candle and the light died in her eyes. The red of her lips grew deeper. 'When he wanted me, he had to remind himself that it was wrong. A sin. That's the very word he used. A sin. He wanted to sin. He said that more than anything else he wanted to sin. If he sinned I'd no longer be his mother. But he couldn't. He simply could not.'

We didn't speak much after that. It didn't seem to matter. I think she realised I was nervous, about being around her. Anyway, she seemed to prefer silence and that was fine by me. We just sat and looked at each other. It was a little unsettling to be so close to something which for so long I had adored from afar; each line of her face, each smile or frown stored in my head. I thought of telling her, of trying to give some sense of expression to the swirls and eddies that were reaching up, crashing, falling into hollows within me. Several times I was on the verge of speaking, of trying to explain. But then, just in time, I remembered to keep my mouth shut.

Gabrielle and I finished our drinks. We didn't talk on the walk back to Veda. The night was clear, the Redhill calm. Fire-flies flickered in far-flung nooks and cranies along the river bank. Dark hair cushioned the face which lit a thousand stars. A cluster of clouds hung lazily around the moon. Elmer Kolchak wandered the grounds, looking for something. Or someone. Gabrielle and I came close to touching, my fingers lightly on hers. Then came a cry from one of the bunks, the unsettled laughter of a prolonged night, startling us.

And after that the moment was gone.

I left her outside her bunk and went back to The Cuckoo's Nest to finish what I'd started: a bottle of lonely Irish whiskey.

I had to see Lucien. Perhaps more because Gabrielle wanted it than for me.

I knew where he'd be. And that's where I found him, in the front pew of the church. Alone. The hinges on the door were loose and it scraped along the floorboards as I went in. Lucien turned round. He'd been crying. Or praying. I couldn't tell which.

I sat by him. He was nervous. We didn't speak. He laid his hand on mine and together we went through the well-worn words of the Lord's Prayer, as we'd done at the beginning. For ever forgiving trespasses...

Afterwards we went for a walk by the falls, still saying nothing. I wanted to kick off the conversation, but I didn't know how. Eventually it was he who spoke. He asked me how I was doing. I said fine. How was I getting on with the patients? Was it still all too much? I said no. My boys were just what I needed. He said he was glad.

Then, by the riverside, he turned and said he wanted us to start again. I wanted the same thing. He was miserable without me. He said he'd missed me and he was sorry he hadn't been there when I needed him most. I told him that was all over now and that I'd missed him.

We walked on in silence a little further. Ice broken. Tension relieved. Those first moments when you breathe easy and begin to believe that everything really is going to work out. Falling back into one another's step. Then he told me, just when things were going fine. Or rather, he didn't tell me, he instructed me in a firm voice which gave no room for disobedience. It was a proclamation and I was to obey.

'You are not to see any more of Gabrielle. Not ever.'

He didn't look at me when he said it, didn't explain, just said it straight out. He was uneasy, chewing his lip, turning over a twig in his hands. I asked him why. He snapped the twig and told me not to ask that. 'Just don't see Gabrielle.' I wanted to know why. I said I didn't see why the three of us couldn't get along together. The Trinity. I reassured him that he gave me something she never could.

'Then why do you need to see her? Why? Tell me, why?'

'Lucien, what is this? Why are you behaving like this? Just when we're working things out. There's too much for us to lose here.' I reached for his hand but he withdrew it, stepping back, glaring at me angrily. Then I heard the squeak again. Like before. Quiet. Like a mouse caught in a trap.

'Benjamin. Stop playing with me.'

'I'm not playing with you, Lucien.'

'Then I don't want you seeing Gabrielle.'

'But why?'

'Benjamin.'

'You're being unreasonable.'

'You don't understand. And you never will.' He called me insensitive and stormed off up the path.

I ran after him.

'Don't follow me!' he shouted. And turned. And fled. Into the trees.

The mare broke into a feisty gallop. She was white. Pure. They called her Dusty. I kicked Kaluah's belly and he took off. I kicked again, trying to catch up. But Gabrielle's horse was too fast for me. She raced the wind, thundering downhill, beating me to the brook, easily. Just like she said she would.

Up ahead the Veda party climbed the blue trail at an easy pace, heading for the wood. Dutch was leading. Dutch had worked on the ranch since he was a boy. His father was the manager until he got caught in a barn fire: took seven horses and him with it. Dutch had nowhere to go, no family, no education; the only thing he had, all he knew about, was horses. Since then every new ranch manager had kept him on, the ranch orphan. And whenever a group from Veda came riding he insisted on taking them out. 'They sure make a change from some of the little brats we get coming here,' he said when the patients arrived. Ellen had chosen Gabrielle and me to accompany the group this time; another favour. There were six of them, all from the lower level. Some of them were pretty good riders too. Grace, whose mother had bought her a riding hat with her initials embroidered on the front, though she'd never been near a horse in her life, Grace was anything but. She flopped along on that horse like a drunken sack of potatoes. Logan on the other hand was all style; knees at the right angle, back straight, head high. But then he did have the most docile horse of them all, even my grandmother could have ridden that old thing and horses scare the hell out of her. Now Charlie, the only rider from B8, he was fearless. He didn't so much as flinch when Dutch picked out Old Ben for him, the biggest horse on the ranch, more hands than a Tibetan Buddha. Charlie just climbed straight on up with a grin, gave the beast a kick, and he was off. But then Charlie was like that, took everything in his stride. From seizure to sex, it was all the same to him.

Gabrielle was spending a lot of time with B8. She was a floater, filling in for counsellors on their day off. But generally she had a few hours spare each day and Ellen said she could work with us. She was great with the boys. The first time she came, Mitchel tried giving her a hard time, moaning and whining, trying the old wheelchair trick. But she didn't fall for it, not like we had. She didn't take any shit, just told Mitch to stop whingeing and act his age. And he did, as near as he could get. Walter wouldn't leave her alone, sitting by her side for hours, nodding and dribbling his heart away. He'd actually do things for her too. She sent him on errands, fetching canteen and the like, things that Joe and I had no idea he was capable of. And Joshua, he was a different person when Gabrielle was around, like he'd suddenly discovered manners and charm. He called her 'Lady Counsellor', inquired after her health, opened doors for her, stopped swearing in her presence, refrained from farting and, for the first time all summer, closed the toilet door when he was taking a crap; became a perfect little gentleman.

One rainy day, whilst the boys were watching *The Karate Kid* for the fifteenth time, Gabrielle and I sat on the porch of the cottage wrapped in our overcoats and she spoke about herself, a steady monotone emerging from under a rain hood. You'd have thought she was reading the business pages such was the lack of emotion in her voice, an absence of feeling, a numbness. She spoke of the most personal things without even a hint that any of it mattered, like she was tired and long past caring. There was no sadness, anger or resentment: just fact, detached observation, as though it had all happened to someone else.

She said that the more she came to know Lucien, the more he reminded her of her father.

Gabrielle's father had been a philosophy professor. He'd been buried in books ever since she could remember. She said her first memory of him was sitting on his lap in the warren of his study, bouncing up and down on his knee whilst he took notes from a book. He was some sort of Spanish nobility, descended from a line. Only the family tree had wilted. He let his lands go to waste. Tired of trying to get any coherent sense out of him, the farm managers took what was owed them and left. After that the whole place fell into decay. And nobody even thought to lift a finger, just watched it all disappear. When Gabrielle's brother came of age there was hardly anything left for him to inherit. Hundreds of years of diligence and effort went down with the sun, and never came up again.

As she grew older Gabrielle got to know her father's strongest trait: absence. Emotional. Mental. Physical. He'd disappear for months at a time. Her mother said he needed time to think. Think! He was destroying a life for thought. Her mother stood by him whilst the family went the same way as the lands; falling apart. One Christmas Eve he came home after a long spell away, gathered the family albums together, photos stretching back over generations, and threw them all on the fire. While they burned he decorated the tree. He wasn't uncommunicative, that wasn't the problem. When he was around he'd sit and talk for hours. Words words words words. That was all she ever remembered. Just like Lucien. Ideas going nowhere. Emotions dissipated in words. Words with no beginning or end. Words without relevance: never words like 'family' or 'love'. Gabrielle grew to loathe words. Anything that needed expressing for her was false and unfulfilling. If you had to explain how you were feeling then the feeling was worthless. The infinite strangled by the finite. Explorations. Explanations. Empty and without value. So much time wasted on words. Words. Words were a curse.

One day, just as Gabrielle had always known, her father didn't come back. Her mother kept believing he would. Kept telling her children as much, kept the dust from gathering in his study. Then, when Gabrielle and her brother were old enough, they persuaded her to move to Cully on the north shores of Lake Geneva to be with her family. Her brother moved out after a year and Gabrielle was left to tend to her mother alone. She was a broken woman. No one knew this in Cully of course, she kept up appearances, doing the social rounds with efficient Swiss panache. And that just made it all the more difficult for Gabrielle to deal with: her mother's disillusionment, bitterness, guilt and anger was reserved for Gabrielle. But

Gabrielle didn't take it on board, didn't let it swamp her. She just hardened herself, realised that life needs a firm hand or it will run around like a street urchin, causing all kinds of upset and pain.

The house in Spain still stands empty, the land rotting, the books on the shelves in the study. Gabrielle said that when her father dies she's going to return and burn the place to the ground, starting with his books. If those damn books had remained unopened from the start, none of this would ever have happened.

The Karate Kid fought his last fight and the film ended. William snap-kicked Walter in the belly. I rewound the film and they watched it again. Gabrielle and I sat on the porch in silence. No words.

I thought I was imagining things at first. But Gabrielle saw him too. Standing in the trees, a scarf tied over his head. Watching us. Not moving. I called out to him.

'Lucien, come over here and join us.'

But he ran off.

'Just like my father,' said Gabrielle.

Lucien took to wandering in the woods up behind B8, weaving in and out of the trees, following some endless trail. You could see his flock of black hair amid the foliage, that and his dark eyes. I sat on my bed and watched him through the window. He knew I could see him, otherwise he wouldn't be there. But still he pretended to be hiding, as though it were all part of some child's game. He was there most days. Every time Gabrielle came, he would sit on a moulding pile of leaves on the edge of the baseball field, the closest he dared come to the bunk, and throw stones. You could hear them knocking against the white wooden boards, an occasional one rattling against the mosquito mesh. He didn't throw them hard. Soft, in a weepy kind of way, just loud enough to be heard. I begged him to come in, several times, at least talk to me. But whenever I went outside, he ran off.

Kolchak granted our request for permission to take the boys to May's Ice-Cream Parlour. Walter got to hold Gabrielle's hand all the way up Sageville road. 'Do it do it do it,' Book chanted. Walter kissed Gabrielle on the cheek, leaving his saliva trademark. 'I wanna make sex!' William shouted, the rest of the boys cheering and howling. All except Dakota, who was a little put out at the sudden change of schedule. It was only by bribing him with ice-cream that we got him to come at all.

We sat them in the back of the old smithworks which had been transformed into the parlour, under the great hearth with the brass plaque commemorating the horseshoes that had been made there during the Civil War, and ordered just about everything on the menu. May was great. She chatted with the boys, doting on Charlie, then gave us a twenty per cent discount. It wasn't like the trip to the Game Farm. This was real. We were just another bunch of customers. No one gawped. We weren't on show. A couple of locals passed by and ignored us, just like we were normal people. The boys really made an effort. I was so proud. I wished Lucien had been there to see us.

Lucien roamed around my head pretty much constantly. Sometimes he'd be walking with the Slavic girl, she a step or two behind, following faithfully as though being led by a rope. He wouldn't speak, he was just there, an effective barrier between Gabrielle and me.

He was there the evening the autistic came. I was lying on my bed listening to Patrick's plane swooping low overhead, chasing the sunset. The odd mosquito buzzed around, looking for a nightcap of blood. It had been a sweltering day. I was sweating even now. Lucien needed time alone. He'd come round, I was sure of that. Sometimes emotions aren't enough. They have to be sorted through, figured out. I only wished he didn't have to make it so hard on me, make me feel so guilty when I didn't believe I had anything to feel guilty for.

Joe was off with Claudia, getting hammered down by the Redhill. Dakota was firing off a round of questions about the new schedule Joe had drawn up for the coming week. I'd stopped re-asking the fifth time around. Rilke sat slanted on my shelf, or was he lying. Words of meaningless wisdom. I was just about to pick him up and go for a browse when the spring on the door squeaked and a patient stumbled in. He was an autistic, one of Lucien's, I'd seen him before. He sat at dinner chewing paper cups. He had lazy muscles, one eye permanently closed and his mouth drawn down in sadness, for ever unable to smile. He stood there, tapping his fingers together, a noise like shy rain on the wooden roof, trying not to disturb anyone as it falls. He wore some sort of frock which was too small for him, like an outsized choirboy. I asked him what he wanted. He didn't reply, just frowned at his fingers. Maybe he was a peace offering. Maybe Lucien was outside on the porch. I went to look. No. Only a grey squirrel eating the stale crusts Mitch had left out for the birds.

There was something tied around the patient's neck. A roll of parch paper with a bow of rich blue. It was tied so tight I had to cut it. The scissors slipped and drew blood, a tiny trickle seeping under my fingernails. The patient didn't like being there. He grew agitated, raising his hand in a flurry of finger tapping. I told him he could go back to his bunk. But he didn't move. He started gazing around the bunk, as if only now realising he was in a strange place.

On the paper flowed a paragraph of the most beautiful handwriting I'd ever seen, so precise in its execution, so loving. It must have taken hours. Hours crammed with care. The patient began to hum softly.

Have mercy on my son: for he is lunatick, and sore vexed: for ofttimes he falleth into the fire, and he foameth, and gnasheth with his teeth, and pineth away. And I brought him to thy disciples, and they could not cure him. Then Jesus answered and said, O faithless and perverse generation, how long shall I be with you? how long shall I suffer you? bring him hither to me. And Jesus said, if thou canst believe, all things are possible to him that believeth. And Jesus rebuked the devil; and he fell on the ground and wallowed foaming; and he departed out of him; and the lunatick was cured from that very hour.

Matthew 17/Mark 9.

23

It was the heat that caused me to stir. They were already awake. I couldn't see straight, there were little white dots doing the polka in front of my eyes. Gorillas had been trampling over my tongue. Joshua sat up in bed gazing out at the flames, chuckling. 'Well now won't you just take a look at that.' A henna haze oozed through the floorboards of the bunk, shadows dancing in the corners. Crackling. Spitting. Intense noise. It must be inside. But it can't be. The boys are not burning. My cheeks singe. I was too close to the sun. What is the sun doing in the trees? Someone's dropped it. Why does it burn so? Sleep. Let me sleep, I'm tired. My eyelids start to boil. A bright bulb implodes by the window, roaring through the glass. Dakota mutters. '...Na I don't like I don't like make it stop pleeze make it stop pleeze...' Come on boys, go back to sleep. It's the middle of the night. It's only a fire. Sleep now. Sleep.

Fire.

I shook. Sparks. Cracking. The flames are real, hammering on the walls of the bunk, mocking my drunkenness. Joe. Wake up. Fire. I didn't move at first. I can't say why. I knew I had to. Had to get them out of there. Lunatics burn like oil. (Burning freaks.) The windows dyed red. (Combustible freaks.) It was close enough to curl the blankets of our beds. Got to get the boys out. But I didn't move. Flames climbed on the backs of the trees, surveying what was left to burn. Looking for wood and the odd loon. 'Well now won't you just take a look at that.' Sparks chuckled. Something splintered, diving past the window, illuminating the night.

FIRE!

I was up. Leapt out of bed. Stubbed my toe. Running around. Shaking beds. Cracking heads. Pulling covers. Yanking bodies. Jesus Christ! It was right there. Right outside the bunk. I could see the flames in front of me. Could count them. Every one. Burning. Singeing circles around the cabin. Up. Come on. Up. Let's go. I shook Joe. He raised his head in drunken stupor, last night's beer pouring from his eyes. I slapped him. Yelling. Fire's here. He cursed. Said I'd flipped. I pulled his mohican and hauled him from the bed. Howling. He saw the flames.

'Holy Mother of God! Why didn't you tell me?'

We ran. This way. That. Down. Back again. Forward. Panic. Tripping over clothes in an angry, raging light. Hot hands on cold iron bed posts. Come on. Please. Faster. Hissing closer. Ever closer. Inferno's infernal chant. Coming for us.

The boys for their part remained perfectly calm. We bustled them down the steps. A few mutters. Rubbing their eyes. But there were no tears, no cries, no fear, no sense of danger or even urgency. It was Joe and I who supplied the melodrama.

Outside, the other bunks were already up. Manic counsellors charging up and down the hill like rabid sheepdogs, hustling sleepy, bemused patients. The fire looked smaller from outside, further from the bunk than I'd thought. It was quite some way back in the forest. But the light! The light pulled the sky down over our heads and the moon burned red.

I bordered on the hysterical. At least that's what Joe told me later. Though I find it kind of hard to believe. I remember being very tranquil, watching the whole episode from afar. Joe said I ran into the trees to take a closer look at the flames. Then came back with sparks in my hair jabbering something about pencils, a camera following me incessantly and the Gospel of St Matthew.

'Fire brings out the crazies in everyone,' he laughed. 'You just have a few more than most, that's all.'

The boys were fantastic. No moaning or crying. No panic. They just stood around, yawning, waiting 'til it was safe to go back to bed. Though William did get excited when the fire trucks arrived, cheering them as they roared down Sageville Road. 'Go go go go! Get it ya sonsabitches! Get it get it!' One of the firemen let Willy try on his hat. The proudest moment of William Alexander Hunt's life to date. A real fire. A real fireman. And Willy in the heart of the action, wearing a real fireman's hat. He never let us forget that.

Around four in the morning the firemen gave the all clear and we were allowed back to bunks. The boys went straight to sleep, untroubled by the night's little interruption. It took me a while longer. I'd never felt such darkness. Except when I closed my eyes, then I could see flames.

The next morning a bleary eyed Veda was tripping on gossip. Speculation filled the breakfast bowls, presumption poured on top, with a sprinkle of postulation to sweeten the taste. Kolchak didn't want it getting out. No announcement was made. But the news got back all the same. One of the locals who worked part-time as a fireman told Fergus while he was out for his morning jog with his two-legged dog. The dog couldn't run, of course. So the fireman carried him. Said it was good for the dog's spirits to get out and about in the early morning air. After all, a two-legged dog must get pretty bored. He was going to get a false leg made by a retired heart surgeon in Woodstock, one day. The fire had been started deliberately. Matches were found by the old disused barn up in the woods beyond B8. Apart from the barn, none of Veda had been damaged. But it was a close call. Veda had been lucky, the fire chief said as much himself. If the wind had been just that little bit stronger...

Rumour rumbled remorselessly. Dave had picked a fight with one of the locals up at May's. The guy had been hitting on Natasha and she'd been responding more than favourably. So Dave took a pop at him. It was a good punch by all accounts. Straight and to the point. Knocked one of the guy's teeth clean out, left a sweet gaping hole. Some said the guy lit the fire by way of revenge. Others reckoned it was more widespread, said it was a local thing. They were tired of having loonies on their doorstep, dragged down property prices. The fire was a warning to Kolchak to pack up and go. Apparently something similar had happened several years back. Fergus said it was the anti-Semites, the area was a red-neck haven after all.

Then Berg surprised us all. He kept his information till last, waited for everyone to gossip themselves out. Then, with great calmness, like a key witness nailing the prosecution, he spoke. He'd been up in that part of the woods last night with B2 during evening activity. B2 were too low functioning to join the football game so he took them off on a treasure trail instead. The trail went well. Joey won first prize: a can of fizzy orange. (Though afterwards Berg gave them all cans of fizzy orange to avoid trouble.) On their way back he saw Lucien wandering around aimlessly, kicking up leaves. He said he was sure it was Lucien. Berg even called to him, asked him if he was coming out for a drink. But Lucien didn't answer. He just ran off.

Nothing was ever proved. But Lucien was found guilty by rumour. After all, he had been acting strangely recently. Holing himself up in his bunk with the autistics, never speaking to anyone. Not coming down to the dining-hall for meals, going hungry. I wasn't the only one who'd seen him moping around the forest in recent days, tracking people who didn't exist. And Dave brought up all that business of him going to the church every day, on his own. I mean, it wasn't natural to go praying so much, was it? Can't be good for you. Warps your mind. Everyone agreed. No wonder he'd started doing strange things.

I didn't go to the Veda Councils any more, hadn't done since the abuse allegations confined me to the bunk. But Joe told me they couldn't get enough of the fire story. This one was running big time. New pieces of evidence were constantly cropping up, and the court had no jury, only judges. Alexandria said Lucien used to play with matches in cookery lessons, she'd warned him about it several times, said he'd start a fire if he wasn't careful. And, well, what d'ya know, she'd been proved right. At least she was happy. Then there was that time when Lucien stood outside the fire station for the whole lunch hour, just staring at the tower. 'I told you 'e was wacko,' Dave said. 'Told you all along, didn't I?' Dave had lost a bit of influence with the counsellors ever since he'd been humiliated by Gabrielle that night up at Dotty's. But here was his chance to make up some lost ground, claw his way back in their hearts, re-establish himself as leader in their eyes. And he didn't waste the opportunity. He suggested the Veda Council undertake its own investigation. If they could find evidence, maybe Kolchak would take action. (And, why of course, he'd be more than happy to lead the investigative team – good ol' Dave.)

As Lucien's ostracism from the counsellor community became complete, I was gradually brought back within the fold. They seemed to forget my past crimes now they had a new object for their inadequacies. Some counsellors even asked me if I thought Lucien could have done it. 'Well, I mean, you do *know* him don't you? I mean, you were sort of, well, *involved* with him, weren't you?'

Poor Lucien. I knew only too well what he was going through. But I wasn't too sure what to do, how to react. I asked Gabrielle. I asked her what exactly had happened between them during that month when they were together. At first she looked away, changed the subject, anything to avoid answering. But I kept on, asking, asking. I needed to know. And so finally, as we lay down by the Redhill in the evening sunlight, mosquitos descending in force, she told me. She didn't want to, more for Lucien's sake than for hers. But she told me all the same.

Lucien wanted her to treat him like a patient. Not right away. At first he just told her about his ideas; they would go for long walks through the woods, simply talking. She was fascinated, both by him and the warped notions that flew from his head. She was drawn to his awkwardness, felt out of step with the world when she was around him, and she liked it. Then, after a while, he said he wanted to try and understand what the patients felt like. It wasn't enough to observe them, he had to get into their skin and the only way to do this was to be like them. Initially it was simple things: he'd ask Gabrielle to talk down to him as if he'd had a mental age of minus three, pretend he couldn't communicate properly, he wanted her to control, chastise or reward him. She felt uncomfortable, but he seemed so excited by the whole thing, so enthusiastic, like he was on to a major discovery. She didn't have the heart to let him down. So she did it. Then things began to slip from her control. He wanted more. He wasn't understanding, she was being too considerate. She had to forget that it was role playing, do it for real. He needed more. He wanted her to feed him, to lead him everywhere by the hand, to shower him, to dress, to wipe his arse, and to give him pills. Gabrielle refused. Said he'd gone to far. Lucien got angry. Then he stopped responding, kept on playing his game, stuck inside a simulation. They'd had a row. Or rather she shouted at him and he cried. She couldn't go on like this. She told him it had to stop. That was the night before the day trip to the Catskill Game Farm. She hadn't spoken to him since.

I asked her what I should do. Gabrielle said I should go to him; forget what had happened and just go to him, he'd respond to me. I said it was hard: he'd betrayed me. 'The hurts and grudges we store up against those we love eat away only at ourselves.' That was her answer. She said I was throwing away something that was good for the sake of the past.

So I went looking for him. He was never in his bunk, didn't turn up for activities, and I no longer saw his black eyes gazing out from the trees.

Eventually I found him. I suppose I always knew where he'd be. But I didn't want to go up there, the place gave me the creeps. It was so quiet and, well, holy. I guess that's what religious people like; nothing to distract them from prayer, no realities to impinge on God. He was in the front pew – Lucien, not God – on the left of the cross.

Only this time he wasn't alone. The autistic with the twisted face who'd brought the message to my bunk was sitting at his side.

I entered the church stealthily, afraid I was being watched, and took a pew. It was cold in there. The sun refused to heat the inside. Lucien's cheeks were flushed, just as when I'd seen him for the first time in Dotty's. He looked like an English rose, except he was French and his expression was more that of a thorn. He was praying, again. When I sat down he put his hand to his lips and I waited for him to open his eyes.

'What's he doing here?' I whispered, pointing to the patient. Don't ask me why I whispered. I couldn't tell you. There was no one else there. I'd never whispered in a church before. It made me feel kind of righteous. 'You shouldn't bring him in here.'

'Why? He has a soul too,' Lucien answered angrily. 'And someone has to pray for it.' He didn't look at me. He stared straight ahead at the altar steps. My heart sank. He was still wounded, bitter. He sighed heavily, as though gathering all the hurt in his lungs and expelling it in one breath, then started stroking my hair. 'Sorry, I didn't mean to shout. After all, you did come didn't you? I mean you are here, aren't you, for me?'

'Yes Lucien. I'm here.'

'For me?'

'For you.'

He tussled my hair, leant over and placed the hint of the beginnings of a kiss on my cheek. 'I knew you'd answer my call.'

The autistic gazed at his fingers tapping together, an eternal acceptance of boredom, chewing some pages from the Bible. I looked closer. It was the Book of Revelation, chapters seven to twenty.

'I gave him those,' Lucien said, watching me watching the autistic devour the Bible. 'He was hungry. He's eating the Beast. He should've been eaten a long time ago.'

'I hope the Beast doesn't give him indigestion.'

'That's not funny, Benjamin,' Lucien snapped, years of learned, pent-up religious fervour forcing its way out.

'Lucien, he's eating the Bible. It's hardly serious.'

'Laugh if you want, Benjamin. They laughed at Jesus you know. They also called him a madman. Did you know that? Well, did you?'

'No.'

'Jesus would've liked Veda. These are his people. Pure. Uncluttered.

This is man before he tasted the serpent's apple. Free from the knowledge that causes pain.' Lucien paused for a response. But I said nothing. Let him speak. You could hear the clunks in his head, whirring away, working things out. 'I'll tell you something. When my brother had his mental breakdown and then began to study for the priesthood, I laughed like a devil. I used to say it just goes to show that you'd have to be mad to want to be a priest. No one in their right mind would want to be such a thing. But now I understand. No one in their right mind *could* be such a thing. Because no one in their right mind has access to true understanding. My brother had to see things from the other side. He had to be free from the constraints of our vision. Madness is the path to freedom. Madness releases us from all the irrelevancies, the pettiness, the trivialities of our daily existence. It empties the mind of the clutter of necessities we need to function in our normal world, leaving room for exploration of the mental uplands. Why do saints fast, lock themselves away, banish necessities from their daily lives?'

'Because they're crazy.'

'Don't mock, Benjamin. The saints are trying to rid themselves of the mental preoccupations which normal life requires. They want to empty their mind of every detail which obscures vision. They need to destabilise themselves mentally if they are to have a chance at enlightenment. With madness, the crowds disappear, the confusion, the bustle, the pain, the noise stills and we are left alone to start again on what really matters.'

The church opened up to the echoes of Lucien's voice. Colours floated through the clear windows, coming to rest upon the altar. The magi adored from the walls and dark clouds gathered over Calvary. In the corner I saw an angel annunciating to Mary. It was the same picture that use to hang above Peter's desk back at school. I didn't like it even then. (So much beauty comes to art via religion, yet Peter's mother was only ever interested in the kitsch.) The autistic finished eating the Book of Revelation and started rocking, the pew creaking softly.

'You see,' Lucien continued, squeezing my hand, 'what I'm trying to say is, I suppose, that madness is a means to an end. I used to think it was an end in itself, a point of finality. I used to see it as the endzone, to be entered for the experience and to be left again at will. But I was wrong. It is just one part of a journey.'

'Lucien.' My voice struck a strange note after the long silence which followed Lucien's sermon, as though it had been tainted by the holy air in which I sat. I didn't want to bring it up. I knew it would upset him. Besides, I didn't believe what I'd heard. But I asked nonetheless. 'Lucien, the fire?'

'Benjamin,' he smiled gently at my foolishness, putting his arm around me, drawing me close. 'Benjamin,' he whispered. I could feel his breath swimming in my ear. 'I knew you'd come. Sooner or later, you'd come. Now it's just us, together. Like it always should have been, from the start. Before her. You know what the Book of Job says? "Women are evil. Three times worse than the devil." She got what she wanted. She came between us. Almost destroyed us. But we're too strong for her. You and me. She won't bother us again. We beat the Devil at his own game.'

'Lucien, what are you talking about?'

'Benjamin,' he pulled me tighter, squeezing the air from my lungs. 'I'm so glad you're here, with me. As it should be.'

'Lucien, what are you talking about?' He was losing me. I pushed him slightly, to ease his grip, just enough so I could breathe freely. He kept repeating my name, over and over again, hypnotising nothing.

'Benjamin. How good it is that you've realised. Benjamin. You've come back. Benjamin. You've seen her for what she was. Benjamin.'

I stood up, freeing myself from his embrace. Lucien didn't seemed to notice, just went on rambling without thinking, some sort of religious chant. I did know what he was talking about, but I wanted to hear it from him. I wanted to be sure. I was saddened. I thought he'd understood, realised, come to his senses.

'Lucien.' I backed into the aisle, my voice ringing through the pews. No more whispers. 'For God's sake, will you tell me what you're going on about?'

'*Her*!' He snapped. The autistic tapped his fingers. Lucien's hand shook. 'Her and her evil.'

'Who?'

'Gabrielle. Who do you think?'

'Please, Lucien. Not again. We've been over this.'

'You agreed!' He jumped up, pulling the autistic with him, waving the torn Bible in my face as though it were a signed confession. 'You agreed. You said you wouldn't see her. You came for me. Remember! You came for me. You agreed.'

'I know I came for you. But I agreed to nothing of the sort. I thought you'd understood. I came for you because I don't want to lose you. I thought you had accepted the way things are.'

'I want to be with you.'

'You can. The three of us, we can be together.'

'PLAYING AGAIN!'

The scream blew the dust from the cross, rattling in the rafters, pigeons taking flight. Spittle flew into the air, changing colours as it sprayed on to the altar. Lucien raged. His lips quivered, like Dakota deep in a fit. His hand flapped. 'Playing again. Always playing. People are just one game after another for you. Benjamin! Don't see any more of Gabrielle.' He slapped the autistic round the face. 'I'm warning you.' The patient stopped tapping his fingers, holding eye contact with me for a brief moment, trying to figure out where the pain was coming from.

'I'll see who I bloody well like.'

'But you love me! Not her. It's me you love.'

I hate tears. Scenes. Emotions cheapened by melodrama.

'Lucien, stop this rubbish. Get a hold of yourself.'

'But you love me.'

'STOP! You're driving me nuts for Christ's sake.'

'Don't blaspheme! You are in the House of God.' Lucien wailed. The autistic began to cry, though the tears were Lucien's. 'You love me. Come here.' I didn't move. Lucien banged his fist against the pew, hymn books scattering across the floor. 'Come here, DAMN YOU!'

'Lucien, I don't need this. Come and find me when you've calmed down. Then we'll talk.'

I stormed up the aisle, crashing against the wooden doors and out into the midday sun. Behind me, from the church, came a howl. It was howl I'd heard from the autistics in Lucien's bunk up across the top field. The howl that swam through Veda at night, keeping us awake. Only this time I knew the voice. It wasn't the howl of madness. It was the howl of the sane, trapped.

24

'I ain't no loonie! Honest to God I ain't! Bejumen, you gotta tell them.'

Mascara slid down Thelma's cheeks, chasing the tears. She held me tight, her purple mohair jumper caught in the buttons of my jacket. Thelma only ever wore purple. I'd seen her knickers once. Same thing. Purple. When she arrived at Veda she kicked up one hell of a fuss. She was in E2, the bunk where Gabrielle slept, came with the penultimate group from the New York institutions. The first morning they tried getting her up for breakfast she lay on her bed biting and scratching anyone who came within range. They bawled her out. So that night she got up and pissed all over the counsellors' clothes. Counsellors refused to deal with her after that and Kolchak was forced to promise she'd be sent back the following day. Kolchak hated doing that, she'd have to return the fees. The next morning Thelma was up before anyone else had stirred. She woke the other patients, showered them, made their beds and led them over to breakfast all by herself. She was better than any counsellor. Her enthusiasm never waned and she didn't need to go out and get pissed every night to do her work. Plus she had more charm.

'Well now, Mr Bejumen, you are looking *fine* today. Hmm. *So* fine,' she'd greet me whenever I visited E2. 'Now you just wait right there. I'll go and get Miss Gabrielle. She right inside. And if she don't be good to you, you just tell me and I'll break her head. She soon be treating you right.'

And now she had her arms flung round my neck, crying an ocean.

'You gotta let them know, I ain't crazy. You know I ain't. I don't belong there. I ain't crazy like them. I'm like you Bejumen.'

It was change-over day on the higher level. Thelma's group was due back at the institution that afternoon, before the last lot of patients arrived at Veda. Gabrielle was inside packing the luggage. Thelma was on the porch soaking my clothes in salty tears. She didn't want to leave. You couldn't blame her. She was from the BCCI – The Brooklyn Care And Concern Institute. However bad Veda got, it was no BCCI. Hell was inspired by that place, the devil took the blueprints direct. A scum of an institution. Built in the fifties when loonies were loonies and just needed a damn strong strait-jacket, the BCCI had hardly altered. Half of it was closed owing to disrepair and the other half was an exercise in self-demolition. Paint peeled the corridors. Windows broke themselves out of frustration. Drains backed up, bringing in half the selected shit of New York City. There was little for the patients to do all day except wander. And that was all the patients did. Wander. If the wards were left unlocked, that is. Oh and there were beatings once in a while, just to break the monotony.

There was an old Down's guy called Doug, been at the BCCI most of his life. Everyone at Veda knew the story. Doug was forty, old for Down's, and pretty high functioning. He used to like the dining-hall doors at the BCCI, kind of like Dakota. He'd press his nose up to the windows and just look in with one hell of a smile. He loved those windows. And then one day they changed the doors. Workmen from the city just waltzed right in and took them away. Put in new ones, with no windows. So Doug couldn't see what was going on. He had to step inside the hall to get any sort of a view. Just inside, not far. That was against the rules. Doug knew that, everyone did. 'Rule N° 7: No Patient To Set Foot In The Dining-Hall Before The Meal Bell.' It was printed in orange on every concrete pillar in the BCCI. But there were no windows. There'd always been windows. Doug had to step inside, just to have a look.

That was where the staff caught him. Red-handed. Inside the dining-hall. Before the bell. To teach him a lesson they bustled him into the kitchen and held his hand over a lighted gas ring.

Now that took place twenty years ago. Doug was dead long since. But things hadn't got much better. There were still stories. New stories with every new group of patients which came to Veda. You only had to stand on the higher level and listen to Frank babble on about 'yeah an' they grabbed this stick an' they shoved it up my ass an' they made this yellow pus come out yeah an' they said I was good an' an' an' they said I was good'. Frank was from the BCCI.

You can understand why Thelma didn't want to go back there. Gabrielle had tried to get permission for her to stay. She went and saw Kolchak down at High Command and asked if Thelma could remain in her bunk for an extra two weeks, just until the end of the season. She even offered to pay the fees herself. But Kolchak refused. Said it would make a mess of the lists.

So back Thelma went. I stood and watched her go. Crying and wailing as the bus took her out of sight, hammering on the windows.

Don't look at me like that. What could I do? Go with her? Take her home?

Talking of home, there was Joshua. Ellen called me out of the pool one afternoon. I was annoyed. It was a hot day. The water was cool.

'It's Joshua,' she said without looking up as I dripped into the office. 'You better sit down.'

'What's the problem? He's up at the pool. He's fine.'

'He is for the moment, yes.'

'What do you mean?'

Ellen let out a long hard sigh. 'Dr Kolchak received a letter from his social worker this morning. It seems that Joshua's foster family no longer wants him.'

'Why?'

'I have no idea. And it doesn't matter. Makes no difference. The fact stands. Joshua Art Hoses no longer has a family. And no family means no home.'

'Well what the hell's he going to do?'

'No idea. I guess the social worker will have to try and find another family for him. But there's less than two weeks of the season left to run. It's unlikely she'll have any luck before Veda's over.'

'So what'll happen?'

'He'll have to go into a home, an institution.'

'But he only came out of an institution last year. That's why he's supposed to have a bloody family, to keep him away from the institution. They can't just dump him right back in.'

'Apparently they can.'

Ellen said she knew how I felt.

Screw how I felt. What about Joshua? There he was, splashing around in the pool while his whole family had just done a runner.

'Look, Benjamin. I know this might be difficult for you and Joe to handle. So if you'd rather leave it up to Kolchak to tell Joshua, she's already said she'll be more than willing.'

'No way. He's our boy. We'll tell him.'

I said nothing for a few days. Then I told Joe. He blew his top, hussing and cussing the bastards. Joshua had been coming on so well. He'd stopped teasing Mitch. He'd even started to help out in the kitchen after meal times, washing up and taking out the rubbish. He'd come back to B8 huffing and puffing so that everyone would notice, wiping his brow, going on at great length about how hard he'd been working. 'Well, you know Counsellor Benjuman and Counsellor Joa, having a job is really much more tiring that I ever thought it would be, well yes it is, I would never have thought you know. A job. Well that's what it is, a job.' We told him to keep at it. We told him that hard work always paid off. And now his family had pissed off and left him.

We had to tell him sooner or later. We waited until the other boys were in bed one evening then called Joshua out on to the porch, adult-like. You know, man-to-man. Out of our useless stuttering, fumbling and half-sentences, Joe and I managed to get the message across. Joshua nodded at our every word, throwing in the odd chuckle and thoughtful scratch of the chin. We took about fifteen minutes to say what could have been said in five, cushioning our every word, letting him down lightly.

'Well, Counsellor Joa and Counsellor Benjuman,' Joshua said after several minutes silence, 'are you quite finished?'

'Yes.'

'Yes.'

'Well, now you know that's quite okay, well yes it is. 'Cos, well, you know I always said now didn't I, they like to go up to Block Island from time to time. Well, yes, you know, and I believe the weather gets pretty nice up there around this time of year, well, you know, that's what they say. And that's okay.' And with that he stood up, looked down upon Joe and me and laughed. 'Now, Counsellor Benjuman and Counsellor Joa it's been very nice talking to you, but well would you mind at all if I took myself inside and went to bed?' And he did just that.

Joshua never made mention of the subject again. Once or twice I tried to bring it up. But he'd just wander off or interrupt me with details of Block Island's weather. He still spoke of his family and home, except he now said 'my ex-father' or 'my ex-sister'.

Louis said Josh was finished.

It was still hot around eight so Joe and I skipped evening activity and took the boys down to Redhill Creek. Louis came too. He and I sat on the rocks. Joe took Charlie out for a swim on the far side, slipping and sliding their way across the moss covered rapids.

Patients weren't allowed in the river. Veda rules (N° 61). In fact they weren't allowed down the rocks (N° 60). But they liked it there. And Charlie was a good swimmer. I built the rest of the boys a little fire and they sat around picking up twigs and sticking them into the flames. All except Dakota, that is. He'd peel his twigs and set them neatly down in a little pile. Only when he had a bunch would he give them to Walter and Walter would throw them into the fire. William splashed about in a rock pool, terrorising waterboatmen. Book sat at the water's edge, eyes fixed on Charlie. He only ever came alive around Charlie these days. When Charlie wasn't there Book slipped into his mental slumber, responding to nothing, speaking to no one. But as soon as Charlie was back at his side he was as loud and mischievous as ever.

'Well, damn,' Louis said, squashing a horsefly with the palm of his hand. 'They put that poor Josh in that place and he won't be coming out normal no more. They gonna fuck him up so bad he gonna be needing treatment.' No family had been found for Joshua. He was BCCI-bound. 'Well take a look at me. That's where they put me. BCCI 503, that was me. Had that fucking number steamed into my brain. I was pretty okay until that damn therapy came along and messed my head. They stuck me in an institution and by the time they finished with me I needed to be in an institution just to survive. Couldn't ever leave 'cos they kept on damn curing me. They gonna do the same thing to your Josh. Gonna fuck him right up. Poor little shit. Well I just don't know. Why they can't go leaving us all alone, I just don't know. Like it's a crime to be crazy. If we wanna be crazy, let us go right ahead and be crazy. What difference does it make to them? What they have to go curing us for. I tell you, that little Josh don't stand a damn chance.'

The river flowed on. Ignoring us. On its way to somewhere else. Charlie and Joe got out and came over to the fire. You could see Joe's goose bumps through the smoke. Charlie didn't have any. I guess his insulation kept him warm, layers of flab wobbling in the evening sunlight; a beaming walrus without the tusks. Book left the water's edge to come and be with Charlie. They stood side-by-side, giggling at nothing, Charlie poking Book's skinny little ribs. Joe gave out the sweaters we'd brought in the rucksack and we settled down in front of the fire. There was more silence in those few moments than there had been all summer. I'd never known B8 so quiet. Another day died.

The river rushed on and if you listened carefully you could just hear a tiny scratching as Dakota peeled another twig.

We all took turns to pee on the flames and, when the fire was out, we trekked through the woods to Veda. Up on Sageville Road, in front of the house of the fireman with the two-legged dog (half a kennel built in the garden), one of the nurses from the infirmary came charging towards us, arms flailing like a malfunctioning traffic policeman, blood streaming from her nose.

'Thank God,' she ran up to us, panting, almost knocking Walter down. He smiled. 'Thank God I found you.'

'What is it Ruth? What's the matter?'

'Please. Come. Come quickly.' She was so distraught her words came out all crooked; you could barely understand what she was saying. One side of her face was stinging red. 'Please,' she gasped. 'Come quickly.'

'Come where?' said Joe. 'What's going on? Calm down. Tell us what's happened.'

Ruth grabbed my arm, dragging me along the road, rambling, tripping over herself in haste. 'You know him, Benjamin. Benjamin, you know him. Please, he'll listen to you. You know. You know.'

I pulled my arm away and shook her until she fell silent. 'Now. Tell us exactly what's happened. Slowly. Make some sense.'

'He just burst in. I was alone, on duty, and he just burst in. I was alone. He bust right into the infirmary, demanding medication. Said he needed medication, said it was urgent. I asked him who it was for but he refused to say. Medication had already been given out. I told him so. No more medication until lights out. That's the rule. I even showed him the rule book; N° 31. But he just kept on, getting more and more angry. "Give me the medication, damn you!" I got scared. He started cursing, turning everything upside down, tipping out the drawers. I tried phoning Kolchak. I was so scared. And he ripped the line out of the wall. Just tore it out. That's when he hit me.'

'He hit you?'

'Twice. He smashed the doors of the medicine cabinet. I ran. He's in there now. I ran away. He's there. He's crazy. Please, Benjamin. Go talk to him. He'll listen to you.'

'Who? Who's in there?'

'That French guy.'

'Lucien?'

'That's it. That's the one. Lucien. Please.' Ruth tugged at my arm.

I gave her a handkerchief to mop up the bleeding. It was dirty. But I don't think she cared. I told Joe to go find Kolchak. Ruth went with him. Louis offered to take the boys back to the bunk. I went to find Lucien. It was time to talk.

The wooden panel on the front door of the infirmary was split, right down the middle, fresh splinters lying on the porch. I pushed it and stared into the waiting-room. Reams of wet paper towels covered the floor, trailing from the sink, wrapped around the easy chairs, stuffed upon the shelves Herbert had made. They were falling down. The fridge door was open, its antiquated motor whirring away, screaming for the warmth to be kept out. On the floor lay an open tin of cherries, sweet syrup mixing with milk spilt from an upturned carton. Above the bench where the drugs were doled out, the cupboard doors had been forced. At the far end was the medicine cabinet. Broken bottles, pills of every conceivable colour scattered across the floor: suppositories, needles, bandages, splints, a broken crutch, a tampon, stained brown. The fluorescent strip bulb overhead buzzed unhappily.

I heard chanting. Soft. Sweet. Coming from beyond the door in the far wall. The simplicity of a child's rhyme. I waited.

Listen.

'*Pleurez, pleurez les anges, j'oserai. Pleurez, pleurez les anges, j'oserai.*'

I didn't recognise the voice as Lucien's at first. In fact, I didn't even recognise it as human. It was angelic.

I picked my way through the debris and found Lucien sitting cross-legged in the midst of a large, square, white room at the back of the infirmary, singing, rocking himself gently in time with the rhythm. *Pleurez, pleurez les anges, j'oserai. Pleurez, pleurez les anges, j'oserai*. I wanted to go up and put my arms around him, hold him. He looked so small, lost, beautiful. His black hair was speckled with spots of white, his long wavy fringe stuck in sweat to his forehead. His eyes were bright, glistening. Happy. *Pleurez, pleurez les anges*... Calm.

In the opposite wall were three large doors. The room was being decorated. You could smell the fresh paint. Tins of white emulsion lay scattered across the floor. Darkness rolled up to the windows, crowding round for a closer look.

At length Lucien looked up. He was singing. Songs for me. My anger faded. He patted the palms of his hands on the floor, splattering white paint which ran from an open can.

He stopped. 'So,' he said, still rocking. 'My pretty little Judas has come. I knew you would. I knew you wouldn't let me down.'

'Oh, Lucien, what have you done?' I tried to drum harshness into my voice, but it wasn't there. 'What have you gone and done? You've really let yourself in for it this time.'

'I've written you a little poem. Would you like to hear it?'

'Later.'

'No. Now. Listen.

'Your Peter plays the Judas, first grabs a stone to throw.
But who would not deny you, while like a cock you crow?
And when they crucify you and your betrayal takes its toll.
Those two thieves beside you will steal your precious soul.

'Isn't it beautiful?'

'Yes, Lucien.'

'I wrote it for you.'

'Thank you. We must get this place cleaned up. Joe went for Kolchak. She'll be here any minute.'

'It's not easy finding something to rhyme with toll, you know.'

'Really.'

'I bet you've never tried it.'

'No, Lucien, I haven't.' I was becoming impatient. No, impatient's the wrong word. Scared. Kolchak would be here soon and Lucien was still fooling around. 'Come on, you're up to your neck in shit. Why did you have to go and hit Ruth? Let's clean up this place. At least that might put Kolchak in a better mood.' I held out my hand to help Lucien up.

'DON'T TOUCH ME!' He screamed, slapping his hands on the floor, splattering paint over his clothes, hollering. 'Kolchak, Kolchak, Kolchak! Is that all you care about? What about ME?' A moth fell from the ceiling. Dead. Suffocated in white emulsion. Lucien's rigid voice was the only sound echoing in a world's chamber. 'What about me? I wrote you a poem.'

'I know. I said thank you. But we've got to get you out of here.'

'When did you ever write me a poem? When?'

I didn't answer. Neither of us spoke for a while. The moth wasn't dead. Not quite. You could hear it kicking, scuttling around on the floor.

'Benjamin, do you remember when we first met?'

'Of course I do.'

'You were drunk.'

'Was I.'

'And you told me that all knowledge was improvised wisdom. Do you remember that?'

'No, Lucien, I don't.'

'No, of course not. Why should you? It's just words to you, isn't it? Words to exploit and roles to play. All for effect. All to corner another admirer, another conquest.'

'Lucien, when you've quite finished assassinating my character, we have to get this place...'

'I haven't finished. You told me it was all improvised wisdom: knowledge, understanding, experience, everything. Well I'm tired of improvising. But you, you just go on and on. All improvisation and no script, that's you.' I stood there, looking down at Lucien covered in paint. Rocking. Frittering away our love. 'But there's never any meaning for you, is there. It's all equally worthless. You never stand by anything because nothing is worth believing in. It can all be proved false in the end, seen through. So why even bother trying. Am I right?'

'No, Lucien. You're a babbling idiot. Now come on. Enough of your selfish games. I'm tired of fencing with your ego.' I stepped forward to take his hand.

He sprang, leapt up before I even saw him move, stamping his feet, shouting. Hideous strangulations. Wailing in the endless whiteness of the room. The doors in the wall slanted and grew ten times. The ceiling pushed down on my head, popping pressure. Temples bending. Lines in my forehead cutting through to the brain. Lucien picked up a can and span round and round and round, paint splashing across the windows, shutting out the darkness. And round. 'There! You see,' he cried. 'I've conquered darkness. I've done what God never could. I've conquered darkness.' He howled with laughter, stamping in the paint. Dancing with no steps. Singing, but no voice. Another can. Paint swirling through the air, plastering me. In my hair. My ears. Eyes. All white. Blurring. 'Look!' he shrieked. 'I made you pure. White as the driven snow. I purified you.'

Lucien collapsed, sprawling across the floor, skidding through emulsional emotion. Panting. Exhausted. 'Oh, Benjamin, you're so funny. I'm sorry. But you see, I'm suffering from cerebral paucity.' He cracked up, ripping his seams wide open at his own joke, pounding fists against the wall. 'Cerebral paucity!'

Two beats of the heart. From within. Out of time. A baby cried. Somewhere. I could see the mother making love to the lover on the sofa. And someone shot a child through the head whilst he played in the garden.

Paint dried. Faces cracked. Lucien rose high on his knees, arching his back, holding out his hands. Damning. Not forgiving. A scream of a force I have never since known to this my dying hour.

'GOD IN HEAVEN. WERE YOU SLEEPING WHEN YOU MADE MY SOUL? Where the hell were you? Answer me, DAMN YOU!' He collapsed. Not even a tear. Just slow rocking. Back and forth. Gentle. Forth. An apple fell without reason. Back. A father rejected a son. And no one knew. 'You have no answers. You dish out all this pain. Send down your only Son to bring misery to my family. Questions upon questions. Dogma and dilemma. But no answers. *Je ne moque pas le Diable. Il reçoit les âmes, mais ce n'est pas lui qui les damne.*' A slight flap of the hand. Flicking ears. Tapping fingers. Humming. Slap of stomach. Lucien's sharp breath rattled around the room, chasing his words. 'You know, Benjamin, madness is the opium of religion. Or is it: opium the religion of the mad? No, no, that's it, it was religion the opium of the mad. Oh, I don't know. You can't make sense of religion. Religion is mystery. You solve the mystery and you destroy God. The mad are the most pure. And the mad have no God. Godless souls. That's why they're pure. I dreamt. You have to pay for your dreams, you can't have them on credit. That's what my father always said. And he never once went to church. How come he came out okay? Answer me that. Godless and pure. Purely Godless.'

Lucien's voice was close to disappearing. I could hardly make out his words. I wanted to move. This time I really wanted to move. Do something, not like last time. But I didn't. I could have. It would have been so easy. But I didn't. I just stood, looking at Lucien scratching at the floor, rocking back and forth, head lolling side to side, trying to dig through to somewhere else.

Pencils.

I saw them coming. I knew they would. He had pencils in his

pocket. Scraping. Shavings falling into paint. Sharpening pencils. Remember, clean through the eye. Perhaps I was crying. Though I don't see a tear. Do you? Lucien saw something. 'Don't be upset,' he said, laying out another pencil on the floor. 'My whole life's been sketched by a child who hasn't yet learned how to draw. It's not your fault. Well, not all of it. It's just a little madness. It always comes in the end. Madness more certain than death. You can't conquer madness, Benjamin. It won't ever go away. Once you're infected you'll stay that way until past your dying day. It might lie dormant from time to time, slumbering, repose, but don't kid yourself: it'll never leave you. It'll come back. Wait, you'll see.

'I asked that sweet nurse for some tablets, to help. But they wouldn't give me any. That's my mother, she doesn't want to ease the pain. She's religious you know. She needs pain.' He lifted the lid of his eye and picked up the pencil, searching for the centre. 'Pain. Madness. Religion. Religion rains pain. Pain flows madness. Flee from pain into religion and find? Madness.' He laughed. The eye flickered on the sharp end of the pencil. 'And then? Don't worry your pretty little head, Benjamin. You have time. Madness still has work to do.'

The middle door in the back wall burst open. Three men ran in. I'd never seen them before. They wore grey coats. I saw the needle go into Lucien. Somewhere. Some flesh or other. He collapsed and his face twisted into a smile. I didn't move. They carried him out right under my nose and I didn't even move. I watched the paint dry. One of the men had a crucifix round his neck. Then in came Kolchak and asked if I'd been hurt.

25

I hate tears. For something so natural, they're damned false. But whatever I thought, tears came all the same. There was the saddest dusk I'd ever seen that day, the day they took Lucien away. Gone. Swallowed up by an ambulance. The sun didn't want to set, refusing to accept it was over. I tried to talk it into staying, frightened it might never come back. After all, why should it? The rain came and I sat on the pile of moulding leaves on the edge of the baseball field, right where he used to sit, watching me. And I could no longer tell the difference between the rain and my tears.

You know, it's funny how we dismiss clichés just because they're clichés. As though we know best. As though our micro-wisdom is any match for the macro-experience of the masses. But believe me, clichés are clichés for a reason. You'll never love someone so much as when they're gone. When I was a boy I used to be frightened of dying in my sleep. I hated the thought of simply not waking up in the morning, trapped in a dream. It might not even be a pleasant dream. Though this fear taught me one good habit: never go to bed angry. Because if you don't wake up, you'll never get a chance to apologise. Lucien left me in the midst of bitterness. And for that, I'll never forgive him.

Louis was good to me and sometimes I tried to convince myself he was Lucien. I'd sit and listen to him natter on long into the night. He would only talk for certain people. There were plenty of counsellors who still believed him to be a non-verbal, thought we were crazy when we told them Louis could speak. Joe and I tried to prove it, tried to get him to say things in front of some of the other staff, but he just refused, remained silent. He'd stay over at the bunk every now and then. Joe and I brought in a bed for him and stuck it in the corner next to Willy. William liked Louis. They'd lie in bed and see who could fart louder. William came out on top, always (long, low reverberations). I forget most of what Louis said. More stories from the BCCI I suppose. Rapes in the shower, being kicked around on wet floors. I didn't say much. Louis didn't like listening and besides, I was going off words.

Though I do remember one thing. I asked him why he talked to me.

'Shit. Well I gotta talk to someone. Kinda keeps me together. I figure if I can hear the sound of my own voice and if I can identify the words then I ain't so crazy. Like it tell me their damn therapy ain't working.'

'But why don't you talk to the others?'

'Don't need to. I already got someone to talk to: you. What's the point talking to anyone else?'

Sometimes Louis would sit up all night talking, just to be sure he was still there.

It was lonely without Lucien. I know I hadn't exactly been on good terms with him recently, but at least he'd been there. I took to going up to the church in my lunch hour. I'd sit in the front pew on the left of the cross, right up close to the altar. Don't ask me why. I didn't expect to find him there. Even had he been resurrected, he wouldn't come back to Sageville. If you got to live your life on this earth again would you spend it in some tiny dot-on-the-map town which America forgot? Nor did I ever pray. I just sat in the pew. I even took Louis up there with me once. He asked why. I told him he had a soul. He said I was damn crazy. Maybe I was waiting for a sign. That would have been a good time for God to make a move. I mean, I was ripe for conversion. But all I ever saw was the midday sun shining through the plain windows. I wished it had been a Catholic church. At least then I could have lit a candle or smelled the incense or something.

Veda started to think about winding up. Activities, for those that still went to them, became more inactive than usual until soon, they just faded away. The last one we attended was cooking. Alexandria, the cookery counsellor, had lots of goodies left over in the stores; icing sugar, cooking chocolate and hundreds and thousands. So we sat and did nothing whilst she made little chocolate cup cakes, top heavy with icing. Then we ate them all. B8 had become pretty good at eating over the last two months. Even Walter managed to get most of the food in his mouth most of the time. He still had a problem with baked ziti though. God knows why but that was the one dish which ended up all over him and his neighbours. Book was turning into quite a pig. He'd stuff his face every mealtime, on a par with William, hiding the food away in his cheeks like a hamster, bringing it up and chewing later in academics. Though he'd only ever eat the food off Charlie's plate. He wouldn't touch it if we put it on his own.

We had fresh fish. It was on a Thursday. There'd been great excitement that morning when Herbert bolted up from the Redhill hollering and bawling. The Lord had answered his prayers. He'd caught a fish. Finally. Hallelujah. A real fish, one which wiggled. And waggled. He showed it to everyone. That was the first fish he'd caught since his wife left him. He'd been fishing every day since, and she'd walked out over twenty years ago. Herbert was so proud of his catch that he insisted Rosetta cook it that night and that the whole of Veda should have a piece. Rosetta didn't have the heart to tell him it was too small even to feed one family, so she went into Kingston and bought fresh fish from the market. 'It's amazing how many servings we got from that fish of yours,' she told Herbert. He looked at her kind of puzzled, like she was some modern day Christ showing off with fishes and loaves. 'I'd never have guessed it'd go so far. Still, just goes to show, you never can tell.' Herbert beamed like a kid who'd won the hundred metres on Parents' Day, bumbling round each table to see how the folks were enjoying it. That night he went up Dotty's to celebrate. He got blind drunk, danced with Dotty in the back room, lifted up her dress for a quick peek (red bloomers) then collapsed and had to be carried home by four counsellors. Dotty looked disappointed, her last chance at a bit of nooky before she croaked, and she'd been waiting so patiently. She didn't want to let him go at first. He was out cold and she was still prepared to get as much of her wicked way with him as the good Lord would allow. But when her kisses failed to wake him, she kicked his usless ass and hit the moonshine. In the morning Herbert woke up with the worst hangover of his life. He went out to his garage and snapped his rods; all of them, one by one. Then, in front of all the counsellors, he solemnly swore never to fish again in his life. Two days later his wife turned up. Twenty-five years and she waltzed into his house without a word, started making the supper. Fish.

Lucien's name slid down everyones tongue for a while, hanging there on the tip, festering. Some said he'd been escorted straight back to Paris, others heard he was being held in a New York institution. Strangely, perhaps, I didn't want to know, nor did I try to find out. Gossip raged, feeding on itself, snowballing uphill...he'd always been crazy, schizophrenic, certified; no, it was Veda that sent him mad, he was fine before; but then all queers are manic depressives, it's only natural, a form of divine punishment; don't listen to them, he was having us all on, the last laugh, he just wanted to get out of Veda...Theories crackled along the grapevine, propelled by an array of tinpot psychoanalysts. Someone, I forget who, even said I was to blame, that my rejection proved too much for him; he and I were supposed to have fought in the infirmary before he was taken away, some kind of loon-lovers' tiff.

To tell you the truth, it was all a little confusing. I half-believed some of what I heard. The windows of my memory misted up. I couldn't be clear what *had* happened, or whether I'd even been there. Perhaps I'd only heard about the whole affair. Perhaps I'd convinced myself I'd seen it, had heard stories and reconstructed the whole episode in my head. After all, I was receiving therapy. At least, that's what I heard. One hour a day with Dr Rosenthal. The only way I could cope (to be expected after such a shock). Perhaps the gossip was true, and it is I who am mistaken. Counsellors certainly looked at me in a new light, charitable pity flooding their eyes whenever I passed. Joe tried to tell them it was all bullshit, that I had never been to a therapist, that I was perfectly fine, just a little upset, that's all. But no one believed him. They even began to look upon him with pity. He'd been around me too long. Poor thing.

But then there was Gabrielle; she's the only thing that halts this whole spiral into self-doubt. If it weren't for her, if it weren't that she was there, everything I'm telling you crumbles into nothingness. If I can't believe what I remember, then all of this is meaningless and I'm lost. If I doubt what I did and did not do, then how can any of this have happened: Peter, New York, Veda, Lucien, everything? No, I'm right. I'm sure of it. Gabrielle was by my side most of the time and she never once made mention of a therapist (unless she was protecting my feelings).

Gabrielle was wonderful, not an ounce of pity in her. She wouldn't waste time on such an emotion. It had no place in her; it is false, conjured up to ease a conscience. She doesn't like to talk about these things, but if you watch her, it's not difficult to see. She stayed with me because she felt it wasn't good for me to be left alone. I told her I wasn't alone, I had the boys. She said it might not be a bad idea to spend a little more time in normal company, though she offered to dribble, flap, and shit her pants if it made me feel any easier about her being around. We sat under the falls (water running off our noses) or hitched into Madingdale to prop up the Mexican bar (frothy beer coating our lips), anything to escape the counsellors.

She held my hand. Hers was soft and the most solid thing I have ever touched, and when I looked at her (staring into those dark brown eyes as if for a for ever first time), I no longer thought of me.

I wanted to touch her, touch her more. You think I wouldn't have tried had I been able? But it wasn't like that. I wasn't the one in control, she was calling the shots. Bang. Everything, every asset I'd ever had, every game, every role, all those false charms, were stripped bare when I stood before her.

We took a day off together, went up into the hills to go whitewater tubing on the Phoenix River. It was cold, wet, goosebumps dappling our skin, and we spent most of our time missing the patients. It was they who provided us with enough emotion for each other. Without them I daresay we would have been too concerned with ourselves, our prides and jealousies. But the normal waste, excess, which surrounds relationships dissolved in the faces of Dakota, Willy, Charlie and the rest.

We spoke little of Lucien. The subject was coated with a thick, sticky embarrassment. Besides, I didn't like the idea of talking behind his back. Gabrielle asked me what he'd been like in the final hours. I didn't really have an answer, didn't know what to say. I didn't want to think about it, couldn't bear to give verbal form to what I'd witnessed, was terrified of bringing it all back. So I told her he was just Lucien, only a little more beautiful.

Gabrielle wasn't surprised by the whole thing. She'd seen it coming. I asked her why she hadn't said anything, hadn't tried to do something. She said what's the point? The mind's a stubborn son of a bitch. If it wants to go, it'll go, when and how it pleases. And nothing you can do can make the slightest bit of difference. What happened to Lucien, she said, was not an aberration of his mind but its fulfilment. Still, she missed him. The loss of his confused sensitivities made Veda a more cynical place.

We left the Phoenix River behind and returned to Veda to find the air still heavy with Lucien. No one spoke of anything else, not until Hank and Robbie came along.

Hank was an institutional from E6. High functioning. He'd help Herbert out with the minuscule amount of maintenance work that was done around Veda. He seemed a nice enough guy, always with a heavy grey stubble, his fat belly erupting out of his shirts. He'd been coming to Veda for years, was one of Norma's favourites.

Robbie was a skinny little kid from B6. Barely a teenager. I don't think anyone was sure what was wrong with him. He never spoke, only giggled. Giggled at everything, his tongue quivering between the gaps in his teeth. He had these enormous blue eyes, like a role model out of a Nazi propaganda film on the purity of the Ayran race, and a snubby little nose covered with freckles with one finger lodged deep inside. He seemed okay, never caused any problems.

It was Fergus who caught them. No one knew how long it had been going on, but the joke went around that this was why Robbie was always giggling. Fergus found them deep in the forest when they should have been at swimming. Hank had Robbie up against a tree, his trousers round his ankles, his little white teenage butt spread high in the air; Hank's penis was out, hard and ready to go. Fergus couldn't say if it was inside the anus or not. Hank was frothing, Robbie giggling. Hank was forty years old. Robbie thirteen. Fergus said he'd never be able to get that giggling out of his head as long as he lived. He ran at them, throwing stones, shouting and clapping his hands like he was trying to scare off two wild beasts. They stood there under the tree, trousers in the dirt. Neither of them moved. Just stared at Fergus. Didn't try to cover up a thing. No embarrassment. No shame. Fergus even had to pull their trousers up himself.

Hank got hauled into Kolchak's office. Robbie was from a private family, someone's blue-eyed little boy. Kolchak called the institution and told them to come for Hank immediately. We never found out whether Robbie's parents were told. Nick, Robbie's counsellor, said the parents never came over, nor made any reference to it in their phone calls. Robbie just carried on giggling.

'It's sick. An old man in the woods with some kid up against a tree, like an animal. Makes my stomach turn.'

'You're too hard on him,' Gabrielle answered.

'Hard on him! The guy was raping the kid up the backside. He's thirteen years old. How can you not be hard on him?'

'Perhaps he didn't think he was doing anything wrong.'

'So why was he hiding in the woods then? No, Hank knew damn well what he was doing.'

Gabrielle and I slouched on the porch of E4. It was my last OD and I had asked to spend it at Louis' bunk. I came up a little after nine-thirty to avoid bumping into Dave. I needn't have bothered. Fergus, his co-counsellor, told me he'd been down at the HCs all evening, helping Norma prepare the end-of-season schedule. Norma liked Dave, said he was reliable and had 'outstanding leadership qualities'. She wanted more of us to be like him. She'd recommended Kolchak give him an extra bonus for his 'valuable services to the Veda ethos'. I listened to Fergus tell me this. I was about to say something, but then thought better of it and kept quiet. Gabrielle arrived shortly afterwards and we sat OD together.

The higher level was the quietest I'd ever known; soft mumurings of troubled sleep eeking out through the wire mesh on the windows. The new group of institutionals were the highest functioning of the season. It was hard to see why some of them were there. They still screamed, rocked and flapped, naturally. But they were a damn sight more *compos mentis* than most of the counsellors, a lot nicer too. There were some I adored, like Dinette with her soft cotton voice, and some I hated, like Jim and his ceaseless unfunny humour, prodding you in the ribs and spitting out half-chewed food every time he made a joke. But I guess that's the way it is: some people are arseholes and some aren't, loonies or otherwise.

Gabrielle and I sat under the care of a beautiful night: untrammelled sky, warm moon, sunburnt stars, deep rich blackness pulled around like a heavy cashmere coat. I listened through the mesh door for Louis' voice rambling along the conversational tracks of sleep. He always talked at night. But tonight he was silent. He was going back in a couple of days. His paperwork had finally been sorted out, but his old institution had no bed for him. So the BCCI said they'd take him. He hadn't taken the news well. He'd been out of the BCCI for five years. You could see him wince when Ellen told him he was being sent back in. He didn't understand: he'd been good, behaved, made progress. Still, at least he'd be company for Joshua.

We were throwing a party for Louis the following day up at the ice-cream parlour. May had agreed to throw in four free flavours, the boys' favourites: chocolate chip, pistachio, cream caramel, and plain old vanilla. Louis would opt for vanilla, he always did. He'd been at Veda for almost eleven weeks, longer than any other institutional. It wouldn't be the same without him around jabbering away on my porch, and I was glad we'd all be leaving shortly afterwards. I promised him we'd stay in touch, I could even visit him at the BCCI. He chuckled and said I might yet end up there. I couldn't wait to see his face the next day. The party was a surprise. He had no idea. He'd be so happy, probably start blubbering. I loved surprises.

'I still think you're being hard on Hank,' Gabrielle said. 'You're being unfair.'

'Oh, and how's that?'

'Well you have sexual desires, don't you?'

'Not to bugger some thirteen-year-old kid in the woods.'

'So big deal, you have the choice. These people don't. They want sex as much as anyone else, only they never get the chance. Think how frustrating that must be.'

'They could at least exert some element of control.'

'What, like you did with Natasha?'

It wasn't an accusation. Just fact. Gabrielle's voice was as calm and gentle as ever, and all the more damning for that. She looked at me and smiled. I tried smiling back, but the muscles in my face refused to budge.

'Do you have to bring that up?'

'No, probably not. I just want to show you how similar you are to these people. You should be a little more careful before judging them.'

A few days previously Kolchak was showing some important people round the more presentable parts of Veda. There was a business man, some entrepreneur who'd set up a string of toilet-paper factories and became a millionaire and a local messiah in the process, a priest and a local county official. I think she was hoping for their backing in her application for some sort of grant or financial support. Anyway, they were up on the top field when Linda emerged from behind the music hut, zipping up her trousers. Shortly afterwards out stumbled Donald, from B6, fumbling in his mal-co-ordinated way with his shirt buttons, putting them through the wrong holes or ripping them off completely. Kolchak's party of dignitaries stopped and stared. She tried hurrying them on, knowing damn well what had been going on. Finally, after a long embarrassed silence in which Kolchak saw her funding slip away cent by cent, Linda bawled out, 'So what yer all staring at? Retarded people wanna have sex too ya know!'

The visit came to an end shortly after that. Though the priest asked if he could come back to look around some more.

And then there was Walter and his constant slobbering over girls. He knew the female counsellors found him cute and he played it for all it was worth, siding up to them whenever he could, feeling their dresses and their hair, nodding in one long, subdued orgasm. And there was Dakota's marathon world-beating masturbation sessions. And what about Willy and his constant cries of 'I wanna make SEX!'

I listened to Gabrielle telling me these things. 'So you see,' she concluded, 'you shouldn't be so hard on them. They're dealing with their sexuality in the only way they know how.'

With me floundering on the argumentative ropes, going down in a hail of empirical punches, Gabrielle leant over and kissed me. Not on the cheek, not a little peck: on the lips, full and unrestrained. I still have the taste, guard it day by day; molten saliva burning across my tongue, a fission of skin. I took her deep into my lungs, blood carrying her through my body, awakening each slumbering organ in its turn. Frontiers came tumbling. I closed my eyes, trying to store the moment afresh for each eternity that was to come, savouring her closeness, thinking about Hank, Robbie, Dakota and Willy.

The door opened with a tentative squeak, unwilling to draw us from the embrace, and Louis stepped on to the porch in his ragged pyjamas.

'Bad timing, Louis.'

He didn't respond, didn't even smile. There wasn't even that far away look in his eyes. Just weariness. Tired. Age crept from behind and clocked up years in those few moments.

'What is it Louis, what's the matter?'

Louis stood there on the porch, looking down. He didn't speak, not a word. It wasn't like him to stay so silent around me. A racoon scampered out from underneath the bunk and into the forest. We waited. It looked as though he was on the verge of speaking, of telling us something. But the words wouldn't come out. They stayed inside in the warm. Then he gave a slight shrug and that was it. Nothing more. Whatever he wanted to say had passed.

I wanted the kiss. Moments were slipping. I wanted the kiss.

I jumped up and took Louis' hand, shuffling him back to his bed. Still he said nothing. He wanted to speak, you could see that. But nothing came.

'We'll talk in the morning, okay?' I pulled up the covers and tucked him in tight. 'I promise, we'll talk in the morning. It can wait. Okay?' I waited for an answer. Louis stared at the ceiling, tired eyes, then patted my hand. No words. So I left him and returned to the arms of Gabrielle.

We made love that night. In the counsellors' lounge. On a cheap broken bed, on sheets that hadn't been properly laundered. Gabrielle took me and placed me inside her, my penis an extension of her vagina: as hard, as soft. Passion floated somewhere over our heads. Desire stretched until it snapped, catapulting past into present. I became lost, in her, leaving me far behind. And I found some kind of peace. In a musty hut in the middle of an uncared for woods in a country thrashed by madness. One orgasm without beginning or end. No heaving bodies. No rising sweat. I climbed inside her and curled into a ball. There was only her body: smooth, endless, a journey far from me. And in that moment – when self no longer existed – was love. I looked outward from the womb and saw other, tortured selves, watered by introspection, attentive self-love, and obsessive quests into inner realms, ripening into sin. But these were no longer a part of me: I had Louis in my head, his sadness and silence, and Gabrielle in my arms. And 'I' was nowhere to be seen.

Was it happiness?

I don't know. There was a fleeting moment, of something. Something Peter had felt that night in our room at school, before the pencil went in the eye. I felt it, like a shiver in the cold, warming. But even then, as it tumbled through my body, I knew it was not mine. Not to keep. It wouldn't stay. Lucien had spoken the truth: madness still has work to do.

'Benjamin.'

It was cold. A half-hearted light filtered into the bunk. The voice came from nowhere. Then there was her shadow hovering by the door, not wanting to be a shadow. A blue bird sat on the railings of the porch, feathers and bone, it's mouth open. But there was no song.

'Benjamin.'

The voice came again, taking on stronger human form. Making a stand against nothingness. I opened my eyes. Early. So early. The boys slept: Charlie sitting bolt upright, hands behind his head. We had mice. (Or mice had us.) I could hear them scuttling around in the back room. A heavier footstep now, squeaking on the dusty floorboards. Gabrielle came into the cabin and took my hand. It was cold, colder than the day. Just beginning. Pushing aside the night. I saw her more clearly as sleep passed from my body. She had brought the new day, heaved up the sun, dragged down the moon. The bed was warm and snug, a kingdom in a cover. (Bed is a wonderful invention. Whoever invented bed was a bloody genius.) Gabrielle's hand was shaking.

Laughter. It was definitely laughter, bitterly light. Though where it came from I have no idea. It raced around the bunk and yet the bunk was still. It wasn't Gabrielle, her lips didn't move. I watched them, carved them in marble. No more than a perfect collection of smooth outlines. Her eyes met mine and I saw a shadow. A shadow of pain with no sun to cast it.

'It's Louis.'

The voice was heavy, the words falling, splintering on the floor.

'What?'

'It's Louis. He's dead.'

'Dead?'

'He just stopped breathing. Just gave up.'

Laughter. Again. Was it me? Was I laughing? Can anyone tell me? After all, you were there. Weren't you? I didn't see myself laugh. What I saw was my self lying there in bed, the early hours of a Veda morning all around, Gabrielle at my side, not crying because she had forgotten her tears. I opened a fresh can of tears and offered her some. (God counts a woman's tears.) She squeezed my hand. I saw it with my own eyes. Or were they somebody else's? They were black. Mine are blue. There was no feeling. Well there isn't when you die is there. It just goes. One. Two. Death. You don't even make it to three.

I sat up with some difficulty. I felt old, my body no longer obeyed my commands as readily as before. I tried pulling on a sweater, but my head was too big. The ego had escaped, causing havoc with the proportions of my body. I saw it run through a crowd of people, head down, growing bigger and bigger all the time. The people were my personalities and the ego was knocking down every one, obliterating them. All that hard work, creating faces, perfecting roles, destroyed by a runaway ego. All comes to nothing.

Then I felt it. On my cheek. A tiny breath. The hint of the beginnings of a kiss.

I jumped down from the bed and fell through the floor. Gabrielle could have caught me, but she let me fall.

I wanted to see Louis, wanted to see the body, one last time. But Gabrielle said they'd taken him away. No point leaving him around

Veda all day, it would only upset the others. I pulled on some clothes and ran from the bunk. Perhaps I wasn't too late. Perhaps Louis could ask death to wait.

But Gabrielle wouldn't let me pass. She held my head tightly, pushing it down on to the cold gravel.

'Don't struggle. You'll hurt yourself.' Her eyes were foreign, they belonged to someone else.

Pressure in the temples.

Then came the laughter again, brushing against my cheek. I knew the laugh – Lucien. I saw him standing behind me before I turned round. The paint in his hair was still fresh, drying for eternity. Highways of tranquillity ran through him. His eyes were alive and dead at the same time, the charm of his smile bright and dull. He stood before me, in the middle of the baseball field, holding out his arms, entreating me. As beautiful as I had ever seen. Faint as the morning light.

'Well, aren't you going to congratulate me on my resurrection?' The voice was Lucien's. I recognised it. Yet it was anonymous, a composite of fears I had shut away. Demons I had never known. The camera was back. Rolling. I heard it at the side of my head, though the picture was fuzzy. I had great difficulty seeing myself. Lucien was inside the camera, operating it, seeing through my eyes. He was inside my consciousness, directing my vision, forcing my self to watch me watch him.

'Benjamin, why are you running? There's no need to hurry. Louis' time is up. He might have had a little longer, had you chosen to help. Why worry now? You didn't when he was alive. Maybe you could have made a difference. Maybe. Had you not preferred the lips of this Jezebel.' Lucien punched Gabrielle in the face, her neck snapping with the force of the blow. Still she held my head, her eyes staring indifferently into mine, her face brightening at the pain. 'But then that's not like you is it, to help people I mean. As long as you don't go under, that's all that matters. You say anything, be anything, do anything and then turn your back when the consequences come. The consequences of your existence. Everything you do matters. Ask them.' Lucien pointed.

An overwhelming greyness sucked colour from every object, submerging visual distinctions. And through the colourlessness, then, I saw her, standing like a willow, the coarse pointed hood casting a purple shadow all around: the Slavic girl.

Touch her. She was there. Clear in the tentative light.

Feel. Her white, dew-soaked skin.

And yet I couldn't be sure. For it wasn't her. Or rather she wasn't whole, a body within which lies another's spirit. What I saw and what I felt had no connection. Sorrow, pity, devotion, spun round inside, a cocktail that had once produced love; though I knew not this girl and such emotions were neither inspired by her nor destined for her. It was for someone I knew, or had known. Someone whose past wouldn't let me lie.

The landscape around her stepped back, fading, and she was all there was. Her bones grew thinner. Her smile, what was left, became hollow. I moved toward her, shifting through the grey; solid matter collapsing, the ground dissipating beneath my feet. Her face withered into transparency and I saw inside her head. It was full of mountains of words, judgments sliding down scree slopes, filling the valleys. The sky was crammed with clouds of cumulus conscience, all tumbling over one another to escape the earth's downpour. And I saw rivers of condemnation, flowing from one life into the next, out into estuaries of self-love, silted with guilt.

And then she kneeled. At Lucien's feet. He smiled. I heard the prayer; the solitary voice which had echoed around the dorm every night of my school days; the clammy hands in a tight grip, fingers running blue; the thin legs, jutting at odd angles from the knee; taut lips, barely moving, the nervous tongue slipping between; the shy eyes eeking out understanding. Memories, which for so long I had tried to bind up, tight, stow away, muffled and strangled, came undone, unravelling at my feet, gasping for air.

I knew.

I knew now who it was, there, praying at Lucien's feet, why the emotions were so familiar, what it was I had loved and lost to self. I knew why the eyes beneath the hood stirred within.

A step closer. I could hear the suffering in the voice, crying to be heard, pleading with those who will never care, a breath so fragile it could cease at any moment.

The praying stopped.

The Slavic girl sat back on her knees and turned to me, lifting her hands, open palms for me to look upon (the tiniest trace of blood, the wear of prayer) and lifted the pointed hood from her head.

And I saw. Clearly. No doubt. Who it was.

Peter.

He was frail, worn, punished by time, the softness of his sad features hardened and cracked. He looked tired, beaten, as though he could no longer muster the will for another breath. But it was Peter. I'll swear on my grave, when I get there. He knelt at Lucien's feet exactly as he used to kneel by his bed before lights out in the dorm at school. His mother would write out prayers for him to recite. He'd always show them to me first and ask whether he should read them. I always said he should if that was what kept his mother happy. And after prayers he'd cross himself and climb into my bed and we'd make love. He'd touch me, then cry. He couldn't live with that: us so close to God; physical desire and holiness under the same covers. But neither could he stop. Prayers. God. Then me. I suppose that's why he got so confused in the end: couldn't tell us apart.

I guess I could have done something. I knew it troubled him. And I let it go on.

He didn't look at me now. He was trembling. But not from the cold.

I went to him, at long last, to offer him the comfort I failed to give once before, to make amends for what was not done.

Father, forgive me...

'Too late. Too late.' Lucien's gleeful whisper wrapped itself around my throat.

For I know not...

Peter shrank from me, on Lucien's command, avoiding my touch. I held out my hand. But the closer I got, the weaker the image became. Peter flickered, struggling to stay whole. The was a pain in his eyes, as if he were trying to resist.

A collection of demons, I could smell them, that was all Peter was. And each one of them belonged to Lucien.

I laid my fingers upon Peter's cheek.

It shattered. The whole face. Dropped to the ground, splintering like glass. Disintegrating without a sound. And through each fragment came a broken image of Natasha: flushed cheeks, sensuous lips, the bluest of eyes and long blond hair resting on a tanned shoulder. I saw her drowning in the sea of stories, believing and swallowing every one. And deep down, deep under the source, I saw me.

I was roles, stories, lies. A swirling collection of impermanences, invented, never real. I was a gospel without truth, a bible of deceits. I was me and me alone; I stood for me, fought for me and believed only on me, no one else mattered, whilst all that was worthwhile collapsed around my blindness.

Then, one by one, the faces of Natasha rose up and changed, into seven bodies; malformed and out of time. Noses too large, mouths too small, awkward, dependent: my boys, standing there, needing me.

Lucien called to them, promising falsehoods. He told them lies and they believed every word. They looked, listened, trusted, then knelt at his feet.

'Leave them alone, you bastard.'

'Why? They're freaks, Benjamin, remember, you said so yourself.'

'They're mine. They need me.'

'Oh, Benjamin, don't go sentimental on me. They're no one's. They're veggies. They don't need anyone. What do you care?'

He wanted to take them, take them from me and so I would have nothing, nothing left to hold on to.

The voice was inside the camera now. It was Lucien, giving voice to my fears. He beckoned to me. I tried holding back, tried not to give in. But self was stronger than I. Self was under his command, shrouded in the demon's cloak. Self listened and obeyed, ignoring me. And it was thus I saw myself go forward and kiss Lucien on the cheek. Then with a sickly sweet smile, a face of concern, of care, trust and comfort, I looked on, horrified, powerless, as I sauntered towards Dakota, lifted my arm and, with all the force I possessed, smashed him across the face with the palm of my hand.

He bled. And I cried.

The blow. The pressure from the side of my head was released. Temple doors opened. I looked around: nothing, no one. I was alone, lying on the grass of the baseball field in my nightclothes in the early morning light, my hair soaked. I remembered Gabrielle, her message. I panicked. I leapt up and charged across the field, tearing into the woods, tripping over roots, kicking up stones, panting: *if only it were a dream, if only...* Branches tore against my nightshirt, hindering me, whipping my bare legs. The sun had climbed higher in the sky and it was colder than ever. Breathless, my heart dipped in acid, I reached the higher level and rushed into E4. I knew it was a dream. It hadn't happened.

But E4 was empty. It had happened. No Louis. They'd taken him away. Dead. Just like Gabrielle said.

I left the bunk, wandering down the steps and into the triangle at the heart of the higher level. Everything slowed.

He'd gone.

The place was deserted. Not a soul. Not a body either. Except for the handful of institutionals who stood in the inner triangle of the higher level, the statues I had seen so long ago, undecided whether to live or die. Louis was there no longer. He had taken his decision.

I came to a halt. My legs just stopped moving. I had nothing to do with it anymore. A bird started to sing, trying to wake his friends. But they slept on, unconcerned by the start of a new day. Veda slept in the peace of the birds. I was weary.

Dizzy. The ground beneath me swayed. Closer now. Further away. Side to down. Up to side. All I could do to keep my balance was to rock slightly, compensating for a world which turned around me, without my consent, out of control. I stepped in amongst the statues. And there we stood, side-by-side, as one, gently rocking back and forth, gently rocking.

26

Tapping. Tap. It wasn't the rain. Rain wasn't falling. But the noise was rain. Only no wetness. It was like rain falling from under the roof, like the rafters were clouds. Tapping came out of the darkness, thicker than night. I reached for my torch. Each bed stood isolated amid trees, as though the forest had grown up in the bunk overnight, as though the walls had simply disappeared, letting in the wilderness. Movement was at the far end. Tossing and turning, iron bedposts rattling on the floor. It was William. He hadn't soiled himself. He moved side to side when he soiled himself, shifting around until Joe or I got up to change the blankets. This movement was more restless, over and over, round and round. Urgent. I climbed out of bed and began the long trek to the far side of the bunk, straddling fences, splashing through brooks, scrambling through hedges. William lay floating on a burning ocean of salty sweat, his pupils so dilated they were spilling out the sides of his eyes. He was bucking violently now, trying to shake something out of him; his eyes open wide, staring at nothing, his subconscious watching me, his blood bubbling, singeing the palm of my hand as I placed it on his forehead, trees around his bed wilting in the heat. Moans as words streamed from his mouth, soaking the bedclothes.

I woke Joe.

We did what we could, mopping William's face with cold flannels, but it was no good. I wrapped him in a blanket and carried him down to the infirmary.

I was wrong. It was raining after all. And cold, as though each drop had been individually chilled before falling. William was heavier than hell. I could barely hold him, a trapped nerve in my arm pleading with me to let go.

Lucien didn't show his face. But he was there. I felt it as I see you now. Pouring concentrate of blame into my veins. Scattering seeds of guilt across my tongue. I could taste them. I tried spitting them out. But he sowed faster than I could spit.

Dr Rosenthal was one hell of a sleeper. I almost had to break down the door before she arrived, hobbling across the porch in her patched up nightdress. She opened the door just a crack, enough to look upon me as I stood there with William in my arms, soaked. She looked as though I had disturbed her from dying, so old and worn.

'It's William,' I panted, angry at the old bag for not letting us in. 'He's ill.'

'Yes,' she replied slowly. 'I suppose he would be, what with coming here in the rain at this time of night.' She squinted at me, wrinkles charging to her eyes to obliterate any sign of a human face. 'I suppose you'd better come in. Yes, put him down here.'

At long last she opened the door. 'Do you have a towel so I can dry him?'

'Yes. Of course we have towels. This is an infirmary. All infirmaries have towels. That's regulation.' She shuffled out of the room without the slightest inclination for urgency.

The moans died. William's moist face peeped from the blanket, his lips quivering so fast they were still. The doctor took her time. In fact she took more than her time, she took mine too. We stood in the waiting-room. Rooms built for waiting, what a waste. It had been cleaned up pretty good. Cabinet doors mended. Wooden panel on the door refitted. It certainly wasn't Herbert's doing, it was too neat for that. The only trace of Lucien was the fridge door which no longer closed properly.

The fossil of a doctor returned, moving with the swiftness of a funeral cortège. 'Yes, well then, was it you who wanted the towel?' I looked around. I was the only person in the room. 'Yes, well perhaps you should tell me his name.'

'William Alexander Hunt.'

'Yes, William Alexander Hunt,' she repeated, savouring each syllable with painful languor. 'Which bunk is he in?'

'Boys Bunk 8. Lower level.'

'Yes, Boys Bunk 8. Lower level. Where's he from?'

'California.'

'Yes, California. Very nice. And what's wrong with him?'

'I don't know, Dr Rosenthal. That's why I brought him to you.'

She stared at me hard. I think she was frowning, it wasn't easy to tell behind all those wrinkles. 'Yes, well, that's quite enough of your sarcasm, young man.' I was beginning to regret coming. The doctor couldn't operate faster than ten words a minute. Every time she opened her dried up old mouth I thought she was going to croak. I should've gone straight to Kolchak. 'Yes, well I suppose we'd better take a look at him. He may be in a dream you know.'

The medical miracle of a doctor bent down, put her lips to Willy's ear and shouted. 'William Alexander Hunt! Can you hear me? Please acknowledge.'

'Is he deaf?' the doctor shouted.

'No.' I shouted back.

'What?'

'I said, "no". He's not deaf.'

'Oh.' She wandered off again, slowly, fearful that the slightest sign of enthusiasm might cause her to fall apart.

'Where are you going?' I called after her.

'Going to get my medical kit, with your permission,' she replied, annoyed at my intervention. 'My, my, what an impatient young man!'

Dr Rosenthal's medical kit comprised a large camping torch which she shone mercilessly into Willy's eyes, a small rubber mallet she'd borrowed from Herbert's maintenance shed which she banged up and down Willy's legs, and an old wooden clothes peg which she used to pinch the skin on his arms. 'Testing the reflexes,' she told me. 'It all comes down to relflexes.'

I tried giving William some comforting words, meaningless things said to the sick. 'I wouldn't bother,' the doctor said. 'I think he's deaf.' She shuffled away again in search of more medical tricks.

There was a sudden thump. I thought the doctor had keeled over and went to help, cursing Kolchak for not hiring proper medical staff. Then, as I got closer to the door in the back wall I heard the faintest of chants, caressing its way through the cracks. Soothing. *Pleurez, pleurez les anges, j'oserai. Sweet. Pleurez, pleurez les anges, j'oserai*. I watched it slip under the door, trying to grab my feet and pull me in. I wanted to stay, listen to the song. Then I remembered William. I had to get him out of there. The chanting grew louder, clawing against its weakening. I snatched up a dry blanket and wrapped it around the bundle of sweat. Lucien was coming for William. I had to get him away. Dr Rosenthal saw me leaving and creaked to the door as fast as her lethargy would allow, blocking my way.

'Where are you going with that patient?'

'I'm taking him to High Command.'

'Oh no you're not. I haven't finished my tests yet. No need to worry. He'll be fine in my hands. I'm a doctor, you know.'

'I know, Dr Rosenthal. But look at him. Don't you think we should get him to a hospital?'

'A hospital!' She spat out the word, barely able to conceal her contempt. 'Why no, no, no, there's no need for that. He'll do just fine here with me.'

The chanting grew louder, more urgent. *Pleurez, pleurez les anges, j'oserai*. An empty chuckle skipped along beneath the notes, filling the house of the sick. The doctor didn't seem to hear. I think she was deaf.

'I'm sorry Dr Rosenthal, I have to go.'

'You'll do no such thing. That's my patient.'

'And he's my boy and I'm not going to let anything happen to him.'

I kicked open the door and ran into the rain, the good doctor standing on the porch fuming. 'Get back here this instant! That's my patient! Get back here!'

Kolchak was a saint. I don't care what they say about her, she was a damn saint. It was close on four in the morning when I hammered on her door. She'd already been woken by a steaming phone call from an irate Dr Rosenthal, screaming for my balls. If such insolence is tolerated for one moment then the whole hierarchy of age and respect will come tumbling down and we shall all be lost. But Kolchak wasn't angry, not for a moment, not even the slightest hint of annoyance. All she cared about was William. She stuck some kind of shower cap on her head, a ragged jumper over her granny nightdress, an undignified mess, and we jumped in her car and raced off for Kingston hospital, me in the back holding on to Willy for all I was worth.

They wanted to keep William in for a few days, under observation. It was worse than we thought. There was some kind of nasty reaction going on between William and his pills. I don't pretend to know about this stuff so I can't really tell you, but the confused frowns of the doctors at his bedside said enough.

Hospitals scare the hell out of me: everyone hanging around gawping in at your organs, no one telling you what's going on. I stood at the end of William's bed, so far away I couldn't reach him. Useless. Kolchak stayed with me through what was left of the sleepless night, then suggested we go back to Veda. 'William is in good hands now.' She offered to stop off at a diner on the way home and treat me to a cooked breakfast. I'd never seen the director close up before. Her features, thin and hard from a distance, softened. She looked a little like my grandma on Mother's Day, happy yet absent, the gentle face of an old woman with that once-removed look in the eye of fading colours which tells you she knows it's all coming to an end. Kolchak had had more than her share of suffering, you could see that. When she smiled the pain lit up, memories she had tried to forget shining like a stubborn beacon. She was somewhere inside, hiding from the light. But it was too bright. I thought of her and Auschwitz, of Hitler and Blatch.

'I know what they say about me.'

That's what Kolchak said. She reached out, touched the sleeve of my shirt and said: 'I know what they say about me'. She had a solemn, reserved tone, like this was her last confession or something. Don't ask me where it came from. One minute we were talking about Willy and his chances of recovery, the next she comes out with this. I hadn't asked her a thing. And why she chose to tell me, I will never know. We weren't on particularly good terms, no more so than any of the other counsellors.

She touched my arm and pulled me close in a whisper, sadness lighting up her eyes, resigned to an undesired fate. I had no idea what to say. She was my boss; I wasn't used to this kind of intimacy. 'You know, you can only try. You think I wanted Veda to end up this way? Half-hearted, half-functioning. They think I'm stupid, that I don't know what's going on. I know. You think that's what I wanted for Veda? Of course not. I had dreams. This was going to be the best institution America had ever seen. This was going to be the envy of the whole country. But you can't escape from what goes before. You think you can. You think you can leave your past behind, but it stays with you and colours whatever you do. And then you realise, on a sad, sad day, that's it's not going to work out as you imagined, that everything will fall short of your dreams. That's when you grow old. That's when you understand: you do what you can and it has to be enough.' She let go of my arm, lowered her head as if in prayer and stepped back.

I thought she'd finished. I started to walk to William's bed, but she checked me.

'You do see, where else would these people have to go if not Veda?' She spoke more urgently now, as though it really mattered to her that I understood. 'The institutions? Don't talk to me about those places. I know those hellholes. Believe me, I know. They have to get away from there sometimes in their life, even if it's only for a summer. And where else would they go if not Veda? You do see that don't you?' She tugged at my arm.

I nodded.

'Growing old,' she continued, 'is learning to live with the least of your expectations.'

Then she picked up her coat and shuffled out the door, beckoning me to follow.

Out in the corridor her face was bright again, her public smile returned and I was just another member of her staff. There was no trace of sadness in her face and no hint of the intimacy we had shared. 'Come along, then. We should be getting back.'

I wanted to stay at the hospital, with William. Kolchak didn't approve at first. 'What about the rest of your boys?'

'Joe's there. They're all right with him.'

She shook her head, tutted, and then said if that's what I wanted she had no objections. Though I shouldn't start loading responsibility on to myself. That wouldn't do anyone any good. Besides, I'd already done all I could. I said I'd like to stay all the same.

The hospital was clean, efficient, friendly and ill. Life kept running down the corridors trying to check out, doctors and nurses racing along behind, dragging it back inside. It might have been a nice place to stay if there weren't so many sickies lying around. The whole cast was there: temperature, vomiting, diarrhoea, infection, all happily prancing from bed to bed, side-stepping treatment. An assault course for mischievous microbes. Bacteria basking in blood. Disease gambling in the body casino, rolling the dice for that elusive first prize: death.

Place your bets.

William's room was on the fourth floor overlooking a huge graveyard – that town had a sick planning department. Masses of crosses piled one on top of the other, a stationary traffic jam of the dead, rushing to beat the crush to heaven, hell waiting for those who didn't make it before closing time. There were two other kids in the room, though what they were doing there was anybody's guess. They both looked fine to me. Doctors came in, glanced at the sheets of paper on the clipboards at the end of their beds, said nothing and left. No pills. No injections. There wasn't the slightest change in them whilst I was there. The freckled one with puff cheeks wouldn't take his eyes off Willy; gawping at his chipped teeth, smirking at his squashed nose, giggling at his cabbage ears. He knew there was something wrong with him. Not sick. Just wrong. Willy looked ill even when he was fine. Though now he was sick, I thought he looked rather well, more normal. The other kid took no notice of us. There was some sort of pocket computer game glued to his hands. He just sat pressing buttons all day. Left. Right. Up. Down. Fire. Listening to little bleeps on his ear phones. No wonder he was sick.

William said nothing all through the first two days. Didn't mumble in his sleep. Not even so much as a fart. His eyes never closed. Wide. Dilated. I don't think I ever saw him blink. I had to take it from the doctors that he was alive. Though he did do one thing. Sweat. I'd never seen so much sweat. The nurse had to change his bed twice a day to prevent the sheets solidifying.

I didn't sleep. Not for a second. I was frightened of letting William out of my sight, scared he'd be taken away. When I was weary I could hear Lucien's chant. Though I knew it was in my head; no one sings in hospital. I sat on William's bed holding his hand, stroking his face, or slumped in the stiff soft chair and watched him do absolutely nothing, the bright lights of the rooms wrapped tightly around my head. Had I known how to pray I would have. God must get a lot of requests from hospitals. I figured He must get pretty fed up with people turning to Him only in times of trouble. Still, I suppose He has to earn His glory.

Ellen came on the second afternoon. We sat for an hour and said nothing. She asked how William was. I said no change. And that was it. We just looked at him.

Later she told me I looked terrible and persuaded me to come back to Veda at least for a change of clothes. I made her promise she'd bring me straight back.

As it turned out I wished I hadn't gone. I was in no fit state to be around the boys. My mind wasn't tuned in to theirs. They were good to me, in their own way. Charlie leapt at me with a great slobbering hug. Joshua and Mitchel stayed well away, taking the argument they were having elsewhere. Although Josh did ask after William. 'Well you know, Counsellor Benjuman, I know what it's like to be sick, well yes I do. There's quite a lot of suffering involved. Now you be sure to give Client Hont my condolencies, don't you go forgetting.' Book crept to my bed and gave me a sock to give to Willy. Even Walter seemed to notice something was amiss. He sat on William's bed in silence, didn't nod once, trying his hardest to look thoughtful. But Dakota, he just had no idea. Things somehow never got home to him. Or rather they did, there was just no one there to receive them.

I didn't go down to dinner. I wanted to take a shower, grab some clothes and get back to the hospital. But Dakota wouldn't leave me be. Joe had left him to follow the rest of the bunk down to the dining-hall, like he usually did. But he refused to budge. I told him to go. Scram. Shift. Scat. Time and time again. But all I got was questions. Questions. Who's opening for the Mets? What's for lunch on Friday? When does the last bag of laundry go out? When we begin the new schedule? Each one repeated dozens of times, tossing and turning in the sweaty sheets of my head. I wanted to be alone. I didn't need this. I was tired. Weary. He wouldn't stop. I pushed him out the bunk. But he came right on back in. What time breakfast? What's on channel fifteen next Wednesday at seven? I pushed him out again. He became annoyed, started slapping himself. My ear got caught in the cross fire, a stinging thwack rattling through my head. I could feel the anger rising in me. I could've headed it off. But it's hard to be calm when Dakota's around. Questions. I gave him answers. But that wasn't enough. Questions. I yelled at him, bawled him out so hard I thought I'd blow the bunk down. There are no bloody answers, Dakota. Leave the questions alone. The stubborn son of a bitch refused to listen.

I didn't want to do it. Didn't plan to. But by the time I realised what I was doing, it was done. Right in the middle of a question on the next Mets home game. My hand sprang with a snap. I caught him clean across the face with the palm of my hand. Real hard smack.

The large red mark throbbed on Dakota's cheek. I think it was his left. You could see the outline of my long fingers. I'd caught part of his eye. That'd be a real shiner in the morning. Stopped him dead. He didn't say a thing. Not a sound. He looked up at me, enormous tears swimming in his eyes, refusing to fall. Pain from nowhere. Out of blindness. Into the light. Misunderstood.

Deep from within, so far away it almost wasn't a part of me, came a cry. I wrapped my arms around Dakota, holding him like he were my own. How I expected him to understand the words that fell with the tears, I have no idea. I couldn't understand them. They were imploring sounds, begging forgiveness. Apologies without excuses. Again and again they came. I wanted Dakota to speak. To say it was okay. To say he understood, he forgave. Anything. Even a sound.

Nothing.

I stood with my arms draped around him, crying whilst the bruises swelled on his face. Why didn't anyone give him speech. Why the hell couldn't someone give him some real words, just for once? But he stood like a pillar. Without sound. Stone. Untouched. Uninvolved. Holding me up. If he collapsed, I would fall.

The hospital was asleep when I returned, the ward bathed in such confused misery that I looked out that fourth floor window on to the graves with a kind of shallow envy. William showed no sign of change. Same and same. The doctors were perplexed. Whatever they pumped into him made no difference, his lack of reaction was the one constant. He wasn't getting worse. He was just there. Motionless. Bug eyes with a temperature. Life sitting on the side of his bed, undecided. I longed for William to do something. Called out to him to shit his bed, thump me, wet himself. Anything. The kids in the next beds looked at me like I was crazy.

In the evening, solitary people came to visit the graveyard, replacing the dying flowers with fresh ones so that they too could die in their turn. One woman in a pink scarf came with an enormous box of flowers. Carnations I think (ask my mother, she knows). She went round to each grave, placing one flower by each headstone until the box was empty. Then she picked leaves off the flowers she'd already laid down and scattered them on the remaining graves.

Lights out and I sat alone in the glow of the red night-lights. Humming. The patient in the end bed had a hell of a snore for a little kid. Perhaps that's what the doctors were trying to cure; if they weren't, they should have been. There weren't as many voices in the corridors outside as there usually were. I couldn't hear the nurses doing the rounds. Our nurse didn't even come in and say goodnight. The hospital was still, as though the sick had all been cured and gone home.

It was the reflection I saw first, feeling its way along the nightlights; a little pale, unwell. Lights were runways, and nothing ever landed. Forever taking off, never resting. It was just like Lucien to creep up whilst my back was turned, in the dark so you could never be sure how much of him was there. I wasn't sleeping. I was looking down into the graveyard, wondering how to fill hours that had no end, trying to make out the carnations. The yellow ones were the only ones you could see at night and even they were just a blur. I saw his face. But the body kept changing. He was wrapped in the false security of a monk's habit. He was in a mountain retreat, high above man-made clouds. Monks shut themselves away from the outside world, and were called holy. Holy for ignoring their fellow man. He was close now, his breath tugging at the hairs on my neck. You could smell him, the only thing in the room not sanitised. Infected. He leant forward to kiss me. I tried to resist. But he squashed my face up against the window, his tongue slobbering across my cheek, clouds of condensation thickening the glass. His eyes were blacker than despair. Wide, opening on to the lake where demons are named.

He didn't speak for a while. He'd always said that love meant comfort in silence. The camera rolled. Flickering. Remorse-less. I tried to step outside. But there was no outside. I was trapped. I didn't want to watch. But Lucien was inside the camera, operating it. So I was forced to look at my self, that which I had made and to which he had given shape. My image was more distant this time, poorly focused. But it was me. It had to be. There was no one else in the room. Besides, I knew self better than me. It did all the feeling, cried the emotions, carried reactions to the thoughts. Self had become the I. And without the 'I' in the world, there was nothing. As for me, me just wandered around, empty, something for self to watch, predict, feel through, avoiding the danger of immediacy. Lucien's smile, once so graceful, grew eternally weak. Muscles wasted away, dragging down the side of his face. If you're quiet, you can hear them weeping. I prayed. Or did I rock? The floor kept slipping around me. A patient died at the end of the corridor. I felt his heart stop. There was a moment when he might have made it. A shudder. But no one came, they'd all gone home.

Death hauled in the bets.

'That was quite a punch you gave Dakota. A nifty right hook. Congratulations. I knew you could do it.'

'Go fuck yourself, Lucien.'

'Come now, Benjamin, there's no need to be unpleasant. I've come to see how William is getting on. Caught a cold, has he? Your last piece of sanity lying in a hospital bed. I wonder how long he'll last.' He leant over the bed, his face close to William's, feeling his temperature, caressing his cheeks.

'Leave him alone.' I tried to stop him, push him away. But the camera wouldn't move. I watched my self stand by whilst Lucien picked up a pillow.

'Let's see what your sanity's made of.' Lucien brought the thick white pillow down across William's face, smothering him. William didn't move. 'This one's going to go easy,' Lucien smiled, his face flooded with its former beauty, his eyes serene. 'I don't like a struggle. It's better this way.' There were screams. It must have been me, I must have been raging, but it was all so far away. Somewhere was a part of me hammering against the window, pleading with Lucien: take me, not William, take me. But he couldn't hear. He pressed the pillow down harder. I kept calling for William to react; kick, do something. I could feel his lungs collapsing, each element of oxygen stretching to keep the body alive. Blood slowed, veins clogging.

Can you hear the voice? Now can you hear it?

Perhaps it is Louis, though it sounds more like Gabrielle. Calling. Words without meaning. I don't understand. *Feeding on guilt*. Lucien pushed harder. 'More resistance than I thought. He'll be gone soon Benjamin, then you'll be with me. We'll be together. Over on this side.' He smiled at me, sweetness. Innocence regained. The voice. Comes again. Gabrielle, a collection of echoes. A summation of disparate hesitations. Carnations dying on the graves. *Feeding on your guilt*. Clearer words. Still no meaning. A kick, from William. Not even. A quiver of the leg, a chicken after slaughter. I am crying, bashing my brain, clawing at the eye. It is the camera which fixes me, immobile. Second-hand emotions. Awareness. *Lucien is feeding on your guilt*. The words; they fall together.

William kicks again. Feeble. Still alive.

Lucien presses. Angry. 'Son of a bitch won't stop breathing.' He's cursing now. Give me humming. Give me pencils. I'll do it. Ram them through my eye. Let him go. Please let him go. I'll do it myself. Just give me the pencils. Lucien is pleased with me. 'Now,' he shouts, still on top of William. Smothering. Oxygen drying. 'Now. Do it now!'

I grab the pencil. Sharp. Ready. Up to the eye. Release. End this pressure. Mind hurts. One stab from relief.

'Now!'

I see Peter. In the led of the pencil I see Peter. He is sitting at his desk in the corner of the room, young again. I am trying to read. If I can only read. Lucien is holding the book, forcing it to my face, words burning me. But I hear Peter's voice and can see him. He is smiling. He loves me. He doesn't blame me. He tells me so. He doesn't blame me after all. I know that now. The light in the room is growing dimmer. 'The camera,' he says, 'the camera.' The voice is Peter's. That one in your head: it belongs to Peter. A voice free from blame. 'Put the pencil through the camera. Smash the lens. Destroy the camera. It is on the outside. Louis was wrong. It's not on the inside. Not the mind. Destroy the self, not the 'I'.' His words are so clear. Crisp golden leaves on an eager autumn morning. They have meaning. They are words and they have meaning: eye for an I. Peter sharpens the pencil and gives it to me.

William is kicking now, bucking like Old Ben up at the ranch, fighting for breath. Lucien is screaming. He's telling me not to listen to Peter. I see him. I see self. William's getting stronger. 'In the eye,' Lucien is crying. 'In the eye.'

I look up.

For the first time I look up at the lens. Directly. Outside of me, inside the camera. I see the one-dimensional, distorted self, reflecting each emotion, robbing it of meaning. I see form dictating to feeling. I see blind self-absorption, the inability to look outward, the quest for self-love, devouring everything in its path.

There is a howl. It comes from Lucien, but it is not his voice. His eyes are no longer black. He weakens. A last surge of energy and William throws him off. Lucien falls. He never stops falling. Disappearing for eternity. And I. I ram the pencil through the camera's lens, shattering self.

Sunshine so bright you can not see. The sky is clear, painted with a fresh coat of blue. There is noise on the other side; splintering components of a pervasive calm.

I am being shaken. I can not see it. But I can feel it. I am being shaken.

I open my eyes and there is the nurse.

'Are you all right?'

I see her. Only once, one image, from within.

'You're not the one who's supposed to be sick,' she laughs. 'What are you doing unconscious?'

The carnations on the graves are in bloom. William is sitting up in bed, his huge lips wrapped around a monstrous peanut butter and jelly sandwich. He looks up at me and burps loudly. 'Ya fat pig!' he yells, grinning meanly.

I feel it. Whatever the emotion is, I feel it. Not second-hand. Not thought about. Not reflected. Fresh emotion of which I am not aware.

Never had I been so happy to see B8. The broken shower, the toilet that didn't flush, the sodden floorboard, the soiled Calvin Kleins in the rafters. It was all so perfect. And there were my boys, waiting for me.

I helped William up the steps and into the bunk where we were greeted by the monstrosity of a mal-co-ordinated ear splitting scream. Prolonged agony. The boys stood there cheering. Out of time and out of pitch. On and on. Ceaseless. Over their heads was a homemade paper banner on which Charlie had copied out:

WELcOME HOME WILLY

It stretched the width of the bunk and was full of little holes, as though the boys had been taking pot shots at it. Joe had decorated it with drawings, the twin symbols of B8: a pillow in one corner, and a pile of turd in the other. Above was a picture of what I suppose must have been William, only with two heads, one leg and arms sprouting from his neck. Crêpe streamers left over from Independence Day raged around the bunk. The boys had silly hats on, and silly faces underneath. Joe blew his party whizzer so hard it broke; it was cheap anyway.

William stood in the centre of the bunk, his grin stretching through the windows, opening and shutting his mouth, mumbling shyly. 'Yeah yeah yeah yeah yeah that's me. Willy Alexander Hunt!' In all the excitement he wet himself. But he didn't seem to notice, so we didn't bother cleaning him up.

Instead we cut the cake. Rosetta had made it in the cottage kitchen.

It was a beauty, hidden in layers upon layers of icing, just how the boys liked it. And Kolchak had given us free soda, two cans each, and chips for the boys. It was a real party. We even threw food. Joshua and Mitchel started it, plastering soggy chips against the toilet mirror. Soon the whole bunk was thick with icing-covered, soda-dunked cake chips.

That night we had a celebratory pillow-fight. B6 asked if they could join in. But we wanted to be alone, with just each other to bash. Dakota hid in the toilet as usual, picking his toes and asking us to stop. But the rest of us had a wild time, fought like never before. Walter's co-ordination had improved to such an extent that he could actually hit you, though it still took a good minute for him to line up the swing. Charlie tried pummelling Book stupid. But Book kept sliding under the beds. Charlie tried to follow, but he was too fat to get through and got stuck, which made him the perfect sitting duck. The doctors at the hospital had said William should take it easy. So we didn't let him fight much at first, not until Joshua caught him square across the jaw with a classic overhead swing. After such inspiration, Willy couldn't resist, charging down and up the walls, cussing and hussing, frightening the shit out of poor Josh.

We slept soundly that night, right through breakfast. It was mid-morning by the time we woke up. The bunk was a tip. Joe and I thought about cleaning it up, then thought better of it and went up to the pool instead. Herbert was emptying it tomorrow in preparation for Veda's end. That was the last day it was open and we were damned if we were going to miss it.

After dinner came the call, down at High Command. It was my father, calling from England. Grandma had died. Heart attack. Keeled over whilst playing Beethoven's Piano Sonata N° 14, her head thumping F sharp as she fell. She was only seventy and had never been seriously ill in her life. Mother and father couldn't believe it, just sat there in shock waiting for her to play on. But I guess she's playing somewhere else now.

I haven't told you about Grandma before have I? Well, I didn't think it was important. Didn't think she was going to go and die, did I? I'd like to tell you about her, only not now. Maybe some other time. She showed me her knickers once in church. Huge frilly white things they were. I never did stop laughing.

Kolchak gave me the rest of the day off. Said perhaps I wanted to be alone. So I wandered down to the Redhill, following the path, picking up sticks and throwing them in the water, watching them being carried away. Father didn't want me to go home especially. Grandma would have wanted me to stay. Our family were never ones for ceremony. I wondered what Grandma would have made of Veda, wondered what anyone at home would make of it. It's difficult to explain if you haven't been there, as futile as trying to convey real emotion through words in a book. She would have liked Dakota. She would've thought him hilarious, could have sat re-asking his questions all day. I thought about Louis and wondered whether anyone would be grieving for him. Probably not. Grandma would have grieved for him, had she known. I wish now I'd told her before she died.

I thought I'd want to be alone. Well you do, don't you, when something like this happens? Need to reflect. Take a little time. Gabrielle offered to come with me. But I refused. Somehow, whatever comfort she could offer only seemed out of place. So I went on my own. Walked a long while, thought a lot of things. But none of it made me feel any better. Even in death you can feel comfortable. Something I needed was missing.

Then suddenly on the riverside track, alone, I realised what it was: my boys. I needed to be with those who understood.

I hurried up though the woods, the darkening sky filtering through through the leaves. Several times I lost my way, rushing along a myriad of tracks, guessing my way by the sound of the river, only it seemed to be everywhere. Finally I came out on Sageville Road, up by the falls, and charged down to Veda as fast as I could run.

They were in bed when I got to the bunk. All seven of them. Joe had already left for Dotty's, a little sympathy note on the door asking me to come and join him. I scrunched up the note and wandered the length of the bunk, stopping to look at each of them in turn. The toilet light buzzed. They were all asleep, except Joshua, who lay staring up at the rafters. He noticed me but chose not to look. I wondered whether he was thinking of his ex-family, or if he knew anything about the BCCI. This time next week that would be his new home. Dakota slept in his Shea Stadium nightshirt, four sizes too big, curled up around a well-thumbed TV guide. Book lay by the side of Charlie under a bundle of covers, their heads touching on the pillow. Walter had a faint smile, a touch of spittle on his lips, dreaming of Gabrielle no doubt. Mitchel still had his headphones on, a blank cassette whirring away inside. And William, he'd soiled himself. There was just the faint whiff of his personalised processed homecoming cake. But he looked so peaceful I didn't have the heart to wake him. The change of sheets could wait till morning.

I went over and slumped down in the corner on the floor. I thought of Grandma and her white knickers and of my boys here, and the two seemed to become one in an indistinguishable warmth.

Up in the rafters over my head was the banner. Part of it had been torn down in the food fight. I squinted through the shadows at what remained, only just making out the jumbled letters of Charlie's writing:

WELCOME HOME

27

'Thirty-five pairs of underpants!' Joe read the inventory form again to be sure he wasn't mistaken. 'Jesus! Did he really have that many? Thirty-five? He'll be lucky to go home with five.'

We searched the bunk a fourth time, enlisting Dakota's expert eye. Joe even climbed up in to the rafters. But five pairs were all we could find. In truth, I knew of an extra two in the wastepaper basket, but they were heavily encrusted with fossilized skidmarks, we couldn't send those home. The other twenty-eight pairs of William's Calvin Klein briefs hadn't made the course, had fallen along Veda's way; mislaid in the laundry, discarded in rubbish sacks, beyond saving, or flung into the forest, a gift to nature, the defecated lumps so mind bogglingly huge and solid they wouldn't respond to human hands.

'I wonder if we should put in a little note for Mrs Hunt. To explain.'

'What for?' said Joe. 'I'm sure she knows she's got a shitter for a son.'

So we packed the five surviving pairs of Calvin Kleins and said nothing.

Not one single item of William's wonderful wardrobe was returning in the pristine condition in which it had arrived: the silk dressing-gown had been torn in a pillow fight, the lambswool sweaters snagged, even the leather soles had come away from his funny French shoes. But then it was the same with all the boys. Veda had taken its toll, left its mark. Everything left soiled, and perhaps much the better for it. None of the trunks looked as immaculate as when we received them. Now the clothes were shabby, ingrained with the dirt that was Veda. Joshua's stuff was the only exception, but then that had been shabby from the beginning.

We packed the trunks and the boys lolled aimlessly around the bunk. Dakota was a help, in a Dakota sort of way, identifying the mounds of featureless possessions which festered in corners and under beds. Though he had no sense of order. Joe and I would finish one trunk, ticking off as many items as we could find on our original lists, locking it and stacking it in front of the bunk for Herbert to pick up whenever his truck gathered together enough speed to make it up the hill, then Dakota would come running to us, shouting and giggling, holding up a pair of socks or a shirt: 'Charlie yeas it is Charlie yeas Charlie's fings'. Every time the clothes belonged to the trunk we had just finished. I'm sure he waited until we'd neatly crammed everything in and squeezed down the lid before charging forward with the newly discovered items we'd long written off. It annoyed the hell out of us. Dakota loved it.

Joe and I thought about getting angry. But we couldn't. We only had him for two more days.

If the boys knew they were going home they didn't show it, at least, they didn't get excited. I tried drawing some emotion out of Dakota, just a drop. He stood over us whilst we were packing his bags. 'Why you pack my bags why why?' I took his hand in mine. He flapped and pulled it away. He would let me touch him these days, a little. But if I tried to hold on too long he grew agitated.

'Dakota. Are you going to miss me?'

'Why you pack my bags yeas why?'

'Tell me you're going to miss me, please.'

'Why you do pack my bags yeas why you do?'

Though I think he knew what was going on. He started asking questions he'd never asked us before: questions about shopping lists, nachos, and visits to Grandpa on Thursday evenings, questions we couldn't answer, parts of his life we didn't even know existed and would now never get the chance to discover.

A sort of excitement came William's way for a couple of hours on the Thursday morning. He stamped his feet on the ground and pounded the bed with his fist. Perhaps it had something to do with his going home. I asked him.

'What you getting het up about, Willy?'

He shrugged his shoulders, whispering shyly. 'Oh no, I don't know.' Then he stopped stamping and went and sat quietly in the corner.

Joshua spent most of the last week in that corner, we'd had hardly a peep out of him. I'd never known him so quiet. He sat as still as a trainee Buddha, watching us whilst we cleaned up; mopping the floor, disinfecting the bathroom, patching up the holes in the wall. Perhaps the news about his family walking out on him was finally hitting home. Perhaps he'd realised where he was heading.

Book also grew quieter as the end approached. Though with him it was different. We'd seen this before. He was withdrawing into himself, hiding in the badlands behind his eyes where we'd first found him. He stopped eating, spent much of the last day in bed, eyes poking out from under the covers, staring at the rafters without the slightest interest in the world around him. Even Charlie couldn't stir him. He tried; pinching him, stroking him, kissing. But Book didn't want to know. Charlie might as well not have been there. So he gave up on his attempts to reach his friend and lay down beside him in silence, heads touching. Book still responded to questions, but only with single syllables. And he no longer answered to the name of Book. It was back to Robert.

We finished Walter's trunk, jumping on it until it surrendered and closed. That was the last. All done. Then came that familiar Dakota snigger. He was holding up a grubby T-shirt shot through with holes, stained down the right side with saliva. 'Walta's yeas it is Walta's,' he laughed. He was right. He was always right. We opened the trunk, shoved the shirt inside, and hauled it out of the bunk before Dakota could find anything else we'd forgotten.

Once we'd got the the boys ready Joe and I packed our own bags. My cubby had been spawning junk all season: empty pill bottles, ear plugs embedded in thick brown wax, schedules never followed, a bra, mangled cassettes, piles of 'hot bitch vixens' fighting it out in the mud. Underneath it all I came across the notes I'd made during orientation. Way back. I hardly recognised my own writing. The paper was yellowing, damp-stained, like an old newspaper whose events no longer have any meaning. Clinically noted, incomprehensible scribbles. I read. Over two months and 'autistic' still didn't mean anything to me – Dakota did.

The sun tried its best but the late-afternoon air remained stubbornly cold. Counsellors ventured out of their bunks with bags strapped to their backs, dumped them on the grass then scuttled back inside. Trunks piled so high they proved gravity false. Herbert had yet to make a start on collecting them. He hadn't ventured past his front gate ever since his wife had returned.

Joe and I slumped on the porch. This time tomorrow we'd be out of here, nothing left but memories to grow old with and dodgy digestive systems from the Veda diet. Joe spoke long of his plans. He was heading out West: California, hitching coast-to-coast, fulfilling his mother's dream. He wanted to take Claudia with him, didn't like the thought of leaving her. They really had something going, I hadn't see them fight once. But he couldn't take her. Worse, he couldn't explain why; not to her at least. He'd dreamt of his journey since he was a boy: standing by the side of a deserted road cutting through the red rocks of the Arizona dessert; shacking up for a long ride at the side of an obese hog of a truck driver; snatching twinklets of sleep in the booths of old diners, an old dime melody to which no one was listening playing in the background – right across America. And in the dream he was alone, there was never anyone by his side. And that was the way it had to be. Claudia would never understand that. So he told me instead and she was left to cry in the dark.

Joe had no idea what he was going to do if he ever reached California. But one thing he did know, he didn't want to return to England. 'Look at my brother,' he would say, time and time again, seeking some form of justification for comfort. 'Twenty-six going on forty. A mind narrower than the Coventry Canal. Small town written all over him. I couldn't handle that.' Joe's brother was everything Joe hated about England: beer bellies, gormless pride, ignorant arrogance held with an irrational passion, punch-ups in the High Street on a Saturday night, puking your guts up on a Sunday morning, a resigned acceptance that whatever was yesterday would be tomorrow, one long passage through sameness.

'What about you, Ben. What are you going to do?'

I didn't know. I still don't. Not that it matters much anymore. Cambridge had lost its shine, the ivory in the towers was cracked. I suppose I felt some kind of obligation to return. I didn't think I'd really follow Gabrielle back to Switzerland, didn't think I had the balls. It was just a romantic notion, a dream. But why not? Romance and reality have been known to get along from time to time. It's not only the stuffing of fiction.

Gabrielle and I had talked about it. Once. Her mother had a big house by the lake. She had people staying over all the time. One more would make no difference. She was the head of a local private school, the chances were she could find me a job teaching English. I could borrow some money from my parents, just to start out. At the very least I could take a year out from Cambridge. I had dreams then.

And now?

I remember what Kolchak said on that first day I arrived at Veda, so long ago where the light of memory begins to fade. It was in her welcoming speech, when she was just a petite elderly woman with a frail voice in a large, dark, cold hall: 'Whatever happens to you here, the experience awaiting you will affect the rest of your lives'.

Did it?

Would I be here in this dormitory full of cast-iron beds, paint peeling from the walls, infernal flies buzzing, lying in my own excrement in this cheap broken bed, drugged up to the eyeballs, barely able to string a sentence together, utterly alone, dying, if I had never gone to New York that summer? Would I be here spending my days watching head-cases wander up and down night and day, flinching each time I hear the screams, wetting myself when the nurse does her rounds, if I had never experienced Veda?

Number 503, that's me. And that's all I am. It's written at the end of my bed, so if you ever come this way you'll know it's me. I'm no longer handsome, nor young. And I'll have nothing to say to you. You might not want to come too close. Last time I looked in a mirror, it was pretty disgusting. And I tend to spit. But at least you'll know it's me: BCCI 503.

Know yourself. Isn't that what they say?

And what if self doesn't want to be known? What if it fights you? What if self is insane?

Know yourself. The quest for self-love is endless. Embark upon that inner journey and you may never again see the light of day.

Gabrielle and I never mentioned our cherished dream again. We both secretly hoped I would follow her back to Switzerland, neither of us wished to confront the truth. I think she knew what was happening to me better than I did, or rather what had happened and could never be undone, an infection that had gone too deep. But she never said anything. She even allowed me to believe, for a moment at least, that a dream can be more than a dream. Early on one of the last mornings, before reveille, when Veda was still abed, snores and mutterings, breeze waking the forest, Gabrielle came into the cabin and, under my pillow, left the key to her house.

My hand was shaking when I picked it up. I showed it to Joe, sitting out there on the porch. He put his arm around me and held on. He knew how the future frightened me.

'Come on, Ben,' Joe jumped up and held out his hand. 'Think about it when it happens. I don't want to sit around getting sad, they'll be plenty of time for that when we're alone. It's dinner.'

Meal times had become quite an event over the last two days, occasions that were eagerly awaited, longed for. And it wasn't just because they broke up the cheerless monotony of preparing for the end. Rosetta had been running the kitchen stocks down over the last week. Only she'd run them down too fast and was now out of food.

She didn't want to do it, went against her principles as a cook. But she had no real choice.

She sent out for pizza.

And we had our first decent meals on Veda in over two months, paradise in large square boxes. It even put a smile on Norma's face.

The following morning Joshua broke his silence to tease Mitchel one final time. 'Well, you know, Client Luckee, I wouldn't go waiting for your mother to be on time too much if I were you, I expect she'll be late. Well, she's been late before and so I wouldn't be so surprised if she's late again. Well you know that's what I think.'

And he was right. Mitchel didn't even bother to fly off the handle, didn't scream, didn't shout, just sat on his bed and let himself be goaded. He knew Joshua was telling the truth.

Geena Luck was five hours late.

When she arrived Mitch didn't say a word, not at first. He said his goodbyes to us, great hugs laden with emotion, then hobbled over to the car and struggled all by himself to get in. And he did. No one helped. He did it on his own. Geena thanked us, half a look in her eye pleading us to go with her. 'He needs a male influence,' she smiled sadly. Then she got in the car and drove away. The last thing I heard as they passed through Veda's gates was Mitch screaming at her.

Dakota was the next to go. We walked him down to High Command, listening to his questions on the next day's menu. Neither Joe nor I felt like answering. I tried, for a while, to explain that there wasn't going to be a menu the next day, nor the day after that. But he just kept on in good faith, asking away.

When he saw his father standing in the car park, he wandered over to him as if he were approaching a stranger, unconcerned, and fired the first question. Richard came over and thanked us for looking after his son. There was no hug, no goodbye, no nothing. Dakota simply got in the back of the car and stared at his belly. I saw his father say something to him, pointing to Joe and me. Dakota raised his hand and, without looking our way, gave us a sort of wave. Once. And then he was gone. Just like he'd arrived. Sudden. Unexpected. And I was left with a gaping hole I didn't even know I had.

Slowly, dragging my feet, I wandered up to the bunk for final checks. Joe and the rest of the boys were down at the HCs waiting for the buses which would take us to Port Authority in New York City. Families were waiting there. Patients would be returned to their rightful owners and counsellors would shrink away to wherever it was they came from.

B8 was ten times larger without the boys, and twice as cold. Never had it looked so clean and lonely, sterilised: the beds stacked at the far end; the pictures taken from the walls; the couch returned to the counsellors' lounge; the dust wiped away, making room for new dust to fall. All that was left as witness to the lives which had been lived there was a broken toilet, clumps of rust trickling to the floor from the cracked cistern. I don't know how long I stayed. Alone. Joe wasn't by my side to haul me away from the melancholic tides wetting my feet. Maybe I would have drowned had I not heard the buses blasting their way down Sageville Road, Norma's harsh rasp cajoling people to hurry, hurry.

There was something in the corner. I looked closer. A pair of Calvin Klein briefs, still fresh and clean in the packaging. I went to pick them up, thought I might use them. But I changed my mind and left them there. Let someone else soil them.

Three silver Greyhound buses stood at the back of the HCs. Empty. Soon to be filled. By the time I reached the bottom of the hill loading was already under way. I waited under a maple tree by the side of the gravel track and watched.

A short fat man bundled his way forward, kicking up stones, his eyes fixed on the ground, his mouth twisted as though trapped inside a laugh. He hummed to himself. Occasionally he tried a whistle, but his lips refused to make the right shape. Yet he'd try all the same, again and again.

A boy catching non-existent flies with his outstretched hands, buzzing. His nose running. Trying to get away.

A rake of woman flopped her way to the doors of the bus, negotiating the route by a series of half turns, weaving in and out of obstacles which were not there. Grey hair falling out. Empty skin drooping from the bone. She was kissing the air, in the hope that there might be some lips around. I stepped forward and offered her my cheek. She brushed her tight lips lightly against it, said thank you, and flopped on.

Josie, a whale of a Down's from E2, stomped up and down throwing her arms around anything that moved, crying and bawling. 'I don't wanna go home, I don't wanna go home.' Her tears were false, they always were. But she got more hugs that way. She came over to me to receive her dues, squeezing the little life had left in me.

'You be a good girl now, Josie.'

'Aw Ben, you a kidder! Course I be good. Now what you expect? I always good. I good through and through, can't be nothing else. That's the way I's made.' And with that, a little more crying, a few more hugs rounded up, she bounded aboard the bus with a shriek. 'Ohooo, I is *soooo* GOOD!'

And then it was our turn, time for counsellors to be checked on to the bus, with the patients. Names and ticks. I was the last to be called. I didn't look back. The next time I looked up at Veda everything was black, a huge tinted window in the way. I sat next to Book, holding his hand. As lifeless as when I first touched it. I gave it a squeeze.

No response.

I only took one souvenir. It was all I needed, all that Veda gave me. A white sticker, placed in the centre of my shirt. Slightly smudged, in the corner, in large black marker pen, was written: BCCI 503.

The brakes hissed and the bus rumbled up Sageville Road. Looking out upon a blackened, empty Veda. Past the boarded bunks, shutters drawn across windows like eyelids stitched closed over eyes. Past the basketball courts with puddles that never dried and nets falling down. Past Herbert slouching against his front gate, scratching his head, smoking his pipe with no tobacco in it, looking miserable with his wife at his side, wishing he was fishing. Past the kitchens, the scene of so may crimes. Past the cottage, sewing and *The Karate Kid*. Past the social hall, broken guttering wilting from the roof. Past the *Welcome to Veda* sign, nails lose, drooping over the gate, still in need of a decent coat of paint. And past B8, far back back in the woods, branches drawn down like a veil.

A bus full of loonies. An air-conditioned madhouse on wheels. Whipping its way from Veda as New York ushered out the used up summer, tugging in an eager autumn. Crammed to the hilt with howling, wailing, flapping, shrieking, screaming, soiling, slapping. And I. I on the inside.

ALLISON & BUSBY FICTION

Phillip Callow
The Magnolia
The Painter's Confessions

Catherine Heath
Lady on the Burning Deck
Behaving Badly

Chester Himes
Cast the First Stone
Collected Stories
The End of a Primitive
Pink Toes
Run Man Run

R. C. Hutchinson
Johanna at Daybreak
Recollection of a Journey

Dan Jacobson
The Evidence of Love

Francis King
Act of Darkness
The Widow

Colin MacInnes
Absolute Beginners
City of Spades
Mr Love and Justice
The Colin MacInnes Omnibus

Indira Mahindra
The End Play

Henry Miller
Quiet Days in Clichy

Adrian Mitchell
The Bodyguard

Susanna Mitchell
The Colour of His Hair

Bill Naughton
Alfie

Dolores Pala
In Search of Mihailo

Boris Pasternak
Zhenia's Childhood

Ishmael Reed
Japanese by Spring
Reckless Eyeballing
The Terrible Threes
The Terrible Twos

Françoise Sagan
Engagements of the Heart
Evasion
Incidental Music
The Leash
The Unmade Bed

Budd Schulberg
The Disenchanted
Love, Action, Laughter and Other Sad Stories
On the Waterfront
What Makes Sammy Run?

Debbie Taylor
The Children Who Sleep by the River

B. Traven
Government
The Carreta
Trozas

Etienne van Heerden
Ancestral Voices
Mad Dog and Other Stories